T0304426

WHITE: A NOVEL

More Praise for *WHITE*

"Every action humans take plants a seed. *WHITE* brilliantly explores the yield of such seeds—good, bad, and ugly. While hate can be cultivated and passed from generation to generation, it can also be dispelled when the right people come into our lives at the right times."

—Arno Michaelis, author of *My Life After Hate*,
Co-Author of *The Gift of Our Wounds*

"Aviva Rubin eloquently captures a young woman's struggle with the intergenerational trauma of hate. While Sarah Cartell fights for a different world from the one she was raised to believe in, she feels unworthy of it. With humour and compassion, *WHITE* shines a light on the complex and transformative powers of family, friendship, speaking one's truth."

—Paula Klein, Psychotherapist

"Brave, moving, and fierce, *WHITE* shows us the deep rot of a family's white supremacist beliefs and a fearless daughter's plan to infiltrate the racist groups she wants to bring down. Taut and compulsively readable, Aviva Rubin's debut novel is as much a sharp psychological portrait of generational racism as it is an unflinching look at the realities and limitations of hope and change."

—Laura Zigman, bestselling author of
Separation Anxiety and *Small World*

"A mesmerizing tale of a small-town young woman's valiant, misguided scheme to combat white supremacist violence. In Rubin's gripping account, anti-Black racism, antisemitism, and xenophobia are terrifyingly present, not only out in the world, but within homes and families. Set in Canada in the 1990s, this surprising yet familiar story echoes back to the 1930s and 1940s, and ahead to our own troubled times."

—Doris L. Bergen, author of *War and Genocide: A Concise History of the Holocaust*

"In this bold debut, Rubin delivers readers to the fringes of society where we find an unflinching story of the things we learn, the things we unlearn—and ultimately, the power of love, family and redemption."

—Karen Green, author of *Yellow Birds*

"A bold and brave novel about the dangers of both loyalty and betrayal when the family and community we love are bonded by negative values that hurt other people and the world. Using the frame of Canadian white supremacy, Aviva Rubin brings us inside the conflicted heart and mind of one young woman who finally makes the break and decides, at great personal cost, to say 'No.'"

—Sarah Schulman, Author

WHITE: A NOVEL

AVIVA RUBIN

RE:BOOKS

Copyright © Aviva Rubin.

All rights reserved.

www.rebooks.ca

Published in Canada by RE:BOOKS

ADDRESS:
RE:BOOKS
Brookfield Place
181 Bay Street
Suite 1800
Toronto, Ontario
M5J 2T9
Canada

www.rebooks.ca

No portion of this publication may be reproduced or transmitted, in any form, or by any means, without express written permission of the copyright holder.

First RE:BOOKS Edition: October 2024

ISBN: 978-1-998206-30-8
eBook ISBN: 978-1-998206-31-5

RE:BOOKS and all associated logos are trademarks and/or registered marks of RE:BOOKS.

Printed and bound in Canada.
1 3 5 7 9 10 8 6 4 2

Cover design by: Chloe Faith Robinson
Typeset by: Karl Hunt

Dedication

For Wendy Coburn. I am so grateful for our conversations about WHITE. I wish you were here to see Sarah make her way in the world. I miss you always dear friend.

Author's Note

This book deals with difficult issues of intergenerational family trauma, white supremacy, hate, racism, and anti-Semitism. It contains offensive language and instances of violence against people of colour and children that are upsetting to read. I have been careful and intentional in all my choices.

1

DECEMBER 1994

Train Line — Montreal to Toronto

THERE WAS A KNOCK ON THE DOOR.

"You okay?"

How did she even get here in this cramped toilet? On this train, with her head between her knees. Wasn't that what you did to get ready for a crash, put your head down? Or was that only for flying? Her crash and burn already happened. This was the part that came after, and it was way worse.

That cop was waiting outside. She looked at the sink and the paper towel dispenser. No sharp edges. Maybe he only got paid for the safe delivery of a live person. It was tempting not to answer and see if he'd bang his way in.

"I'm fine." *Not loud enough.* She cleared her throat and said it again, this time too loud.

Sarah felt dizzy when she stood up and grabbed the counter. Her greasy-haired reflection made her pull her wool toque down further. Luce had suggested a shower so Sarah didn't offend anyone who could fuck things up for her. But she hadn't bothered. How much more fucked up could things be?

Back at her seat, she sat crunched against the window. She and the cop had been only inches apart since they left her apartment hours ago. Sarah had no idea why he was even there. Something about it being *for her own safety*, he'd said.

"Cartell, you sure you're okay?"

Why did he keep asking? Of course she wasn't fucking okay. She was being *accompanied* to a loony bin for safekeeping. She'd accomplished nothing in a year and a half of trying.

A pile of unfinished assignments and missed exams she'd never bothered begging extensions or making excuses for lay trashed behind her at McGill University. Not that the cop knew that part of the story. He'd probably only heard about how upset she was at the police station after Aravinda was attacked. Her fault. Maybe the frequent visits to the toilet had him worried about a urinary tract infection. Or a drug addiction.

"I'm fine. Like I was five minutes ago."

Ignoring the sarcasm, he offered her half of his egg salad sandwich, which was kind, but while she was hungry, she was not *that* hungry.

"The wife made it."

The wife. Like wives were all interchangeable. Egg salad made her think of Luce again, who hated it too. And then about how the plan, when Sarah had left Goderich for McGill, had felt clear and controllable, how she hadn't noticed it getting away from her, but Luce had. She waved *no thanks* at the sandwich.

Sarah's hand rested on the poster tube jammed between her thigh and the window—the White supremacy at-a-glance mural that had taken years of research and still wasn't done. *Just finish something.*

The attendant breathed egg beside her. His eyes were closed, but she could tell he was awake. She wished she could sleep—not that it helped stop the images. A laughing Aravinda with his worn leather bag of demo flyers banging against his skinny ass, planting kisses on Sarah's cheeks. He was pretty much the only person she let do that, even though it was Montreal, and everyone kissed. Then there was his broken body, which she hadn't seen but conjured anyway. It felt like weeks, but it was only days since everything happened.

Her eyes rode the power lines over passing fields. Grey and brown mostly, the odd red house, blue car, yellow sign. Luce, always covered in flecks of paint, had made Sarah notice colour.

At Sunnyside Mental Health Centre (who named these places?), the cop handed an envelope to the woman behind the admissions desk. Sarah wondered what was in it. She'd always been good at keeping to herself. How was there even enough information to justify funding this stay?

"Good luck to you, then." He squeezed her shoulder. "Say hi to your uncle Carl for me."

The cop turned and walked away before she could think of what to say.

2

DECEMBER 1994

Montreal — Two days earlier

SARAH PRESSED HER HIP BONES HARD AGAINST the counter at Le Plateau Montreal police station. Pain was preferable to shaking. It was calming. Did she seem calm? She was aiming for calm. "It was my idea, my plan. I'm responsible."

"You planned what, exactly?" The officer glanced at her, not nearly interested enough, his half smile patronizing.

"I told you. The break-in. The computers. St. Catherine Street. What happened to . . ." *Ara. Ara. Ara.* She unsuccessfully tried to clear a passage for his name. What came out was a squeaky, garbled noise.

"Slow down, dear. Why don't we go sit somewhere quiet? I'll get you some water, then you can start from the beginning and we can get this down."

Sarah pulled away from the counter. *Dear*, he fucking called her *dear*.

The officer slid his hand back slowly as if she was a feral

animal who might be set off by quick movement. He buzzed her in and gestured for her to come through, then led her to a small room, sat her in a chair, and left. The only sound was the clock marking seconds. Half an hour passed. Maybe the cop got lost on the way to some corner store.

By the time he returned with two cups of water, Sarah was curled up on the floor, cheek to linoleum. She ignored the hand he extended. Someone else came in. No uniform. Maybe a detective. They sat facing each other on metal chairs for what seemed like hours of questions that had nothing to do with her part in the attack on Ara. She answered them all, hinting at the project she'd been working on for years, minus the details. The detective asked how she knew Marc Scott. How she fell in with that group of people. *Bad eggs*, he called them. Because that's what neo-Nazis were, bad eggs. It all boiled down to mistakes and unfortunate choices. *What's a nice girl like you doing in a place like that?* She shouldn't have yelled, but he wouldn't listen. Then, she was left alone again.

Someone put a hand on her shoulder. She must have fallen asleep with her head on the table. Luce.

"What are you doing here?"

"Taking you home," she said. "We have a couple of days to organize and pack everything."

"Pack? They're arresting me?" Sarah almost smiled. "Don't they just do that right away? Why are they letting me go?"

"No. No arrest. But they're recommending you go somewhere to get better. Got the feeling it's not a choice."

"Better than what?"

Luce winced. Sarah felt sure her friend had messed up the plan to turn herself in.

"What did you tell them?" Sarah asked.

"Does it matter?"

It did. But she had no energy for this. In the end, she betrayed Luce, and Luce betrayed her. That's what mattered.

"Ara?" Sarah whispered.

"Still in a coma." Luce contemplated the two paper cups on the table. "To bring down the swelling before any surgery."

"Right."

Luce put a hand on her shoulder.

"Please don't."

Back in her apartment, Sarah stepped around papers and markers, gripping the chipped Happy Face mug that the junk shop guy had thrown in along with the plaid armchair and space heater she bought that boiling hot August day when she'd first arrived in Montreal. He'd given her a pair of the mugs, but one of them broke on the way home. In Grade 11 English class, she learned that was called foreshadowing. As in, this person would remain alone.

Life had definitely taught her she belonged by herself. She took a sip of her lukewarm tea, then reached for the cat who preferred rubbing against boxes and furniture. Melrose was the perfect pet for her.

Luce assured the police that she would stay with her friend until it was time to go but after Sarah begged, or more like argued her case, she agreed to let her have that couple of days to sort through everything alone. Luce felt no allegiance to the cops, still, she made Sarah promise to answer the phone every time it rang, or else she'd be over and wouldn't leave. She called a stupid amount, and Sarah yelled at her for interfering each time. They argued non-stop about whether it was safe to store all the research stuff at Luce's studio. Well, mostly Sarah argued.

"It's only until you get back." Luce said it like she believed Sarah coming back was possible.

"It's risky. People are named. They could come after you." Sarah knew she sounded paranoid, but it was true. Those boxes were filled with White supremacists. Dangerous people who didn't want to be exposed.

"Just give me the fucking things. You have the better choice?" Luce's English always made Sarah smile.

No, she didn't have *the better choice*. Melrose and the couch—pink, garish, and stiff—would also go with her. Sarah later regretted never telling Luce she was the only person who made it look comfortable. The rest of the stuff could be left there. Some of it was Harrison's, but she couldn't think about that. He was her closest friend in high school, her only friend almost. He gave her this apartment when he moved in with Ara. Now, he'd probably never talk to her again.

Sarah turned back to the mess. Fourteen hours until Luce arrived with the truck.

White Supremacy at a Glance was still pinned to the wall. A messy colour-coded mural with hundreds of sticky notes stuck on with tape. She didn't trust the adhesive. Luce said it reminded her of a Jackson Pollock painting. Sarah had to look the guy up.

Ku Klux Klan: red
Heritage Front: purple
Aryan Nations: turquoise
Western Guard: brown
REAL Women: pink
Silver Shirts: silver
Campaign Life: yellow
Church of Jesus Christ Christian: green

The colour added a layer of irony to the mural. Linked to the organizations were hundreds of names: leaders, prominent figures, flash in the pan skinhead thugs, Wolfgang Droege, Malcolm Ross, William Dudley Pelley, Carl Cartell, Thomas Franklin Cartell, Jim Keegstra, Terry Long, Ernst Zundel, Marc Scott, Bruce Gotteral. Beside the names were as many photos as she could find. Sarah had taken the ones of Marc and her uncle Carl, who ran True Canadian Heritage. In a box in her grandfather's attic, she'd found one of him as a teenager in a fascist uniform, the words *hero for a bright White future* handwritten on the back. Others were forwarded through anonymous connections or cut from newspapers and pamphlets. Stapled to the top left corner was a list of books: *Web of Deceit*, *The Real Holocaust*, *The Turner Diaries*, and *The Hoax of the Twentieth Century*, which was illegal in Canada.

A timeline spanned the bottom of the mural, capturing key events beginning with the establishment of the Ku Klux Klan in 1865 and ending with what had just happened, her own name pencilled in. Sarah photographed the mural in sections with a disposable camera for safekeeping.

One box had stuff about women in the movement. Another held memorabilia; a Confederate flag, a toddler-sized *My Canada Includes Nazis* t-shirt, a RaHoWa sweatshirt, two baseball caps (*White Pride* and *White Is Might*), a key chain with the number eighty-eight, and a mug with a slogan printed across that she'd kept because it was so stupid. *Drink Canada White.*

She sealed each box, first with packing tape, then window insulator, finishing the job by going at them with a blow dryer.

Sarah put the camera and a master list of all the contents in an envelope and addressed it to the P.O. box in Goderich. She was grateful Mrs. Broder, the librarian, had kept it active. *Think about her later.* Sarah wiped at her eyes as she carefully rolled up the mural and slid it into the heavy cardboard tube.

She looked around. Aside from the mural, whose supposed artistry was completely accidental, the only truly beautiful things she owned were from Ara, who single-handedly undermined her penchant for functionality. A bunch of hand-painted ceramic containers *for all her jewellery*, he'd said every time he brought a new one over. They'd both laughed because all she had was her mother's wedding band that she wore on a silver box chain and never took off. The containers were too magical for paper clips, thumbtacks, and matches. But that's what they held. Two devil masks with wild eyes and toothy mouths, one in the living room and one in the kitchen, watched over her. A Buddhist tapestry she kept meaning to hang but instead used as a bedspread.

If you keep bringing presents whenever you come over, I'll have to stop inviting you, she told him. He never did stop and neither did she.

If only Ara was there to help. But then, none of this would be happening. Last spring, when all the unfinished assignments had piled up, Harrison was so angry that she'd made White supremacy her priority and was fucking up what really mattered—her only way out. Ara came over with dinner and lit incense. He told Sarah that Harrison called him an enabler and was pissed off that Ara had taken it as a compliment.

Ara also brought over a book that had just been published, called *Bird by Bird*. It was about writing, but the relevant bit told of the author's panicking brother who had ignored a huge school project on birds until the night before it was due. The kid's father sat down beside him and told him not to worry. They would do it bird by bird. And Ara sat with Sarah until she got well into two of her papers.

She pulled the tapestry off the bed and wrapped it around her shoulders, then opened the window and lit a cigarette.

Sarah wasn't surprised when Luce arrived early, messy hair, polished police boots tied neatly to the top. She stared at her coldly, resentful of all the help her friend continued to offer. Luce had every right to be pissed off, but she was refusing to play her part.

Harrison left only one whispering croaky message right after he found out; *had she heard, could she please come.* It was before he'd talked to Luce, before he'd heard Marc's name on the radio or read it in the paper. News of the crime was everywhere. Yet, her name was nowhere. Invisible, behind the scenes, blameless as usual. Harrison hadn't called again.

"Thanks for going to the cops to clarify." One last pointless dig. Either Sarah's sarcasm didn't cross the language divide, or Luce wouldn't let it.

"It's at least I could do." Luce looked around. Not clean, but more or less tidy.

"*The* least," Sarah said.

"What?"

"That's the expression. It's *the* least I could do." Sarah walked around the room touching boxes and pretending to look for things she might have missed.

"Ara's parents don't want Harrison at the hospital. They arrived and took over with some polite nod of appreciation for his having stepped in. *We're here now, so you can leave.* They're pretending they don't know there's a relationship, ignoring the newspapers which say 'gay activist' all over."

Sarah winced and turned away. Luce had to tell her, but nothing Sarah could say would make things right. So, nothing it was. "I guess I'm ready to go."

They stood there, neither of them moving.

Luce's friend Rodrigo knocked on the open door. He was wearing a pink *Out and Proud* t-shirt and a *Ford Built Tough* baseball cap.

"All set?" He looked back and forth between them. "I can come back. But the truck's by the hour so . . ."

"No. Now's good," Luce said.

"I want to pay for it." Sarah looked around for her bag.

"Send me a cheque from the joint," Luce said.

They both laughed. Sarah had taught her all the meanings of the word "joint" one night when they were stoned.

"Here's the extra key for Harrison, in case."

In case what? In case he needed to come back because he couldn't bear to live where he and Ara had lived? Because Sarah had destroyed his life?

"And one more favour. Sorry, but I have no stamps." She handed Luce the envelope. "Do you mind mailing it?"

"No problems." Luce took the key and the package. She started to say something but changed her mind.

Rodrigo picked up two boxes, and they carried everything out to the truck. Luce and Rodrigo insisted on moving the couch themselves. Sarah didn't bother arguing. When everything was secured, Rodrigo walked away and lit a cigarette.

"I'm sorry, Luce."

Luce put her fingers on Sarah's mouth, and Sarah covered them with her hand.

"Don't lose it in there," Luce whispered.

They stood like that until Rodrigo started the truck. Luce took a quick breath and pulled her hand away. Sarah knew that would be the last time she touched her.

She watched them drive off, then went back upstairs. Locking the apartment for good would be as easy as shutting an empty filing cabinet. It was hard to remember what good had happened there.

3

DECEMBER 1994

Sunnyside Mental Health Centre

THE CENTRE WAS A CLOSED FACILITY THAT smelled of cement, bleach, and something fake floral to cover something mildly barfy. No leaving without permission or accompaniment. Not that there was anyone to go with or anywhere to go.

The woman at the desk shook the poster tube, popped off the lid, peered inside, then grabbed a yardstick to poke around before handing it back. Luckily, Sarah had secured the sticky notes. What did the woman think was in it? Rope? A knife? A bomb? Sarah almost laughed. When a box of tissues was pushed across the counter towards her, she realized she was crying.

"Someone will show you to your room."

Like the bellhop? She wanted to make a joke. She'd been working on her humour. It helped pre-empt pity she didn't need but often got. Her stomach cramped and she winced before she could stop herself.

The woman's head tilted in that *I'm so sorry* way.

"Thanks." Sarah picked up her backpack and stuck the tube under her arm.

The roommate, long brown braids and a *Little House on the Prairie* dress, was lying on her bed reading. The Laura Ingalls Wilder look was accompanied by a pair of worn boots, like the ones Luce wore.

"I'm Becky. That's *your* bed. Obviously, since I'm on this one. You can hang around today, unpack, but starting tomorrow, it's program city. Oh, and I snore. Post-nasal drip."

She sniffed, as though that was evidence. Sarah wasn't sure if Becky was funny or just really literal. And it wasn't clear what was wrong with her. She seemed pretty normal.

"Got a name?" Becky asked.

Sarah hesitated. *Answer her.* "Sarah. And don't worry about the nasal drip. I've got other things to keep me up."

Why did she even say that? The girl might ask for details. But she didn't. She just looked back at her book.

Out the window, there were some sad little trees and peeling wooden benches that had once been painted with cheery rainbows. Winter flower boxes were filled with what looked like oversized cabbages. She blew air out slowly. *Keep it together.* Keeping it together and never losing her shit used to be her superpower.

She pushed the poster tube under the bed and tucked Beans, hardly identifiable as a stuffed rabbit anymore, under the flannelette sheet and wool blanket. She couldn't bring herself to throw Beans away. Even brought him to Aryan Fest.

How many White supremacists, she'd wondered, had brought their stuffed animals? Or was it only infiltrators who travelled with them?

She unwrapped the smallest of Ara's ceramic containers and put it on the bedside table. She'd allowed herself to take only one. And one devil mask, for juju. Devil masks and juju were a mash-up of cultural messages, Ara had said, but everything worked best when it was mixed. It was one of her favourite things that Ara believed. It was where her purpose and his way in the world met and kind of fell in love. But look where that had gotten them. She wiped at her eyes with the back of her hand.

"Those are amazing," Becky said.

Sarah pretended not to hear the comment and pushed the rest of her few things into the two dresser drawers Becky had indicated sarcastically were *all hers*.

"Not much space," the girl said.

"Not much stuff," Sarah answered.

"You want the tour now?"

So that was her role. Girl Guide. Sarah nodded.

"Then we eat."

The idea of eating in some smelly cafeteria, like high school but with even more mental cases, made Sarah's stomach cramp again.

"Food any good?"

"Unmemorable but generally inoffensive." Becky shrugged. "By some standards, that's good."

The roommate pointed out rooms for arts and crafts, a gym, a bunch of admin offices, the medical wing where Sarah was scheduled for some intake appointment with the psychiatrist, the yard that their room faced.

"Cabbage?" Sarah pointed at the flower boxes.

"Ornamental," Becky said. "My mother loves them. God forbid there should be nothing decorative outside the front door in winter."

They continued, peering into rooms. Sarah feigned interest with dumb words, like *nice* or *cool*, that Becky clearly didn't need.

"And here's the dining hall," she said, pushing open a door. The girl registered Sarah's look of disgust.

"You'll get used to it." She grabbed a tray.

The appointment that first afternoon with Dr. Blowhard—his name was Bladdard, but Sarah was sure the nurse who weighed her and took blood had said Blowhard—took less than five minutes. The psychiatrist who wore his lab coat like a protective art smock had no couch and asked no invasive questions. That suited Sarah fine.

Lying in a twin bed that first night, monitoring Becky's breathing and occasional snorts, felt awkward and oddly comforting. Being the only girl in her family, Sarah had never shared a room before. She took inventory of the footsteps, loud whispering, doors opening, toilets flushing. Every new sound, no matter how faint, kept her too vigilant to slip into the promise of the Ativan some sickeningly sweet nurse had handed her in a tiny paper cup. "Here you go, dear." *Dear, dear, dear.*

She listed the events that brought her to this place, then

she listed them again, then again, like counting a flock of ugly sheep. At some point, it must have worked.

In the morning, Sarah kept her eyes closed as Becky dressed and left the room. Then she pulled on what she'd been wearing the day before, beige cords and brown hoodie, and headed to breakfast. She grabbed some toast and tea and sat down at Becky's table. It would have been too weird to sit alone.

"Hi," she said.

Becky smiled up at her, then went back to the book, letting Sarah off the hook.

After a few minutes, she got up to leave. "Art therapy for me. Hope today goes okay."

Sarah felt something akin to disappointment as her roommate walked away. Disappointment that she was now alone, which she thought she wanted, but even more, that Becky had read her as needing pity or compassion, which felt like a failure to protect herself. She made a mental note to stop wiping her eyes and nose on the worn-out sleeve of her hoodie.

Sarah's first therapy session was at 10:00 a.m. The certificate above the therapist's head read PsyD and other letters that didn't spell anything. Mona Rubinoff, orange plastic glasses on the bridge of her nose, was part of the mental institute package, like shampoo or a terry cloth bathrobe in a fancy hotel room.

"I'm Mona." The woman stuck out her hand and looked unoffended when it wasn't taken. She pointed at the chair across from her.

Sarah sat down and braced herself for mushy solicitation.

Mona Rubinoff smiled but remained quiet.

The room and everything in it was orange, beige, or brown; even the macramé plant holder with its half dead plant and the dry leaves on the dark beige carpet underneath it. The silence felt unbearable. Sarah was used to other people filling the gaps.

"Do you want me to say something first?"

The therapist shook her head. "A Wandering Jew, in case you're interested."

Sarah tried not to look shocked. Was it a test?

"The plant you're staring at, it's called a Wandering Jew. And no, I'm not expecting you to say anything. First time's a freebie, a chance to check each other out."

"Can I pick someone else, if this turns out to be a bad match?"

Mona laughed and leaned forward. "I'm afraid I'm it. Take it or take it."

The room was cluttered with what Sarah could only assume were therapy toys to occupy hands. Other people's junk always made Sarah feel claustrophobic. Through the window in the building across the way, she could see adults holding crayons and paint brushes. She scanned for Becky.

The therapist put on her glasses. "Says in your file that you've come from Montreal. That you had a trauma-related breakdown."

Mona placed the open folder on the table, then fiddled with her glasses that hung from a chain of brown plastic loops. It reminded Sarah of a Barrel of Monkeys. That and

Pick-up-Sticks had been their childhood rainy day games. Her brother Blair's tactic, on the rare occasion that someone else was winning, was to make them laugh. He was a genius at rubber face humour, stretching his lips in impossible directions, rolling one eye at a time. The weird noises that accompanied his expressions made ignoring him impossible. Once she cracked up, it was game over. Her strand of hanging monkeys would collapse.

Was "trauma-related breakdown" what they called it when your boyfriend attacked one of your best friends?

"I was told some bullshit about being here for my own safety." Sarah leaned forward trying to read the notes in her file.

Mona pushed it closer. "Have a look. Tell me what needs correcting."

The offer caught Sarah off guard. She leaned back, not wanting to seem desperate.

"Everyone's here for their own safety," Mona said. "It's not actually a form of punishment, although it seems that's what you were looking for when you went to the police station."

"What about homicidal sociopaths, delusional psychotics?"

"No need to worry. There aren't many of them here."

Did she look worried? All she felt was exhaustion from the horror running on a permanent loop in her head. She tried to calm the noise by going back over the steps she took to pack up her apartment—the boxes, the information they contained, lists, tape, careful wrapping of all things breakable. When she drifted off into how much time it took to acquire and organize everything, the exercise stopped working.

"I guess they've explained the routine." Mona took the glasses off. "You'll see me three times a week."

"*Fan*-tastic." She knew her tone was childish. The woman was just doing her job, pointless as it might be. Sarah shifted in her seat. Three hours a week. The better-out-than-in approach that worked when Sarah had too much beer just seemed ridiculous with feelings or memories. Where was the shit meant to go?

"Nurse says you're 5'6 and 104 pounds."

The sentence hung there.

Ya. So? There was a paper plate with a half-eaten cookie the size of a frisbee on the desk behind Mona. Crumbs everywhere. Sarah felt her nose wrinkle. "I'm not anorexic, in case you're wondering, just unenthusiastic. Is there a force-feeding plan for that?"

"Mostly we just look over your shoulder, maybe encourage a bit."

Sarah thought about being watched in the dining hall, about going to sleep and waking up in a little room with a stranger every day, about communal everything. How she was doing. What she ate. What she weighed. What she felt and thought. It was funny that surveillance had always been *her* gig, what *she* did best.

"What's funny?" Mona asked.

Did she laugh out loud? She hadn't meant to. Not only was there no lock on the door to her room and no walls between herself and others, but it seemed even the barrier between inside her head and out her mouth had been breached. What if she really didn't know the difference between what she was thinking and what she was saying? Sarah put a hand over her mouth, like after the fact might help.

"You okay?"

Sarah sighed. The universal question that always signalled some perceived imbalance. It wasn't pity, but it was close enough. She pulled her t-shirt away from her hip bones. "Yeah, I'm great."

Mona pushed the box of tissue towards her, her face sympathetic. Sarah wouldn't call what she was doing crying. More like leaking. Her body kept betraying her.

"Dr. Bladdard put you on Zoloft, Ativan, and iron for anaemia. Ativan's just temporary. I know that was only yesterday, but any reactions?"

"I'm nauseated and I have the shits, but I feel perky." She made up the last two. Nauseated was pretty much a permanent state.

Mona picked up her pen and scribbled something on a yellow pad.

"What are you writing?"

"A note about what Sarah Cartell looks like perky." She winked.

Sarah's laugh came out like a snort as she tried to stifle any hint that she might find Mona remotely entertaining.

"I'm sure the doctor told you it takes a few weeks to feel the difference."

"That's pretty much all he told me."

Mona mumbled something about doctors and self-importance.

"It's okay. No need to waste *his* time too," Sarah said.

Mona looked like she wanted to say something but changed her mind. “Hanging around in your room isn’t allowed. They have you pretty tightly programmed.”

“I’m looking forward to arts and crafts. I like collage.” That wasn’t even a lie.

“Across the way.” Mona swivelled in her chair and pointed out the window.

Sarah wondered if it was possible to see into the therapist’s office from there. Not that she planned to reveal much, but some people were good lip readers.

“How long do I have to stay?”

What difference did it make? She had nowhere to go. Montreal was poisoned, home to Goderich wasn’t an option. Maybe this would be a place to rest.

“An hour, but we can cut it short today.”

“How long am I going to be at *Sunnyside*?” She emphasized the word to make it sound stupid.

Mona glanced at her shaking leg. Sarah clapped her hand down on it.

“I’d tell you if I could, but I honestly have no idea.”

Sarah wrapped her arms around her legs. “I think the cop who dropped me off was a friend of my uncle’s.”

“Makes sense, he and your father organized this stay.”

If they were behind this, what did they know? It was easier to believe the Montreal police had randomly decided to send her to Toronto. Her stomach cramped.

“Sarah,” Mona said gently. “There’s no conspiracy here. You’re not well. Your father asked your uncle to get you here safely. He wants you to get better. We only talked briefly, but according to him, you haven't been okay for a while."

"You talked to him? Isn't that a violation of confidentiality? I am over eighteen."

"I hadn't met you yet, so I had nothing to violate."

Fuck. "Can I go?"

"Sure. I'll see you Wednesday," Mona said.

Sarah pulled the door closed too hard just as Mona said, "You can leave it open."

4

JANUARY 1995

Sunnyside Mental Health Centre

THE DAYS BLED ONE INTO ANOTHER, punctuated by too much forced conversation and a lot of buttered toast. Christmas would have gone unnoticed, but for the flashing tree in the main lobby and the holiday dinner that had them all trapped for two hours listening to the Sunnyside choir sing carols in a cafeteria that was thinly disguised with white tablecloths, electric candles, and Christmas crackers. It reminded Sarah of all the painful school concerts her dad and her aunt had sat through. Maybe *she'd* be here singing next year.

Kitchen staff paraded two enormous turkeys through the room—a Sunnyside tradition that brought cheers from everyone except an Orthodox Jew, who was yelling about latkes and dreidels, and Sarah, who remained silent in solidarity. The birds were carved out of sight. Bones were not allowed at the table. Seems they were a self-harm or potential weapon risk.

Missing the bleak Cartell Christmas meal was the only gift Sarah received and it was appreciated, although Blair's comic antics were missed. As for New Year's Eve, mental institutions do a pathetic job. Noise makers were handed out and expected to be blown at 9:00 p.m. The calendar was flipped to 1995. That was that.

Sarah was in her pea coat and toque having a smoke before her session with Mona, when Simon, the guy from art therapy who could be counted on to say disturbing things that were not supposed to make Sarah laugh, ran up waving his arms. "I'm gonna bludgeon you."

No boundaries, delusions of something or other, anachronistic vocabulary, and impulse control. Supposedly, those were Simon's issues. Otherwise, he was fine.

He pulled to a stop then leaned in and asked sweetly for a puff.

"Gross. Who wants a puff of someone else's cigarette?"

"Gross, ya. Sorry."

Simon shuffled back and forth, then absently patted her arm. Sarah usually pulled away when it even looked like someone might touch her, but the fact that Simon didn't realize he was doing it made it not matter. It was weird that the constant *invasions of her space* as Mona called them, didn't bother her here.

"You can have the rest." She held out the cigarette.

His face lit up as he grabbed it. "Thanks Sar." He turned and wandered off.

She laughed. *Sar.* Simon had given her a nickname.

"Been outside?" Mona asked. "Your cheeks are quite rosy."

"At least something is rosy."

"Things feel worse before they feel better." Mona tapped her pencil with her finger like ashes might drop off.

Sarah sighed loudly enough for Mona to hear. Therapy was a ridiculous waste, paying for the privilege of feeling more miserable than they already were. Not that she was paying. But people did.

She'd heard that only the catatonic or the *out of their minds to the point of utter non-compliance* got to forgo the chatting sessions. At night, her and Becky contemplated sneaking into that locked wing, to gather proof.

In group therapy, one or two *sharers* battled it out for time, interrupting each other with complaints and sad stories about the food, their parents, their roommates, even their pets. What did Davie, the guy who wore only black clothes and eyeliner, think would happen if he let the gerbil play with the snake? The group leader singled people out. "Do you have anything to share with us today, Sarah?"

Sure, I brought my collection of Whites-only mugs and key-chains and my banned books.

But one-on-one was hard work, raking her crappy memories into a pile, jumping in, then doing it again. So much for *that* leafy childhood memory.

Sarah hadn't anticipated the blown-out memory floodgate. Who knew her mind was in the business of cryogenics? Now, unfrozen by Mona the human space heater, things she hadn't thought about for years rushed in to join all the ones she couldn't stop thinking about. They interrupted her while she peed, ate, lay in bed. She remembered gargling competitions with Blair and Keith when they were home sick to see who'd wuss out and spit the salt water first, running through the house on her dad's back yelling *the cavalry is coming*, laughing so hard she almost fell off. Hate and more hate. Kneeling on rocks. Curtis.

Luce was evidence it was possible to wear your feelings on the outside and still get shit done. But feelings had never been particularly useful to Sarah. What was happening now, this snotty mess with no apparent on-off switch, at least not one that she could find—who chose this?

Don't lose it in there, Luce had said. Maybe Sarah had been well on her way already. The border between *going crazy* and *being crazy* seemed unmarked. Would she even know when she'd arrived?

"You have to be willing to help yourself," Mona said. "It's a lot of work but it'll be worth it."

Sarah wondered how many hours of therapy clichés she'd have to listen to. The drugs weren't helping. She'd hoped for numb. This felt like numb mixed with electric shocks that hurt but not enough to flatten her. All those tears near all the open wires. A hazard for sure.

She stared unfocused out the window, grateful for the blur of the art therapy class. In a life of fooling people and convincing them that she was someone else entirely, focus was everything. Now, if she could spend all her time out of focus, she would. But Mona wasn't having it. She shifted her head into Sarah's sight line and dragged her back.

Sarah looked around the room to buy herself time. On the

low table lay a pile of distractions—bean bag balls, number puzzles, and coloured pencils covered in other people's stress and germs. She pulled a piece of paper off a small orange pad and rolled it into a thin tube, liking the pain of pressing it hard between her thumb and forefinger.

The heavy leatherette chair Mona sat in reminded Sarah of the den at home. "My dad has one of these. The vinyl throne."

"He called again yesterday. Wants to know when he can come. Maybe with your Aunt Jean."

"Did you tell him anything?"

"He knows you had a breakdown and that you need rest."

Sarah laughed. Unless it was his car, or a salt sorter at work, the word *breakdown* was meaningless. Plus, Cartells didn't break down. They just didn't run that smoothly in the first place.

While she now knew that her Sunnyside vacation was no secret, it was upsetting to think about her dad and uncle discussing her, arguing the way they always had when Carl was home, maybe blaming each other for Sarah being friends with "some paki."

Sarah imagined her family gathered in the visitor's lounge. Katie the artist in her flowing colourful tops from Africa or Thailand and her cowboy boots—always keen to mix her metaphors. She'd be slumped artfully and say *fuck* a lot. Aunt Jean would be buttoned up neatly in some shade of pastel, sitting erect like a backbone could save her. Maybe it had. Her aunts would insist it wasn't her fault. They'd be prepped by Mona, and they'd probably want the long version of what happened. Sarah couldn't deal with all the things she'd be expected to explain. But no one had showed up yet, had they? Didn't they even care?

"I'll give it some thought," she told Mona. "About seeing him, I mean. How many times has he called?"

Mona smiled. Like the question itself revealed something profound and needy. "A few. He loves you. He's concerned."

Sarah exhaled her annoyance. "That is not my point. He's my dad. Of course he thinks he should come."

The therapist tipped her head to the side, the way people so often did when offering pity. As a kid, there was a lot of pity that often resulted in unsolicited physical contact; a hand on her arm, or worse, her face. *Poor dear with the dead mother*. She kept a studied distance, getting pegged as standoffish but not sociopathic or anti-social. Somehow, she'd known how to do that since she was five. Head in a book always helped.

The orange lady wasn't easily derailed. Despite the tilting head and upturned voice, Mona was paid to pick at mental scabs, and really seemed to love it. But it wasn't just that; the way Sarah was feeling and what she said seemed to matter to Mona. She reminded Sarah of Mrs. Broder and that was dangerous. It involved too much caring. The librarian saved her life. Of course, she'd blown it apart first, but she was the only adult who made Sarah feel truly safe.

The therapist dunked an oatmeal cookie into her coffee, then tapped it lightly on the edge of her mug. There were nicotine stains on her fingers. She wouldn't have pegged Mona for a smoker. Junk food anonymous, maybe. The woman was always surrounded by crumbs. If she ever needed to find her, Sarah could Hansel and Gretel it. She cringed at the memory of sitting on her grandfather's lap, loving his variation on the story where the wicked Jew witch was getting ready to stuff them in the oven with the Passover bread, but the heroic Aryan children pushed her in first. It was the only book he ever read to them.

"I shouldn't eat during sessions," Mona said before swallowing. "Seems we have a mouse problem. But it helps me focus. You don't mind?"

She was pretty sure Mona didn't care if she minded. What grossed Sarah out wasn't the food, but the imagined wet mess in the mug that brought back memories of Sunday lunches after church, and her grandfather's habit of dunking all his bread or cake in tea. It was funny until it was time to wash up. There was no dumping the contents in the sink. That risked clogging the pipes. Sarah had to shove her hand in and squeeze the liquid out of the mush.

"Do what you want," she told Mona, whose mugs were thankfully not her responsibility.

"Would you like a piece?" The therapist offered the half-eaten cookie. Sarah held up her hand too forcefully, like a crossing guard might do. The therapist laughed. A piece of coffee-logged cookie fell to the desk, and she popped it in her mouth.

"I come from a family of sharers. Sticking a forkful into someone else's face is an expression of love. When I wasn't looking, my dad used to grab food off my plate." Mona must have read disgust on Sarah's face. "Oh, it wasn't that bad."

Sarah imagined dinner at the Rubinoffs, duelling forks, food, and words flying. The Cartell table was either silent or dominated by her grandfather's never-ending lessons. No one else was ever allowed to raise their voice.

Mona listened as Sarah described her childhood meals, and laughed when she imitated her grandfather pontificating and dunking his rolls in the weak milky tea he loved so much. She and her brothers pretending to gag and trying not to crack up.

"It's no wonder you don't like eating very much," Mona said.

Wait, what? That's not what she said. It was one stupid story. Everything in therapy had to have two or three meanings. Sarah pulled at her t-shirt. People always commented on her being skinny. She ate. This was just the way she was.

"All I was saying," Sarah said. "Was that it wasn't very pleasant. No talking with your mouth full and all that. No talking at all really, not even at Christmas."

"Don't you think it's possible that if none of your experiences around eating were associated with joy or fun, that maybe food wasn't all that appealing?"

"Have I told you what I do with mac and cheese?" Sarah joked.

Shit, was she crying again? She grabbed a tissue too fast and a bunch of them flew out of the box. She reached to pick them up. "I guess it's possible."

"In my experience, it's more than possible. It's likely." Mona waited a moment, giving Sarah time to put the tissue back. "You don't need to fold them."

But Sarah did.

"Last time, right before we ended, you said you were crying constantly for no reason. But things don't just happen.

I can't force you to look for reasons. But in my experience, that's a good place to start. Maybe track the crying, see if there's a pattern."

"Like in a little journal? I should write down why I think I'm crying?"

"Write it down or don't. But try to remember. It seems your family is almost always a factor. You get upset when you feel you've lost control or think you've been exposed. It's a useful exercise."

"You say you can't force me to do anything, but I do feel forced, to say things, to remember. What's the point? It feels the opposite of useful. What am I supposed to do once I figure out what makes me cry? At least research to stop organized hate serves a purpose." She wasn't all that certain anymore, but it felt important to say.

Sarah bunched and unbunched the tissue. She thought she knew what was useful and what wasn't, but maybe it wasn't clear at all. She had a flash of all the guest cabins her grandfather had made her Uncle Carl and her dad, then later her brothers, build and rebuild. Not that anyone ever stayed in them.

Then she thought about the boxes of hate group material she'd meticulously gathered for years. Even if Professor Pichon was interested in maybe co-publishing something, that was so beside the point; the main objective was to end things, not document them.

"You know what might be useful, Sarah. A shower and laundry."

Wow. Total non-sequitur. Sometimes therapy was like a boring walk by some strip mall, and other times it was an amusement park ride that jerked her in different directions. "I stink."

She knew she did. But only on the left side. Her body was weird that way. What was she trying to prove by not bathing? It wasn't like it kept anyone away. Not in this place.

"You could use a shampoo. Your ponytail looks pretty slick."

Sarah patted her head. "I'll wear a toque next time."

"Good to hear you laugh," Mona said. "It's good you're here. It's where you need to be."

Sarah sighed. Mona couldn't just leave it at a joke. She had to make another stupid comment. *Where you need to be.* What did she know?

Mona loved playing therapy poker, shuffling and dealing different combinations of the same lines. The cards were hers to play. Sarah kept folding and Mona kept dealing.

"I don't want to be rude or anything," Becky said. "Everyone has their reasons and maybe you've got some water phobia, but your head looks like the Exxon Valdez spill and you kind of smell."

Kind of was generous. "Not you too," Sarah said.

"Who else?"

"The therapist."

"She's not wrong."

"No phobias. I . . . I've been busy."

Becky laughed, which was how Sarah hoped she'd respond. But the beds weren't nearly far enough apart, and Sarah hadn't given a thought to how the roommate might be bothered.

"Trying to score some indifference points?" Becky asked.

"Maybe."

"It does the opposite. I tried that and it landed me here. Unless you want more attention, which doesn't seem like your thing."

"God, no."

"Then I suggest a shower."

It was time to end whatever unhygienic demonstration of resistance she was aiming for. Sarah grabbed her towel.

"There won't be much hot water left. You can wait until the morning."

"That's okay. Serves me right."

"Isn't being here punishment enough, Sarah?"

That was an interesting question.

5

SUMMER 1982

Goderich, Ontario

IT WAS THE LAST DAY OF SUMMER HOLIDAYS, and Sarah and her brothers were back kneeling on rocks while her dad tossed them out into the water. They were in trouble again.

A person could almost throw a rock from Goderich, Ontario to Forestville, Michigan. Hardly anyone lived in that town, so it wasn't like somebody could vouch for a landing. But that didn't stop Sarah's dad from trying. When he was a kid, he'd go to the beach and perfect his pitching arm. That's what he told her and her brothers. He never admitted he was hiding from his father. He didn't need to.

Perched on the bluffs overlooking the oceanic Lake Huron (some great lakes were greater than others), Goderich was known as one of the prettiest towns in the country. Between Canada Day and Labour Day, it swelled to many times its size. Thousands camped at the Pinery dunes a little way down the coast. The Cartells never went to the beach when it was hot and sunny, but the wind carried screams of kids bodysurfing and bobbing in the waves. The beaches close to town were a hike down the bluffs to miles of mismatched stones. Even though tourists took home buckets full, they never seemed to run out.

The shops in Goderich's famous octagon sold beach balls, flip–flops, date squares, and maps of the Sifto salt mines, whose tunnels ran miles under the lake. Tours were popular on rainy days.

When people tired of the beach, they could go to the rivers that weaved by old stone houses and fields on the grid of unpaved township roads that blew up hot, yellow dust. Local kids rode in the back of pickup trucks and jumped off bridges into the running water.

Happy people talked about beauty all the time. *Wasn't this lovely* and *wasn't that breathtaking*. If you were a Cartell living in one of the prettiest towns in the country, beauty was a liability.

"Tag, you're it."

Sarah was always it. Even if she ran her fastest, which was fast. And not just for an eight-year-old girl. She'd be turning nine in a few weeks and liked to rub in the fact that she and Blair were the same age for almost two months. Her oldest brother Keith was ten. Ten months between each of them. *Pop, pop,* and *pop*. That's what her grandfather once called them, which was dumb since they weren't triplets. It was the only time Aunt Jean raised her voice, which was more like a loud, hissy whisper. "Dad, please. How thoughtless." She didn't point out that his logic made his own children *pop, pop, pop*, and *pop*. Their mother Margaret had died when Sarah was too little to remember, and Keith was just old enough to claim he did. Blair never said yes or no, and he told Sarah to shut up every time she asked.

Home by three, their dad had said. Everyone had to wash their hair, organize their backpacks, and make lunches. Her father hated a scramble in the morning.

Keith was timekeeper since he had the watch. Sarah coveted it, but the burden of being *on time or else* was heavy. They went to the park and when they got bored, they headed over to the high school to race around the track and jump into the sandpit.

"Hey, can I play?"

They all turned to stare at the boy, then at each other.

"What's wrong with you guys? You stunned or what?" the boy joked. He was taller than Keith. His pants were too short, like he might have outgrown them that morning. He was wearing new Adidas, and he was really Black.

Sarah opened her mouth to say nothing was wrong, but Blair spoke first. "How old are you?"

"My birthday was last week. I turned nine."

Sarah and the boy were almost the same age.

"You sure? You're awful tall."

"I think I'm sure," the boy said, laughing again.

"Let's see if you can run as fast as they say."

The kid looked puzzled, like he wondered who'd been talking about him. "I'm Curtis. We just moved here."

Sarah and her brothers glanced nervously at each other.

Blair's eyes had that crazy saucer look he got right before he did something that might get them all in trouble. But there was no one around and trying out this forbidden kid was too exciting to pass up.

"Like from Africa or something?" he yelled.

Curtis clearly thought it was a stupid thing to say. Probably he wanted someone to play with, so he went along. "Like from near Detroit," he said.

Every possible running or jumping competition was tried.

"Let's race around the track, then skip."

"Let's jump then summersault."

"Let's hop around backwards."

He wasn't super fast, but he had wacky ideas. Sarah looked around to make sure no one else had come to the track.

"How about a three-legged race?" Keith asked.

"Sure," the boy yelled.

Keith pulled two pieces of rope out of his pocket. He always had rope and his jumbo green and orange marble in there. Sarah glared at him. She knew who was going to be stuck up close and touching.

"Here's the best way to do it," Curtis whispered in Sarah's ear, so close it tickled. "I'll call *middle* and we start with the tied-up legs. Then *sides*. Move your leg when I say."

He smelled like cream soda and his lips were pink like hers. "Now put your arm around me."

She felt squirmy. This was wrong, she knew how much trouble she could be in, but the chance to beat her brothers won out. Blair and Keith made kissy faces at her.

"On your mark. Get set. Go." Keith called it.

Curtis whispered *middle* and they were off.

They won the first three races. Blair and Keith kept tripping until they caught on, and then everyone was yelling instructions. They raced again and again, tripping, laughing their heads off and almost forgetting.

"What's going on here?" Her dad's voice was loud and sharp.

The Cartell kids looked up, shocked to see him making his way towards them. How did he even know where they were? Keith glanced at the watch and his face fell.

"It's four o'clock," he said.

Sarah jumped away from Curtis taking them both down.

"Get in the car." Her father didn't need to yell.

She fumbled with the knot. Curtis untied it easily, like a boy scout.

Her stomach cramped. She gave him a dirty look.

"We shoulda never let you play," she whispered. His face fell, but he stayed silent. "You'd better get out of here."

Sarah knew they were in for it. Curtis looked at her once more, then took off across the field.

The siblings moved slowly towards the station wagon in a tight, snotty pack. Their father opened the door and pushed them into the back seat. Yelling would have been better than the silence that filled the car as they drove to one of *God's masterpieces* her father selected for punishment. This time it was the stone beach.

"We're really sorry, Daddy." Sarah liked to get the penal process going.

He never hit them. Ever. Not wanting to replicate his

own childhood experience at the hands and boots of Grandpa Thomas. Soul searching was *his* punishment of choice, while kneeling. On rocks.

He stood between them and the water.

"You understand what you did wrong?"

All three nodded, Sarah bobbed her head the hardest, like the gesture itself might minimize the damage.

"He just showed up, Dad. We were trying to beat him," Blair said.

"You were tied together with a ribbon. Looked like a barrel of fun to me. What have I said about mixing? We don't. Look what happened with your grandmother and that oversized pygmy. Abandoned her own children to spawn a bunch of half breeds."

They'd heard the story many times.

"It wasn't a ribbon," Sarah whispered.

He didn't hear the words. He wasn't meant to. "That kid's father just got the janitor job at your school. About right. If they've got to be here, that's what they're good for. These do-gooder churches that haul them over. Should have left them naked and voodoo dancing in Africa. You kids keep away from that ni——er."

He scooped up a handful of rocks and sent them flying, one by one, way out over the water. "Still got it," he mumbled.

To take her mind off her cramping legs and aching knees, Sarah stared down at the mismatched stones; sparkly white quartz grafted onto smooth blood red, grey and white granite, lumpy brown ones that looked like tiny potatoes. She picked one up and put it in her mouth. It was smooth and warm. She shifted back slightly to take the pressure off her knees and looked over at Keith.

He glanced at the watch and mouthed *twenty-five minutes*. The punishment never went longer than thirty.

"You understand why I'm doing this?" Her father moved from anger to lesson mode. Always the same question to bring things to an end.

"Yes Dad," Blair said.

"I guess we're done." He tossed the last rock effortlessly into the waves and took a deep breath. "Isn't it beautiful here?"

Rain was falling as they drove home through town. Sarah saw their neighbour Miss Eckles rush to her car with a bag of groceries and thought about a game they sometimes played, hanging their heads over the seat and looking out the back window of the station wagon.

Dad always started it. "There's Miss Eckles. Can you see her underpants yet?"

They'd collapse into giggles, screaming, holding on to treasures he threw away like McDonald's hamburger wrappers.

"Come on Dad, what else? What else?"

There were dogs pooping upside down, babies that weirdly didn't fall out of strollers. It was all great fun until it wasn't.

"I see Mr. Saunder's bum." Blair would yell something like that.

They'd push the game to its inevitable end, hitting invisible trip wires. That time, it was the lack of logic that made him snap.

"Even if he was upside down, you wouldn't see them, would you? He's wearing pants, not a dress or a skirt like some faggot. What's wrong with you? Sit up, you'll make yourselves sick."

He'd hit the brake, and they'd fall back into their seats.

The drive home was taking forever. Sarah's legs stuck to the seat, but she didn't dare open the window.

"I'm disappointed in you kids. Maybe you still need to go to the library after school."

"What?" Blair yelled. "But you said me and Keith were old enough now to come straight home."

"You've proven you're not."

Her brothers looked deflated. Sarah felt bad for them but worse for herself. She loved the bright yellow library, the books, and Mrs. Broder with her sparkly eyes and wiry grey hair. For the boys, it had always been totally boring and they ruined it for her. When they were younger, Blair ran all over and Keith flicked his stupid marble and then crawled around after it. The moms looked at Sarah with patronizing smiles and made clicking noises off the roof of their mouths, like *those poor Cartells with no mother*, but really, they meant *why can't they sit still and behave like my children?*

Maybe her dad would forget about the boys having to go to the library after school.

Once the punishment was done, it was done. He changed the subject as they turned onto Mooney Street.

"Did I tell you what happened at work?"

A health and safety inspector at Sifto salt mine, he talked about the place a lot. He'd gotten a job there right out of high school and worked his way up. He was proud of its history.

At the 1867 Paris Exhibition, Sifto took a first, outclassing even the English. Biggest underground salt mine in the world, he reminded them regularly.

"Why don't they win any more awards, Dad?" Keith was all about medals.

"I don't know. I guess no one gives out prizes for great salt anymore."

Prizes for salt did seem kind of dumb. Wasn't salt just salt?

Her dad was full of facts. The crystal catacomb was almost as deep into the earth as Toronto's CN tower was high above it. One and a half miles wide and two miles long. It was as slippery as ice, so the miners wore crampons on their safety boots. Her dad made sure of that. He might not have gone to college, but he'd done lots of health and safety courses.

"A worker sculpted a table and chairs out of salt. Ate my lunch there Friday. Isn't that something? And guess what I said."

"Pass the salt." They all yelled.

He laughed. "You know it. Pass the salt."

They finally pulled into the driveway.

Pencils were sharpened and the washed sneakers were set out in the front hall. Sarah tore open the three-pack of Bic pens, the erasers, and the binders. Her dad always joked that they had three kids because stuff came in packs of three. Blair and Keith had no interest in opening school supplies. Sarah loved doing it.

Sitting in the bathtub washing off the boy's germs, Sarah watched as the beach stone marks faded and thought about the first day of Grade 3.

Blair knocked. "Get out already. It's my turn."

Sarah dried herself quickly and pulled on her pajamas. She pushed past her brother and went to her room and closed the door. It was too early to go to bed, but she didn't mind. She had lots of books to read.

Blair and Keith shared a room, so they had each other for fake farts, real farts, and goofing around when the lights were out. She liked her room well enough but wanted her walls to be the same yellow as the library, like a lemon. Supposedly, her mom had picked plain old light yellow, almost not a colour, because it was peaceful. Her dad didn't want it to change.

Her friend Virginia who sometimes came over after church told her she should get a lace bedspread with a skirt. *You need a lady's touch.* Sarah never wore skirts and had no idea why her bed would need one. Virginia had a thing about lady's touches. She talked about them a lot, then looked sorry because everyone knew there was no lady doing any touching at the Cartell's house.

Sarah's room was simple and she liked it that way. Aunt Jean bought her a bright yellow shag carpet. The white dresser with the sticky drawers once belonged to her aunt Katie. The colourful flowered curtains on the window that looked out on Mooney Street were made by her mother before she got too sick. She decorated her sons' room with ocean things like boats and whales. There had been a plan for Sarah's room too. On her sixth birthday, her dad gave her an envelope of fabric swatches. It was a weird present. Maybe he thought she'd want them as a souvenir or something. The curtains didn't match anything and that was fine.

Beans, a birthday gift from her mom when she was two, and a bunch of books competed for space on the bed. Sarah and Beans spent nights in conversation, the rabbit between her chin and shoulder, one long ear tucked behind her own, the other wearing thin between her thumb and forefinger.

I won't ever do that again. That Curtis kid is bad. And anyway, that's how you become a race traitor. It starts with cooties.

He was nicer to you than Blair and Keith ever are.

Beans had a point.

That's their sneaky plan. Some black magic spell. And then you run away together.

But it was pretty fun.

I guess. But Dad lost his mom. She didn't even die. She just took off.

Curtis didn't take her.

Duh. That was silly. *No, but mixing.*

If you run away . . .

I won't. But when I do, I'll take you.

Beans seemed confused too. Sarah picked up a book. It was eight, and there was still summer light to read by.

The Black kid's full name was Curtis Otonga and her dad was right, his father was the new school janitor. Sarah was sure he was staring at her on the playground. She glanced at him when she knew he wasn't looking.

"You know what?" Sarah leaned in close to Mortimer Jones, a boy from their church. "That janitor and his family were all wild and naked in Africa until they found Jesus and learned to read the bible and eat with a fork."

"Were they really naked?" Mortimer giggled.

"Maybe just a loincloth."

"Loincloth." Mortimer yelled and slapped his leg.

Freddy Beacher appeared out of nowhere. "Where'd you get that stupid story? Mr. Otonga was a doctor in Nigeria before they moved to Michigan. We've been hanging out all summer. You don't know anything about Africa. They have buildings and governments and churches."

"Do not."

"Do too."

No point arguing with Freddy. He was wrong. She did wonder for a minute what other games Curtis liked to play.

In class, the teacher gave them a choice of novel to start with. *Watership Down*, *Bridge to Terabithia*, or *The Lion, the Witch, and the Wardrobe*. Sarah asked to take them all home. Some kid hissed *browner* under his breath, but she didn't care. For history, they had to pick a non-fiction book. She mentioned to her dad that night at dinner that she might use one of the books in her grandfather's attic for a book report.

"No," he said. "That's not a book that everyone will appreciate. It could tank your project. Most people don't understand what we believe. For the time being, we keep it under wraps or talk about it in church."

Sarah started reading the books in her grandfather's attic when she was six. They'd been playing hide and seek before lunch one day, and since her brothers didn't love it up there, it had taken them a while to find her. By that point, she'd found a pile of books and was sounding her way through one that was filled with pictures of bent ugly men with hooked noses making Passover bread with Christian blood. Quite gory actually.

The teacher had said it was too many books to carry home. But Sarah insisted, and she'd agreed. She'd even smiled. The heavy backpack felt full of prizes. It was a good first day.

Sunday was always church. Only fevers or barfing kept them away.

Sarah and her dad walked towards the cinder block building with tiny square windows that didn't even open. Blair and Keith ran ahead greeting friends.

"Do you think we'll ever get stained glass?" she asked him.

"Jesus was born in a manger. Stained glass is pure vanity. It's what's inside that counts." Her dad punched his chest lightly. "Humility has the loudest voice."

Actually, Grandpa had the loudest voice, Sarah thought, pulling away and running towards the tall, neat man in a thin black tie, a silver-grey shirt, and grey flannel pants. Aunt Jean called it his all-season uniform, worn with his favourite socks and undershirt.

"Too fast." Thomas Cartell put his hand on his granddaughter's head, discipline and greeting in one spare gesture. Sarah stood as still as she could.

Thomas Franklin Cartell started the Church of Purity in earnest after his wife Charlene abandoned their children for *the African*. He was its pastor and spiritual leader. A group of folks from the United Church of Christ who agreed that what had happened was a violation of both God's will and common decency happily joined.

Sarah stood beside her grandfather as congregants lined up to greet him before the service. It annoyed him that many forgot to address him as Pastor Cartell. But still, they were there. Most people in Goderich belonged to the United Church, which, he repeated from the pulpit or from anywhere anyone would listen, was *a hotbed of miscegenation—short on dogma and weak on heavenly guidance.*

Sarah and her grandfather walked into the church together. It made her feel important to be by his side. Believers were packed in on folding chairs, not pews. The air inside always smelled like B.O., but the first Sunday in September for the end of summer picnic was the worst, with all the plastic containers and tinfoil packages of egg salad and sandwich meat under the chairs. Sarah and her brothers practised holding their breath and breathing through their mouths.

A life-sized paint by numbers picture of Jesus washing poor people's feet hung behind the pulpit. Sarah and Blake always commented on who had it worse in terms of bad smells. At least Jesus was outside.

Her grandfather delivered his sermon, arms flapping, words punched out for emphasis. We *must* (punch) be *prepared* (punch) for the *White revolution* (punch). On it went about the natural order stated clear as day in the Bible, the Lord's plan for White folks to rule, firm hands, people in their rightful places, and of course, Richard Butler and Hayden Lake—the Aryan heaven on earth. The sermon was kind of boring, rarely changing from week to week, but still, it made Sarah angry that people rolled their eyes or whispered to one another while he was speaking. Support got yelled from the folding chair section, and folks kept showing up, but her grandfather complained that they were too lazy to heed his calls to action. *Adrift on a sea of mediocrity and indifference,* he liked to say.

"So long as there's beer on the raft," a friend of her dads once said.

Her grandfather carried his frustration home where it got reheated and served to the family with lunch.

After the service, everyone carried chairs and folding tables into the yard. The kids were playing hide and seek. Sarah was under the food table hoping not to get found. She could identify people by their feet. Nancy Hunt was wearing white nursing shoes, Hillary Garand, her Dr. Scholl's.

"Church is supposed to make you feel good. I'm so tired of hearing about Hayden Lake and Richard Butler and fighting the good White fight. Can't we live decent White lives? I refuse to feel guilty about not making things better. I make things plenty better for my family every day." Mrs. Garand bit into something. "What's *he* doing anyway?"

"He did have to raise those kids on his own. After his wife's, you know, betrayal."

"That was over twenty years ago. He never tried to get over it. Lots of ladies would have married him."

"Lots of ladies? I doubt it." Mrs. Hunt lowered her voice. "Honestly Hill, he gives me the willies."

"Maybe it was true love and he never got over her."

"He really seems like the loving type." They both laughed.

Her grandmother leaving with some Black man was a story Sarah heard her whole life. No details were ever provided and there was no one to ask. People said things when they didn't know she was listening, like it would have been better if she had just died. Either way, there was always pity. On top of laziness, what her grandfather hated most was anyone feeling sorry for him. *We spit on pity*, he always said to his grandchildren. *Understand?* Sarah did. No one wants to be a charity case. That was all she knew about the man her grandmother took up with. He was a charity case. His whole family was.

"Frank Cartell's a looker, but around Daddy, he turns into wet noodle salad," Mrs. Hunt said. "I don't understand why he never left like his brother Carl."

"I liked Carl."

"Who didn't? Keeeyute! I wish he came to the CPC."

The CPC was the Church of Purity Club. Purely social, although always with a *Whites Are Right* theme to activities, which was a challenge when it was bowling or mini golf. Her grandfather hated everything about it and insisted they change the name to keep it separate from church, but it stuck. Only thing pure about it, he said, was pure pointlessness.

Sarah liked her uncle Carl too and wished he visited more. He and Grandpa didn't get along, which was curious because he ran True Canadian Heritage in Montreal and was a proud believer.

"Remember their sister Katie—that wild hippie?" Mrs. Garand said. "She left two years after the mother did. I bet she was pregnant."

"Pregnant? Are you kidding? She was a lezzy, for sure. And sad sack Jeanie still living at home, serving the Pastor. Didn't she make that dress she's wearing back in Grade 8 home ec?"

Their laughter was followed by the slurpy noise of fingers being licked. Gross. Sarah wouldn't touch any of that food.

There was Cartell family history and then there were the stories people told or made up. The truth was impossible to know for sure. Sarah rubbed a twig between her fingers until it hurt. She was tempted to jam it into Mrs. Garand's scaly heel. Sweaty and bored, she finally crawled out from behind the plastic cloth.

"Sarah Cartell, were you eavesdropping?" Mrs. Hunt's open-mouthed embarrassment revealed half-chewed muck.

"Nope. Hide and seek."

Sarah ducked as Mrs. Hunt reached out to pat her head.

"How's your daddy?" Mrs. Garand sucked another finger.

"Fine." She shuddered, then turned to walk away. Talk about wet noodles.

The other non-negotiable was Sunday lunch at her grandfather's house, the house where her dad had grown up. The same place her grandmother and her aunt had fled. Even Uncle Carl left. He lived in Montreal with some girlfriend they'd never met, and only visited at Christmas. Grandpa Thomas had more success bossing around what was left of his family than he did at church.

A week after the picnic, Sarah was still thinking about what she'd overheard from under the table as she prepared to be quizzed by her grandfather. The Sunday meal in the dark dining room was washed down with a second sermon in front of a captive audience. There was less flapping. It featured a cast of recurring characters and events that, by age four, Sarah knew by heart. She always loved competing with her brothers to call out names and locations. They'd almost stopped trying, but her grandfather hadn't noticed.

"Who took meals at my daddy's table?" he asked.

"William Dudley Pelley, Dr. Wesley Swift, Reverend Gerald L.K. Smith," Sarah called out.

Their great-grandfather was a dead American who had eaten a lot of meals with important people. Everyone that got mentioned was a source of pride, a champion of hard-working White folks. Pelley, who almost got the United States to back Hitler, was the founder of the Silver Legion (otherwise known as the Silver Shirts) and the reason why Grandpa Thomas wore them.

"Did you meet them, Grandpa?" Blair asked.

He didn't answer, just waved the air, frowning as if someone had farted. "As you know, Swift started the Christian Identity movement."

He waited for his grandchildren to nod—the obligatory response to any statement that began *as you know*.

"No offense to the old British Israel believers, but Swift knew we had to take matters into our own hands. Sometimes, God takes his sweet time bringing about the promised change."

He glanced upward with an apologetic smile, as though he and God had an understanding and God was not to take offence. "Dr. Swift was a prophet, even if he was a little off on his dates. We weren't rid of Jews by 1953, but I appreciated his optimism. Poor fellow died in a Mexican hospital. Better that than having some Jew doctor poison you."

Rather than answering Keith's question about why they were even allowed to be doctors, he moved on. "Jews are responsible for what evils?"

"Communism, both world wars, the Federal Reserve Banking system, homosexuality, abortion, the United Nations." The kids tried to out-shout each other.

"No yelling. You missed tooth decay."

There was never a winner. The bucket of offences was bottomless.

Her grandfather dipped his dinner roll already soaked in gravy into his tea. Blair stuck the tip of his finger in his mouth, crossed his eyes, and made a weird gagging face. Sarah and Keith muffled giggles with napkins.

"I keep telling Carl to take a lesson from Richard Butler."

Richard Butler and his supposed upcoming visit were what drove Grandpa to drive others to build and maintain all the cabins on his property. The day would come when Butler would show up with his little army, and he would be ready to house them. Many letters of invitation had been sent over the years. *Butler is a very busy man*, Grandpa responded when the question of when he might actually arrive came up.

"Look what they are doing out there in Idaho. I don't mean to be blasphemous." Another wink upward. "But it's pretty much heaven on earth he's building out there in Hayden Lake."

Sarah was curious to know what heaven on earth might look like.

"Butler posted a sign, right out in the open. *Aryan Nations.* You got to be bold in this world." He sneered slightly at his son. "Right, Frank? By the way, how's that kyke boss of yours doing? What's his name, Goldberger, Hamburger? Still waiting for him to recognize your talents and give you that promotion? It's embarrassing to beg a Jew for anything. The opposite of bold."

"So far I haven't had to get on my knees, Dad."

"You got no sense of humour, Frank."

If anyone had no sense of humour, it was her grandfather. What he called his jokes were all insults, mostly focused on her father.

"Watch what you're teaching these kids. It's only when everyone is in their rightful place, when good honest White folks rule this world, with a firm fair hand of course, that God will smile down on us every day."

Clearly, her grandfather was also waiting for that day to come before *he* started smiling.

"How about a little reading from my granddaughter." He slapped a pamphlet on the dining room table. *Who, What, Why, When, Where Aryan Nations.* Sarah had been reading out loud for years. She was a little old for that, but her grandfather never seemed to tire of it.

Kiss ass, Blair mouthed.

"You might *look* like that no-good daughter of mine, but you aren't anything like her. You're a good girl."

When she'd finished reading, he handed the pamphlet to his daughter. "Put it with the others."

Commands could never wait. Aunt Jean got up from the table and filed it away in a drawer in the front hall credenza.

When they were doing dishes together, Sarah asked her aunt if she really did look like Katie.

"I suppose."

"Would you show me a picture?"

"If I can find one." She never could find one.

"Mrs. Hunt and Mrs. Garand were talking about her at the picnic. Mrs. Hunt said she left because she was pregnant, but Mrs. Garand said she was a lezzie."

"Good Lord." Jean picked up a glass and started wiping it.

"You already dried that one, Aunt Jean. What's a lezzie?"

"People like to make up stories. She was just different. She liked painting."

"Are we Nazis?"

Her aunt coughed and twisted her mouth. "Goodness, that's quite a conversation you all were having. There are no more Nazis, Sarah. What a strange thing for them to say."

"It wasn't them that said that. Someone at school did. Like an insult. But it would be a good thing, right? If we were?"

Jean wiped the counter in wide circles, missing crumbs in the middle. "I might know where I can find a picture of Katie."

"Finally," Sarah said.

Her aunt swatted her lightly with the towel. "Impertinent."

Her grandfather came into the kitchen. "What's all the excitement?" He didn't wait for an answer. "Come on Sarah, we're going for a drive."

"But the dishes."

They were never optional.

"Jean will finish them this once. Right Jean?"

"Should I tell Dad?" Sarah asked.

"They're fixing a shelf in Pelley." The cabins were named for people he respected. "We won't be long."

The kids never got to ride in their grandfather's car. They were too dirty and sticky, he said. Even though they weren't anymore. Grandpa seemed almost as proud of his spotless fern green metallic Ford Cortina as he was of his stories. He only ever drove Fords. Henry Ford was a hero, he always told them. A framed portrait of him hung in Adolph Hitler's office. Ford was one of his inspirations.

"Front seat," he barked.

Front seat *never* happened. Sarah even had permission to crack the window. The mild wind blew her thin blonde hair around.

"May I turn on the radio?"

"Not too loud," he said. "When I started Church of Purity, we didn't gather where we do now. I hate that building."

"Me too." She hesitated. "It's ugly."

"Sure is. We have a proper church. That's where we're headed. Robert Mintleig willed it to us for services. He was a true believer. It wasn't that far out of town, but people whined about the drive. Jesus, they go that far to Tim Hortons."

"Does it have stained glass windows?"

"It has nice windows. You'll see. You're a lot like me, Sarah. Those folks who have the gall to show up at church, they're a bunch of lazy ne'er do wells. I'm counting on you to revive this congregation. Whip them into shape."

"You mean now?"

Her grandfather laughed, a sound she barely recognized. "It can wait a couple of years."

The church they pulled up in front of wasn't what Sarah hoped it would be. The long windows did have arches. But two of them were broken. The steps were worn but the doors were glossy wood with shiny knobs.

Sarah took her cue from his adoring look. "It's really nice, Grandpa."

"I come out here sometimes, put a coat of wood stain on the door. A place of worship needs a welcoming entrance." His eyes, half shut, seemed to be seeing something altogether different. "The place needs work. I'm going to get started soon. But look how beautiful it is. Can't you just feel God?"

Despite all the years at church, Sarah still had no idea what God felt like. She nodded anyway. Her grandfather pulled his heavy keychain out of his pocket. Sarah always wondered about the big metal one. He unlocked the door and stepped in ahead of her.

"Jesus Christ," he yelled.

Sarah peaked around him. There were empty soda cans, candy wrappers, half a bag of Wonder bread, and cigarette butts on the floor. It looked like pews had been moved around. There was a dirty blanket and pillow on one of them.

"Wait here," he snapped.

He hurried past a warped pulpit through a door at the back and Sarah heard him going down stairs. She waited for a minute then followed.

The cellar was dimly lit by one bulb that hung over a large worktable. Her grandfather was peering around and scraping at the dirt floor in the corner with his shoe.

"Is there a broom, Grandpa? I can help clean."

"What did I tell you?" he screamed. "Get the hell out of here."

She froze for a moment then tore back up the stairs,

scraping her arm on the stone wall. It felt like a long time before he came back up. He stopped to force the bolt on the back door closed, mumbling to himself about vagrants. She didn't ask what he was doing in the basement.

"You're bleeding," he said, pulling a hankie out of his pocket and dabbing it on the cut. He folded it carefully then tied it around her arm.

She couldn't tell if he was still angry at her. "I'm sorry Grandpa. I-I thought I could help."

"I needed to make sure there was no intruder. It's not safe down there, as you now know. I never want to hear that you or your brothers came here without me. Understand?"

How he thought she'd ever find her way back, Sarah had no idea. And the cut wasn't exactly because it was unsafe. He patted her head almost absently, like she might have been anyone. "You're a good girl, Sarah."

She smiled warily and leaned against him. "Aren't we going to clean up?"

He patted her again. "Another time."

When they arrived back to East Street, her father was pacing by their car. Her brothers were already inside, she could see them wrestling in the backseat.

"You were gone a while, Dad. You could have told me you were taking Sarah out. Offered to drop her home. I've got stuff to do too."

"I was showing this daughter of yours what we Cartells are made of. Jean knew we were gone. And anyway, you all were busy. Did you redo the shelves in Pelley?"

"It's done."

Her grandfather grunted a supposed thanks and walked by with a half wave. "I'll check it later."

Sarah glanced at her dad. His face was red, more scared than angry, like he wanted to say something to his father, but didn't dare.

"Goodbye boys."

There would be no more talk.

"Bye Grandpa," they yelled.

"We're going," her dad said quietly.

"But Aunt Jean has a picture. Can't I just . . .?"

"I said we're going. You take the front seat, Sarah."

She smiled at her brothers and pulled open the front door. As she slid in trying to keep her legs from touching the hot vinyl, she knew that it was not a reward, just an opportunity for interrogation.

Turning to the right as he pulled out of the driveway, her dad noticed the bloody hankie. "What happened to your arm?"

"I scraped it on the wall of the old church basement."

Her father stiffened, his eyes wide. "He took you into the basement?"

"He was checking for vagrants. The church was full of food and garbage and a gross blanket. But it had real pews."

"He never should have taken you down there."

"I followed him. Then he kind of yelled at me to get out. But he really loves it. And it doesn't stink. We're going to fix it up so we can use it. And I'm going to be the pastor."

Blair and Keith started laughing.

Her father jerked the car to a stop at the side of the road and turned off the ignition. He said nothing for a minute. The kids stared at each other.

"You won't be the pastor at that damn church, Sarah." No one laughed this time. "You will never go back there. None of you. The place is a death trap. It's full of evil. I'd burn it to the ground if I could. If I ever find out that any of you have gone, even with Grandpa, there will be hell to pay."

"But what if he asks us?" Keith said. They all knew that saying no was rarely an option.

"If he asks, you make an excuse; homework, sports meet, pneumonia, I don't care. But no one goes. I'm sorry for yelling. I'm not angry at any of you. But I *need* you to make this one promise and keep it."

Their father's hands were shaking as he turned the car back on. They all nodded.

6

JANUARY 1995

Sunnyside Mental Health Centre

"THAT'S A MESSY AND COMPLICATED PILE OF feelings tearing around your grandfather's table every week. He really doled it out, a different dish to each of you, with leftovers to take home," Mona said.

Food metaphors seemed apt, despite the fact that meals at her grandfather's were at best unremarkable, and Sarah rarely cared what she ate. The anti-cherry on top was definitely squeezing the liquid out of the mushy mess at the bottom of his teacups. Gross.

"He played you off one another, leaving everyone suffering their own abuse differently. Your dad defending and proving himself. Blair trying to keep everyone laughing with his rubbery humour. Your aunt stuck in that house at her father's beck and call. And you, trapped in the impossible place between impressing your grandad and defending your father. Irreconcilable demands."

The first time Mona used the word abuse, Sarah didn't understand. Was getting in trouble abuse? Was making fun of someone abuse? Was everything her grandpa did or said abusive? The rock kneeling and anything that felt like mockery upset Mona. Turns out abuse was a popular therapy term to refer to pretty much anything that was done intentionally to make someone else feel bad, which, it seemed, made a lot of people abusive a lot of the time. *Spot the abuse* was a therapy game Sarah felt forced to play. She caught on to this pretty quickly and realized she was downplaying the shitty things, which, Mona said, would get in the way of the healing that comes of facing certain truths. This *process of illumination* skewed her entire childhood towards awful. In pretty much every session, Mona encouraged Sarah to make a pile of childhood shit so they could sort through it, with Mona labelling what was what.

The process, as Sarah understood it so far, was to unearth an emotional mess, label it abusive, then stick Sarah's nose in it. If she was a puppy, the goal would be learning not to poo in the house. The goal here seemed to be hanging out in the shit in order to learn something about oneself and one's emotional relationship to that shit, and somehow figure out how to live with it. Surely there had to be a balance between feeling emotions all the time and not feeling them at all, which Mona seemed to have decided was at the root of Sarah's problem.

It's only by facing them that they go away. That was the argument. So far, facing them just helped Sarah get a clearer understanding of how crappy things had actually been.

"Isn't it even occasionally better to leave things be?"

"I don't get paid to leave things be," Mona said. "Your father loves you. I can tell even from the short conversations we've had, how concerned he is. You're worried about what he knows and how betrayed he might feel if he learns the full truth. But I wouldn't focus on that. He doesn't seem to. From everything you and he have told me, his attention is focused on you getting better. He wanted to protect his kids from his father, you most of all because you're the one your grandfather clearly favoured and had expectations of. That scared him."

Mona seemed convinced by this protection theory, but Sarah had never felt scared of her grandfather. He wasn't warm or kind, but he never hurt her or her brothers. Her dad's fears went way back, and they made sense, but they were his, not hers. As for being trapped between conflicting needs, to prove herself and impress her grandfather, and to deflect the humiliation that he threw at her dad, maybe she and her father had that in common. Being torn between proving themselves and protecting others.

"Your father did whatever his father asked, anticipated what he wanted, even played the tough disciplinarian to show that he wasn't weak."

Sarah thought about how trying to shift her grandfather's attention away from her dad mostly backfired. How it was easier to encourage him to go on and on with his sermons. It was an unspoken pact between Sarah and her brothers. *Tell us more about Hayden Lake Grandpa, tell us more about Henry Ford.* Less damage that way.

"I hope my dad didn't know we were doing it. When I think about it, the kneeling on rocks . . . it sounds horrible and maybe it was. But it felt like his heart wasn't really in it. As soon as it was done, it was done. Half an hour, max, and then he wanted to be fun dad again."

The rocks were not okay. Sarah knew that. But her dad almost never humiliated them.

"I used to think he was jealous of my relationship with my grandfather, the way he was of Uncle Carl. Not that what I had with my grandfather was a relationship exactly, more like I was the pupil in his White supremacy school. Grandpa spent so much time focusing on what a disappointment my dad was. He would build me up by taking my father down. And my dad took it like a punching bag. I don't get it. He had a good job, he raised the three of us alone, he stayed in Goderich, he did everything he could for his father. What the hell? Carl took off, barely showed his face at his father's house, and he was the golden child."

"You wanted to be that golden child too," Mona said. "And you were heading in that direction. But in order to win that place of honour, you were expected to sell out your dad. Your grandfather knew exactly what he was doing. By offering you the opportunity to bypass your uncle, and join with him, he hurt your father and made him proud at the same time."

"That's so fucked up." Sarah sighed.

Sarah didn't want to admit it to Mona, but as awful as it was to see it all exposed, like in a TV crime scene with ultraviolet light revealing where the blood was, it felt worth knowing. Maybe. It surprised her that as hard as it was to see herself as a victim, it was worse to be a perpetrator. Mona suggested *manipulated participant* might be a better way to describe it.

"It's a lot to take in. Sometimes weeks will go by at a manageable pace, and sometimes it's like a log jam gets unplugged. It can be heavy."

"I guess there's no chance of my ever becoming pastor of the Church of Purity. Damn. Pastor Sarah has such a nice ring."

Mona looked grateful for the humour, so Sarah decided to offer a bit more. It wasn't all doom and gloom. "Grandpa couldn't hear well in his right ear, so when Carl would come for Christmas, he'd sit on his bad side and say silly things and then pretend he'd said something else. Once, Grandpa was going on and on about how True Canadian Heritage should be more like Hayden Lake. It was pretty much his favourite topic to raise with him. Uncle Carl said, 'Guess I could sit on my ass in the middle of nowhere trying to pull some non-existent strings.'

"Grandpa jerked his head, kind of like a chicken, to hear better. That always cracked us up. He was yelling, *What's that?* So Uncle Carl says, *we're in the middle of trying to change some things.*

"In the end, my grandfather poked at him one time too many, asked why he didn't have the guts to put up an *Aryans Only* sign outside his club. Carl screamed, *in a strip mall in Dorval? Where's your fucking sign, anyway? Not outside Cartell Hardware. Not even inside, if I remember correctly.* And right there at the table, Grandpa punched Carl in the chest. Once he caught his breath, he got up and left. Not a word. Never came back to that house.

"I remember watching my dad watch his brother and knowing that, despite all their bad blood, he wanted to get up and leave with him. And as if he knew, Grandpa said, all mocking, *where you gonna go, Frankie?*

"My dad was trapped. Uncle Carl wasn't."

Sarah sighed. Maybe most of it was doom and gloom.

Sarah thought about what happened later that night when she found her dad and her uncle in their backyard fighting about him storing crap in their garage and why he didn't just use one of Grandpa's cabins. In the end, her father agreed to store Carl's giant hockey bag.

"You know what's funny, Mona? That bag was filled with his White supremacist shit. I could have looked at it any time. Instead, I waited years until my dad dropped me and the bag off at Carl's house a couple of weeks before I started at McGill."

"Maybe your father was afraid you would choose your uncle over him."

"But he's my dad."

It was never about feeling closer to her uncle. It was pragmatic. That anything she had done might have made her father feel more insignificant, made Sarah sad.

"When I was old enough to see what my grandfather was playing at, I started finding things my dad and I could do together. We didn't have much in common. It's not like we both loved books. But we could play darts."

"Darts?"

"Yup. I actually got pretty good."

7

OCTOBER 1987

Goderich

SARAH'S DART LANDED IN SAMMY DAVIS JUNIOR'S one good eye. On Barbra Streisand, it was the nose they all aimed for. Cheers broke out and the men clinked their beer bottles against Sarah's pop.

They'd been playing darts in the basement for years, but a few months earlier, her dad had started bringing her to dart night at CPC. Because she was at the library so much, Sarah was now responsible for dart targets. Her dad gave her a handful of dimes out of the petty cash, and she'd bring home photocopies from magazines. Jews and Negroes mostly. Shepp Brankstone tried to argue that Muhammed Ali should get an exemption because he was Muhammed Ali. *Float like a butterfly. Sting like a bee.* And O.J. Simpson, who was almost White.

Most agreed that there was no such thing as almost White. And so what if they could play? That's what those ni——ers do. Muhammed and O.J. were fair game.

The boys had pretty much stopped going to the club altogether, but it was family night and someone was bringing pizza from a great place in Detroit, so they agreed to come. Blair and Keith hated how good Sarah had gotten and made fun of how she stood on her toes and pulled her arm back three times before letting it fly. She didn't care. Making fun of something well done, that was just jealousy.

"You run faster, throw harder, hit farther. Let her have this one thing," her dad said to her brothers.

Sarah knew she had more than just one thing, but let them have sports. The rest they didn't care about anyway. Blair blew a bubble, then popped it while she was taking aim, and her dad smacked him on the side of his head.

Sarah pinned up fresh pictures and told everyone who they were and why they were worthy targets. She looked over at Blair and Keith, glad they had agreed to come, even if it was for pizza.

"Yit hack?" Blair asked.

"The Prime Minister of Israel," she explained.

"And this ugly kyke?" someone else asked.

"Woody Allen. He makes popular movies," Sarah said. "He's on the cover of magazines."

"We can't take shots at just anyone. Waste of a dime," Shepp said.

Shepp was hands down the most out of shape police officer on the Goderich force, her dad had told them. With a gut that hung way over his belt, he couldn't catch a perp if his life depended on it. Thankfully he had seniority, so it did not.

"Why didn't you bring a picture of Curtis Otonga or his dad," Keith suggested, totally out of nowhere.

"It's about famous people, young man," her dad said, then looked resentful that he had to acknowledge that any of them were famous or made more money than all the members of their church combined.

"No matter who's on the wall, this kid's got it." He clapped Sarah on the back. "You're ready for Olympic darts."

"It's not an Olympic sport yet," Sarah blurted. "But official dart organizations are really pushing."

"Jesus, Frank. The kid's quite a know-it-all," Shepp said.

"She's my know it all." He put his arm around his daughter.

At Sunday lunch that weekend, her father couldn't help himself but brag about Sarah's prowess. "Dad, you got to come to the club and watch Sarah throw darts. Perfect shot almost every time. She'd blind that Sammy Davis Junior completely if he were actually in attendance." Sarah shot him a look as if to say this seemed risky, and her father quickly added, "Not that he'd ever be there."

It wasn't purely wishful thinking that made her dad bring up the club. Unfortunately for him, Thomas Cartell was not one hundred percent consistent in his disdain. On rare occasions, he showed interest in some random happening, and Frank couldn't help but hold out hope.

"My son," Grandpa said with snarky false pride. "Always taking aim at the deep problems of our times, supporting chip and beer companies, and funnelling dimes through the library photocopier." How he knew about the dimes and the photocopies was unclear. Sarah often wondered if he had a plant. "My granddaughter has better things to think about." He winked at her. "Protegés so often skip a generation."

"It's just fun. Nothing wrong with some healthy fun or a little target practice. Sarah could prove useful, you know, when Hayden and his boys arrive."

Sarah watched her grandfather consider whether he was being mocked, but let it go.

"I got no problem with fun, Frank."

Sarah and her brothers looked anywhere but at each other.

"Cake," their aunt almost yelled and jumped up to serve it.

The last two weeks in October, there were track meets every weekend. Keith and Blair both ran track when it wasn't hockey or baseball season. Over dinner that night, they discussed the competition for the regional meet on Saturday. What felt like hours of strategy, skills, and insults.

Curtis Otonga came up as usual. Not because he was a great athlete. He wasn't. Maybe because of the years-old humiliation of getting caught with him, Blair and Keith remained obsessed. And because now, in Grade 9, it was clear the kid was an exception to the Negroes and sports rule.

"The Fluke can't play for shit. Must feel like a total loser when he hangs out with his African cousins," Keith said.

He and Keith called him the Fluke because he was smart in school and totally average at all the things *normal ni——ers* were good at.

"A fluke. Like an accidental race traitor. Get it?"

"Ya, I get it." It didn't really make sense, but Sarah wanted Keith to shut up.

"Drop it already," her dad said. "Let's focus on this weekend."

The Cartell boys, with Sarah in tow, arrived early so their dad could give his pre-competition tips for that last minute advantage. Curtis was there with the junior high team. Someone had to come in tenth or fifteenth. That silly motto from gym that made nobody feel better seemed to actually work on him. *It's not whether you win or lose. It's how you play the game.*

Keith was running the 400. Her dad was on his feet beside her sweating like it was his race to lose. Someone screamed for him to sit down. Sarah pulled at his pant leg.

He cupped his hands around his mouth and yelled, "Boot it, Keith. That guy's catching up."

Keith glanced over for a split second and the other kid passed him and took gold.

The bleachers emptied. Her dad ran off to give post-competition tips, like *the next time I'm making an ass of myself in the stands, don't turn and look.* There was advice whether they won or lost. Anything less than gold was a defeat. Sarah always wanted to punch her brothers in the arm and tell them they did great. But there was no place for that.

Curtis threw his Detroit Tigers baseball cap on the bench near Sarah. His father ruffled his hair then hugged him. A younger sister jumped around cheering like he'd won.

"Hi Sarah," he said, then grabbed his sister and swung her onto his shoulders. "Let's go find Mom."

Sarah waved but he'd already turned away. Her reaction to the happy little scene, some mix of envy and annoyance, like they were showing off that they were so normal, felt confusing. When the Otonga family was gone, the Tigers cap lay forgotten on the bench. She stuck it under her t-shirt.

At home that afternoon, she put it in her dresser drawer without bothering to wash off the cooties. She didn't want to want to see Curtis again, but she did. She told herself that the curiosity, fed by her brothers, was more about knowing your enemy. But he didn't feel like an enemy. And his dad was a janitor, a much crappier job than her father had. *Taking over* was what her grandfather worried about, but that was mostly the Jews.

The next Monday after school when Sarah was at the public library doing research for a project, Mrs. Broder pulled her aside and told her they got funding to hire a student. "No one knows their way around here better than you. It's not much money, but it beats babysitting."

"I've never babysat." She had no interest, and no one ever asked. "But the library, I'd work here for free."

"No need. You've put in years' worth of volunteer hours."

Not exactly. But it was nice of her to say. Sarah was concerned that her father wouldn't agree. He didn't mind using the library as a free place to drop his kids or get dart targets, but this was different. Grandpa had nothing good to say about public libraries. They occasionally found their way onto the list of awful things Jews had created (the Jewy-decimal system—ha ha ha). *It's filled with lies, that's why it's called a liebrary.*

"I'll have to check with my dad. I have chores and I make dinner."

"Leave that to me. Give me your phone number and I'll call him tonight."

Sarah was unsure how that would go. He wouldn't be rude, but he might have all sorts of excuses. Mrs. Broder took the piece of paper and put a warm hand on Sarah's shoulder. She stiffened and the librarian moved away. She didn't mean to go rigid. It was just what happened.

Sarah was washing up after dinner when the phone rang. She could hear her father in the other room saying things like, *Oh isn't that nice. I hadn't realized she'd learned so much about the library. She does love it there. Keeps begging me to paint her bedroom bright yellow.* Sarah groaned. *Well, every teenager should have a part-time job. Builds character. Next Monday. Sounds good. I'll let her know you called.* Like a totally normal parent conversation.

"Looks like you'll be working at the library," he said proudly.

Sarah surprised herself by hugging him.

"Oh, okay." He patted her back. "Dinner's still your job."

"For sure."

"Total nerd job for a total nerd," Keith said when they were brushing their teeth. "Remember that time you got caught sticking your nose in the books? *Oooh, these smell soooo good.* And Mrs. Broder said they smelled like a thousand people had loved them, and you were like, *Ooooh ya.* That was totally gross."

Sarah had to laugh. "What's your great job? Oh right, cabin building for no dollars per hour."

"It's for the revolution, Sarah. We get paid in glory."

Mrs. Broder clapped her hands in excitement. "You're here. Officially. I got you a name tag." It was metal and it read *Sarah Cartell—Library Assistant*.

Sarah smiled back, hoping to match the librarian's glee. Grown-ups were often hurt when she didn't show enough enthusiasm, but she really was excited.

"How about we spend some time learning the ins and outs of reshelving, not that you don't already know most of it, then you can pick anything you want and read or do homework."

"I can do homework at home. I want to do library stuff."

"Library stuff it is." Mrs. Broder smiled.

Over the next weeks, Sarah learned the Dewey Decimal system; the microfiche; the magazines, periodicals, and literary publications.

When she approached people and offered help, they always looked surprised. Because she was a Cartell? Because she looked young? It wasn't clear which, but it stopped soon enough. On Thursday, Curtis's dad came in after work to read the *Economist*, *TIME*, and *Newsweek*. Turned out this was a weekly thing and he always stopped to have a chat with Mrs. Broder. If he heard any of the rumours about Sarah's family, he didn't show it; just smiled when he caught her eye, and she started letting him catch it more often.

Within a couple of weeks, she was greeting him with the

magazines before he even had a chance to put his coat on the back of his chair. "Here you go."

He laughed kindly. "Why thank you."

Sometimes Curtis came with him. They'd talk and laugh quietly. When they left, he always said, "See ya, Sarah."

Was he trying to force her to act nice? She'd make lists of the things that were wrong with them and repeat them to herself. It had stopped being convincing.

"See ya," she started saying back.

In the weeks since she'd started her library job, she'd taken to wearing the Detroit Tiger's baseball cap. Only when she was alone in her room.

Keith barged in without knocking, and she had to resist pulling it off. She stared at *The Catcher in the Rye*—weirdest book she'd found yet in her grandfather's attic.

"Nice hat. Looks kinda familiar."

"Knock much? What do you want?"

"Ni——a lova." He wiggled his hips in something he considered a move off *Soul Train*. A show he found really funny. "Honky."

He knew the hat belonged to Curtis.

"I'm looking for my protractor."

Sarah cracked up. She knew he was bored. "Sorry. Not here. Have you checked with your compass?"

Keith stared at her. "Where did you get the cap?"

"Get out." Sarah went back to reading some scene about a high school bully wandering the halls, snapping a soggy towel at kids for no good reason. If she had towel right now.

Keith got tired of no answer and left. She pulled off the baseball cap and threw it in the corner. She had to give some serious thought to why she was wearing it. No chance Keith would drop it. He'd make her sweat.

It was Thursday and since Cartell Hardware stayed open late, Aunt Jean brought over dinner and Sarah didn't have to make it. Sure enough, Keith brought up the cap. Like it was a joke.

"Got a tiger in your tank?" he asked.

"Funny." Her stomach flipped. He could ruin everything, even the library.

"Da-ad," he whined. "Make her stop wearing it. She's trying to bug me."

"Wearing what?" Her father glanced up then back down at the *Guns and Ammo* magazine next to his plate. "Do you really care what your sister's wearing, Keith? Thinking about getting ourselves a little skirt, are we?"

Like she ever wore a skirt.

"Perfect Curtis's team."

"What are you talking about?" Her dad finally looked up.

"Go get it and show it to Dad, Sarah. It's a Tiger's baseball cap."

"We're eating," her father said.

Just keep eating Dad. Please. Sarah could smell the sweat. Her left armpit was like a highway sign—*Scared Shitless, This Way.*

"Do you have a new hat?" Aunt Jean smiled, like Sarah had been to the millinery and bought an Easter bonnet. "More meat, Frank?" Was she trying to distract him?

"Keith, take your plate into the kitchen. The rest of us are having dinner and you're spoiling it." Her father smacked his palm on the open magazine.

"But Dad, Sarah . . ." Keith said.

"Go on, git."

She was hesitant to call it *going her way*, but the library, and now this. Good things. Whatever it was, she wasn't paying for Keith's shit, not that night anyway.

The next day, Sarah was sitting in the schoolyard, her back against the fence. Twenty more pages, then she was done. She hadn't decided whether she liked *Catcher in the Rye*, or why it was such a big deal. Holden Caulfield was not succeeding in pushing the memory of her dream out of her head. Curtis's voice was jarring.

"What are you reading?"

She scrambled to her feet. He had never talked to her at school. Why today? In the dream, she'd been wearing his hat and one of Keith's gold medals around her neck. He'd kissed her and she tried to run away, but they were tied together at the ankles with a ribbon. She tripped and fell. *I can't touch your hand*, she'd said when he reached out to help her up. Cooties. Instead, he bent down and kissed her again. Then she woke up. Freaked.

He'd been on her mind too much and she was always looking for him at the library.

Sarah held up *Catcher in the Rye*. Curtis was standing too close. She could smell his minty breath.

"Cool." He hesitated a minute. Did he expect her to say something else? She wanted to, but looked back at the book instead, only glancing up as he walked away, both grateful and disappointed that he didn't turn around.

All through Sunday service, Sarah worried about how her plan would play. A few weeks ago, she'd decided to show Mrs. Broder one of her grandfather's books. *Hoax of the Twentieth Century*. She'd looked through the card drawers and hadn't found it under Holocaust (there was no section on *no* Holocaust) or World War II or German history. Even the microfiche on books published in North America didn't reference the book.

Sarah never worked on Sundays. The library was closed, and it was the Lord's Day. Her grandfather insisted. Not that he hesitated to make his son and grandsons work on the cabins. But that was God's work. She'd asked Mrs. Broder if they could meet, and the librarian had agreed. Sarah told her dad there was a special shipment that needed to be unpacked and shelved. He agreed to let her go once all the dishes were done.

She'd gone by her grandfather's house on Friday after school, grabbed the book from the attic, and dropped it off for Mrs. Broder so they could discuss it. Sarah wasn't sure what kind of a response she'd get, but the fact that she'd slipped the book into a brown paper bag, like a bum on a street corner hiding a cheap bottle of rye or cough syrup, suggested she knew it might not be positive.

It was raining when her dad dropped her off. Mrs. Broder left the back entrance open. The door to her office was unusually closed. Sarah knocked.

"Yes."

She assumed that meant come in, although Mrs. Broder didn't sound welcoming. *Hoax* was face down on the desk. Sarah felt a rush of panic that the spine might be broken. She looked at Mrs. Broder. The expression of horror on the woman's face didn't suit her.

Sarah tried to sound normal. "Did you read it?"

"Enough of it. Where did you get it?"

"It's my grandfather's. But I've read it a couple of times."

Mrs. Broder's expression kept mutating. Now it looked like disgust. "So, you know what it's about."

"It's about the invention of the Holocaust." Sarah felt the words shrivel as they came out.

"Did he give it to you to read?"

"I took it myself. I first read it when I was six. I didn't do too bad." Was she trying to impress her? "Now I know this stuff inside out. He's even tested me on it."

"He must be very proud," Mrs. Broder said.

"I tried to find this in the library, but it isn't here, or in the system."

"It's banned in Canada, Sarah. Any idea why?"

Sarah talked fast. "Because it's hard to disprove such a massive hoax that most of the world has bought into? Because Jews have that much power. My grandfather says there's a Jewish conspiracy, a cabal that secretly runs the world."

"Any idea why the rest of your grandfather's books aren't here either? You went looking. You must have found other books on the Holocaust. We have quite a few. Did you look at them?"

Sarah stood frozen.

"I know the church your grandfather runs, and the ideas

he and his congregants believe come directly from God. I've heard the story about your grandmother, and I know that's not where his hate comes from. But this, Sarah." She points to the book. "This is an utter fabrication. It makes me sick. I thought you were different. You love the library and learning. You run to bring Felix Otonga his magazines. I see the way you look at his son."

Sarah stared at the floor. There was nothing to say. Suddenly Mrs. Broder's feelings and opinions mattered more than anything. No one else cared. Not about things like this. She could please her dad with a bull's eye, never get her grandfather's full attention. Her aunt was always busy trying to keep what was left of their family, a family, by almost never talking. Mrs. Broder saw her.

The woman let her stand there another minute. The muscles around her mouth gave slightly. If it was pity, Sarah was willing to accept it, would be grateful for it even.

"Sit."

She dropped into the chair. The invitation to stay, at least for now, was the best she'd ever gotten.

"The world is full of hatred and mistrust based on prejudices and false beliefs about who people are and how they behave. Jews have always been a target."

She knew Blacks kind of were, and Indians; she just wasn't supposed to care. But Jews? Didn't they own everything? What did they have to complain about?

"Do you know any Jews, Sarah?"

She hesitated. "No. Maybe Mr. Goldberg, my dad's boss, but I've never met him."

"I think you know others."

Mrs. Broder must have wanted her to squirm because she waited. Sarah braced for the blow she suddenly saw coming.

"You know me."

Sarah laughed then clapped her hand over her mouth. It wasn't funny. It was crazy, because of course if someone in this story was going to be Jewish, it was Mrs. Broder.

The librarian's horror and disgust were replaced by something else. Only someone who cared could look almost kind after saying they hated everything she believed in.

"I didn't laugh because that's funny."

"I know that." No matter how angry or upset the rest of her face got, Mrs. Broder's eyes never hardened. She seemed to be offering Sarah a chance. And before she knew exactly what it would mean, Sarah knew she would take it.

She told Mrs. Broder about Sunday lunches and second sermons, about competing with her brothers to win every pop quiz her grandfather threw at them, until they didn't care anymore, so she kept on impressing him herself. She told her about the old church in the country and how he wanted her to lead it one day, about finding it weird that her father was so against the idea. She talked about Richard Butler's Aryan Nation and Hayden Lake and how her grandfather expected the man and his followers to carry the armed insurrection across North America right to Goderich, where they would stay with him in the cabins he stocked with food. Mrs. Broder was quite impressed with the list of problems that Jews were responsible for, including the invention of the public library.

"Well done us," she said.

Sarah listed a few more things, including her grandfather's growing anger and frustration that the world was clearly going to hell, and no one was doing anything to bring about the glorious change. The White Revolution. How stupid it was that a revolution was even necessary, one had only to look back a few decades to find the right track and get back on it.

"He doesn't seem to actually do anything though, does he?" Mrs. Broder asked.

Sarah thought about it for a moment. It was true. Other than complaining and bossing his family around, he wasn't even any good at inspiring others to do things. Sure, he blathered on at the pulpit and at his own table, but otherwise, he kept pretty much silent and yelled at others, mainly his sons, for not speaking out.

"That's what a great preacher does. Inspire." Mrs. Broder asked Sarah if she'd heard of the Reverend Martin Luther King Jr.

Only enough to know he'd be a good dart target, which was way too embarrassing to say. Mrs. Broder was noting down books and articles for Sarah to read. The list was growing longer. Their tea got cold. She reheated it and it got cold again.

Finally, they went out into the library, and she started pulling books off the shelves and passing them down, giving a quick summary of each. A pile accumulated on the table. *Night* by Eli Weisel, *The Diary of Anne Frank*, *Treblinka* by Jean François Steiner, *Why We Can't Wait*, by Martin Luther King Jr.

The Cartell worldview, held together by a homemade glue of conspiracy theory, biblical literalism, and crude stereotypes, started crumbling under their weight before Sarah opened a single one.

They'd been at it for hours. "Call your dad and tell him you're going to be a little longer. I'll drop you home."

"Why would someone write a book that's full of lies you can disprove so easily?"

"A book legitimizes their values. For some people, all it takes is one. We humans have always believed things that seem easy to disprove. Take the most popular books of all—the Old and New Testaments. Filled with horrifying nonsense."

"But you're Jewish. The first one's your bible."

Mrs. Broder laughed. "The other one's yours. I pick and choose what's important to me. Most people do. Some swallow it whole, but that can choke you. We *have* made progress. We don't sacrifice animals or stone women for adultery anymore. At least not here."

Sarah thought about the books she'd read. The importance of keeping separate. The fact that Jews and Blacks and other immigrants took jobs away from White Christians. Was none of it true?

"It's complicated." Mrs. Broder pushed her palms into the small of her back. She'd been going up and down the step stool for the last hour. "Sometimes giving rights and opportunities to people who've always been denied feels like trampling on the people who had them first. It makes them angry. And of course, there are lots of White folks who don't have it great either. But it's not because they're White. It's for all sorts of other reasons."

"Maybe some people like how it feels to hate."

"Some do. We get attached to our ways. And it's comforting to have a target for frustration and disappointment."

Sarah thought about all the dart photocopies she'd made at the library. One day, she'd tell Mrs. Broder. Right now, she felt run over by truckloads of things she'd never considered. Things right there on these shelves, in this place she loved but didn't deserve.

What a jerk she was, always thinking she was so smart. Turns out she was simply good at memorizing and spewing bullshit.

Mrs. Broder pulled her blue sweater across her body, like it might hold her up. "Don't let it paralyze you, Sarah. You couldn't have known any different."

"Maybe I did know different. Maybe I just looked away."

"That's a lot of maybe. You're only fourteen. Everything you believe won't change in an afternoon. And your family will always be your family."

Sarah thought about her dad's insecurities, his beliefs—how nothing could topple them, but nothing made him stand up for them either. Out in the world, he denied everything and hid all his supposedly sacred beliefs behind his back, like they were stolen. That part she couldn't bring herself to tell Mrs. Broder. Something made her want to protect him from looking wishy-washy, which was almost stupid.

A few hours. Was that really all it took the librarian to dismantle everything Sarah believed was true? Had it always been that unstable? Maybe her dad's shame, something he didn't even know he felt, started that process long ago, making it easy to knock down.

The idea of going home felt like stepping willingly back into a kind of jail. "Now what am I supposed to do?" Sarah almost laughed again.

Mrs. Broder sighed. "Whatever you can to feel safe and normal. The next couple of weeks will probably be the hardest. The contradictions will be glaring. You'll feel like you're constantly sneaking around, being untruthful."

She didn't say lying. Maybe she though the word was too harsh. But Sarah knew that's what she'd be doing.

"It'll settle. I promise."

She couldn't know that, but Sarah chose to trust her. Was there a book in the library on feeling normal? "So I'm supposed to fake it?"

"A bit. You still have to live your life. But you have this place." She gestured around the library. "And you have me. I'm here." She reached out and touched Sarah's hand.

Sarah did her best not to flinch. *I'm here.* Those words gave her comfort. It was a feeling she almost didn't recognize, something she never knew she needed or wanted.

It was almost dark. Neither of them had thought to turn on a light.

Sarah stuffed three of the books into her backpack and turned to take another two.

"Perhaps not all at once, dear. You can store the books here. Read them whenever you want. There are empty lockers in the office. Use them."

Sarah started putting them all away, neatly, spines facing out. There was so much to learn and unlearn. All these facts and stories that countered all the lies she'd grown up with.

She thought about what Mrs. Broder said about successful preachers like Dr. King. She needed to know who was out there preaching this hateful gospel, the one she'd been raised to believe.

"My grandfather and my dad may not accomplish anything. But lots of people do, like Richard Butler and probably hundreds or thousands of others. I need to start tracking them. Maybe even exposing them one day."

"We can do that."

We.

Sarah turned to put the last of the books away. She picked up *Hoax of the Twentieth Century* and slid it back into the paper bag, like it had cooties. It was the first of many times she'd feel Mrs. Broder's protective eyes on her. The way out the librarian was pointing to, like an underground passage, had zero guarantees of reaching somewhere safe, and piles of risk. But now Sarah knew what she knew, and she couldn't not know, so she couldn't not take it.

Rather than feeling trapped, Sarah kind of felt freed. The conversation with Mrs. Broder gave her permission to do things differently. Carefully, but differently. And not just at the library. Once she had decided on her next big move, she busied herself reading and figuring out how to navigate her new world order, leaving no time to second guess it. It was a few days before she found Curtis alone in the schoolyard at lunch. He was usually surrounded by friends.

"Hi." Sarah took a breath and went on. "Want to hang out after school?"

He looked surprised, shocked even, but not in a bad way. It took him a few seconds to answer. "Okay. I guess."

Sarah let out her breath, a little too loud, then laughed. She was relieved he hadn't asked why.

"Meet at the front door at 3:45? I have to talk to Mr. Carlton about a project first," Curtis said.

She couldn't meet him at school. What if Blair or Keith saw them on their way home? Just standing here was bad enough. "By the tire swing in the ravine at four o'clock."

He looked unsure. "Embarrassed to leave together or something?"

"No."

"But you don't want anyone to see us?"

"You know my brothers." Maybe it was a bad idea. And he really didn't know her brothers at all. If she were him, she wouldn't agree to meet.

"Sure, Cartell, tire swing at four." He turned and walked away, arms swinging.

Her arms never moved like that. She couldn't say how she knew that was what ease looked like. She just did. Sarah moved towards the school testing out the movement, certain she looked like a weirdo. But even forcing it made her happy.

When he arrived at the swing, she was wearing the Tigers cap. Curtis grabbed it off her head. "Hey, that's mine."

Sarah snatched it back. "Finders keepers, and anyway, I could have bought it myself in Detroit."

"Like the last time you were there for a game? Wouldn't have figured the Cartells for Tigers fans."

"I don't do everything my family does." She hoped that sounded light and funny.

"It has my initials in it."

"Get out, it does not." Sarah had seen the lettering inside the cap. C.G.O. Neat block letters perfectly sewn. "Okay, maybe it does."

"My mom. She puts them on everything for us. He pulled off his jacket and showed her the initials on the inside collar."

"Cool. What does G stand for?"

"Never mind, it's goofy."

"Your middle name is Goofy?"

They cracked up and couldn't stop. One would try to start talking but the other would say "Goofy" and they'd end up doubled over and snorting again.

Sometimes characters in books laughed until they cried, but that had never happened to Sarah before.

"Now you've *got* to tell me."

"Promise not to tell anyone."

"I promise." She held up her fingers like she was in Girl Guides.

"It's Gloire. It's Congolese. The word's French." He spelt it out.

"What does it mean?"

"It means glory. Dumb, eh?"

"No way. It's great."

"It's embarrassing. Like if my name was Fabulous. Good thing it's not my first name."

"That would be rough."

It was awkwardly quiet for a moment and Sarah realized she hadn't thought the plan through any further than getting there with the baseball cap on. She knew what she liked about him, at least so far—he was smart and kind. Also, he laughed easily, and he was interested in what was happening in the world. Or he just pretended he was to please his father, but she doubted that. That was the Cartell way. No need to assume everyone else did that.

Since current events were a relatively new area for Sarah, she thought she'd jump in with a different take on something old.

"Have you heard of John Demjanjuk? Eleven Holocaust survivors identified him as a guard at the Treblinka death camp." She liked the way the words sounded familiar and easy as they came out. Her grandfather had been outraged by these *false* accusations and the extradition. What a sham. Sarah was now looking into it for herself, finding the truth. "Ivan the Terrible, that's what they called him. He's been deported to Israel to go on trial."

"I might have read about that." Curtis looked a bit surprised by the turn in their conversation.

Learning about the Holocaust and understanding what had happened, in all its horror, had the surprising effect of making Sarah's stomach hurt less. So, she went on.

"Eight hundred and fifty thousand Jews were murdered in the Treblinka death camp. And the Auschwitz commandant, Rudolph Hoess, he and his family lived in a house that was right against the wall of the camp. People were slaughtered and the bodies burned just on the other side, all day. Then he would come home, eat dinner with his kids, probably read them bedtime stories, and the next day he went back to work. They used incinerated Jews for fertilizer in their gardens."

Curtis said nothing so Sarah continued.

"And what about your own history; slavery, lynching, torture, and sitting at the back of the bus? Your dad trained to be a doctor, and instead he's a janitor. It must make you so angry all the time."

Sarah wanted Curtis to know this new version of herself. Wanted to yell it at him, it seemed. Maybe make it more real. Otherwise, there was only Mrs. Broder who knew. She kind of forgot that Curtis didn't have *any* version of her yet, other than the person who worked at the library.

He stared at her like he was unsure what she wanted him to say.

"Sorry," she said. "A bit heavy."

"Maybe a bit heavy on the horror stories."

"I thought you'd think it was important."

"I didn't say it wasn't important. It's just . . . Goderich is pretty great. People are nice. Mostly. I don't walk around being Black all the time."

"But you do."

"Okay I do, but that's not what I mean."

Oh God. She was totally messing this up.

And in that moment, it felt like the only way to salvage this wreckage she was building to prove she was no longer an actor in the horror story, but rather a potential down the road hero or foot soldier, was to change the topic so drastically that it threw Curtis off balance. She had a flash of her dream. Restart.

"Do you think the French invented French kissing?"

Curtis laughed and looked relieved, like an awkward conversation about making out might help clear the air of all the bodies. "I've wondered that too. Do the Spanish or the Germans call it French kissing?"

"German kissing would be disgusting. That's for sure."

He looked worried for a second, that "German kissing" might take them back to the Nazis.

"Want to French kiss?" she asked.

Sarah kissed him. Frenching required tongues. That much she knew.

Two days later, they met up again. Sarah insisted and was a little surprised he agreed. Had he thought about the weird middle part of their sort of date and wondered why she was such a freak?

Neither of them had very much time but she wanted to come clean, or at least a bit cleaner. Otherwise, this friendship would never work. She liked him enough to take the chance that he might walk away and never talk to her again.

When she got to the swing, he was there.

"Breaking up with me already?" Curtis asked.

Oh. He was way ahead of her. Sarah knew she was supposed to laugh and instead just looked uncomfortable.

"I have to tell you something. You need to know, in case we maybe get together again. The other day, when we kissed, when I asked you to French kiss. Maybe it felt kind of abrupt and like I was changing the subject. Well . . ."

"Spit it out Cartell. How bad can it be?"

"Bad," she said. "It's about my family. Maybe you've heard things. Like . . . they're bigots." She paused. Bigot sounded like an inoffensive place to start, like her dad or her grandfather was Archie Bunker or something—a loveable hater.

"Like White Nationalist types?"

Sarah laughed. "Jesus, Curtis. Cut to the chase."

"Everyone kind of knows, Sarah. How can you not know that? That first time we all played together when we were nine. *Let's see if you can run as fast as they say. Like from Africa or something*. I never forgot that shit."

"Why did you stay?"

"I didn't have anyone else to play with. And it was pretty fun, at least the part between the *bigoted* comments and when your dad showed up."

"My family believes people should stick to their own kind and I always believed it too. Until recently."

"What changed your mind? Me?"

"Ego or what, Glory?" She laughed. "Sort of. You were nice. Your family's different. They go to the library a lot. And you're really smart."

"Is that supposed to make me feel good? Like we're an exception? Different from all the dumb Blacks?"

"No, I mean you're different from us. No one in my family does any of that stuff, except maybe my aunt Katie. She's an artist, I think. I've never met her. And my grandmother, Charlene. Don't know her either. She was married to my grandfather, but then she took off and married a Black man. That's all I know." Telling him felt good. "But it wasn't just you, although I was having feelings I didn't know what to do with. It was Mrs. Broder. I didn't realize it, but I was ready to see it all. I gave her a Holocaust denial book that belonged to my grandfather. She had a reaction, to put it mildly. She explained a lot of stuff about the way my family sees things."

"And you just changed your mind about everything, like that?" He snapped his fingers.

"Sort of."

"I like the crush version of the story better."

"I'm sure you do."

There was so much more to tell him, but she'd said enough for now and they both had to get home.

"In case you were wondering, I've noticed you too for a while. But because of, well, everything, I was not going to be the one to make a move. But now I can."

He leaned in and kissed her.

8

FEBRUARY 1995

Sunnyside Mental Health Centre

"WHEN I WAS LITTLE, THINGS FELT CLEAR. Allegiance was allegiance. Family was family. Betrayal was betrayal. What Charlene did to my grandfather was clearly betrayal, and betraying family was the worst thing. I never considered that *we* might be the bad guys. I believed in my grandfather. He was mean and cranky, but he had good reason. When me and Keith and Blair laughed at him and my dad, it was to make the shitty stuff funny. We only ever did it amongst ourselves."

"And then you began questioning and opened yourself to Mrs. Broder," Mona said. "At fourteen. And she encouraged what turns out, according to your hierarchy, to be the ultimate betrayal." Mona tapped her pencil on the desk.

Suddenly, Sarah felt trapped in an argument she hadn't known she was making. "I'm sure it wasn't her intention. She was helping me see the truth."

"You were a little young to face that kind of truth with all its implications. To step into a double life from which you couldn't extricate yourself. At least not for years. Mrs. Broder was fully aware that you couldn't walk away from them."

"It all unravelled so fast. I brought that book to the library. She was so angry and upset."

"You were a child, a young teenager Sarah, left with a huge burden of truth and betrayal."

"What was the choice? Should I have stayed believing all that crap? Should she have let me? It was already crumbling, because of Curtis and just being at the library. Why are you turning me against Mrs. Broder? Why make *her* bad?"

"I'm not making her bad. I'm making her real. She's flawed, Sarah. Same as we all are. You haven't betrayed her."

Betrayal? Deception maybe. Sarah felt like she was being tricked into something.

"You had your reasons for misrepresenting your life to her. But she cared deeply, and you weren't letting her in. Maybe you always believed she was too good for you. And you worried that she'd see the path and the people you chose as shameful. Instead you rationalized things like not telling her about Marc, as a desire to protect her. Then you exaggerated what might be possible with Professor Pichon. Why do you think that is?"

This line of reasoning, toppling Mrs. Broder from a supposed pedestal, pointing out how she may have failed Sarah by encouraging her to do something she was too young for, all in order to push Sarah back towards her, was making her spin. "I needed her to think I was safe."

"But she knew you weren't, or suspected you weren't. Sometimes the things we imagine are far worse than the truth. You've effectively cut her out when she's one of the most important people in your life. For no good reason. This is not taking care of her."

Sarah's head hurt. "How is it possible that you get paid to do this?"

Mona's laugh was more like a bark. "Hopefully one day, the answer will be clear."

"To me?" Sarah rocked back and forth, her arms around her knees.

"That's the way this works."

"Couldn't you let me hold onto one thing in my life that was completely good?"

"Kind of the opposite of holding on. And the idea you have of Mrs. Broder as perfect has forced you to leave her behind. You can salvage this. Get in touch. Ask her to visit. And who knows what other relationships might become possible. Like your grandmother. Give her a chance to care. I'm not saying you have to give anything back. But if someone has an explanation for their actions, it can be worth hearing them out."

Was all this dressing down of Mrs. Broder just a way to get her to change her mind about seeing family? "Seriously Mona, that was a slimy move. A little bait-and-switch where suddenly I've agreed to tea, oversharing, and salvation."

"It's not a move."

Sarah hadn't exactly let go of Mrs. B. She sent letters and they talked every few weeks for at least half an hour until everything blew up. But she had altered or avoided the details of her day-to-day life, which made calls more awkward. Sarah didn't love the phone anyway. She couldn't turn away and shelve some books then pick up the conversation later. She had told the librarian about True Canadian Heritage, which had started feeling benign anyway, about going through her uncle's papers and how that was a frustrating waste of time. She talked a lot about Ara, who Mrs. B had met when Harrison brought him home for Thanksgiving. They weren't exactly out, but Sarah suspected she knew. And Melrose. Sarah talked about Melrose, as though she were a full-on cat person, which she absolutely was not.

Mona was right that she wasn't protecting Mrs. B or herself. She knew how much she missed her and that without something close to the full story, there was almost no point.

9

FEBRUARY 1995

Sunnyside Mental Health Centre

SARAH SAT ACROSS FROM HER FATHER IN the visiting room, wishing she had a cigarette. Not that she'd smoke in front of him. But it would calm her down for at least a few minutes. It seemed a silly thing to hide from him when she was locked in a mental institution for way worse behavior. But she was now the Queen of Revelations. Not a predicter of an apocalyptic future like in her grandfather's favourite book of the New Testament, but an exposer of wrongdoings, and even worse, how she felt about them. Formerly a locked vault, Sarah was now a sieve. So, it was hard to know what she might eventually tell her dad. Of course, her father never dug. Mona was a tireless digger and pusher. If asking nicely didn't yield results, she picked up a tool. Her dad was content to sit quietly together, which felt almost as good as smoking. Why had she been so worried about this visit?

It bothered her a little that he'd waited almost three months, that he hadn't insisted on coming. But that was her fault too. She wasn't ready and she'd put him off a bunch of times. That he hadn't seemed to mind, or forced his way in, was likely a function of his way in the world, and not a measure of how much he loved her. At least that's what Mona had claimed the day she first floated the idea of a visit a few weeks ago. It had struck Sarah as a ridiculous thing to say, when the therapist really had no idea what her father was like or how he felt. She'd just assumed Sarah needed to be reassured when she didn't.

But love. Whether or not there was or wasn't any. Especially in her family. This question, planted by Mona, was impossible to dislodge, making what was already an abnormal situation even worse. When had she ever worried about how much or if he loved her? Whether anyone did? But the idea took root. And like a weed, it was choking out all her healthy self-protection.

Now she felt a bit sad for the missed time. Sitting here together was nice, comforting almost. Her dad looked at her, not staring, just looking, content to sip his coffee and eat a donut with his daughter.

"You look nice," Sarah said.

"Thank you. Fresh haircut." He pushed his hand through his thick hair—greyer than it had been a few months ago. "And a new sweater for this special occasion."

Sarah frowned a little. Like, *My kid's lost her mind. This calls for a new sweater*. Is that what he was thinking when he hurried into Munster's Men's Apparel, maybe after work yesterday, to pick the right institutional wear.

"How often do I get to the big city?" he said too quickly, correcting his mistake.

His blue and grey plaid shirt matched his blue cardigan. A cardigan? Had Sarah's incarceration, as she liked to call it, driven her father into a Mister Roger's Neighbourhood-style middle age? She'd never seen him in a cardigan. She was unsure whether she'd seen *any* Cartell wear one. But he looked nice, or maybe relieved. Maybe he had been scared about what he would find when he got there, the way she'd been scared about what he might know or want to know.

"You look good too," he said. "You've put on a couple of pounds, which I'm glad to see. You were a stick the last few times you were home. I was worried."

"Lots of toast and peanut butter." Sarah reached for a second donut.

They talked for a while about things at home. Her grandfather was still at the hardware store every day but seemed to be having some memory problems, so Jean was helping him. The boys were okay. Keith was liking work at Sifto more than he thought he would. He'd even signed up to do a health and safety course.

"How about that?" her dad said proudly. "Blair's still jumping from one thing to another. He dropped out of the clowning class, now he's making pizzas. Gourmet. He wants to take a cooking course. Maybe at Fanshawe College. Anyway, that's the plan for this week, and in the meantime, we are all benefitting." He patted his stomach. "I've been bugging those boys to get their asses down here."

"I'm sure they will."

Without a joint to smoke together, Sarah worried a visit could be awkward.

"Have you been talking to Uncle Carl much?" She didn't want to know.

"Nope. Been too busy." That was all he said about that. *If* he was being honest (and he was a shitty liar so likely he was), then her fears about all the information they'd shared had been a waste of energy.

"I did run into Mrs. Broder at the grocery store last week. She's a nice lady, Sarah. She's worried about you."

Sarah tensed. "You told her I'm here? That's not yours to tell, Dad. You shouldn't have . . ."

"Whoa there." He put up his hand as though to catch her punch. "I did not say anything. She asked how you were and said you hadn't answered her last few letters. I said you were living somewhere else and that you might not have received them. That's it. Not a lie. But she didn't look particularly convinced."

Maybe Mrs. Broder already had the whole story, or at least Harrison's part of it. And was there another part to it? Not really. Nothing was within Sarah's control anymore. Nothing was containable.

"You'll get in touch when you're ready. She'll come visit, or you'll see her when you get home. I'm sure that won't be too long. There's nothing that can't be fixed, Missy."

He was wrong about that, but it was sweet of him to say. She'd think about it later. About what pieces might be salvaged.

"I don't think you failed. If you're worried about that."

She blinked back tears. He was different. Or maybe she'd known him as little as he knew her. His concerns about her failure had not made her worry list, but his belief that they had was confirmation of what he didn't yet know.

"University and all that work Carl had you doing at TCH, it's a lot of pressure. Every time you came home, you looked so worn out."

"I want to go back to McGill. When I'm up to it." Sarah wasn't sure that was true. But it didn't feel not true. And it was reassuring just to say it. She wanted to reassure him. Maybe she wanted to reassure herself.

Her father looked relieved. "That's my girl."

In the end, she didn't have to confess anything. His analysis of the breakdown suited her fine and the donuts were good.

10

FALL 1989

Goderich

SARAH WAS BUSY AND HAPPY. Grade 10 was a whole new thing from junior high, and all the clubs, extracurriculars, and group projects made meeting up with Curtis a lot easier. There was still church and Sunday lunch and making dinners, although Blair was showing some interest in the culinary arts and had agreed to cook twice a week.

"What the hell are you smiling about? And get out of Dad's chair." It wasn't the first time Blair commented on her mood like he was jealous. "Little Miss Library attendant."

"Assistant, not attendant. Attendant is like a bathroom attendant." Sarah licked her lips. They were always chapped. Too much making out. And she was constantly buzzing. Curtis had switched something on. She had no idea how to turn it off and didn't want to. He made her feel normal. At least she hoped this was what normal felt like.

"Dad's not here, so I can sit where I want."

"You're acting way too happy, like dopey."

"Dopey? Did you call me dopey?" They both started laughing but the observation made Sarah nervous. "I like the library. If that makes me dopey, who cares. I think it makes me smarter. At least I have a job and my own money."

Did he suspect anything? He seemed to be sneaking up on her a lot lately.

"Come on, let's go do something. I'm bored."

Blair never asked her to hang out anymore. Keith had something that resembled a girlfriend and wasn't around much, so maybe Blair wanted company. Sarah dropped the book and jumped up. "Okay."

Blair winked at her. "Naw, forget it. I'm hungry." He turned and walked into the kitchen.

It was a test to make sure he was still up there on Sarah's list of things she loved to do. *Asshole.* She went back to reading.

Sarah was taking meatloaf out of the oven when Keith walked into the kitchen, hips moving like he was swinging a bat. "Talking to the Fluke are we now?"

Sarah leaned into the fridge for too long, like she was looking for the lost Catalina salad dressing. He was making it up. He had to be making it up.

"As if."

"Don't think people don't talk, Sarah. Because they do. Things get around, and I saw him leaving the library the other day."

"Sure, with his dad. They come every Thursday."

"You know his whole schedule?"

"Jesus, Keith. Don't you get tired of your own bullshit? As you know, we were put together to do a science project. Not my choice of partner. Actually, he's a nice person. There. I said it. Someone can be nice without being my best friend."

"Like you have friends."

That was true. But Sarah wouldn't take the bait, although maybe she should. Get him off topic.

"You like him, don't you?"

"I said he was fine."

"You said he was nice. Remember how much you loved the three-legged race?"

"That's your evidence? Seriously? That was six years ago. Wow, you're on a roll, Nancy Drew. Following him around or what? Sounds like *you* might have a crush."

"Fuck off. Maybe I'll tell dad." He hadn't seen them together. That was clear. But it didn't matter. If he felt like making trouble, he would.

"Go ahead. There's nothing to say anyway."

Keith was grinning. "Maybe there is, maybe there isn't."

October fifth, Sarah's birthday. No one ever made a big deal about birthdays in her family. But she was happy it fell on a workday. Mrs. Broder snuck in a cake and Sarah was pretending she didn't know.

"I'm done with the returns. Don't forget to tell me if you find anything out of place." Sarah stood in the door of the library office.

"Believe me, I'm always looking for mistakes. Either I'm getting too old or you're getting too thorough."

"You're not too old."

"Could Sarah Cartell actually be saying something positive about herself? Is this a sign of maturity?"

Mrs. Broder straightened a stack of library cards, a sound Sarah would now recognize anywhere.

"I'll take them."

She laughed as she handed them over. "What am *I* supposed to do around here?"

"As if you just sit around eating bagels and cream cheese." Sarah enjoyed tossing around Jewish references.

"You're looking happy these days."

"I love working here."

"It shows."

Mrs. Broder winked, and Sarah pretended not to see it. It was clear what she meant.

When she came out of the office carrying the lit cake and singing, everyone in the library joined in and Sarah was both mortified and a little thrilled. It qualified as the biggest birthday party she'd ever had, not that these strangers were guests. Other than Curtis and his dad, Mrs. Broder had made sure they'd be there. Everyone sang with gusto.

Sarah and Curtis had a plan to celebrate on the weekend.

"See you Saturday," Curtis said as they were leaving.

"Enjoy your birthday, Sarah." Mr. Otonga waved.

It was mild and sunny, and Curtis had brought a picnic to the beach.

The unspoken plan was third base for her birthday. She was not sure if it technically included both hand jobs and fingering, but that was the idea. They were starting with Curtis.

"Are you sure you want to keep doing this? You look weird."

Did she look weird? That wasn't how she felt at all. Maybe a little nervous. "This is how I look when I'm concentrating."

"Concentrating? It's not a test, Cartell. It's meant to be fun."

"It is fun. I'm just trying to get it right. Do I go up first or down? The manual was unclear." Curtis bent over laughing and Sarah lost her grip.

"You crack me up."

"See, I'm having fun. Now pass it back to me."

"Pass it back? If you don't stop making me laugh, we won't be able to pull this off."

Pulling it off sent them back into fits of giggles.

They finally managed to focus. Curtis led her hand up and down his penis. "You okay? Is that okay?"

"Ya."

"Faster. A little faster." His voice dissolved into a whimper. And then his limp dick lay in her hand covered in slime.

"Hmm. So that's how it goes." She let go and examined her hand. "Where are the seeds?"

"The seeds? Like the ones for growing vegetables in the packs from your grandfather's hardware store?"

Sarah laughed, but the mention of Thomas Cartell made her stomach flip. She held her hand out toward him.

"Gross." He banged it away.

"Get a grip, Goofy. It's *your* reproductive material," Sarah said.

"Reproductive material. You *have* been researching."

Sarah walked over to the water and rinsed her hand. "How was I? I mean compared to friendly efficient self-service."

"You were great." He kissed her and put his palms on her small tits. She pushed her hips against his, feeling damp and excited. "Will you do me?"

"*Do* you? Don't you want your actual birthday present first?"

She shook her head no. Her breath quickened. "I've never done this before."

It was his turn to look nervous. "Duh, me neither."

She leaned against the tree. Curtis undid her button and fly and pushed his hand down between her legs, checking in with her at each increment. "I'm following the heat."

Sarah giggled, a weirdly unfamiliar girly giggle.

"Is this good?" he asked.

"Ya." Her breath was getting short.

"What about this? Is this okay?"

"Stop asking," she said.

"You're messier than I am." He whispered the words into her ear. Her legs felt jiggly. She moved them apart to steady herself. He pushed a finger inside. The sound that came out of Sarah's mouth involuntarily was a squeaky groan. Curtis pulled his finger out. "What's wrong?"

She pushed his hand hard against her pubic bone. "Put it back. I'm really fine."

"Me too. I'm so fine too."

The air was still warm enough and the beach was empty, so they took off their clothes and went in quickly, barely looking at each other. Naked was not a place they'd gone to yet. They splashed at each other, and he pulled her into a hug. It was easier under the cover of water.

"You get out first," she said.

He was beautiful, Sarah thought, staring at his back as he pulled on his clothes.

"You're looking," he said. "I can feel it."

Sarah was smiling. "I am. Okay, so what's my present?"

When she was dressed, he handed her a bright yellow envelope. Inside was a thin silver box chain. He put it on her, and she touched it. "It's beautiful."

"Like you," he said.

"Get out." She laughed, embarrassed, then changed the subject. She'd been meaning to ask, but wasn't sure she wanted the answer "Does your dad know that I'm your . . . that we're . . ."

"That you're my girlfriend?"

"Ya, that."

"My parents both do. Not the details or anything. They like to know what's going on with me." He didn't ask her the same question.

"Of course, they do. That's nice." Was it awful to feel jealous that his parents knew? That he could tell them? She touched the necklace again. "I guess we should get going. I need to be home by five. I love my present."

She took off the chain, put it back in the envelope, and put it in her pocket. "I can't wear it home. I'll figure something out. Maybe I'll tell them I bought it for myself."

She wished Curtis didn't look so sympathetic when he smiled. But he did. "You can show Mrs. Broder," he said.

She would.

11

NOVEMBER 1989

Goderich

"THOSE NEGRO BOYS WERE IN THE STORE YESTERDAY. Planning to make *janitor dad* a present." Grandpa Thomas laughed like he'd said something funny, then bit into his soggy bun.

Curtis told Sarah they'd been by Cartell's Hardware and that her grandfather had been polite and helpful. She wished they would shop elsewhere but Cartell's had the best stuff, and when her grandfather was in salesman mode, he was almost a pleasure. Curtis's dad's birthday was close to Christmas, and he and his brother and sister were making him a musical instrument.

"They needed Brazilian rosewood and fancy glue for making a *marimba*." Her grandfather made the word sound silly, or what he thought was African. "Got to special order it all if I can even get it. Can't buy regular wood, like regular people. Or go to a music store. Anyway, I'll try Simonson's in Stratford.

Kids will come by in three weeks. If I got it, I got it, if not, well too bad for them."

"You're going to sell them stuff?" Sarah asked. She took a bite of ham and looked at him expectantly.

"Money's money."

Her dad's smile was both condescending and alarmed. "Money's money," he repeated.

Sarah was reaching for a box on a high shelf at the back of the attic and knocked a book off. Even though her grandfather rarely went up there, she always made sure to put things back in their place. She stuck her hand behind the bookcase and pulled out a thick pile of discoloured newspapers with yellowed scotch tape. She carefully unwrapped it, saving an article on the Apollo moon landing to show the boys, and found four paintings signed by Katie Cartell. In each one, a threatening dark form loomed large over four small ones, huddled, egg-shaped, arms wrapped around legs, heads down. One of the forms had bits of bright colour, but mostly it was all grey or black.

Sarah banged the book against her thigh and put it back on the shelf, then carried the paintings downstairs.

"Look what I found." Sarah held them out in front of her aunt, who was peeling potatoes for the potato pie her grandfather requested for lunches that week. One meal done, another started.

She glanced at them then looked away, as though one second was more than enough. "I'd forgotten all about them. Not very pretty, are they? Katie left them behind to make a point that got the rest of us into a lot of trouble. Whatever you do, don't let your grandfather see those."

Jean pushed Sarah's hand away with a frown claiming the dirt would get all over her potatoes. "Still lives, or barely, with eggs. I think that's what they were called. Says so on the back."

Unlike Sarah's dad, whose face filled with hate on the rare occasions Katie's name came up, Aunt Jean didn't reveal anything; not love, or anger, not even ambivalence. When she got up and left the kitchen, Sarah assumed the subject was closed. But her aunt came back and handed her a box of old photos, then picked up a potato and continued peeling.

It was just pictures, but Sarah's heart started racing. She'd waited so long for these. The week after the old church blow out, Sarah had reminded her aunt about the photo of Katie she'd promised to show her, but it never materialized.

In the first picture, Carl and Frank's hair was slicked down and they wore matching pullover sweaters. Katie and Jean had long braids. Sarah was shocked to see how much she looked like her aunt. Not the hair, hers was thin and limp; Katie's, despite being tightly pulled back, looked thick and unruly. Her eyes were bright and direct. Jean looked away from the camera, hands clasped.

"This was after your mother left?"

"Maybe a week later. That was the last Christmas portrait, the last time your grandpa pulled out the camera and tripod. He was still insisting nothing would be different. We couldn't mention her. No talking about 'before.'"

Sarah stared at the picture while her aunt talked.

"At first, we were lost. Keeping everything the same was impossible. Aside from grocery shopping, which your grandfather turned over to us as soon as Frank got his driver's license. He did nothing she used to do. He worked late at the store, and we were left with the rest."

Sarah nodded, not wanting to interrupt the story.

"We fought. Your dad and Carl decided that nothing our mother had done was boy's work. Katie said that was fine, they could see how long they'd be happy going to school stinking of sweat and poo, because she for one, was not washing their clothes."

"So *you* did?"

"I couldn't stand the yelling. But the silence was even worse. It's not like what we talked about with Mom after school or at dinner was so important—someone's dog dying, the teacher throwing a piece of chalk across the room at a kid's head for drawing a moustache on the Prime Minister, try-outs for track and field—but when it was gone, we almost stopped knowing each other."

Aunt Jean looked surprised, like she had just found a piece of a puzzle. "She left on a Tuesday, two years to the day after the African family arrived. They were sponsored to come here from the Congo."

"By our church?" Sarah joked.

"Right. They wanted to import a few slaves." Aunt Jean almost never made jokes, if it *was* a joke. "The church my mother grew up in. The United Church. Your grandfather had started Church of Purity by then and expected Charlene to attend every Sunday with us kids. That day, it was a Tuesday, he got home from work and the four of us were sitting at the kitchen table. The radio was playing like it always did when Mom was making dinner. He asked where she was. 'Dunno.' Only Frank opened his mouth. He was always such a pleaser." Aunt Jean's comment was surprising. She judged even less than she joked.

"'Dunno is not a word, Frank.' Even in a crisis, Dad couldn't let it go. I thought we should call the hospital. Mom was always home after school. Maybe she had an accident. Carl said it was weird. Dad said he hated the word weird."

"He really hasn't changed much," Sarah said.

Jean shook her head in agreement. "He mumbled something about those Africans, then sat down to wait with us. Leaving the table would mean acknowledging something was wrong. I made baloney sandwiches and forgot the mayonnaise. I remember how it stuck to the roof of my mouth. At ten, he sent us to bed. Someone from church called the next day and told Dad they'd seen Mom and Diallo Duoma, not together but separately, carrying luggage."

"Diallo. He's the one she ran off with?"

"He's the one. Very tall and very Black. I wanted to ask his sister Bunny where Mom was, but Dad forbade us from going near them. I saw Bunny again only once a couple of months later, when their nine-year-old son went missing. She was going from house to house. I had a million questions, but Dad was in the kitchen when she knocked. He could hear us, so I just shook my head no when she asked if I'd seen him and shut the door. This kitchen. This table."

She patted the table and looked around the room then back at Sarah.

"Your father was really upset. Not sure why. He didn't know this kid and we were all mostly angry at that family. It wasn't exactly their fault, but if they'd never come to Goderich, none of this would have happened. Dad took Frank out for a drive, and we were all jealous. None of us went for drives. Maybe he wanted to calm him down."

Sarah wondered if her grandfather had taken her dad to that old church. Maybe it was the only place he took kids for drives. He loved routine. He hated change. Sarah knew from what her aunt had told her that nothing ever changed in Thomas Cartell's house. Nothing, she thought, except for the people who left.

"Police said the Black boy ran off to Toronto to be with his uncle and my mother," Jean said. "Not that they even looked. Told the family to wait twenty-four hours. Supposedly, the kid turned up. Or so Dad said. They left town within a week."

Sarah handed Jean another potato, worried if she stopped peeling, she would stop talking. But she rushed on like she needed it told.

"My mother and the *African* was all anyone talked about until six months later, when Rudy Brindle drowned in seven inches of water. He was six. After that, people rarely mentioned her again. But they felt betrayed, like she'd done something to them. Rudy made people sad and worried, but a mother abandoning her children was an affront. Even the ones who didn't like your grandfather felt she'd violated decency and were outraged on our behalf. Katie held her head up. I mostly looked down."

"Didn't she call or send a letter?"

"Your grandpa picked up the mail at the post office so nothing made it home. He riffled through drawers and under beds for signs that she'd infiltrated his barricades. He never found what he was looking for, but he found other things and punished us for those—a pack of cigarettes, a short skirt, a brochure for art school, a girlie magazine, *The Catcher in the Rye*."

"I found that book in the attic. Katie's name's in it. I'm surprised he didn't burn it."

"He probably forgot all about it. I must have stuck it back up there. There were too many things for him to keep track of. Too many things to punish us for."

"Did Grandpa ever make you kneel on stones at the beach?" Sarah had never mentioned that to anyone. Aunt Jean didn't seem to understand the question.

"To pray?" she asked.

"As a punishment." Sarah was sorry she'd opened her mouth.

"Your dad does that?" Her voice was shaky.

"Only a couple of times." That was a lie. "It's been a while." That was pretty much true.

"Your grandfather liked a more direct approach. In addition to hard labour." She looked up at Sarah. "That kneeling. It's not okay."

"It was never for long, and we always deserved it."

Aunt Jean raised her eyebrows but moved on. "You can piece our lives together with what's up in that attic. You must have found a lot of things."

"I didn't think you knew."

"Not a lot gets by me." She looked at Sarah for what felt

like a few seconds too long. Another moment where something could be asked but wasn't.

"Why didn't your mother take you with her or try to get you?"

"She did. A friend of hers made all the arrangements. There were train and bus tickets and plans to put our things in garbage bags that she would pick up and transfer to suitcases. She'd get us to the bus and send the rest of our can't-live-without things to Toronto once we were settled. It was a lot of sneaking around."

Sarah could imagine the kind of surveillance they were under. Aside from the mess he made of tea, her grandfather was meticulous and controlling.

"Katie was excited, no hesitation. I was anxious. How would Dad get along without us? What would we do in Toronto? What about our friends and our stuff? A million holes in the plan, it seemed to me. I stopped sleeping. Katie worried your father would give us away and wanted just us girls to go first. I was surprised your dad agreed to leave at all. Mom's friend told us she needed all four of us. I guess not having any one of her children was inconceivable. Maybe she should have thought of that before she left.

"Mom's friend invited us for dinner. Chicken pot pie and banana cake with chocolate icing. I remember it so clearly because no one made us dinner anymore. She outlined the plan. Your dad was quiet. Carl fired off in all directions; happy, confused, interested, suspicious.

"Dad watched us like a hawk, but he missed the clues. Didn't notice Katie smiling like a monkey, Carl climbing the walls, me forgetting laundry in the machine and burning things on the stove, which I never did.

"Did my dad rat you out?" Sarah wanted the worst part confirmed.

"The day we were meant to go, he left school early and went to the hardware store to find Dad. When we heard the front door open, Katie took the stairs two at a time, ready to go. She saw them both standing with their arms crossed, Frank looking more sheepish than self-satisfied, almost resigned to his fate. Carl and I were on the landing watching her ponytail swing back and forth. Katie never spoke to him again."

Charlene had escaped and left her children trapped. Sarah hated her and hated what her dad had done. Aunt Jean stopped peeling and reached out to pat her niece's hand.

"We were kids. He was a kid."

The photo trapped in Sarah's hand was bent and damp. Too many over-peeled potatoes lay in a pile on the table.

"Sorry," Sarah said trying to smooth it out.

"It's okay." Her aunt smiled weakly. "I hate that picture."

"When did Katie leave?"

"Almost two years after my mother. She'd have left sooner but it took that long for Grandpa to let down his guard even a little."

"Did she go to Charlene's?"

"She did, but it wasn't a happy reunion. I didn't know that at the time. I fantasized that it was perfect."

"How did she get away?"

"We were at church. Katie stayed home sick with a fever. Grandpa checked it himself. She must have drank hot water.

She'd pulled that stunt a few times, but Dad always left Frank at home with her. Maybe enough time had passed. Maybe he needed Frank to help at church. When we got back, those four paintings you found were taped to the living room wall.

"He yelled for Katie then told me to check our bedroom, as if she might have put them up, then climbed back into bed. Her drawers were empty. He drove around town. Katie was too smart and too desperate to get caught. When he got back, he stomped around the house, taking inventory of what was missing, mostly paints and brushes she'd bought herself. Then he noticed that the jewellery box he made Charlene for their second anniversary was gone. It was the only artistic thing he'd ever done. Hundreds of tiny pieces of inlay wood.

"'She stole it. Sneaky bitch, just like her mother.' Strangely, he'd been angry his wife hadn't taken it when she ran off. It turned up in the kitchen cupboard, where Katie had hidden it just to mess with him.

"'We're better off without her and her stupid paintings,' your dad said. 'She's useless. Jeannie does everything.'

"Your grandfather opened the box, preparing to be vindicated. Everything Thomas bought Charlene, including her wedding and engagement rings, was there. Katie had taken what belonged to Charlene's mother and a cheap necklace we all chipped in and bought her one Christmas. Dad threw the box against the wall and it splintered.

"I rescued Katie's paintings from the garbage and hid them in the attic. Your grandfather was apoplectic. He already hated Katie because he couldn't control her. Nothing he took away from her had mattered enough, and it made him crazy.

I thought he'd be happy she was gone, but I guess it was another affront to his authority."

"Maybe that's why he's never very nice to Uncle Carl. Because he kind of ran away too."

"Maybe."

What hung in the air unsaid was why he wasn't nice to Jean and Frank, who stayed behind and did his bidding.

"Do you talk to Katie? Have you seen her since she left?" Sarah asked.

Jean hesitated then shook her head. No, but not quite no.

Sarah didn't ask how she knew about the reunion with Charlene and how badly it went. If she wanted to say, she'd have said.

They heard the door open, and Grandpa Thomas call out. "I'm ready for my tea."

"Can I keep the paintings?"

"Do what you want with them, and the photos, they're yours. But keep them hidden. No one but you is interested in those family things."

"Do you think Uncle Carl might bring Marcia for Christmas?"

"No, I don't. You ask every year Sarah."

Sarah banged her mittened hands together. It was four weeks until Christmas. It wasn't their day, but Curtis asked if they could meet. They hadn't gone off the schedule since the time Sarah told Curtis what he already knew about her family.

"Sorry I'm late. The math group was meeting. It's kind of cold for fooling around. But we could try." She pushed up against him.

He didn't answer. Something felt off.

"We're leaving." Curtis didn't look at her.

"But we just got here."

"Not you. Us, my family. Goderich, we're leaving Goderich."

"What do you mean . . .?"

"We're not going to live here anymore. We're moving."

It was like all the oxygen got sucked out of her. Her mouth went dry. She kept blinking. Everything was on repeat. If she asked enough times, she might get a different answer. She walked in a circle banging her hands, then turned and walked in the other direction.

"Can you please stand still?"

She stopped, then swallowed hard and chose new words. "Like for good?"

"My dad was fired."

"From the school?"

"No, from his other job as a brain surgeon."

Sarah laughed, some awkward barky laugh that died halfway out of her mouth. "But everyone loves him. He's so great."

"Thanks. So great at being a janitor." Curtis knew how much she adored his dad. How she always asked him questions about everything. He was upset, not angry. "He was accused of stealing money."

Sarah stopped breathing. Keith. That fucker. The topic of Curtis never came up again. There'd been no blow out. Sarah stupidly assumed he'd dropped it. Now she knew he hadn't.

"But Curtis . . . he didn't. Whatever they say, I know he didn't do anything wrong. It's my fault. It's Keith. He said something. Then my father . . ." Sarah started to cry.

Curtis touched her face. "You don't know for sure. And anyway, my dad can do better. It's a crappy job. He's been looking for a reason to move to Toronto. We have cousins there." Curtis looked like he was trying hard not to cry too.

"It's not a crappy job. But maybe he can go to medical school now."

"Maybe."

They both knew how likely that was. He said maybe because he didn't want her to feel worse.

"We're leaving in a couple of weeks. Right after school closes for Christmas break. We can hang out until then."

"Sure." Sarah looked down at her hands, then over at Curtis. "But you love it here," she whispered.

"Shut up. Please just shut up."

Sarah came in the back door, kicked off her boots, and went straight to her room. It took effort not to slam the door.

"Dinner in five," her aunt yelled.

Thursday. Family dinner. She washed her face and went down to help set the table.

"Guess you heard the big news, eh Sarah?" Keith motioned at her with his fork.

She wouldn't give them any satisfaction, just raised indifferent eyebrows and pushed the boiled corned beef into her mouth.

"Otonga stole money from the school office. And they are pretty sure he's the one who took cash from the church too. He's getting fired."

Sarah kept chewing,

"How much money got taken from the school?" Jean asked.

"I heard it was $247," her dad said.

"That's a pretty precise amount, Dad," Sarah said.

"It's what I heard, Sarah."

"And how much specifically was taken from the church?" Jean asked.

Sarah's dad shrugged. "How would I know?"

"I happen to know, since it's my job to count it and lock it away. It's $38.74, almost all in change. We were well on our way to getting all those petunias for the church garden this spring."

"You seem awfully sarcastic tonight, Jean," her dad said.

"It's a man's job that was taken, Frank. A whole family displaced. I sure hope they got the right thief. Is there evidence?"

"I heard there was an eyewitness who talked to the police. It was Shepp who took the call."

"Well then, I suppose that's that," Jean said. "I wonder what they're planning to do with all that money. Maybe organize a race riot."

Sarah almost broke out laughing. Her dad glanced up. "You can't trust them." He reached for the bowl of peas.

"Are you crying or something, Sarah?" Keith asked.

And then she lost it. "What did he ever do to you? Do any of you even know Mr. Otonga? I saw him at the library every week and he was always kind, always nice to everyone at school even though his job was to pick up everyone's shit. Some of it dumped intentionally." She glared at her brothers. They looked dumbfounded like she was finally making the confession they'd been hoping for. But she didn't care what they thought.

"Enough," her dad said.

Sarah thought about the story her aunt had told her about another Black family that was run out of town, about the police not caring when their nine-year-old was missing. But this serious crime of just under $290, and they rush right in to catch the perpetrator and save the day. Her father was behind all this. She felt sure of it. Back when he was sixteen and Charlene had left, he'd destroyed their chances of leaving. What else had he done?

It depressed her to think about all the times she'd bleated out his wisdom. Her punishment for all the years of following blindly was finding Curtis, and now losing him.

Maybe she could leave too; the way her grandmother had. Suddenly, that choice made a whole lot of sense.

12

FEBRUARY 1995

Sunnyside Mental Health Centre

THERAPY WITH MONA STOPPED FEELING LIKE A tug-of-war. Whether the meds kicked in and dulled the inclination to resist, or the struggle was no longer protecting her, was unclear. Maybe it didn't matter which. She was starting to trust Mona. It was more than patient-client confidentiality. Sarah had decided Mona wouldn't betray her, wouldn't use what she was telling her against her. The therapist did throw Sarah's feelings right back at her or force her nose into them, but she had nothing to win by hurting Sarah, no investment in the game going badly. It had taken Sarah months to figure out that Mona was there *for* her, not *against* her.

Complicated may have been Mona's favourite word, but trust was the holy grail. No relationship could work without it, she always said, unless it was purely transactional, like a business deal. Sarah was also learning that trust wasn't an either-or proposition. Things could mess up, people could hurt each other, and it could feel like betrayal, but it didn't mean trust was gone, like poof. It might go underground for a bit, but it could be unearthed.

"Maybe your problem with trusting others," Mona said, "is that in your mind, people have no reason to trust you. And we mostly understand trust as a two-way street. You were forced to be deceptive, which must feel like the opposite of trustworthy. So, you are unworthy of it. You don't feel you've earned it. That started early. When you were fourteen. Even if you had no choice, and you didn't. You trusted that what your family believed was true and legitimate. That trust was violated and left nothing but deception. You know what I mean?"

Sarah did. It made too much sense. "But if I'm not someone to be trusted, then all I have to work with are transactions. I give you this if you give me that."

"That's your perception of yourself. It's not an objective truth about you. You are not categorically untrustworthy."

"But I do lie a lot."

"Let's leave that aside for now. Who are the people you've trusted? Don't overthink it. Just go with your gut."

"Curtis was my first real friend. He knew me and he liked me anyway. No one else knew me. Mrs. Broder doesn't really count."

"Sure she does. She was actually your first true *trustee*, outside of family. As little children, we trust because we have no choice. We trust we'll be fed when we're hungry, that sort of thing. But you're right, Mrs. Broder is different from Curtis. She was an adult looking out for a child she cared about. She felt responsible. Curtis had no responsibility to you. He made a choice. You both did. You took a leap of faith. In part because you were both outsiders."

Sarah laughed. "Outsider? Curtis? He was so popular. I like to think I was unpopular by choice, but I was unpopular."

"You know what I mean. Why do you think he accepted your offer to hang out? And then kept hanging out? If he was an *in* kid who could have any friends he wanted, why you? Why not someone as popular as him?"

Sarah smiled. She hadn't thought about it like that. He *had* agreed. And it lasted almost two years. She didn't exactly miss Curtis. But she missed the feeling of how easy it had been, aside from all the sneaking around terrified that they'd be caught. Easy in all the ways that counted. All the non-transactional ways. Now that Sarah was familiar with the term, it was hard not to apply it to all her friendships. Was this a transaction? How about that? Everything was suspect.

She and Curtis had spent hours figuring out how each other's bodies worked, laughing about what didn't. They'd talked about everything. Ideas, news, jerks at school, who they thought would do something great, or something illegal, or something disgusting. Who would blow up their lives. Sarah knew Curtis would do great things. As for herself, she hadn't given it much thought. But now, with everything that had happened, she was relieved he no longer knew her.

"You two were so young. You're still really young, Sarah. Don't forget that."

"I thought I didn't miss him anymore, but I do."

"You trusted him. You had to. But you wanted to. And he trusted you. And it sounds like you loved each other."

"For a while." Maybe the stories she'd invented about how great things were for Curtis and his family were to make herself feel better.

"Not your fault," Mona said.

"Not my fault," Sarah agreed. "But kind of inevitable."

"Let's stick with trust for the moment."

"I think I trust my aunt Jean. Even though there are so many things I don't know about her."

"I think you do too. I think you've always trusted her intentions."

"And maybe Luce and Harrison, even though I gave them no reason to trust me."

"That's not even remotely true. We'll get to all the reasons. In the meantime, look at you with all these folks you trust. You're on a roll."

13

MAY 1990

Goderich

OVER THE MONTHS SINCE MRS. BRODER HAD made the storage offer, they'd started their research project in earnest. Well, mostly Sarah, but the librarian was all in. Worried from the get-go about the attention that might be drawn to Sarah and the Goderich Public Library by an influx of questionable material, Mrs. Broder rented a post office box under the name Ellie Mae Tucker. The obvious southern-ness might have been an unfair association, but they kind of fell in love with Ellie Mae, who had an outgoing personality, a flare for fashion, and a love of line dancing and the rifle range. When the occasional letter went out seeking supplementary information, the details helped.

Sarah started by photocopying the pamphlets in her grandfather's credenza—mostly the old guard. Not very current. But names, phone numbers, and addresses were often included. No worries about exposure. Ellie Mae would follow up with slightly flirty letters of introduction that Mrs. Broder edited for friendliness. Naming conventions went from the obvious say-it-like-it-is, *Aryan Nation*, to any combination of patriot, proud, nationalist, freedom, liberty, front, guard, militia. Some used the words Israel or Israelite, and there were all sorts of *Moms For Saving Something*. Leave it to moms. Some material was well designed, others just crappy flyers for events that already happened. It was too disjointed to call a movement. It had no centre. It was more like cancer with mutant cells popping up everywhere.

Mrs. Broder tended to be more vigilant than Sarah. Paranoia, she believed, was useful in small doses. Healthy paranoia. They called it "HP sauce." I'd add a little HP sauce to that Sarah, she'd say.

Once Sarah read all the books Mrs. Broder had lent her and they were re-shelved, she used the lockers for everything they were gathering. They quickly ran out of space and started storing things in cardboard boxes in the slightly damp basement. Not a permanent solution.

It was early May and still a little chilly, but yard sale season was well underway. As long as there was no snow in the forecast, people were happy to haul their old shit out to the front lawn and pull up a chair, as much for the conversation as the money. Sarah had discovered this source of storage units—boxes and filing cabinets, anything that could be locked—while biking home from the pharmacy one Saturday morning before work. Turned out she had a talent for talking people into donating.

Sarah mastered pedalling quickly and assessing potential at the same time, barely needing to slow down. When she spotted the old filing cabinet, she pulled her bike over.

"This your stuff?" Sarah said to Irving Harrison, who seemed to be in charge.

She'd seen him around school and at the library. He was a grade ahead. Same year as Blair, but they weren't friends. Maybe to compensate for how tall he grew before anyone else, Irving was always bent forward, braced for a headwind. He wore a military duffel coat, and his hands were always in his pockets. Occasionally, she'd seen him taking inventory of what he carried in them; a little leather-bound notebook, a lighter, a pack of gum, gloves with the fingers cut off, a roach clip. He was a good-looking version of the prototype for Shaggy from Scooby-Doo.

"This for sale?" The rusty metal cabinet had three drawers and layers of flaking coloured paint.

"No, just airing it out. It's an heirloom."

"I can tell."

"Seriously, I love this thing. It's beautiful right? But my mom redid our basement and it'll rust even more in the garage. So here it is. Side of the road, waiting for a good home or the scrap metal guys."

Sarah saw storage potential, not beauty. She opened and closed each drawer and they squeaked.

"Just needs a little oil. You're Sarah Cartell of the sporty Cartells."

"Only darts for me. My brothers handle the rest."

"Planning to take it on your bike?"

Sarah laughed. "Yup. Got some rope?"

He laughed too, then pointed to a long thick coil in a basket. "We got everything."

Sarah glanced around. "You really do."

Irving Harrison arrived at school in Grade 4. He was pretty short then and showed zero interest in sports. That was his first problem. His second problem was a weird name that other kids made fun of. One boy started pulling his bubble gum out of his mouth and stretching it as far as it went, saying *Uuuuuurving*. Then everyone was doing it. His third problem was that he didn't seem to care at all. Didn't run crying to a teacher or say, *That's my name don't wear it out*. The gum pulling stopped. When Irving hadn't reacted, it made them look like idiots for doing it. And now, he was good-looking, didn't much care for general popularity, and hung out with an arty farty (that's what they were called) crowd.

"For prices, talk to my mom. I'm just here to protect the merchandise. Someone might steal that peach bridesmaid dress from 1969. What's the cabinet for?"

"I work at the library. We need more storage."

"I've seen you there. You're kind of an unlikely librarian."

"Really? What's a likely librarian?"

"That's a great question for which I have nothing but stupid answers. Don't they get municipal tax dollars for new things that don't need oiling? You have to ride around on the weekend buying old crap for the public library?"

"It's a long story. But I like riding my bike."

"Great job, working at the library."

Sarah looked at Irving, wondering if he meant it. The

library was generally seen by kids over twelve as a deeply uncool place, and Irving was at least sixteen or seventeen. "It is."

"Maybe I should get a job there. Delivering pizza is a drag."

"Money's pretty tight. Not even a storage budget." They both laughed. "Can you hold the cabinet for me? I'll be back in a couple of hours."

"Sure. But we haven't settled on a price. And I'm guessing it will be in high demand."

Sarah jumped on her bike. "Maybe your mom wants to donate it. Good cause," she yelled as she rode off.

Sarah locked her bike to the pole outside the library and took the steps two at a time.

"I found a real beauty."

"Not another cabinet, Sarah. This is the third one. There's barely room to swing a cat."

Seriously, who swung cats, Mrs. Broder had asked the first time she used the expression.

"Just one more. I need it."

Mrs. Broder shook her head. "Fine. One more. But that's it. Eat up, then we'll go get it before we open. Are they selling blankets? The wagon's getting all scratched up."

"Plenty of blankets."

Mrs. Broder's station wagon with the fake wood panelling was already held together by what she called schmutz. Jewish glue. If she washed it too well, she claimed the thing would fall apart.

Sarah bit into the bagel and cream cheese. The first time Mrs. Broder made her one, describing it as *Jewy* food (which Sarah found a bit shocking, but the librarian said was perfectly fine coming from a *Jewy* person such as herself), it tasted like heaven in her mouth. Mrs. Broder's sister brought bagels from Montreal by the dozens and the librarian jammed them into a freezer chest bought specially to store them, and something called blintzes. The name made Sarah laugh, but they tasted great.

"Alrighty, let's go pick up that prize cabinet."

Assessing all "the project" material that arrived got easier over the next few months. At first, it was hard to categorize things since the little groups themselves seemed to have no focus. A lot clearly thrilled to simply spew hate. Sarah read every word of every pamphlet that arrived for Ellie Mae. She listed organizations, contact people, addresses, and phone numbers, flagging places where the most activity was happening, then filing things as best she could according to an ever-growing list of themes and categories:

- Antisemitism
- White Nationalism
- Anti-Government
- Anti-Immigrant
- Neo Nazi/Aryan Nations/militant
- Subhuman races/Pseudo–science
- Holocaust denial
- Father's rights

- Christian Identity (all sorts of Christian, God's work and such)

Most could fit under several headings and Sarah had figured out a colour-coding system for cross-referencing. It involved construction paper and markers, which made the back room off the office look like a kindergarten class. Coloured dots from the hole puncher flew around whenever the door or window was open.

Soon she could just skim the contents—same set of beliefs with varying degrees of heartfelt venom and grammatical skill—and pop them in a file. The more spelling and punctuation errors there were, the happier it made her. Sarah's favourites were the ones that tried to sound sophisticated.

> *Join us in the fight for Racial Purity. God made man in his image. Beware the Jew wearing a White man's mask to ensnare you. Exercise caution. Breeding with Hebrews is an insult to God. Fear the anti-Christ that could grow in your womb, taint your jeans, and bring shame upon our White nation. Propagating with the Blacks beneath your feet will bring filth to your lineage and soil your pedigree.*

They'd actually spelled "genes" *jeans*. And bummer about those dirty pedigrees. No amount of scrubbing would help.

Every group had a pamphlet of their own. The White supremacy marketplace was flooded with calling cards. Some went directly to a file marked comic relief.

Sarah researched the guests who'd supposedly graced her

great grandfather's dinner table. Dr. Wesley Swift, founder of the American Church of Jesus Christ Christian, was the inspiration for their Church of Purity. *Christian* was code for White. Dr. Swift took to preaching in his teens. Grandpa Thomas claimed the same gift. Unfortunately for him, the right people weren't listening.

And then there was the Reverend Gerald L.K. Smith, a Christian nationalist, who established the America First party and ran for President under that banner in 1944. His simple strategies for building a mass movement assumed that most people were sheep—stupid and in constant need of herding. *Keep it superficial for quick appeal, fundamental for permanence, dogmatic for certainty, and practical for workability.* Get them hyped up, give them tasks, but don't ask them to think, don't even let them think. Her grandfather might have had more success if he'd bothered to keep his sheep happy rather than herd them by yelling criticism. Much as Mrs. Broder hated to admit it, Reverend Smith knew a thing or two about human nature.

The man was a follower of William Dudley Pelley. Supposedly the two of them had reached out repeatedly to Adolph Hitler to discuss the *semitic* problem and anti-German propaganda. He founded the Silver Legion in 1933 and ran for President in 1936 for the Christian Party. His followers were called Silver Shirts. That was why her grandfather wore what he did to church; more grey than silver, but it made him feel connected to his roots.

The two pals died in the 1970s, but their followers were still around. You could get copies of Swift's essays for two dollars, or three for five. Sarah ordered *God, Man, Nations, and the Races, Were All the People of the Earth Drowned in the Flood?* and *Give Not That Which Is Holy Unto the Dogs.*

Richard Butler, of Hayden Lake Ohio fame and the founder of Aryan Nations, was a disciple of Swift. The loose ball of "Christian" hate took little to unravel.

People started sending pictures with notes. *Nice Silvershirts right? Send us your picture Ellie Mae.* Captions were helpful, like *Ducky Franklin (me) and Richie Deward—White Night, Keene New Hampshire.* Lots of teenage boys with acne.

Curtis had been gone almost eight months. At first, he sent postcards and letters. He was taking Grade 11 math and science summer school courses to get ahead. He'd gotten a job at a library. It wasn't yellow and there was no Mrs. Broder, but it was a good job and the smell of books reminded him of Sarah. He liked Toronto well enough, White but not nearly as White as Goderich. Sarah always planned to write back, but everything she wanted to say seemed pointless. It was easier when the letters stopped coming and the memory of someone who really knew her, and maybe even loved her, started to hurt less. Mrs. Broder made her feel less alone, but she couldn't spend all her time at the library. Her friend Virginia had shown back up and thrown her commitment behind new lady's touches; makeup and padded bras, whose effects she studied daily, frontwards and sideways, in the mirror of the girl's bathroom at school. They officially had nothing in common, but she made Sarah laugh with heartfelt popularity tips she pretty much ignored. And there was Harrison, who was starting to feel like a friend.

On the weekend when neither of them was working, they'd sometimes hang out. It was easier not having to hide from anyone. He was a weirdo for sure, but he was White and anyway, he wasn't her boyfriend. Keith and Blair made the occasional snarky comment, more out of habit than because they actually cared, and even invited them to the odd party. It was more like, *come if you want*, but still.

Sarah was trying to read when she heard her brothers laughing and singing off-key—a Cartell skill. It was Saturday but her dad was on some emergency call at work.

"Shut up," she yelled a third time. The hall smelled of pot. She pushed the door to their room open to find them sitting on the bed blowing smoke out the window.

"I can smell it in my room."

"What the fuck? You don't even knock?" Keith looked more nervous than angry. Blair giggled and took a big puff off the joint, then made chokey noises as he held in the smoke.

"Like *you* ever do."

"Why are you even home? Isn't it library day?"

"Since when are you interested in my schedule?" It felt nice to have the power.

"Want some?" Keith held out the joint. It was a test of allegiance.

She'd never tried it and had a split second to decide. She could say no and use it against them, or she could join in and hope it created goodwill. She took the joint. Keith smiled.

They spent the next hour laughing at things Sarah would

otherwise never find funny, like armpit farts and bad imitations of kids at school. It felt kind of great.

High school had a different set of rules. Being neither popular nor unpopular, Sarah managed to avoid the random directives that controlled kids who had a long way to fall, or a long way to climb. People who sought popularity at any cost seemed happy to see others strung up and ridiculed. That they themselves might be next seemed inconceivable. But someone needed to give a shit in the first place, otherwise the rules didn't work.

For some strange reason, she and Harrison often found themselves witness to notable events. Sarah arrived at school one morning in the pouring rain, at the same time as Petra Grinder got there. Petra had thick blonde hair and an attitude that predated the boobs she'd grown over the summer.

When she was seven, the girl had been on a local TV show where kids walked around in a circle balancing books and bowls on their heads. She never got over her stardom. Neither did anyone else. Sarah would watch girls trip over themselves to eat lunch beside her and do her bidding. She could make or break anyone who cared.

Dressing for weather created a divide between the kids who thought they were cool, and those who had figured out that if their mom sent them to school in ugly rubber boots, they could take them off before getting there. Sarah went for warm, dry, and stable.

Petra walked open-coat and umbrella-less to the edge of the road, pushing and pulling damp strands of hair away from her face, mindful of applying the right smile. At the curb, she paused and cast about to see who was watching her, then stepped into five inches of puddle.

The shock signal took its time getting to her face. Still smiling, head jerking side to side, she lost what was left of solid footing. Her arms flew up, hoisting her red leatherette purse like a flag up a pole. Her mouth collapsed as she sank down on her knees and came to rest on the fabled D cups.

A gaggle of lesser mortals appeared out of nowhere, mixing high-pitched concern with poorly concealed glee, as they held out their hands.

"Just take the fucking purse," the girl snapped, batting their arms away.

Sarah, the occasional butt of Petra's nastiness, took the high road and kept her distance from the scene. She caught sight of Harrison, shoulders heaving with laughter.

"Hands fucking down, that wins this year's best moment," he said. Sarah smacked him on the shoulder, snorting, which made them both laugh harder.

"Makes me believe there's a God," he said.

Sarah nodded. Definitely the kind of God she could get behind.

Later that day, Harrison dropped into a seat beside her at the library. "What's the mailout for?"

He scanned the envelopes addressed to American Patriot Vanguard and Aryan Nations–Church of Jesus Christ Christian. It hadn't occurred to her to cover anything. None of her *sort of* friends came there to work. She didn't want to make up a bunch bullshit. It was time to say something to Harrison.

"Research on White supremacy."

"For school?"

"No. Personal interest. Mrs. Broder is helping. That's what all the storage is for. I'm tracking people and groups or clubs, neo-Nazi shit."

"Looking for one to join?" He laughed, a bit uncomfortable.

"Pretty much the opposite. I already left."

He registered no shock. "Your family? That church?"

"Basically. I came by it naturally. Now I'm trying to flush my DNA or make up for it. People know more about my family history than I like to think they do, but I'd still appreciate it if this stayed between us."

"Your secret is safe with me. I wouldn't tell even if I had people to tell."

He wouldn't. She didn't have proof. She just knew.

"Irving Harrison came by yesterday, ostensibly to check on his filing cabinet." Mrs. Broder handed Sarah a pile of magazines. "He confessed he was in fact looking for a filing job. No wonder he was wearing a blazer. I suggested his aspirations were too low and gave him a pop quiz on the Dewey Decimal system." She winked at Sarah. "He did not pass. But he impressed me with his knowledge of the history of revolutions. He said you can give him a reference. Yard sale management skills. Very transferable. We had a lovely visit. Did you tell him I was looking for another student? You might have raised his expectations."

"Not exactly. I said I'd ask. He thinks the library's cool. Virginia's jealous, but only that I make money which I then spend on neo-Nazi pamphlets. I guess it's obvious I'm not investing in my *look*, which she insists is critical to raising my social status."

"You might occasionally venture off the brown to beige spectrum."

"This has an orange stripe." Sarah gestured at her turtleneck. "Anyway, Irving would be great."

"I'm sure he would. He's a lovely boy. Don't you think?"

Sarah smiled. She knew what Mrs. Broder was trying to do.

"But right now, there's no money. We'll see what happens."

14

FEBRUARY 1995

Sunnyside Mental Health Centre

"WAS HIGH SCHOOL DIFFERENT? Did you make more friends?" Mona looked very unlike herself in a loud boxy jacket with football-sized shoulder pads.

"Those pads for protection? Doing a lot of tackling these days?"

"Some new administrator suggested I *spruce things up.* Seems government officials and potential donors could turn up unexpectedly with pockets full of cash. Nothing like a floral jacket to prove I'm having a real impact."

"I can vouch for you," Sarah said.

"What a lovely offer."

"Anyway, you look nice."

The outfit was more silly than stylish, but who was Sarah to say? And it would have been strange to not comment. Like if she showed up in a clown costume and Mona said nothing.

"It got easier by Grade 10. Sort of. Smoking dope helped.

Blair and Keith wanted to hang out a bit more. They were popular, so I was sometimes included by association or obligation. And Virginia seemed to have taken me on as an unsuccessful makeover project. Turns out people didn't exactly dislike me. They just thought I had no interest in them, which was pretty true. I was weird. But not weird enough. I stopped sitting alone in the cafeteria. I almost looked like I fit in."

"Maybe you liked it a little. Being 'normal.' Is that possible?" Mona leaned forward and the sleeve of her jacket dipped into the container of soup. "Damn. Some people shouldn't be allowed to wear blazers."

"I think you need an art smock."

"What I need is a stylish green garbage bag."

Sarah started looking forward to her dad's visits every few weeks. They were easy. He always brought donuts and coffee, and expected little in return. He gave her updates. Grandpa Thomas was slipping. Seems he had some kind of early dementia or Alzheimer's. Mostly he was pleasant, if she could imagine that, but occasionally there were violent eruptions of disappointment or frustration or total oblivion. Like the time his entire dinner roll fell into his tea and floated there for a minute. The rest of the family watched it bob then sink, but he didn't even notice. They felt bad for laughing but couldn't help it. Even Jean had to laugh.

Keith was driving the Cortina. The deal was he had to pick up Grandpa from work in the afternoons. Jean managed the store, but everyone pretended Thomas was still in charge. He was mostly being babysat but he did remember the name of every screwdriver head, every saw, every nail, and where each one was stored. Luckily for Jean, he'd never cooked, so on the rare occasions that he was home alone, he didn't turn on the stove.

"What happened to the old church?" Sarah asked. She didn't know why it popped into her head, but if her grandfather was losing his mind, no one was doing even basic upkeep.

Her dad said the church was planning to put that broken-down building on the market. Seems people were paying decent money to turn old country churches into stylish country homes. Good bones, or something, and a river ran through the property.

But the deed was in Grandpa's name and that complicated things. Now a lawyer was involved. Her grandfather didn't want to let it go. Kept calling it *his* church. Her dad looked uncomfortable even talking about it.

"Have you been?"

"No. I hate that place. Your grandfather hasn't been either since he stopped driving. He was a hazard. Went up on the curb and almost hit Miss Eckles. Poor thing had to jump out of the way. That's when we took the keys. Had to get Shepp involved. There was a lot of yelling, but he's adjusting to being chauffeured around."

He seemed to be steering the conversation away from the church.

"It would be good to sell it, right? It's just sitting there."

"Sure. Jean and I are working on power of attorney. Dad's in no shape to meet with a lawyer or sign documents. He just blurts things out and doesn't understand." His shoulders sagged. "I should probably fix the place up a little. Get what we can for it. Extra money for tuition."

"Good thing you didn't burn it down."

Her father grunted, like he wasn't sure about that. "Legal stuff's kind of nerve-wracking. I'm a salt of the earth kind of guy. Jean's good at this, but she's annoyed that I'm getting in the way. She wants it done."

Mona pulled a cookie out of a bag and put it on a plate, moved the coffee mug into the centre of the desk, then straightened some files.

"Mona?"

"Your grandmother called. She wants to see you," she said, making no eye contact.

The news dropped like a cement block. The words were impossible to make sense of. Sarah stared at Mona's coffee mug, half expecting it to fall to the ground, like she might, from the shock.

Mona tried again. "She's concerned. She thinks she might be able to help." Which only made it worse.

Everything about those short sentences was ridiculous. A grandmother. A concerned grandmother. Help, and what *she wants*.

"Your dad's mom, Charlene."

Could she shut the fuck up for a minute.

"Thanks for the clarification." Sarah hated being caught off guard. "Now? She wants to see me now?"

"Not right now, she's not outside the door, but she wants to find a time."

"I know it's not this fucking minute."

Sarah put her face in her hands. There were so many questions and they all seemed absurd.

"Did you even think about how this would make me feel? She's not only estranged, she's a fucking traitor. She abandoned them. How did she even know I was here? God, I hope she sounded guilty and miserable. What did you say? No, don't tell me."

Mona waited.

"Okay, tell me."

"I said I'd ask. Maybe your Aunt Katie contacted your Aunt Jean, and Katie . . ."

"Shut up."

"Sarah. Take a breath. You're angry. I get it. You need time to think."

"A breath?" she yelled. "That's your suggestion? A breath. I'm done."

She knew there was no being done. At least not anytime soon. This over-reaction was evidence of that. She walked to the door, tempted to turn around and see Mona's face, but that would be a sign of weakness. So she kept going.

Back in her room, Sarah lay still to keep from puking. She wasn't allowed to be there, but no one had stopped her.

The sum total of what she had in the world was packed up in boxes, at Luce's place and at the Goderich library, waiting for Sarah to probably do nothing with. She'd never follow the map she'd created to take down or expose all these fuckers, never write a book or co-author a paper. Even her cat, the only sentient being she'd managed to maintain a relationship with, not that Melrose had a choice, was gone. Mona was supposedly a confidential sounding board, but she'd ratted her out. Now Charlene was calling. And Katie. Just like that, the Cartells (half of whom she didn't know or barely) were a concerned family. And Mona was inviting them in. As if they could save the day.

Sarah took a bite of the buttered toast she and Becky snuck into their room. There was always something available in the cafeteria, but no food and drinks allowed out. Sneaking it had turned into a nightly ritual for them. Occasionally they got caught, but there were no consequences, just warnings about bugs and mice. Sarah grabbed the snacks while Becky distracted staff with sleepwalking stories they knew were fake and didn't care.

"She wants me to invite all these people to come visit. And now my fucking grandmother who abandoned her children, screwed up my dad, and hasn't shown her face once in my life. So what? I'm supposed to let her in to explain? Take the kind help she's decided to offer? At least my dad isn't under any illusion that he can do something magical to fix me. He just wants me better and hopes donuts will contribute calories to the process."

"I don't know. Is it really that bad an idea?" Becky asked. "You don't have to be nice. You could get some answers you've always wanted. Think about what might be in it for you, as opposed to what she gets out of it. Also, you could use some practice on your human interaction skills."

Sarah threw Beans across the room at Becky.

Becky smiled, kissed Beans, and threw him back. "I could help you strategize about what to say. You would have to give me a little bit more of your story than the post-therapy frustration spew."

"That's a lot more than most people get."

"I'm honoured," Becky said. "Aren't you curious about meeting your father's mother? It might explain all sorts of things about him."

"Things I might not even want to know."

"Maybe, but information is power. Anyway, you don't have to decide right now." Becky licked the jam off her toast, testing Sarah's gag reflex.

"Thanks for the offer to help me prep. I'll take it under advisement."

Becky was a lawyer. Well, almost a lawyer. The breakdown, at least the final stage, had happened in the middle of her Bar exam. She'd taught Sarah the expression and it got used regularly.

Charlene Duoma showed up at Sunnyside three times that week and twice the week after. Staff knew better than to let visitors pounce on patients unannounced, but each time, Sarah had to be called into Mona's office to contemplate the offer while her grandmother waited at the front desk. She was either patient or stubborn, because it often took an hour or two before being turned away. Didn't she have anything better to do?

The news of each arrival did feel like less of a bomb in Sarah's day. Mona thought reconnecting with family could be helpful. The therapist was particular about language and suggested it was problematic to call Charlene a traitor. But for someone so semantically precise, perhaps she should drop the "re" in reconnecting. The woman was a complete stranger.

For someone so smart about human beings and their stupid interactions and motivations, Mona shouldn't be tossing around the word *family* as if it had some fixed meaning, like a hammer or a toaster that could always be relied on to do the same thing. She seemed obsessed with good guys and bad guys. Traitor might be the wrong word for Charlene, but just because her grandfather was a bad-guy didn't make her a good-guy.

Two different stories about her grandmother ran on a loop: the heroine fleeing evil, and the unfaithful wife abandoning her children. Both served as escape fantasies. Now, this person who was responsible for everything her father was, wanted in. Maybe Charlene *should* get what she was asking for, the story of how she had failed them all in gory detail.

"Aren't you a little curious about her? Would seeing your grandmother break some rule you've established?"

According to Mona, people were masochists by nature and set stupid rules for no good reason that they could flagellate themselves for violating.

"It's not a rule. I just don't want her to think she won."

"So this way *you* win?" Mona asked

Sarah pulled at her t-shirt. "She shouldn't have left."

"Having two unhappy parents isn't guaranteed to be helpful."

"I wouldn't know. Dead mom, remember." She knew Mona hadn't forgotten. "Becky agrees with you. She thinks seeing Charlene isn't a bad idea. I could get some answers. So what's the harm? But there can always be harm. I get that now. And maybe I only thought I wanted to know."

Was she angry that Charlene found love, escaped, started a completely new family, didn't look back for decades? Hate might not be in her blood, but she'd still been capable of something horrible. Maybe leaving her kids behind broke her heart, but she did it anyway. How much more information did Sarah need?

Did Mona manage to chip away at her resolve, or did she decide making the grandmother feel worse might be worth it? Either way, she finally agreed to see her.

15

SUMMER 1991

Goderich

ANOTHER SUNDAY. ANOTHER LUNCH. Another flattery session. Sometimes Sarah drafted the questions for her grandfather in advance. When it didn't look like her father was going to be dragged through the mud, Blair and Keith just glared at her, resenting her for extending the torture. She would, as they suggested, chat him up on her own time, but these days he always napped after lunch. And anyway, there was a point to evoking the glory days in front of his entire family, even if the glory was all in his head.

While Sarah now knew way more than her grandfather ever had, she still fished enthusiastically. Partly out of some faded sense of respect, partly so he didn't suspect anything, partly to retain his sense of himself as king of the castle, not that he would be easily dethroned. It was, however, a balancing act. And she worried about sounding too eager to show off.

"Why you asking me all these questions?" her grandfather said.

She had to tread carefully. The answers he didn't have annoyed him most, and right now he looked irritated.

"I've organized a bunch of your materials, some of the stuff in the attic and all the pamphlets and flyers in the credenza."

He nodded.

"I'm trying to find out who else is doing what you and Dad and Uncle Carl do. Identify this incredible network."

"Sounds worthwhile. Nothing's going to change if we don't build a stronger movement. And do watch out, there are plenty of idiots on our side."

That went without saying. More than plenty. Sarah was getting tired of sending letters from Ellie Mae Tucker to pumped up adolescent yahoos across North America. The excitement of hearing back had faded, and the effort net more of the same. She hoped that connecting photos and names to one another would help her identify whatever network existed. Mrs. Broder was endlessly encouraging, telling Sarah that this was the way it went, a lot of digging and sifting through rubble and garbage to find the occasional gem. That was the nature of journalistic research. Following false leads to confirm they were false.

"Talked to your uncle Carl?"

Sarah looked over at her dad, who rolled his eyes. "I want to find things myself. I'll talk to him at some point."

Her grandfather grunted. "All on your own?"

"Yup," she lied. It came so easy now. "And anyway, I want to go to university, so I can develop more skills. I was thinking about McGill since I already know someone in Montreal."

Neither he nor her dad looked particularly pleased. But the idea was now out there, and no fits had been thrown. Bringing up university was a risk. Her grandfather claimed higher learning bred liberalism. But getting to Montreal and making personal connections with people Carl knew would expand what was currently theoretical, so it was best to get him used to the idea. It was her dad's support she needed, but he often deferred, so this was the way to go. Name-dropping Holocaust deniers who had university degrees helped make the case. Sarah suspected the real issue was that *he'd* never gone beyond high school, so he couldn't see why anyone else needed to.

"Who knows, maybe I'll start my own group."

"You got *my* brains girl." He looked at his son.

Compliments were always accompanied by insults, real or implied. *The soup is good Jean, much better than last week's. That dress is nice. I didn't much like the green one.* He was a big fan of killing two birds with one stone. Nothing good comes of a swollen ego, unless it's one's own.

"Pass it to me." Blair reached for the joint.

"You just had it. You're too stoned to know how a circle works. I pass it to you, then you pass it to Sarah, and she passes it to me. That's a circle."

"This generation rules the nation," Blair yelled in a Jamaican accent then started singing. "Pass the dutchie to the left-hand side." Then they were all singing.

"Where do you get all this weed, anyway?" Harrison had asked if she could get him some.

"From Randy Nutterson. He's a total stoner. Loves all this Rasta shit."

"The guy always reeks of the ganga." Blair grabbed a handful of potato chips out of the bag.

"He's stoned at every CPC club meeting. Giggles and licks envelopes. Says he likes the taste. The guy cracks me up. We'll have to get stoned for this next event, that old famous Nazi writer guy. How not fun does that sound?" Keith asked.

"Definitely," Sarah said. She was relieved that most of the club meetings happened when she was working. They were a total waste of her time. Her father made a deal with Blake and Keith. They could use the car for every time they went.

"At least we get to go to Toronto. It's not totally planned yet. Hush hush. The guy that's coming is a total ass." Blair started laughing. "Remember, Keith? Guy's name is Butt or something."

"Arthur Butz?" Sarah asked.

"You know all the shit. You're such a nerd, Sarah."

"Is there a flyer yet?"

"Want to put it up on the wall in your room?"

"Maybe. If Butz is cute." She knew he was not cute.

"Totally ugly, I'm guessing." Keith laughed. "But I don't really know your taste in men."

"Randy's mom's making them. I'll get him to bring one to the party on Saturday."

"Mad dog!!" Blair yelled. A mad dog party was a party someone really popular hosted at the house of someone who aspired to be popular, when their parents were out of town.

The place was heaving with kids whose ability to drink and stay standing ranged from professional to non-existent. The cheerleader-types always ended up puking on the lawn. Maybe if they bounced and fake laughed a little less, they might keep it down.

Randy grabbed Sarah's elbow. "Heard you want a flyer." She shook her arm away. What was it with guys and elbows? Grab the rudder and steer.

Randy handed her a plastic cup of beer and stood too close. She gulped down half of it. The music pounded. She could feel the bass through her feet. A bunch of arty kids, Harrison included, were thrashing around. The floor was sticky. Virginia came over and leaned on Sarah's shoulder, emptying a mouthful of smoke into her ear saying: "Ooh Randy, hadn't thought about him that way. I guess he's kinda cute."

Sarah hoped Randy hadn't heard.

"Gotta pee." Virginia stumbled off.

"Wanna dance?" Randy started swaying.

"I don't dance," Sarah yelled.

"Ya well me neither."

"Got a joint?"

"Always."

"Let's go outside."

"Cool." He seemed relieved. When he grabbed her elbow again, she jabbed him in the rib. "No fucking elbows, man."

"No fucking elbows," he repeated, laughing.

When they were sitting on the ground passing the joint back and forth, he pulled a paper out of his jacket pocket. "What do I get for this?"

Sarah grabbed it. "You get to smoke a joint with me."

"No kiss?" He leaned in and she pushed him back. He laughed as he rolled onto his back, too stoned to be disappointed.

"Where's Jed?" Sarah asked.

"He's inside entertaining."

A tractor accident had left Randy's older brother Jedidiah barely able to speak or do much of anything but smile or furrow his brow at nothing in particular. He liked ice cream, was fed too much of it, and was getting harder to move. Randy helped. He drew the line at bathing but was willing to push his brother around town to meet friends. They got him stoned blowing shotguns into his open mouth, then wiped away the spit. If there were steps, a bunch of guys carried the wheelchair up and down. The pot made Jed a party attraction, but no one mocked him. Randy made sure of that. He was a good guy. Not very smart, but nice enough. Sarah was tempted to let him kiss her. She missed kissing and it might be fun to do it with someone who didn't work up a sweat for anything. But the idea of his tongue lolling around in her mouth was not appealing enough.

"You should come to Mexican night next week."

As a kid, she always had fun at Mexican night. It was bright and colourful. People singing *Ay, ay ya yay. I am the Frito Bandito* at the top of their lungs. Every one of those church club guys owned a sombrero. Even though Mexicans were borderline verboten, depending how Mexican—no marrying, no partnering for business.

"They wish tacos and enchiladas could have gotten to North America by themselves." Sometimes Randy was really funny.

"What do you call a fat chink? A chunk." He laughed.

But not always.

"Let's go back inside."

With a little effort, she could probably convince Randy to change sides. But why bother? A totally stoned White separatist becoming a totally stoned liberal. Not very helpful.

Heavy block lettering under a photo that looked like a caricature of a scientist from Saturday Night Live read *Dr. Arthur Butz*. She recognized the photo from the jacket of *The Hoax of the Twentieth Century*. Under his name in a different font, it said *A White hero for our times.* A circle around the word Holocaust had a dark line through it with the words *We Were Right* underneath. Randy's mom could do with a graphic design class, but Jed kept her too busy. The event was two weeks away on a Saturday in a suburb of Toronto. Location: WOM.

It had taken Sarah months of studying event flyers to figure out that WOM stood for Word of Mouth. A bunch of clubs from across southern Ontario and Michigan would probably show up.

At the library the next day, Sarah stuck the flyer in front of Mrs. Broder. "Guess who's coming to speak? Well, to Toronto or near Toronto. Arthur Butz."

"Where'd you get this?"

"From Randy Nutterson. Bit of a club sponsored event."

The librarian had forced her way through *Hoax*, becoming one of the few people who read it before criticizing it. It was a five hundred page and curiously compelling waste of time banned in Canada. The flaws were hard to spot, particularly if someone was unmotivated to look for them. Butz was no dummy. He was a professor of engineering at Northwestern University, with a doctorate from MIT. His science background might not impress Thomas Cartell, but it gave him credibility in other myth-building circles.

"Were you planning to go? Is your family going?"

"Maybe. Unless you think we can get it cancelled?"

"We can try."

"Or maybe I *should* go. See who shows up. Listen to what this guy has to say."

Mrs. Broder looked concerned. "I think we know what it's all about. Do we want to give him a platform? Isn't it bad enough that his book is out there? He shouldn't be allowed to speak."

Sarah wasn't sure about that. Know your enemy might be better. It wasn't like forcing them underground made them go away. In the end, they sent a letter marked urgent to the news desk at the Toronto Star, signed "a concerned citizen." Maybe anonymous tips were ignored, but giving their names seemed a bad idea.

"Never mind Arthur Butz. I'm going to an event next week that I think you'd find really powerful. A Holocaust survivor, Gita Lieberman, is speaking at the University of Guelph. It's on a Wednesday. I think you have a PD day."

"I'd love to come."

The Cartells drove up to the strip mall in Etobicoke. It was Sunday. The stores were closed, but the place was swarming with eager beavers of all ages, cops and journalists, some protesters, and guys with *JDL—Never Again* signs.

"What's JDL?" Blair asked no one in particular.

"Jewish Defence League," Sarah said too quickly. He gave her a weird look.

"What? Know your enemy."

"They don't look like Jews. Way too pumped. Probably hired thugs. People will do anything for a buck. Hell, I'd probably do it."

Sarah laughed too hard.

She looked around. Some Aryan Nations guys were holding signs that read *~~Never~~ Again*! The two sides were inching closer to each other. Cops stood chatting. Any second, it could blow. A couple with a food truck, *Czajakowski* printed in red letters on the side, were selling Polish and German sausages and schnitzel at a discount. The woman was wearing a dirndl dress. Someone else had a t-shirt and hat table. *Right to be White* was selling well. It was like a carnival with no rides or games. An hour passed. The food truck pulled out of the lot. Butz never showed.

Maybe the letter had sabotaged the event, maybe Butz just bailed. Sarah regretted sending the tip to the press. An event like that would be packed with people she needed to know about. Next time, she'd do things differently.

Sarah leaned forward in her chair. Gita Lieberman had survived Mauthausen concentration camp in Austria.

Everything about her, except for what she said, suggested a tidy unruffled life. The green suit with a silky cream-coloured blouse, neat blonde-grey shoulder-length hair, pink lipstick. Her voice was steady, generous, lyrical. But forty-five-year-old pain was no less painful. She'd arrived at Mauthausen when she was fourteen.

The audience was made up mostly of Grade 6 classes from local schools. During the question and answers, kids asked what adults never dared. *Do you still miss your sisters? Did they hurt you? Do you remember everything? Was there enough food?* Then a man in a loose cotton shirt with beaded bracelets, someone's dad or maybe a teacher, asked the woman if it made her feel better to talk about what had happened. Gita Lieberman hesitated for only the briefest moment, and Sarah suspected it was to consider the embarrassment she'd cause him, then she looked straight at him and said "no." Nothing more, simply no. What else was there to say? She turned to take another question.

Sarah wanted to jump over the seats and yell in his ear, *HOW DO YOU NOT GET IT*? A fourteen-year-old girl watches her mother and younger sisters get murdered in front of her, followed by years of unspeakable horrors. Gita used that word *unspeakable*, not that she couldn't speak the words, only that she wouldn't, because they were unhearable. Then *liberation* to a lifetime of remembering. What part of reliving through telling might make anyone feel better? *She's doing this for you, you jerk*, Sarah wanted to scream. *For us*. But the room was filled with twelve and thirteen-year-olds, and she could only hope the man felt ashamed, and would never ask such a stupid question of anyone again.

They drove home saying little, Mrs. Broder glancing over occasionally to make sure Sarah was okay.

"People have a hard time placing themselves in anyone else's experience, even with the best of intentions and imagination. They listen. It makes them feel horribly sad but then they step away. You have to. And anyway, empathy can only get you so far in understanding."

"She's old."

The librarian laughed lightly. "Not that old, but I'm sure she seems it to you."

"No, I mean how much longer will Holocaust survivors be alive? Then who will talk about what happened?"

"I think about that a lot," Mrs. Broder said. "Even with documentation projects, videos, and memoirs, nothing compares to live testimony; bearing witness to someone who has borne witness."

"Thanks for taking me. If you ever go again to hear Gita or anyone else. I want to come."

Mrs. Broder found four months of funding to hire Harrison through a summer student program. The first week he was there, she showed him the materials she and Mrs. Broder had gathered. Sarah convinced the librarian they could trust him completely. He seemed particularly interested in her organizing principles.

"Holy shit, Cartell. Your system is really sophisticated. Where did you learn that?"

"Made it up myself, I guess. It's complicated when so much needs to be cross-referenced."

"Someday you'll have a computer and it'll be simple. I bet you find work for some prof in Montreal. Maybe not right away, but when you're in second or third year. You're still planning on McGill, right?"

"That's the plan. I've started convincing my family. My grandfather's the tougher nut. To say he doesn't place too much value on higher education is a huge understatement. If *he* didn't do it, it's a total waste. My dad will fall in line if he does. I'm hopeful. My uncle lives in Dorval, a suburb of Montreal. He's a contractor, builds houses. But he has his own group too."

"Is it in the whitey files?"

"Yup. But not that heavy duty. At least not from what I know so far. Plan is to find out more. It'll give me a leg up when I get there."

"Will you be attending university as well while you're there?"

Sarah laughed. "Of course. I'm going to take as many prerequisites as I can find for library sciences. But that's a graduate program, so it's down the road."

Harrison looked relieved, which was what Sarah wanted. No need to make everyone panic. She had no idea what Montreal might bring.

16

AUGUST 1992

Goderich

LIFE BEYOND GODERICH BECAME HER NEW FOCUS. The most valuable use of her time was getting the grades she needed for a scholarship, and identifying who in Montreal was bombing synagogues or chasing neo-Nazis.

"You could write an entire doctoral thesis with everything you know already. You barely need to take another course. In fact, you could teach one." Mrs. Broder was excited for what she believed was Sarah's goal—fighting hate with solid, well-researched arguments.

Sarah didn't dissuade her, and of course, she'd keep gathering information and take courses on how to organize it all. But her primary plan was to infiltrate a more hardcore group; find out how they were connected to others and what actions they were organizing. She didn't want to write a book that twelve people would read. She already belonged. Her family pedigree would get her access to more extremist circles.

According to her grandfather, information that may or may not be based on wishful thinking, her uncle had contacts. She knew how to dig for evidence. By the time she got to Montreal, she'd be ready.

Out of nowhere, Aunt Jean was weighing in on university. She didn't seem too keen on McGill and suggested University of Victoria, where Sarah's mom's mom and some cousins lived. She told Sarah she'd been putting money away from her grandmother, yearly birthday gifts for her education. Aunt Jean said her grandmother had MS, which was why she'd never come to visit. Couldn't travel. Sarah had no idea who these people even were, but it was nice of them to honour their daughter through their grandchildren.

"Don't mention the money to your dad. It'll make him sad," Jean had said. "It'll be our secret, okay. When it's closer to the time, we'll sort it out. I've heard residence is very fun."

Sarah couldn't imagine anything less fun than sharing a tiny room with a total stranger. And where would she keep all her things? No need to worry yet. There were still a few months before she had to decide.

Sarah sat in the library reading an article about a firebombing at a Jewish School in Montreal. Mrs. Broder ordered a subscription to the *Montreal Gazette* when she found out Sarah was considering McGill. The photo of a demonstration outside the trial of the accused showed Canadian Jewish Congress members in suits next to anarchist activists from some group the article identified as Anti-Racist Action. They called themselves ARA and covered their faces with bandanas to protect their identities. One of the pictures caught the supposed allies looking at each other with what seemed to be disgust and suspicion.

Sarah had heard of ARA. They also tracked links between *wholesome*, life-starts-at-conception Christian groups like *Focus on the Family* and White supremacists.

"Look at this. A standoff between troublemakers." Sarah handed the newspaper to Harrison. The article described a confrontation at a neo-Nazi march. "Fucked up, right? Who thinks anti-racist activists and neo-Nazis are equally bad? Wear a suit or kakis, and everyone assumes you're an upstanding citizen."

"People don't like the fringes, Sarah. They're full of freaks. ARA may do great work, but they don't look like your neighbours, right? Weird equals scary."

Sarah had been to Harrison's a couple of times to help him pack up all the stuff he wanted to take to Montreal. He didn't know anyone else who was going to McGill, but he was excited and ready.

The two of them lay on their backs in the park by the tire swing where she used to come with Curtis. They were a little stoned.

"It's only mid-August and it's like you've already checked out."

"That's not true," he said. But it kind of was, and she had already started to miss him.

"I'm glad you're going. I just wish you weren't going so soon, or that I was going too."

"Is that your way of saying you're going to miss me?"

"Possibly. Mixed in with a little jealousy that you get to leave." She didn't look at him. Why did she feel like crying? Sarah had been thinking lately that it might be smart to have more than one real friend at a time, to cushion the hard landing when they left.

He reached for her hand and squeezed it. "I'll be back for holidays. And then before you know it, you'll be in Montreal."

She slid her hand away. "I won't miss you that much, man. Don't flatter yourself."

Sarah looked at the wavy brown hair he pushed back behind his ears. Longer than anyone else wore it these days. He smelled like herbal soap. She bought some to start using once he was gone. She'd never tell him that.

"Do you think we should make out?" Yup. She said that out loud. Every now and again, she wondered why it never happened, but didn't give it too much thought. He *was* sort of perfect.

"You think we should?" Harrison looked uncomfortable.

"No. For sure no." It came out too quickly. She giggled.

"Wow. Now you sound so certain. Something wrong with me?"

"Let's see, where do I start?" Sarah poked him in the side.

"Actually, I would. I mean, you're fantastic. Beautiful even maybe." His words dropped awkwardly. Did he feel obligated to say something nice?

"Only maybe?" Sarah asked.

"Definitely. At least according to me. But what do I know?

It's just . . ." He took a deep breath. "Well, if I liked girls, you'd be the girl."

"Oh," was all that came out. It felt like he'd kicked her. How had she divulged every fucked up thing about her family and herself, and he'd omitted this huge piece of critical information? She said nothing.

"Jeez Sarah, I just told you my deepest secret, something that could get the shit beaten out of me, and all you say is '*Oh.*' I would have thought you'd be cool."

"You think not being cool is my problem? Like I'm not saying anything because I hate the homos?" How could he know so much and barely know her? "Were you ever planning to say anything?"

"I guess I didn't think I had to, since there was nothing to tell. And it was just too hard."

"Too hard? I've spilled my fucking guts about hideous things." *Spilling guts* was a bit of a dramatic overstatement. But more than she had ever spilled.

"That's different."

"Oh really. Let's think for two fucking seconds about who wins the shame competition. Oh, I think it's me."

Harrison looked at the grass, the trees, the sky, and then the grass again. Sarah could make it easier for him but didn't want to.

Finally, he spoke. "You're right. Shit. I'm sorry. I'm really sorry."

And that was it. He didn't need to say anything else. There'd be more later, but for now, the air was clear. He got it and she knew he got it.

"I do think you're beautiful."

"Oh ya, right. Well thanks."

They both laughed.

"Have you . . .? I mean who?"

"No, not yet. There was some guy at a bookstore in Toronto. He stood really close to me, and I didn't move away. But nothing happened. It was just a look. And anyway, I was there with my mom. She was in the gardening section. Not far enough away."

"But how can you be sure?"

"For one thing, I didn't want to make out with you."

"Good point."

If he knew, he knew. Maybe that was why she never felt that buzzy thing she had always felt with Curtis. She shifted to lay her head on his stomach. "I wish . . ."

"That I was heterosexual?" He laughed awkwardly, like it was him who needed to be cool with it.

"That you weren't leaving. Seems like anyone great goes away."

He twisted her hair. "You have Mrs. Broder. And anyway, it won't be long, and then you'll be leaving too."

The Sunday sermon had fallen rather flat, and Sarah's grandfather was doing the post-mortem over lunch. It was never what was wrong with *his* words. Rather, he'd pick a badly behaved congregant (according to a set of criteria only he understood) and explain how their lack of commitment and enthusiasm was an offence to God.

The smell of ham and cabbage hung like a low weather

system. Ham and cabbage was not an August meal, but if he asked for it, he got it. When he bent over his plate, Sarah could see the comb lines on his head. They seemed farther apart. His starched grey shirt was worn at the elbows. Blair and Keith were playing pick-up basketball. Not usually their sport, but they'd made some plausible excuse to get out of lunch and her dad seemed to be insisting less these days. It was always worse when her brothers weren't there. The anticipation of Blair's antics made it more tolerable.

"Bun?" Aunt Jean held out the basket. Her grandfather reached for one without looking up. "Can't you take off the apron when you're at my table, Jean?" It was always *his* table.

Sarah waved them away. Since bagels and challah had been introduced, she'd lost her taste for white bread. "No thanks."

"Sarah and I have been doing some research that might interest you, Dad," Sarah's father said.

She'd been getting him to help her collect contacts with groups around the province. He enjoyed making the calls and creating lists. She felt a little guilty using him to do the opposite of what he thought he was doing, but they both enjoyed reviewing the stories, some pretty wacky, that people shared. She'd convinced her dad that dropping Carl Cartell's name wouldn't hurt. It was, after all, him doing the work of getting people to open up. He had a knack for it.

Her father kept talking. He wasn't a gambler, yet he always bet on the longshot of a favourable response. The words landed on the lunch table with a dull thud. Grandpa chewed slowly.

"Dad?"

"What kind of research might that be Frank? Beyond salt and darts, how helpful can you really be?"

He looked at Sarah, as though she might echo his assertion that her father was useless. Which she had never once done, although her grandfather often heard what he wanted. She glanced at him, then at her dad. Rock and a hard place. She cleared her throat.

"He's made a lot of great contacts that'll help build our movement, which you've always wanted." *And never did yourself.* "These folks are committed, not like the people at church."

He continued to chew.

"Grandpa?" Sarah started counting the seconds in her head. "Grandpa?" This time she said it louder.

"Isn't it time for cake?" He pushed back his chair. It was hard to tell if he was being an asshole or if his brain was misfiring.

After the dishes were done, Sarah went out to find her dad in the yard and see if they could leave. An essay was due the next day and she still had hours of work. She'd been dialing back the library research and focusing on grades. The only way to McGill was a full scholarship, or close to it.

She was about to call out when she heard her father. "You think you make yourself look important by taking me down in front of my kids? Seems that's one of your only pleasures, Dad. Doesn't it get tiring?"

Sarah had never heard him talk that way.

"They know what you are. You'll never get anywhere or go anywhere. You and me Frankie, we're attached at the hip. You don't have the balls to leave or the guts to kill your demons."

"I only have one demon, Dad. So you're right about that.

But here's the thing—I am somewhere. I don't need to go anywhere else. I'm not unhappy. You are. You don't win by being mean. Have you ever thanked Jeanie for everything she does?"

"I thank your sister plenty. If you were around here more, you'd know that."

Sarah felt pretty sure that wasn't true. Gratitude was for others to express. It was always expected but never on offer.

She ran back to the house before they saw her and headed upstairs, her hand sliding along the worn banister. The sliver went under her nail bed and started throbbing immediately. She'd once heard that bits of wood could start growing in the body, cause deadly infections, and even kill a person. She went to get a needle from the sewing kit in the tiny guest bedroom.

Something was jamming the dresser drawer, so Sarah started emptying it. Under some folded hankies and a set of flowered bed sheets, she found a thick brown envelope of postcards, each with a picture and description of a different native Ontario flower. They weren't dated, stamped, or addressed, so they must have come in envelopes, but there were none there.

Sarah forgot the splinter and started reading.

Dear Margaret,

Thank you for the newsy Christmas letter. I like nothing more than hearing all about the children, and of course, Frank. I know how crazy it can be with three little ones at home. Please tuck away the university money somewhere safe. I won't tell you what to do, but if you can keep this a secret, I'd very much appreciate it. It's exciting to think of the kids making good use of it. Perhaps one day we'll meet.

The signature was clear, leaving no doubt who it was from. Charlene. Aunt Jean lied about which grandmother had sent money. The third card wasn't addressed to Margaret.

> *Dear Jean,*
> *I was devastated to hear about Margaret's passing. Poor Frank. I understand that I am no comfort. Margaret had been kind enough to give me a family update once a year at Christmas. I don't expect the same from you but would appreciate if you could put away the holiday and birthday money I've been sending for the kids' education, as I understand Margaret had been doing.*

It was also signed Charlene, not mother or mom.

She flipped through the rest of the cards. Each said more or less the same thing, offering no additional information about the sender. Maybe she assumed no one was interested. Maybe Aunt Jean knew more than she let on.

Sarah sifted through the pile of flowers once more: Dragon's Mouth, Ontario Aster, Beechdrops, Northern Bluebells, Pink Lady's Slipper, looking for some hint of what prompted the correspondence. At the bottom, she found the Trillium. The card simply read, *Thank you. Thank you.*

Her finger started aching. She stuffed the cards back in the drawer and found a pin. Then she went to the bathroom to soak it in hot water before trying to dig out the splinter.

17

MARCH 1995

Sunnyside Mental Health Centre

"YOU HAVEN'T TALKED THAT MUCH ABOUT your last year of high school. It must have been lonely once Harrison left."

"It was and it wasn't. I needed that full scholarship, so I busted my ass to get it. Between studying and working at the library, I didn't have too much time to miss him. Occasionally, Blair got me to go to a party by calling me the biggest drag of all times, or a shrivelled social outcast, and I'd cave. Not because I gave a shit about the insults, but because he was the most fun person to hang out with. And I needed that sometimes. We'd drink too much or get too high and pay for it the next day. If the party was on a Saturday night, which most of them were, the two of us would pinch each other awake during church, trying to leave bruises.

"I got the marks. Even in math, which is so not my subject. I joined a study group and had some math mates. The year dragged and flew by at the same time. It was good to get my head out of the White supremacy."

"I guess you managed to talk your dad into university? Or do you think he secretly wanted you to get away?"

"He definitely wanted me away from Grandpa, who seemed to like me, as much as he could like anyone."

"Not to take anything away from you Sarah, but your grandfather likes anything that reflects a shiny version of him back to himself."

"I hope that doesn't mean I'm a lot like him."

"It's more that he believed that he could mold you into an image of himself. Your father has been so hurt by him and projects potential hurt on you. You haven't been hurt in that way. When you were a kid, you felt flattered by your grandfather. That fed his ego and put a wedge between you and your father. You two were in this great project together while your dad was a failure. Which, by the way, he was not."

"I don't think my dad wanted me around Carl either, but maybe that was the lesser of two evils. He didn't like Carl, but he trusted him. Every time I mentioned helping out at True Canadian Heritage, I got a look I assumed was jealousy. I wanted my dad to feel better, so I convinced him that McGill was his idea."

"You felt sorry for him."

"How ironic is that? Pity is the emotion I hate the most, and I was feeling it all the time. It was easier when he was angry. Hurt and disappointment was so much worse. In the end, Grandpa was gung-ho for True Canadian Heritage. Gung-ho is a bit strong, but maybe he saw Montreal as my choosing him over my father. My dad promised he'd visit and bring my aunt and my brothers. They never came. Was my father scared? Was he content? What did my grandfather mean when he told my dad that they were attached at the hip? Jean didn't go anywhere either. How is that different? With my dad, it felt like a threat."

Sarah realized that the brochures for Disneyland and the Grand Canyon that he occasionally dangled when they were kids weren't to tease them. He was genuinely excited. He believed they might go. As for her grandfather, he had never gone anywhere either. His excitement, if it could be called that, was limited to domination and judgment.

"I'm starting to realize that my father might not have been scared about anything happening to him, but more worried that something could happen to us if he wasn't on guard. My aunt was a dutiful daughter, stuck there because she has no children and there was no one else to take care of him."

"Ever wondered why she never married?" Mona asked. "There was no space in her life. Sure, it's a choice. But sometimes choices are not really choices, they only seem like it. Moving away was impossible. At least you got to."

"I did. And it's what I wanted. But despite everything, I fit in at home. I didn't want to. I hadn't wanted to for years, but I did. Leaving meant losing that. My family made sense to me. I knew how everyone would react to things. I knew what to expect. Even after my worldview got blown up, and after my dad did what he did to Curtis's family, I still felt that way. And of course, I had Mrs. Broder. Not at all like my family, but the library was the one other place I belonged. I was about to give up everything. Maybe everyone who goes off to university feels this."

"Not the same at all." Mona said, "You must have been excited about seeing Harrison."

"I was, I guess. But I think being misfits at high school and working together made us feel more the same than we were. When he heard I got accepted, he sent me a postcard with Super Man and Wonder Woman. *The dynamic duo together again!! Coming soon to a university nowhere near Goderich. By the way, nice to hear from you. You're the shittiest correspondent ever.*

"We hung out whenever he was home, but it wasn't the same. He had this whole new life. He loved Montreal and McGill. He found his people, organized demonstrations, fell in love, let his guard down. There was some hard stuff. His roommate was a homophobic creep, so he moved into an apartment in January. But it all worked out. It was an adventure. That was always his plan. I mean who doesn't at least have that as a dream? Except for me. I didn't."

"Is it possible you didn't *let* yourself have it? Didn't think you deserved it?"

"That's kind of not how my brain works." There was something abnormal about not wanting to fit in, but it never bothered Sarah. Maybe she didn't want it badly enough. She worked at it when she needed to; when there was a point. Mona talked a lot about feeling undeserving. She never saw it that way.

"Harrison kept saying, 'Just wait until you get here. I felt the same way you did.' But he didn't feel the same."

"Even if you didn't feel like you fit in, you still built meaningful connections, to Curtis, Luce, Harrison, Mrs. Broder, and Ara."

Is that what people told themselves all the time? Hurray. I'm meaningfully connected. Hearing Ara's name spoken was always unbearable and Mona knew it.

"Ara wasn't like anyone else. He never took no for an answer. But not in a bossy way. You know how I am with bossy."

Mona laughed.

"Ara got his way because he wasn't trying to. It was never to say *I told you so*. He didn't push or insist. Sometimes I had no idea we were going somewhere and then we were there. Once, I finished an entire essay because we were in the same room. He knew that's what I needed. Not information or actual help. Just company. Which is funny because I never needed company."

"Sounds like Ara would make a great therapist," Mona said.

Sarah made a face. "That would spoil it. And I'd be jealous if I thought he did that for anyone."

"Interesting. So, there are so few things you want for yourself."

The words made her feel uncomfortable. "Being around people, even the ones I kind of love, makes me feel like a weirdo. Maybe I'm missing that piece of the brain that sets off normal human responses. But I'm not sure what those are. I'm supposed to miss having a mother. I'm supposed to be lonelier, but I'm not. Sometimes I think all my friendships . . ." Sarah laughed. The word *all* was kind of excessive. "That they're accidents I stumble into, or the other person stumbles into thinking, *oh, this will be fun or nice* . . . but ultimately, it's not. I frustrate them. I don't know what they see in me or get from me. And I don't mean that in a pathetic, poor me way. Just that I'm a crappy friend. I don't put out. Ara never made me feel that way. Like deep inside him, he doesn't judge. Everyone else does. That's pretty normal. I do it. But it's easier not to worry that I'll fail someone."

"What you and Ara had—have—is rare. He's special."

Sarah put her face in her hands.

Mona let her cry for a minute before going on. "As for most people, they are drawn to different things. Sometimes it's that simple. *You* may not understand what they're getting. But *they* do. Or they don't, but they're happy to be there. It's not your job to warn them off. But fooling people. That must have felt . . ." She hesitated. "Complicated."

"Not complicated enough. My dad was totally fooled. In the end, he sent Carl some glowing letter telling him I'd be the best thing to ever happen to TCH. It was embarrassing. He bought me a computer so I could do well at school."

"That's an expensive gift."

"Kneeling on stones was easier. I was almost relieved to leave Goderich. Everything was so awkward. Even with Mrs. B. We sorted through all the stuff we'd gathered, but there was suddenly all this silence we never needed to fill before.

"On the day before I was leaving, she told me how excited she was for me to go to real libraries and do real research. Make a real dent in the problem. She kept saying *real* and I knew my plans, the ones she thought she knew, were not real in the sense that she meant. They wouldn't be building blocks to some better life. Researchers and journalists had been exposing shit for years and all it did was make people bolder or better at hiding. I had no interest in that.

"She knew about True Canadian Heritage, but not that it was a bridge to something worse. I presented it as a destination in itself. Maybe she had her suspicions. She warned me that the people we've been tracking are dangerous and not to chase them down. *That's what the police are for. Aim for the sky Sarah, because why aim lower? Disappointment will be there one way or another. No need to search for it.* But what if my sky was the hell itself?"

Sarah's voice cracked. "I loved that place. I love her. *I'll miss you, my Sarah.* That's what she called me. *My* Sarah."

There was no one in the world Sarah wanted to belong to more. She wiped at her face. Tears had never served her the way they did others. They stole control, and left shame. But that last day in the library with Mrs. Broder, she let herself cry, and it felt okay. The librarian didn't ask why or reassure Sarah that she'd be home soon enough. She understood, like Mona did, that the origin of the tears was much more complicated than that.

"She hugged me. For maybe a whole minute. And I let her. Didn't even squirm."

18

AUGUST 1993

Montreal

THERE WAS MUCH DISCUSSION ABOUT HOW SARAH would get to Montreal with her stuff as well as her uncle's hockey bag. Until the last week, it was unclear whether her dad and Aunt Jean would take her, or maybe Blair and her dad, or Blair and Keith. She could sense her father's hesitation. The drive was close to eight hours, which meant staying the night in Dorval at Carl and Marcia's with their kids. That would be awkward, since none of them had ever met her, and things were always tense between her dad and his brother. In the end, Grandpa settled it by getting some kind of flu bug, so Keith and Blair worked at the hardware store and Jean took care of him. Sarah and her dad made the trip themselves. It was nice. Quiet and nice. The hours of classic rock with stops at two Tim Hortons and a minimum of conversation, not uncomfortable, just easy, went by quickly.

It was only as they crossed the Quebec border that her

father ventured something more than, *please change the station, I can't stand John Denver* or *we can stop anytime you need to.*

"I should have some fatherly advice to give you. Maybe? Eat green vegetables and brush your teeth. You're the first one in our family to go to university. In a few weeks, you'll have advice for us. I will say this, don't do anything you don't want to do. I'm not sure what your uncle is up to with True Canadian Heritage. I know he's excited about getting your help organizing all his paperwork and files for him. But you're there to study and have new experiences and make friends. Don't feel pressured. Enjoy it." There was a long pause, then he said, "Your mother and I had our honeymoon in Montreal. Spent five nights wandering around fumbling with her high school French and eating great food. It's a beautiful city."

It felt like that little story, as short as it was on detail, was the most intimate thing he'd ever shared. He never talked about her mom. But now he had, and it made her feel curiously okay about leaving. Like she knew that things between them were fine.

The night at Carl's was too hectic and short to be uncomfortable. They had a couple of beers and joked with the kids. Marcia talked about *finally* meeting them all. Then it was time to go to bed. The day had been long, and Sarah and her dad were both exhausted. He hugged her hard. No need to get up with him the next morning, he told her. He planned to get on the road really early. She was awake when he left but didn't go down. It would have been too hard. She stood at the window of the bedroom and watched him pull out of the driveway.

The plan was to stay with her uncle for a couple of weeks and slowly gather whatever she needed for Harrison's old apartment in Montreal. That's where she'd be living. Carl wasted no time inviting Sarah to a True Canadian Heritage meeting so she could meet people and start in on the library.

Her uncle pulled his truck into a spot around back of a strip mall. The low grey building (White supremacists liked their cinder blocks) had no distinguishing features. What did she expect? A flashing neon swastika? *Aryans only*? Over the door was an unobtrusive sign. *True Canadian Heritage.* There was a mail slot.

"Don't want just anyone picking up our mail, do we?"

Carl held the door open. Sarah looked around. The walls were covered in posters of blonde families in meadows with wildflowers. Just like at church. Had her grandfather bought a bunch in bulk years ago, or was it standard White pride fare? That was it for décor.

A heavy-set woman, tight Hello Kitty t-shirt and platinum blond hair, was organizing a table—four boxes of donuts, an urn of coffee, cream, foam cups, sugar cubes, artificial sweetener packets. She pointed to a pile of envelopes, then smiled at Carl.

"I opened the mail. Mostly junk flyers but there's something from Ernst Zundel's people. Looks like he'll come in January."

Zundel, Canada's most famous Holocaust denier, spent most of his time barricaded in his downtown Toronto house that was painted black and covered in surveillance equipment.

"Great. Thanks for setting up. This is my niece, Sarah."

The woman turned away, barely waving.

"Don't mind her. Not very social. They're not all like that."

Sarah didn't mind. Any effort to be friendly would have demanded a response in kind that she was happy to forgo.

Fold-up chairs were set out. Blackout curtains were drawn over the windows. People started to arrive.

Carl introduced her. Women were far outnumbered by men in suits, khakis with ironed-in seams, and black leather.

In the middle of a discussion about homosexuals (which followed the topic of immigrants—not the preferred word), some kid yelled out, "Castrate the fucking queers!" Sarah glanced back at a bouncing teenager whose mouth was covered in powdered sugar.

"A little decorum please. No need for that kind of talk here." Carl was smiling and shaking his head. Some version of boys will be boys, *supremacists will be supremacists*.

"They just want to get out there with a bat," he whispered to Sarah when he sat back down. It wasn't clear whether he thought this a good idea or a bad one. Maybe he just saw a version of his younger freer self in those rowdy kids.

Those types didn't last long. The dues-payers were mostly middle management, middle class, middle-aged, middle of the road, not too rich, too educated, or too sharp. Dabblers, mildly dissatisfied with their own lot, resentful as hell of what they figured came easy to those who didn't deserve it.

After the meeting, Carl brought her into what he called the library, a glorified storage room he wanted organized to live up to its name.

Supplies were piled on a flimsy metal shelf. She allowed herself a minute in front of the coloured file folders, markers, sticky notes, pads, paper clips, and labels—the raw material of a future archive. She'd delay the thrill of breaking open the packages until she had a plan. There were two stuffed duffle bags. One, that had lived in her garage all those years. The other, filled with what was gathered since.

"Play a lot of hockey?"

"Not enough." Carl laughed. "It's papers. Movement stuff."

"Nice filing system," Sarah said.

"That's what you're here for. At least it's all in one place."

"It's all yours?"

"Nope. People started giving me their shit to hold onto. They knew I kept everything. At home, I have one tiny room in the basement. Only thing Marcia lets me keep in the living room is my signed Gary Carter baseball. And that was a fight. Keeping meticulous records is important."

"The basement at your house has more of this stuff? Do I need to get at that too?"

"Naw, those are my personal treasures." He laughed. "Marcia calls them toys. But one man's garbage . . . I'm either the default archivist, or the junk collector. Depends on who you're talking to. I'm going to chat with some folks, then we'll head out. Why don't you poke around."

Until she'd gone through everything, it wouldn't be clear what organizing strategy would work. She'd made that mistake before and labelled colourful folders and boxes with fat black magic markers before she knew what she was dealing with. Start with sticky notes and pencil. Test a system before committing to it.

She opened the first bag, unprepared for the greasy, vaguely cat-pissy smell. Breathing through her mouth, she reached in and pulled out a few papers, then unzipped the second one to let it air.

There were faded receipts, pamphlets, notes, newspaper articles, event flyers, paperbacks, application forms, letters, old airplane tickets. Dozens of Tim Horton's receipts. She feared she'd become the default secretary, organizing meaningless crap. Couldn't the lovestruck coffee and mail gal from earlier do that? Sarah reminded herself to mask the skills she didn't want abused by others.

She spotted writing on the back of a receipt. *June 22, 1990. Meeting with Michel Larocque, Francis Pigeon, Rejean Cadet. Re: funds for Carney Nerland.* He was the head of the Saskatchewan KKK and Aryan Nations.

The names evoked a twisted giddiness. Sarah picked through others. On the back of bills, her uncle had marked the who and where of every expenditure going back years.

Maybe Carl was the genetic source of her gathering and categorizing inclination. "Let's go," he said, popping his head in the door. "Looks like you're on your way. Good thing this stuff has some time to air out."

The rest of late August was spent getting her bearings in Montreal and taking any interesting papers to a copy place around the corner from her apartment then back to the suburbs for filing.

Montreal was crowded and dirty. It smelled of things collectively foreign and kind of stomach turning. In Goderich, fast food fried chicken dominated. It was like the Pied Piper of smells. Maybe it worked on some people, but Sarah preferred not to be mugged by the scent of her next meal.

It took focus and a lot of dodging not to rub shoulders with strangers. It didn't seem to bother anyone else. Sarah hoped her discomfort was introversion and agoraphobia, not judgment. But old prejudice dies hard, and Montreal was not Goderich. When they popped up, those shitty beliefs of *yore*, she'd beat them back, and force herself to stay on the crowded street like some kind of aversion therapy.

After her first week of walking (she preferred it to the bus or metro, which offered no quick escape route), the full-frontal assault on her senses receded a bit. Strong cigarettes, coffee, bread, car exhaust, falafel, the head coverings, and languages finally began to distinguish themselves. She'd been buying so-called groceries—instant coffee, milk, cereal, baloney, and beer—on an as-needed basis, at the depanneur. The corner store, that Montrealers called "the dep." One day soon, she'd get to an actual supermarket. She had plans to learn to love everything about Montreal. At the moment, she was on her way to tolerance.

Sarah arrived early for the Sunday meeting and found Carl in the TCH office, thumbing through a file marked British People's League. Had he discovered something missing?

"Best time." He waved a flyer at her, the look on his face some combination of nostalgia for the girl you had a crush on in Grade 6, and smashing windows in an abandoned building.

"Minden Ontario, last summer. Fucking crazy."

"What happened?"

It didn't take much to get her uncle talking.

"You know Mark Bauer? Aryan Resistance Movement?" Sarah nodded. "Well, they organized an event. Save Canada Day. Great name, right? Mostly skinheads. We sent flyers to Ottawa, Toronto, New York State, even Alberta and BC. They booked two bands, Cross and Cyclone; not my thing, too head banger, but the skins love them. It was on John Beattie's property, just outside of Minden."

"Beattie, as in Canadian Nazi Party, British People's League? Isn't he kind of past his prime?"

"Sure is. You really know your stuff, Sar."

After years of riffling through the same information to see what matched up, she could now toss around details like well-worn family gossip.

"Anyway," her uncle continued. "The guy strutted around like king shit, putting it on for the press. But Bauer was in charge. There were skins from all over Quebec, plus Michel Larocque, KKK, and some of his boys."

Sarah recognized Larocque's name from the back of the receipt. "How'd you get to go? You're not exactly one of the gang."

"You think not?" He gestured at his plaid permanent-press short-sleeved shirt and chinos. They both looked at his loafers. "I shaved my head two days before the event."

"No way." Sarah laughed.

"Nearly cost me my marriage. I walk in the door. Marcia's standing at the counter in the kitchen chopping. She turns around and just stares at me, then she loses it. The kids are laughing and pointing at my head. She screams at them to go upstairs."

"Holy shit."

"I'd given no thought to an explanation. 'I just wanted to see what I'd look like bald.' That's what I came up with. Cancer fundraiser would have been much better, but who can think that fast. She threw a wooden spoon across the kitchen. I'm lucky it wasn't the knife. Beaned the side of my head." Carl was laughing so hard he could barely continue.

"'You look like a fucking idiot and we have my cousin Bethany's wedding in two weeks. What the hell were you thinking? How old are you anyway?' She never says fuck. Like ever. She went up to the kids' room and slammed the door. I didn't see her until the next day. Of course, I had to explain the bruise over and over to all the guys. Marcia calmed down, even offered me some of her concealer makeup, insisted actually. What could I say? I've got my limits? I draw the line at makeup?"

Sarah wiped tears of laughter on her sleeve. She almost never laughed like that with her dad. Carl's kids were lucky.

"Not sure she's completely forgiven me. The pictures from the wedding were awful. For months, Marcia would stick a photo on my pillow just to rub it in. She'd written 'Dickhead' on it. I literally looked like a dick. Uncircumcised of course."

"Gross, thanks for the lovely image, Uncle Carl. So what happened?"

"We stayed together."

She swatted his arm. "In Minden, what happened? It sounds awesome."

"It *was* awesome."

"Why were you even invited?"

"I'm pretty involved. I keep a low profile, but I know

what's up. I help a lot, raise money, move flyers and materials around, get people into Canada to speak. It doesn't hurt that I pass for an upstanding citizen."

"I bet the shaved head fucked with that misconception."

"Lucky my hair grows fast. It was a stupid move. Mid-life crisis or something."

"Is that actually a thing?"

"Oh ya. I told Marcia we got off easy. Some people drop fifty grand on an RX 7. If I ever did that, she'd leave for sure. Anyway, I got there a day early, brought all the *God is a Racist*, *Race is the Issue* flyers. You probably saw some in the bags. Bauer and a bunch of his guys from Ottawa were doing security. The next day, about two hundred skinheads got there. Unbelievable."

"Wow."

"Media helps. Flyers are nothing compared to negative attention from the press. There were about three dozen O.P.P. officers too. Probably wanted to be over on our side. Beattie told some journalist it was just a party. We weren't doing anything illegal. When anyone else gets together to celebrate, it's fucking multiculturalism. Thanks to that fag, Trudeau."

Sometimes Carl sounded like his dad. Cartell men did share certain traits.

"Anything get out of control?" Sarah asked.

"A bunch of guys got drunk. Bauer's boys escorted them away from the gate before they beat up protesters. No one wanted that kind of trouble."

"I thought Bauer was a pro-violence guy. Wasn't there some lady shot in the face through her living room window?"

"Friends of his, not him. Mark's a good guy. He helps a lot of young skins get off drugs and stay clean, get their lives on track. I walked the perimeter with them. There's a picture of us somewhere."

Sarah grabbed one from a pile. "This one?" She'd seen it already but hadn't recognized her uncle, posed like a kid at Disneyland with his favourite superheroes. The shaved head looked a bit lumpy, but not as bad as Sarah expected.

"You'd have loved it."

"Any girls there, any women?"

"My niece, the feminist," Carl said, laughing. "Just the ones cooking up the grub."

Sarah gave him the finger.

"But maybe this year." He waved a flyer in front of her face. "Want to go?"

Sarah grabbed the letter.

Comrade:

You and your White friends are invited to the first annual Alberta Aryan Fest to be held 8 Sept, 1993, 4 miles west of Provost, Alberta, at the acreage of AN leader Ray Bradley. Festivities will begin at 1:00 p.m. on Saturday and will include speeches, taped music, and fellowship, followed by a steak supper and cross lighting. Festivities will end at 1:00 p.m. Sunday. Cabins are limited. Bring a tent or RV and a sleeping bag, as well as $20 for the cost of the meals. All Klansmen bring your uniforms. HAIL VICTORY!!!

Terry Long

"Are you serious? Yeah, I want to go. But isn't it kind of late?"

"I'll arrange it. And don't worry about camping gear. I'll score us a cabin. Ever flown?"

"Never. Should I shave my head?"

"Not sure it'll suit you. And anyway, who'd shave off this Aryan calling card." He ruffled her hair. "It won't be as big this year. More inner circle people."

Would getting where she wanted be this easy?

"My dad will never let me go."

"Maybe we don't tell him this one thing. It's only three days."

On the Friday before leaving for Alberta, Sarah officially moved into her apartment, a three and a half room walk-up in the Plateau on Rue Rachel. The bathroom counted as a half. The place was long and narrow (typical Montreal, Harrison had said), with wooden floors worn so thin she'd bought hydrogen peroxide and pins in case of splinters. Slippers got added to her shopping list. The big window in the main room looked out on the street, pocket doors opened on to the middle room that he had used as his bedroom, and the kitchen was in the back—fridge and stove from the sixties. Harrison said she was lucky. Most Montrealers owned their own appliances and took them when they moved. There was a fire escape to climb out on.

Carl drove her into the city with a microwave, some blankets, a pot, and two stuffed animals the kids had given her for company.

They carried it all upstairs and set up her computer on the table in the front room.

"I can help you organize if you want. I've got time."

"That's okay. It'll give me something to do. Got to get used to being alone." He had no idea how used to that she already was. She didn't need him tripping over the files of TCH stuff she'd shoved into the middle room.

"Anytime you want a break from the wild city, just hop on the bus. We're going to miss you, kid. Anyway, we still have Aryan Fest. I'll pick you up Thursday at 8:30. Sharp."

She walked him down to his truck. "Thanks Uncle Carl, for everything. I'll miss you guys too." She meant it.

He hugged her hard then drove away, waving back over his head.

She dragged the futon couch into the living room. Harrison left a note about how to fold and unfold the thing. She wouldn't bother closing it again unless she was having a party (ha ha). What she referred to as WC (White contraband) would live in the middle room. In Britain, WC stood for water closet, as in toilet. Perfect.

Sarah waited years to have a blank wall of her own. She had a vision of plotting everything she knew on one large piece of mural paper. It would be a road map pointing the way to what needed to be done. When she had doubts, she could remind herself by looking at it. A mural like that would say something different to each observer—a display of pride over what has been achieved, or a plot to dismantle it. Her goal might seem childishly unrealistic, like wanting to be an astronaut, but people did become astronauts.

She'd bought a twelve by five inch length of mural paper, a large pack of coloured markers, sticky notes—yellow, pink, orange, and green—and masking tape. One of these days, she'd start building her visual Coles Notes of a movement. That was the idea. She taped Katie's paintings to the wall.

With the lights off, lying next to the window, she could see the sky and the street. Conversation, footsteps, headlights. She wondered how people slept. There was never no one around. It was her first night alone. Ever. Beans didn't count. After years of wanting it, solitude felt different than she expected. Less free.

Saturday morning, on her way to find coffee that was weak enough for her to tolerate, she met a couple carrying a satiny pink striped couch with intricate woodwork. It could have come from a whore house, a fortune teller, or a palace.

The woman caught Sarah staring and smiled. "*C'est joli n'est-ce pas? Vous le voulez?*"

What the hell had been the point of high school French, she wondered. The only word she recognized was jolly and that hardly described the couch. "Pardon?"

"You want this? We are giving it for a new home. It is lovely yes but not so good for sleeping."

Sarah nodded. The couch was pink and fussy, the opposite of her, and she wanted it. They dragged it up, stopping on each landing laughing and negotiating turns.

The woman collapsed on it when they got inside. "Maybe this should stay here forever."

Then they insisted on rearranging her furniture. When Sarah offered them instant coffee, they laughed, and when she reached for her wallet, they looked insulted. Was everyone in Montreal this nice?

19

SEPTEMBER 1993

Provost, Alberta

IT FELT LIKE CRAZY TIMING TO BE running off to Alberta when she was just getting things sorted in Montreal and classes were starting. But it was frosh week, which she would have none of. She already registered for her courses and Aryan Fest was mostly on the weekend, so no downside. And anyway, she might never have another opportunity.

It was only three days away, so she'd agreed to her uncle's suggestion and didn't ask her dad for permission. It felt like deception, but then, what in her family did not? No allegiance had been switched. If people were being fooled, Uncle Carl was getting the worst of it. He had skin in the game, more to lose. What Sarah stood to gain in exposure to new players, and possibly their big plans, was worth it. As long as the plane didn't go down.

Uncle Carl claimed it as a business expense. Professional development. An investment in the future. Hers and his. It felt only partly like a joke when he said it. Nervous as she was, the feeling of her body being pressed into the seat as the plane gained speed for takeoff was one of anticipation, not fear.

Uncle Carl squeezed her hand briefly. "Chew that gum so your ears won't pop."

They rented a car in Lloydminister, Alberta, 107 kilometres from Provost. The heavy rain felt appropriate. Sunshine would have been wrong. Her uncle almost squealed when he spotted the soggy red flags Carney Nerland told him to look out for.

At the turn off to Ray Bradley's property, CTV, CBC, and local media in rain jackets milled around with cameras and recording equipment. Word about the Aryan Fest had clearly spread.

A group of men with rifles, BB guns, and masks or bandanas over their faces leaned against the fence that displayed a *KKK White Power!* sign with foot-high stencilled black letters. One *Stop the Dilution* t-shirt. Otherwise, the uniform was plain white or black and fatigues. Something about the umbrellas they held made Sarah want to laugh, even though they were mostly black. Someone with either guts, a sense of humour, or a screwed-up sense of direction held one that was violet and yellow plaid. To the right of the sign, a banner read *BHORP Welcome's Aryan Nations.* Brotherhood of Racial Purity—a ridiculous acronym. That, and the incorrect apostrophe made her relax a bit. Sarah felt armed with good grammar.

Carl rolled down his window.

"You made it good and early." A chubby, small-faced man wearing dark sunglasses, a brown shirt, and a swastika armband made his way over and patted Carl on the shoulder. He peered into the car. She recognized him from pictures she'd seen. Family hero.

"Sarah, this is Carney Nerland, *the* Carney Nerland. Carney, this is my niece, Sarah. She knows all about you, and you should know her. Next generation working for the cause."

"Violating child labour laws there, Carl?" He smiled at Sarah.

"Who me? Naw, she just looks young. Hey, Terry!" he shouted over at the man Sarah assumed was the head of Aryan Nations, Terry Long. There was no response. Sarah saw her uncle wince. He didn't yell again.

"Why don't you head in and get yourselves settled," Carney said. "Ray's wife Janet will show you where to leave your gear. Then come on back. This is where the action is. At least for now."

Until that moment, it had been theoretical—every pamphlet, book, letter—all two-dimensional. This was live and in colour (although mostly black and red). Some combination of adrenaline, terror, excitement, and revulsion would take her through the next two days.

They drove past a huge Nazi battle flag nailed to a barn and waved at skinheads.

Carl punched the steering wheel. "Shit. Marc Scott's here. How the hell . . .?" He adjusted his demeanour to something more befitting an adult.

"Which one?" Sarah asked.

Carl gestured vaguely at a young man strutting along the side of the road.

"The bald guy? With the white T-shirt and the combat boots?" They both laughed.

Marc Scott didn't look any different from most of the thuggish types they'd seen so far. He had nice teeth.

"His dad's Reverend Phillip Scott. He runs our church. Pile of family money he throws around, so no one tells him what to do. The son thinks he's hot shit, but he's a pathetic show-off. He's at least twenty four. Maybe time to get his shit together rather than sniffing for cash from his old man to support his little cell. That's about all he gets from the guy. The Reverend talks up a Christian storm to cover a wandering prick. Brings a lot of comfort to the lady parishioners and the Sunday school teachers. God knows how many little Reverend juniors there are running around the parish. Poor Marc thinks he's the sole heir."

Despite all the blatant violations of human decency, Carl seemed to be applying a moral code, sounding indignant. Sarah almost laughed.

Janet showed them to a neat cabin with a set of twin beds covered in military blankets. How many properties across the country were ready, how many hosts waiting?

By the time they wandered back to the front gate, there was action, like Nerland promised. A man around sixty, dressed in a concentration camp inmate uniform, was carrying a sign. *Racial Hatred Leads to Auschwitz.* He challenged Nerland to take off his sunglasses.

"You come take them off." Nerland beckoned with raised fingers. "You think you're some kind of a fucking war hero just cause they didn't work you to death. More like a parasite, sucking off us now."

"Why don't you go play victim somewhere else," yelled

a short, younger man with a crew cut who Carl identified as Kelly Lyle, leader of the ultra-violent Final Solution Skinheads. Marc Scott stood beside him, smacking a fist into his palm.

Nerland kept yelling. "You lying son of a bitch. You tell everyone they got what? Twenty million people at Auschwitz, that they made fucking soap out of your auntie and luggage out of your uncle?"

"Dumb fucking kyke, how many guys did you blow to stay alive?" Marc Scott screamed.

Wasn't that more insulting to Nazis than their prisoners? No one seemed to notice. Too busy laughing. Years of lunches with Grandpa Thomas had not prepared Sarah for this. She hoped her face didn't betray her.

The man in the Auschwitz costume held his ground. Sarah overheard two journalists discussing him. Janikowski, a Polish Catholic, not a Jew, who spent four years in the death camp starting at seventeen. She used the factual error to steady herself.

Just smile. Like she's enjoying it. The whole weekend was going to be like this. Janikowski gave her a dirty look. She stared at him too long.

Sarah got noticed. Plenty of comments about the lack of committed Aryan daughters, all the kids who had bailed for grunge. Carl introduced her like she was God's gift to the movement.

"This girl knows everything. Everything."

"Oh yeah, what about me, what's my claim to fame?" Lyle was small but carried a lot of weight with this crowd. The others looked at her expectantly.

"You did some fine redecorating on the outside of that Synagogue in Calgary, convicted of aggravated assault for that righteous deed." Sarah hoped her voice sounded cocky but admiring. Lyle smiled, repeated the word redecorated, and nodded his approval.

"See? What did I tell you?" Carl blurted out.

It was like being on a Nazi version of Jeopardy, a show Mrs. Broder loved watching. *What is the burning of the House of Israel Synagogue?*

There were only forty or so people at the gathering. Some big names in Canadian White supremacy, a bunch of folks gunning for recognition, and some hangers-on, like Bruce (no last name), an older man who looked giddy, starstruck, and out of place. He was dressed like the others, but his fatigues and t-shirt were stiff and clean, like he'd popped into a department store on the way there. Same with the combat boots, straight out of a box. When Sarah asked Carl about him, he laughed it off, saying now and again people paid big bucks for the experience.

Carl wasn't invited into the closed meetings and had to be content with what a few show-offs let slip. Sarah was disappointed she'd miss out on any actual plans, if they were even planning. More like a lot of yelling about blowing up synagogues and cutting dicks further down to size. Sarah monitored her uncle's reactions and made a list of everyone there.

Despite her impressive litany of White supremacist trivia, she was still expected to help make meals and wash up. Janet was prone to gossip, which suited Sarah. Two eighteen-year-olds were there with men at least a decade older. They giggled and actually pulled down their pants to show Sarah and the others their inner thighs—matching swastika tattoos with the boyfriends' initials. The fourth woman, Klaudia, barely said a word. Her red splotchy face clashed with bottled orange hair. Huge breasts formed a shelf on her stocky body. She could have supported a dozen steins of beer at the Hofbrauhaus in Munich while Hitler outlined his twenty-five tenets of the National Socialist program.

"What about Carney's wife?" Sarah asked.

"Never comes to nothing. Not invited. She's trouble. What was he thinking marrying her? If he doesn't keep her locked up in that apartment, she's running around showing off bruises, screaming abuse. And that poor little girl of his. Sometimes he brings her. Sweet thing, you can barely tell her mom's from Chile. I like the man, don't get me wrong, but boy he makes some crummy decisions. Wheeling and dealing with riff raff. Owns his Pawn and Gun shop with an Indian." She pronounced it *In Jun*.

The fact that Nerland had a license to buy and sell guns while being investigated for involvement with American neo-Nazi groups was either police stupidity or collusion with people in high places. Likely some combination of both.

"You're not like them, Sarah." Janet nodded her head toward the tattooed pair. "Can't even count buns or spread mayo right. You seem real sensible."

Sarah smiled at her. If she had any clue just how sensible, she'd be praying for more tattooed groupies.

On the last night, the inner circle gathered to light the cross while the rest watched. Thirty feet of metal wrapped in diesel-soaked burlap meant to send a long-burning message miles beyond the property. Edgar Foth, in the black and red robes of the Klan Wizard, was honoured with lighting it. The others lit torches off the flames. They screamed *White Power! Heil!* and *Death to the Jews.*

It was everything Sarah had anticipated: the ritual, the theatre, the buffoonery, perpetrated by costumed thugs. But nothing could have prepared her for the awestruck, moist eyes staring up into the flames with the fervour of religious salvation.

At the airport in Edmonton, Sarah spotted a headline about a US Air flight that crashed outside Pittsburgh the day they left. One hundred and thirty-two people dead. She gripped the armrest the entire trip back. The terror felt like payback.

20

SEPTEMBER 1993

Montreal

SARAH'S PRESENCE AT ARYAN FEST CEMENTED her credibility. With the praise of Uncle *go-tell-it-on-the-mountain*, and the assumptions that went with it, her reputation built itself. She'd have to have sex with a Hasidic Jew on St. Catherine Street to crack it. Nothing she did was suspect. She copied documents, attended meetings, pretty much did as she pleased.

Sunday was usually her day in Dorval. She'd been meticulously sorting but hadn't found the kind of plans or incriminating information she was looking for and had to ask herself occasionally why she even hoped it was there. Wasn't it better that these TCH people and their associates turned out to be more garden-variety racists, rather than armed and malignant vigilantes? Still, folks were out there somewhere, transforming hate into devastation. Best someone be looking.

Carl usually drove her back into the city after Sunday dinner, but it was late and he'd had a few beers, so she stayed over. When everyone else was in bed, he opened another beer for each of them and launched into a rant about his parents. It was hard to tell who he hated more.

"After Katie left, Dad adopted the twenty-four-hour military clock and tacked chore lists to the kitchen cupboard. Ever look closely? There are thousands of pin holes. He was always smacking us in the head or kicking us in the ass for suboptimal work on those fucking cabins. Dad was the hostess with the mostest, except no one ever came. I did learn how to build stuff, do drywall, plumbing, simple electrical, and I figured out that people are better at taking direction if they actually like you."

A lesson her grandfather never bothered with. But then again, he wasn't big on the lessons he wasn't giving.

"I quit school and left town two weeks after that fight. A month before I was supposed to graduate. I finally got my diploma a couple of years ago. Matter of pride."

"What about Charlene? Did you see her again?"

"That selfish bitch. We fucking needed her. We were kids."

"But she tried to take you with her."

"Jean tell you that fantasy? Can you imagine the four of us in a hole in Toronto calling some ni——er 'Dad'?"

Sarah cringed. Charlene escaped. But so had he. He had a nice life, in a nice house, with a wife and kids he loved. "She must have been really unhappy to have left like that."

"For fuck's sake Sarah, we were all unhappy. Lots of people are unhappy. She had four kids. She screwed around, then she took off. Jesus, I wouldn't expect you to take her side."

"I'm not taking her side, it's just . . . Grandpa."

"We got dealt a shit parent hand." Carl took a long gulp of beer, then shook his head.

"You and your brothers didn't do much better. Well, you almost did. Your mom was so nice. Your dad really loved her. I don't think he ever got over that. I'm sorry, hon."

So he had met her mother. Maybe on their honeymoon. She could ask about her. But she didn't. There were other questions that needed answering. Like why Grandpa hated her father when he did so much for him. Sure, some people were mean in their core, but it felt like more than that. She suspected her uncle didn't have answers.

"What about Charlene. Do you know where she is?"

"Somewhere in Toronto, downtown, with two mixed brats and grandkids. If you can believe that. And I'm pretty sure she's happy. Doesn't deserve to be, but she is." Carl walked to the fridge and grabbed another beer. "You want one?"

"No thanks."

He stared out into the backyard, pushing at a toy stroller with his foot. His face twitched, exaggerating the lines around his eyes and mouth Sarah hadn't noticed before. In anger, he looked almost ugly.

"Does my dad know?"

"I tried to tell him, but he wasn't interested. Chicken shit."

"Not everyone needs to know everything. You're a little hard on him. Maybe you're both hard on each other."

"Fair enough," her uncle said.

"What did you say when you saw your mother?"

"Don't call her that. And I didn't say we talked. I was in town for a Heritage Front get-together. Tracked her down.

Parked outside her house a few times. I wanted to know what her life looked like." He took another sip. "That's not exactly true. I had a speech planned but never gave it."

How did he even know she was happy? "What about Katie?"

"You're on a roll, aren't you? Not like your dad. You're someone who wants to know."

Sarah shrugged. "No one talks about any of it, except the same old stories. It's my family too."

"I didn't look for Katie. She's some hot shit artist. I get why she took off but it left Jeannie with everything. I hated her for getting out." He sighed and finished what was left of his beer. "I don't hate her anymore. Waste of energy."

"You got out too."

"Yep, I did. I'd had enough. Your Grandpa was fond of putting his foot down. On his kids. I was eighteen when I finally punched back. Got a boot-shaped bruise and a black eye for my trouble. Dad got a broken nose." He put an arm around her shoulder. "Now you've gotten out too, right?"

Sarah tried not to recoil.

The lines on his face disappeared and she understood why her father and Aunt Jean looked so much older. Their lines were dug in permanently. What caused them, never let up.

"You're quite the organizer. That library is really taking shape."

"Don't give me too much credit yet. I'm just getting started," Sarah said.

Carl laughed. "We can use your skills. I hate to admit it, and I'll deny it if you quote me, but we don't always draw the smartest crowd. A lot of yahoos in the movement just want to bash heads. That's not what we're about, Sarah. But you know that. We're about restoring order." He smiled at her. "Marcia doesn't know a lot about TCH, and I like it that way. She's a real bleeding heart in her way."

"Don't you want her to get it?"

"No need. She's not tough. You're tough. I can tell. You understand there are hard choices to make."

What made people think she was tough? What passed as tough, anyway? A thick skin? Was she not mushy enough, feminine enough? And why did tough feel so flattering?

"Don't get me wrong, Marcia's no raving feminist or pro-choice." He laughed. "Love that term, pro-choice. Sorry God, just making my choice. Those Jews and all the abortions they do. Probably trying to even the score. *Dr.* Henry Morgentaler, king of the *survivors*. Probably not even a doctor. Holocaust survival's a fucking industry. Movies, books, boatloads of Mercedes buses shipped off to Israel. There's probably an Auschwitz prisoner bobble head doll. They're clever. I'll give them that."

Nodding agreement made her feel sick. It had taken almost no time to convince him he needed her. But she'd have to learn to control the gag reflex. If this made her sick, she had no hope.

Almost a hundred years of the immigrant experience was ground into the thin, once red carpeting in the musty entrance hall of Sarah's building. When she got past that slightly nauseating idea, she loved thinking of herself as one of the most recent in a long line of people her family hated.

In her everyday wanderings, Sarah found a junk store in the north end near Jean Talon market and bought a beautiful old fan that could cut off a finger if she wasn't careful, two lamps, a vintage laminate table, and a plaid armchair to clash with the pink couch. The owner threw in two yellow happy face mugs. Housewarming gift, he said, for you and your boyfriend. Then he winked.

Sarah spent a lot of time on the fire escape, smoking cigarettes, or eating bagels and writing postcards to her aunt, her dad, and Mrs. Broder, describing the city in detail.

She was starting to understand what humidity felt like. Goderich was cooled by Lake Huron, so it never felt this oppressive. Her cut-offs and t-shirt stuck to her constantly. It was a city of extremes. Hot and cold, French and English, Separatist and Federalist, Fairmount and St. Viateur. Those were bagel stores. People had strong opinions about them too.

She hadn't seen Harrison in ages. He'd gotten home to Goderich to visit his mom the day after she left. Sarah felt both nervous and excited about his visit.

"Harrison!" She yelled, pulling the door open before he had a chance to knock. She'd spotted the familiar loose gait ambling headfirst up the street before even recognizing his face, which sported some curious half beard.

He threw his arms around her.

"You." She punched his back and pushed her head into his neck, surprised by the sudden desire to cry.

"You good?"

"I'm fine. Really. Great. You're back."

She hadn't realized how accustomed she'd grown to being on her own, how much she'd missed him, or how much of a stranger he now was. For a second, she wished he could move back in. Sarah pulled away and gestured to the living room.

He looked around and laughed. "That couch. Where the hell did you get it? It's so not you."

"It was a gift from Montreal. Where's this Ara? That's his name, right? I thought you'd bring him."

"That's his name. Aravinda in full. I needed time just with you. You'll meet him soon. You'll love him, everyone does. Hey, maybe you want a pet to keep you company. His cat had kittens and we're trying to find them homes. You like cats, don't you?"

"I do. But I already have one. It's made out of glass, and I take excellent care of it. I dust it regularly." She gestured at his face. "What's this? A bottomless beard? Sixties sideburns?"

"New look. You like?" His hair had grown even longer. His wardrobe looked upgraded. Maybe Ara was driving the fashion agenda.

"I like. I think." Sarah felt a twinge of embarrassment that nothing about her ever changed. "I should get a colourful scarf." They both cracked up. "Beer, pop?" She pulled him towards the kitchen.

"Got any Perrier?"

"What?"

"Kidding. It's expensive soda water from France. People here seem to love it. Beer's good. How about the place? Cozy, right? Not sure what look you're after. Eclectic late-century shabby furniture showroom. Talk to me. Tell me everything."

"First, I made us lunch. Go try out the couch. I'll get it."

"I bet I know what we're having."

Sarah handed him a bowl of buttery macaroni noodles. Harrison crunched the bag then poured pulverized cheese puffs into his bowl and passed it to Sarah. One stoned Saturday afternoon in high school, they invented Mac and Cheese Puffs.

"Careful with the orange powder. No fingerprints on Mrs. Pinky. I named her Mrs. Pinky."

"Perfect," Harrison said after a few spoonfuls. "Talk."

It was unclear where to start and what to mention. She was still processing her feelings about Aryan Fest but was hesitant to bring it up. Instead, she told Harrison about her perfectly pleasant stay in Dorval and how her aunt made Indian food and the kids ate with their hands. Then about her last visit with Mrs. Broder, how hard it had been saying goodbye, and her fear that things would never feel the same. Was it only Mrs. Broder she was talking about? Harrison raised his eyebrows a little, then reached out to squeeze her arm.

Sarah figured she'd better lighten the mood and told him the story about her uncle's shaved head and the wooden spoon. She knew Harrison would find it funny in that people-do-the weirdest-shit-to-fit-in kind of way. *Spot the costume* was a game they'd played often in the high school cafeteria. Then she finally told him about Aryan Fest, blowing through it quickly, hoping he wouldn't ask much.

"Jesus, Sarah. That sounds really fucked up and terrifying."

"It wasn't that bad. And I could hardly turn down the offer, could I?"

"I don't know. It's not like it was a U2 concert."

Even though Harrison understood what Sarah was trying to do, he had been arguing for activism. His letters were all about fighting for good rather than exposing the bad. The world was moving steadily in a better direction, it just needing kicking in the ass. He and Ara did a lot of that, and he was excited to get Sarah involved.

Maybe telling him what she was up to wasn't a great idea, but she needed one person from whom she didn't keep everything a secret. Maybe minus the details.

"Please don't tell anyone about Aryan Fest. They wouldn't understand."

"I don't understand. You took a huge risk. Everything could have blown up. I'm shocked your dad even let you go."

Sarah offered him the cheese puff bag. "More?"

"You didn't tell him, did you?"

"It would have made things worse between him and my uncle."

It wasn't clear he believed her. But Harrison dropped the subject. He told her about Ara and the trip to Europe and their hippy pad. When he was almost ready to leave, she asked him about the anarchist group Anti-Racist Action.

"Do you know how I can connect with them? Funny that your boyfriend's got the same name. A.R.A."

"They show up at demos now and again, but I have no contact info. You'll just have to look out for them."

"What's a demo?"

"A lot to learn, my friend," he said, laughing. "I'm so happy you're here. You're going to love it."

Sarah decided, despite no evidence that she could keep another being alive, to take Harrison up on the kitten offer. Or at least to check it out.

They didn't live far, just the other side of St. Denis, on the corner of Berri and Roi.

Ara opened the door.

"I'm Sarah Cartell."

"You are. Aravinda da Silva." He leaned in and kissed her on both cheeks then laughed at her surprise. "You better get used to it. It's the *bise*. It happens all the time."

Sarah looked around. "The bees?"

"The kisses, on both cheeks. It's called making the bise."

Maybe she hadn't been paying enough attention. Were people kissing in the streets all the time and she hadn't noticed? The couch lady *had* leaned in close then pulled back, which had clearly been a reaction to Sarah's surprise. Ara hadn't been put off, not that there'd been any time to recoil.

"From now on, I'll be prepared. Harrison here?"

"Nope. But don't worry, the kittens might bite, but I don't."

No biting, only kissing, which was possibly worse. They were still standing awkwardly in the narrow entrance way. Sarah tried not to stare. Brown and slender with long eyelashes, Ara wore a collarless cotton top over jeans and pointy leather slippers. Silver bangles on both wrists made tinkly sounds. A canvas bag covered in political buttons hung on the handlebars of a bike.

"You guys carry your bikes up three flights?"

"We do. We're building so much muscle." He flexed a thin arm then gestured for her to follow him down a dark hall that opened into a small bright kitchen.

"Want tea?"

"Sure."

She would have preferred to simply grab a kitten and run. She wanted to know Ara, eventually, but could do without the trial by fire. Harrison knew she'd be uncomfortable meeting Ara alone. Life lesson or something.

He handed her a mug of what he called chai—spicy, milky, and sweet. Sarah swished it around in her mouth.

"You can swallow. It's cardamom. It's Sri Lankan. Well not only Sri Lankan, but we drink it too."

"De Silva doesn't sound Sri Lankan." Sarah had no clue what Sri Lankan sounded like, but his last name seemed Spanish or Italian.

"It's Portuguese actually. Colonizers like to name their possessions."

There didn't seem to be a good answer to that. She glanced at a black poster with a pink triangle that said *Silence = Death*. Growing up a Cartell, silence ensured survival, but she got the point.

Ara's family lived in the capitol city of Sri Lanka, Colombo, and would disown him if they knew he was gay. Otherwise, they were lovely people. Did Sarah know about the civil war there? The Tamils and the Sinhalese? He sighed. Ireland, Sri Lanka, Nicaragua. What was wrong with people? His parents encouraged him to study abroad. He spoke French and English, so he had choices. Not France, nice place for cheese and architecture (that's what he was studying), but never to live. He picked Montreal. McGill. Met Harrison at a demo.

Thankfully, Sarah didn't need to ask.

They talked for over two hours. He refilled her cup three times. The bathroom that she'd had to use twice was full of beautiful containers for Q-tips and soap and shampoo.

He finally led her to the bedroom where every surface was covered in coloured fabric. Four kittens climbed over each other in a wooden box. There was a canopy over the bed. It reminded her of Ali Baba and the Forty Thieves from Mrs. Broder's reading circle.

"A bit of home." Ara smiled.

A weak *meew* brought Sarah to her knees. She reached for the orange one, then hesitated. "Can I pick her up?"

"It's a him. He's my favourite too. I'd keep him, but it's the kitten or Harrison. Hard choice, but I'll give Harrison a bit more time and see how that goes."

"Melrose. That's his name." Sarah had no idea where it came from.

Ara put him in a shoe box with holes poked in the top, then threw in a tinfoil ball. "Melrose's first toy and new mom." He held out the box. "Mazel tov."

Sarah felt panic rise. She'd never been responsible for anything other than herself. "Wait. I don't know. I'm not sure I'll be good at this. In fact, I won't. Maybe you should find someone more maternal." Suddenly the responsibility felt huge. She should have thought about it longer before just showing up.

Ara put down the box and let the kitten out. It didn't run away. It started climbing into Sarah's lap, which required some effort. She went to help it, but Ara put his hand on her arm to stop her. She didn't flinch or pull away.

"When a baby kangaroo is the size of a lima bean, it has to climb all the way to the mother's pouch, with no help."

The kitten made it up and toppled into her lap.

"Sarah, this kitten knows where it wants to be. And don't worry, they're very hard to break. I'll come check on you two as much as you need. But I have a good feeling."

Professor Agnes Pichon stood at the front of the Quebec history class Sarah had chosen less for any interest in the province than because Pichon taught a second-year course called *Modern Quebec: A history of hate, intolerance, and exclusion,* and was known to emphasize research methodology. She also taught higher year courses on archiving and indexing, and Sarah needed the prerequisites. So, Quebec history it was.

The professor, short and pudgy with kinky shoulder-length hair, heavy eyebrows, and a worn leather bag across her shoulder, walked into the amphitheatre and started talking with only the slightest trace of an accent. No platitudes. Straight to the point. She got instantly taller when she opened her mouth. In the middle of reviewing the curriculum document she handed out, she glanced down at the heavy bag she seemed to have forgotten still hung against her hip, like it was a nuisance someone else had placed there. She pulled it off and threw it on the desk sending two pieces of chalk flying. Ignoring the giggles, the professor glanced up at the students with a look suggesting if they'd followed the chalk, they were already missing the point. Sarah liked her already.

"Notes are your best friend in this class. If you don't understand a concept or need clarification, feel free to ask or come see me during office hours. Don't tell me you didn't get it. Make your case for my time. If you missed something I taught because you were, say . . ." She shot a look at the girl sitting next to Sarah who was busy with an emery board. ". . . filing your nails, you're probably in the wrong place."

She gave a brief outline of the Indigenous peoples whose land had been expropriated, the French explorers like Samuel de Champlain who were responsible, and the colonial rivalry between the British and the French. She mentioned the first fort built in 1608, then referenced how boys loved building forts.

First assignment. *Select a topic related to the course material and provide a short outline of how you'd research it—bibliography, other sources. Due October 12.* Agnes Pichon's class would not be a bird course.

Harrison met her after class, and they walked over to eat lunch outside the library on McTavish.

"How did it go? She doesn't dick around, right?" He took the same class the year before.

"She does not. I will stay on my toes and not file my nails in class. She's kind of prickly. I really like her."

"Of course you do."

"Did she give you the research outline as a first assignment last year?" Sarah asked.

"Yup. Why? You want to copy it? She'd know. She has an insane memory."

"No, jerk. Just wondered what you picked. I have an idea, but it might be too soon to launch into my particular field of interest. I want to get off to a good start."

Some of what she'd collected with Mrs. Broder was from Quebec. Carl had other stuff. It wasn't exactly academic, but there was something there. What the prof wanted for now was an outline, not a pile of research in the form of greasy invoices. Did it have to come from a library to be called research? Aside from *Hoax*, there hadn't been any serious books involved. Lists of creepy, stupidly named neo-Nazi groups, like *White-on* and *Black-out*, and papers from a hockey bag hardly seemed like legitimate sources.

"I did it on the October Crisis. FLQ, the War Measures Act."

"Good topic." She had no idea if it was a good topic.

"Lots of people pick it. Kind of an obvious choice. I can find it if you want. And don't worry. You'll get the hang of it."

Would she? At least she liked astronomy, maybe because it was so out there and required little guess work.

"What are you eating?"

Harrison had something that wasn't a sandwich. "Roti with curried potato. Want a bite? Ara made it for dinner last night."

Foreign or ethnic food was still not an area into which Sarah ventured, despite Harrison's attempts. Even poutine—the weird mash-up of French fries, cheese curds, and gravy, none of which she minded on their own—fell into that category. Plain and unlayered served her well. She waved her bagel at him. "No thanks. Brought my own."

She'd landed on Fairmount Bagel. Not because she could tell the difference, although she pretended she could. It was just closer. She didn't mind the line ups, more time to smell them coming out of the oven on the long wooden boards.

"No self-respecting Jew buys a cinnamon raisin bagel," she'd heard someone say as she was about to order half a dozen. Not that she'd be mistaken for Jewish, but she went with sesame just in case.

A flap of processed meat hung over the round edges of her sandwich.

"Is that really baloney? Are you even going to try to fit in here? There must be some law against baloney on a bagel."

Since when was Harrison a culinary or ethnic anything expert? "I didn't have any other bread." She wasn't sure why she bothered with such a stupid lie. At least it wasn't baloney on cinnamon raisin. She took what she hoped was an enthusiastic bite.

"Ara makes delicious chai tea."

"Look at you, all adventurous, drinking chai. I actually think I won the lottery. Ara studies like crazy *and* works at the bookstore *and* at his cousin's computer store on Ste. Catherine. *The Cheapest, the Best, and the Cheapest*. Isn't that a hilarious name? There's a t-shirt. I think he was wearing it when you were over. And he still packs me lunch."

Would Sarah even know if she won a lottery? "I want one of those t-shirts."

"I can ask. It's almost crazy how nice he is. He thinks you're great, by the way."

"I know he's really busy, but any chance he could help me figure out my computer some time?"

"That's your response to his compliment?" Harrison shook his head and laughed. "Always the pragmatist, Sarah. I'm sure he'd be happy to help."

"I assumed you'd told him everything." She'd assumed nothing of the sort. In fact, she'd given no thought to what Harrison might have said about her. Sarah knew that her conversation generally lacked human filler. Mrs. Broder had said it kindly, not that she herself required it, but that most people did. Phatic function was the formal term for the parts of language that serve to establish or maintain social relationships rather than impart information. That stuff seemed to come easy to most people, but not to her.

"That's not the point." Harrison jabbed an elbow into her side.

Sarah took the last bite of her culture clash sandwich. "Guess we should get back to work. By the way, I'm loving Melrose. He's a bit of a terror and I'm worried about his relationship with Mrs. Pinky. Kind of abusive. But it's nice to have company."

It wasn't until mid-October that Sarah made it to the Concordia Women's Centre. McGill had nothing of the kind. Concordia University was supposedly the hot bed of radical activism, at least for Anglos. Sarah scanned the bulletin board—full of flyers and notices for volunteers and roommates, a lesbian basketball league called Rainbow Hoops, choir, used bikes, a potluck coming out group, some gathering called *investigate yourself—BYO speculum*, plus all kinds of support to all kinds of *womyn*.

The girl behind the desk wearing a baggy *feminism works* t-shirt had four piercings in one ear and another in her nose. She walked over, clearly judging Sarah's outfit, neither colourful nor black. "Need help?"

"Anti-Racist Action, ARA. Do they ever put anything up?"

"What are they? A feminist group?"

"An anarchist activist group. Anti-fascist."

The girl looked annoyed that she'd been caught not knowing something radical. "Nothing I've seen. But this is a women's centre. You go here?" She sounded borderline suspicious.

"No. McGill."

The response was a raised judgmental eyebrow.

"Thanks." Sarah grabbed her backpack off the floor. What was feminism working on anyway? Not being helpful? Maybe she could buy herself entry with a purple *smash the patriarchy* sweatshirt. Twenty-five bucks. One hundred percent cotton. The centre was selling them to raise money. Maybe for the sisterhood. Maybe to subsidize the purchase of speculums. She'd expected Montreal to be a political buffet that she could step up to. Finding a route into that other world where it was now obvious she didn't belong wasn't going to be easy. Something would give. She needed to be patient.

Sarah was half listening to the political science lecture when she spotted the little pin with a red bar through a swastika on the canvas backpack. The girl it belonged to, sitting two rows in front of her, had messy light brown hair and rested unscuffed police boots against the seat in front of her.

When class was done, Sarah rushed to catch up to her, hoping to get noticed. What did she plan to say? Nice pin. In the end, her approach was less than subtle. The gal stopped to do up the lace of her boot and Sarah plowed into her. "Oh God, sorry."

"No harms." She smiled then turned to walk off. Her t-shirt had no slogan.

"I'm Sarah Cartell." It came out as a squeak, and she felt herself blush.

"Luce Belanger." She kept walking.

"Do you want to get a coffee?"

"You're asking me for a date?"

"Oh God, no." She was certainly invoking God a lot. "I mean not that I . . . just . . ." Sarah stuttered.

"I never pay for coffee. I work at a café. I do need to eat my sandwich. Join if you want." She shrugged.

Sarah fell in beside her. They sat on a bench.

"You don't eat?"

There was no way Sarah was pulling out her bagel and baloney. "Ate earlier."

Luce seemed interested enough in what Sarah was saying. She wasn't rude and asked for no feminist or anti-fascist credentials. They talked about the class and the professor's not-so-subtle obsession with the failings of counterculture and radical political movements, and his refusal to acknowledge their disruptive or transformative qualities.

"What he knows anyway?" Luce said.

"You certainly understand English better than you speak." It came out before Sarah realized it was insulting.

Luce laughed. "And you say what you think."

"Sorry. That's why I mostly keep my mouth shut, but if you disagree, why don't you say anything?" Sarah asked. "There's no debate in the class. Everyone just sits there like lumps, sucking it up."

"What are lumps?"

"In this case, it's something that sits around not doing much. Or else it's sugar cubes, as in *one lump or two.* You work in coffee and tea, haven't you heard that?"

"I think that's a British thing, this lumps word. And I didn't hear *you* open your mouth to object. Anyway, I'm auditing the class." She winked at Sarah. "Not exactly supposed to be there. Working on my English and learning some things or two."

"Some things or two is good," Sarah said.

"In my real life, I study art at UQAM and make coffee. You live in residence?"

"Nope, I have an apartment and a new roommate—kitten named Melrose. Just got him and he's a little crazy. I can get you one if you want. A kitten." A little forward maybe. Sarah was surprised at how perfectly gregarious she was being. Well maybe not perfectly. Maybe overly. "This guy Ara is giving them away."

"Hey, I know this guy from demos. He's an activist. He offered me one too. But I'm not so much for pets. And fur in the paint is not good."

"You know Ara? That's a coincidence since I know exactly two people in Montreal."

"Now you know three. And I'm late." Luce collected her things in one fluid movement and waved. "See you, Sarah." Both the 'a's were soft.

She waved back. That wasn't too hard.

They fell into a routine after class. Sarah decided to brave it and eat her baloney on a bagel in front of her. Luce never commented.

Instead of probing her about the Montreal anti-fascist scene, Sarah took an unfamiliar tack and went with something a little riskier. Friendship.

"I could use a job. Any chance your milky cat café needs help?"

The place was called Comme un Chat au Lait, A play on café au lait, which literally translated as *like a cat to milk.* It was on the Plateau, not far from where Sarah lived.

"You know how to make coffee?"

"Add water, right?"

"Right." Luce laughed.

21

LATE OCTOBER 1993

Montreal

LUCE MADE NO SECRET OF HER POLITICS but seemed to share the depth of her involvement in measured increments, taking her time, sussing out whether Sarah was worthy of confidence. Trusting Luce was an unfamiliar leap of faith. Sarah's trust list was short. Curtis, Harrison, Mrs. Broder, and weirdly for such a short amount of time, Ara. But she was working on it.

Despite her embarrassingly limited coffee making experience, Luce scored her a job, trusting that Sarah's claim to be a fast learner would extend to working small appliances. Comme un Chat au Lait or "Olé" as Luce called it, on the corner of two narrow streets off Ste. Laurent, was a hodgepodge of mismatched furniture—wood, metal, laminate, some padded, some hard-backed and spindly. When a chair splintered under the weight of a patron (which happened not infrequently, since most were garbage picked by staff—part of the job), apologies and free coffee were immediately offered. No questions asked.

Thick pine floors exposed layers of coloured paint dating back to 1919. Supposedly it had been a greengrocer, then a butcher, then a doctor's office. A few old pieces of equipment, cabinets mostly, a table on wheels with stirrups that people fought over, and an old dental chair, complete with the little spitting sink. The second floor had supposedly been a makeshift synagogue. The big windows (glass panes encased in metal) had never been updated, so it was always either too cold or too hot, but prime real estate nonetheless.

"Espresso. First you taste, then we make." Luce put a tiny cup in front of her. "It's kind of a required taste. You know like Roquefort cheese or stout beer. Bitter."

A required taste. Sarah didn't like correcting Luce even though she'd asked her to. "That's all I get? It's so small." Sarah reached for the sugar.

"That's all you need. Wait, no sugar yet." Luce touched her hand. "Try it first."

Sarah dipped her tongue in. Bitter was an understatement.

"It's good, no?" Luce had obviously been drinking it for years.

"Yes, it's good no. Can I add sugar now?"

Luce pushed the bowl of misshapen brown and uniform white cubes across the polished wooden counter. "Lumps."

Sarah dipped one in the coffee and stuck it in her mouth. The square fell apart against her tongue. She grabbed another.

"That was four cubes, Sarah. At this rate, there will be no hope for your tooth."

Sarah laughed. No hope. She looked up at the menu on the blackboard behind the counter. A long, coloured chalk list of beverages. Coffee, it turned out, was not one thing. And it was crazy that students or anyone paid so much for it.

"It's like rent," Luce said. "They stay for maybe one or three hours for the price of one coffee. And regular coffee's not so much to pay. I'll show you how the machine works. The hard part is making an art with the milk. It's a new thing we do. If it looks like a marshmallow or an apple instead of a heart. No worries."

The stainless-steel cappuccino machine was beautiful and terrifying. Supposedly it could make three cups at a time, as well as steam milk. Luckily, the café was quiet, so Sarah got to keep trying. Coffee was free for staff, and by the time she left, she was buzzing, knew the difference between lattés, cappuccinos, short and long espressos, and succeeded in making a passable abstract milk design.

Sarah's favourite class was astronomy. It had nothing at all to do with any aspect of her life. Even before the class got a look through an outdoor telescope, she enjoyed sitting in the dark amphitheatre looking at slides of the universe. She loved learning in the dark.

Sarah pulled off her toque as she stood behind two other girls waiting for her turn. It was their first time at the astronomy lab. Once they'd spotted at least six constellations with the naked eye, they got a turn with the telescope.

The cool quiet was interrupted only by the odd sniffle, a pencil scratching on paper, the sound of fabric rubbing. The professor was gesturing for the next in line to come forward. Silence was understood.

Gloves off, Sarah leaned her forehead against the metal, still warm from the person before her. The big dipper, part of Ursa Major, the celestial great bear, Orion, Aquarius. She loved the lack of practical utility this knowledge served. She wasn't concerned about finding them, she knew where they were. It felt like floating. At some point, there'd be an actual exam about the science behind these lights in the darkness, but for the moment, it was simply a starry night and she was in it.

It occurred to Sarah that God's masterpieces, the beautiful settings that had formed the backdrop of so many childhood punishments, never included the night sky, and for that, she felt grateful.

She arrived for her first official shift at Olé feeling nervous even though Luce assured her that the four to eight shift was always quiet. The stiff *espress yourself* t-shirt, unlike Luce's that was well worn and hung perfectly, held its square shape. On top of that, there was a full apron—coffee coloured. No one liked a stained server.

The hours passed without incident. Maybe one or two of the espressos were too long or too short, but no one complained. While Sarah was wiping down the counter, she noticed a stack of postcards advertising an art show; part photo, part painting, part collage. The image, a group of turn-of-the-century women in a canoe, had bits scratched away. The text was handwritten and difficult to read. *Yes, we are not drowning.* Printed across the bottom of the card in small bold letters was *Katie Cartell. Micheline Beaudin Gallery.* The opening of the show, her aunt's show, had been a week ago.

"Sarah? You're fine?"

Sarah tried to rearrange her face so she didn't look like she'd been jumped in a dark alley, then showed Luce the card. "Did you go to this?"

"No. We get lots of promo cards. You could go to a show twice a day in Montreal. Katie Cartell. I think I've seen this things before. In my women and mixed media class."

What the hell was mixed media?

"You know her work?" Luce asked.

"No, but I know her. Sort of. She's my aunt. I think."

"You think?"

"The gallery is open until nine o'clock. It's the last day. Can we go after work?" As soon as she'd asked her, she regretted it. Too late. Sarah popped a sugar cube in her mouth and closed her eyes, narrowing her focus to sweet only.

"Of course. It's around the corner."

Was this how she'd meet Katie?

As Luce predicted, the artist was not there. Usually, they only showed up for openings. They were alone in the gallery, except for the owner who let them wander the small brightly lit space and examine each of the eleven pieces. Sarah let Luce explain. Bold colours over fragments of newspaper stories, photos and torn cheese cloth, buried under layers of lacquer and acrylic, a range of artistic techniques known as media. Kind of beautiful from a distance, more disturbing and disjointed up close.

What Sarah could make out referenced missing women, *marginality* (another unfamiliar word), *femmes perdues, disparues, manquées*—missing from culture, from institutions, from systems of societal engagement. They were nothing like Katie's paintings in her apartment.

"Holy shit. They're really expensive, like thousands," Sarah whispered.

"And all of them except one are sold," Luce replied, pointing to little red stickers on the descriptions.

The owner came toward them, neat shiny dark hair that didn't move on its own, fancy slacks, and an oversized crisp shirt, collar up. A chunky necklace of colourful glass balls rested on pronounced collarbones.

"Bonjour. Micheline." She stared, not quite open-mouthed but almost, at Sarah.

Luce was reading the bio on the wall.

They all looked at Katie's photo, half smile, almost turquoise eyes, swathes of coloured fabric around her neck and shoulders.

"She looks like you. With more colours," Luce said.

The bio said Katie Cartell was originally from Goderich, Ontario, currently living between New York and Berlin (like in the ocean?). No mention of a husband or kids. All her materials, the photos, the fabric, were originally sourced. Some from family archives. Family archives? That was a fancy way to describe the boxes in the attic.

"You are her daughter? This is quite a surprise." The gallery owner's smile was forced.

It felt like an ambush. And didn't the bio say no kids?

Sarah felt obligated to respond. "No. She's my aunt but I've never met her."

Micheline looked shocked then disappointed that she had not in fact uncovered a great secret. "Katie is a very private person. Much is written about her art but not her personal life. Everyone likes to speculate, but she mostly says nothing."

At least in that way, Katie was a member in good standing of the *keep-it-to-yourself* Cartells.

"I happen to know her girlfriend." Micheline continued, "She teaches at the Univerität der Künste Berlin, the Berlin University of the Arts. You know it perhaps?" she directed this comment to Luce. "We met years ago when we were both studying there. It was so lovely to catch up with Katie."

Sarah did what she could to keep a straight face. It was funny that Micheline might be trying hard to impress the person least likely to care. "Thanks for letting us have a look," Sarah said. "I'm not sure that last piece is likely to sell." One had to look close to see the swastika and the burning crosses, but they were there.

Luce took Sarah to a bar around the corner and ordered a bottle of gold liqueur called Pineau des Charentes. She told Sarah about her super Catholic family in Lac St. Jean, northwest of Quebec City. A beautiful but depressed region that made its own drink called Du Bleuet.

"Like Dubonnet, but from blueberries."

Sarah nodded, no idea what either drink was. Other than beer, she had little experience with alcohol. Aside from a badly proportioned episode with rum and coke after a high school exam (Virginia, only slightly less hammered, had gotten her home and into bed. Her bright yellow carpet never recovered.), Harrison had only just convinced her to move beyond beer and try wine.

"Lots of people have little money and the wild blueberries are free. So there's a lot of Du Bleuet and blueberry wine." Luce made a face. "Confiture, like jam and jelly, soap and special made tie dye t-shirts. The t-shirts were my idea. Tourists are suckers." She smiled, like Sarah understood that you do what you have to do. "Everyone gets what they want."

"You don't talk so much about your family. According to Micheline, your aunt doesn't either," Luce said.

"Family trait. Silence is golden." Sarah was only slightly annoyed that some gallery owner knew more about Katie than she did. Luce offered her a cigarette, then lit her own and poured them each a third glass. Her arm rested on the back of the booth. The smoke caught in the twinkly white lights running the length of the bar and made it difficult to focus on anything. Luce was messy and neat, beautiful, but not exactly pretty. Her graceful movements, some kind of ease in her body that was unfamiliar to Sarah but reminded her of Curtis, was neither recognizably female nor male. Unlike Sarah, who even after a third drink, was still poised to flee because who knew what might be coming, Luce never seemed in a rush.

What was familiar was the neither *here* nor *there-ness* of Luce. Except that Sarah's middle ground was one of non-belonging. She usually didn't bother with envy, but it was hard sometimes not to wonder what it felt like to relax.

"Was it hard tonight, to see all this things?" Luce asked.

Sarah rolled the unlit cigarette between her fingers. "It was fine," she said. It wasn't fine.

Katie had been that close, one week ago, eating cheese, drinking wine, explaining the layers, shaking hands, maybe pushing pieces of her hair out of her face the way Sarah did. Did she know her niece was in Montreal? Her brother? Was she in touch with Jean? Did she give a shit? Cartells were fucked up.

In a normal world, with a normal family, she'd have been eating the cheese too, they'd have gone out for dinner together, Katie would have dropped by Olé for a coffee, cappuccino probably. Growing up, a normal grandfather would have said, "You look so much like your aunt. Katie, don't you think she's looking more and more like you?"

For glimpses of such normalcy, Sarah had taken to looking in people's windows at night. Not in a creepy way exactly, just from a distance.

"My family . . ." she started to say. "You saw the piece with the swastika, the burning crosses. The only one that wasn't sold. Who would hang that in their living room, right? Except maybe my grandfather. That's what he believes, and what his father believed."

"He was a Nazi?" Luce pronounced it Nazee. She was clearly trying not to sound appalled.

"Maybe. A sympathizer for sure. That's why Katie left, or at least one of the reasons. And he hated her art. So maybe he wouldn't hang it in his living room. That's why I've never met her."

"Oh." What else was Luce supposed to say? "And your parent is the same?"

"My mother died when I was two. My dad believes that White people, at least Christians, are . . . you know . . . better, best. They don't do very much about it, which is a good thing, but still bad. They throw darts at pictures of Sammy Davis Jr." She laughed. What a stupid fact to share.

She started to sweat and could smell her armpit. She wasn't telling it right. "I don't feel that way. Obviously. But I did when I was younger and I didn't know any better."

Luce barely nodded.

Sarah went on about Mrs. Broder and the revelations and the project, about Curtis and his dad being fired, and her father being responsible. When it all felt too convoluted, she skipped to her uncle and TCH. "I'm trying to find out what they do and how they're connected to other groups. I've been researching for years."

"I'm sorry for you," Luce said. Sarah sighed. Great. All she needed was pity from Luce. "Your family. That's fucked up."

Sarah's head felt heavy. Too much Pinneau. She rested it on her arm. Luce touched her hair.

"I have to go." Sarah pushed her chair back too quickly. Luce went out of focus, caught in the twinkly light. She shoved her arm in the sleeve of her jacket, but it was inside out. Luce stood to help, and Sarah gave her a look that wasn't meant to be mean. The girl sat back down. Sarah turned to leave and realized too late that she'd left the cigarette on the table. Going back for it felt rude.

"Thanks for the drinks," she called out, not caring enough if Luce heard.

Sarah walked back to the gallery. It was locked and dark, but still, she pounded on the door. She needed to know how to contact her aunt. Maybe the owner was in the basement, maybe she lived upstairs. Sarah paced the sidewalk out front, then knocked again.

She bummed a smoke from a well-dressed couple walking arm-in-arm. Gitane.

"Do you have a light too?"

The woman fumbled nervously in her purse then handed Sarah a plastic lighter.

"Keep it, really, keep it," she said in accented English, waving her hand. The woman was at least five-ten, and her boyfriend was taller. Was Sarah that scary?

She sank to the pavement, her back against the gallery door smoking and flicking the lighter. She'd get Katie's address. Send her a letter. No kids, no husband, what else did she have to do besides mix her media? Had she ever thought that Sarah might need her?

She started walking towards the mountain, ignoring the astronomy prof's warning that women shouldn't be there alone at night. She'd be fine. After all, strangers on the street were afraid of her. Sarah stared up into the overcast sky. The leaves smelled good. The darkness felt like protection. She walked for a couple of hours, thinking up versions of what she might say to Katie Cartell, who was no more an aunt than Charlene was a grandmother.

For the next three days, Sarah worked on the letter, ignoring assignments that needed her attention. Shredded bits of the first three drafts (why did she tear them that small?) covered the floor around the oil drum she used for garbage. Too pathetic, too stoic, too fuck you, too much information, too little.

Katie would have answers, but why would she provide them? Aunt Jean was stingy with details, except that one time. Maybe she just hated reliving it, although she kind of did every day. Could Katie explain what kept her sister there?

It was two weeks before she got back to the gallery. Micheline promised to get it to Katie in New York. The way she said it, it sounded like she'd take it there herself.

There was a miniscule tug of war before Sarah let go of it, and the gallery owner placed it gently on the desk, like she was ensuring its safe passage. Sarah couldn't be sure the woman wouldn't steam it open and read it.

"Merci."

"You're very welcome. And good luck," Micheline said.

Right. Luck.

Sarah checked the mail every day—eager, upset, angry, indifferent, then finally over it. It didn't matter anyway. Katie would only complicate things. That's where she was at when she got a note, not from her aunt but from an assistant, printed on a promo card, scheduling lunch four weeks later at some restaurant called Air in Old Montreal.

Regrets only. She didn't plan on going, but she never sent regrets.

Sarah was heading out to Dorval every other week now. She had too much schoolwork to do and the TCH meetings were shedding no light. It never ceased to amaze her how much people loved the sound of their own voices. When she was there, she took stealthy inventory of the comings and goings, in case.

On this particular day, things had deteriorated into a poorly refereed name slinging free-for-all, from *butt fucker* to *arse bandit*, *bum driller*, *anal assassin*, *fudge packer*. (So this was where their creativity lay?) The meeting had started with a rant against homo rights inspired by proposed legislation in Ontario that had barely been defeated. Carl waited until the insult choices got thin to call an end to it.

According to a couple of men who'd headed to Toronto to witness the vote, police had smartly worn latex gloves to protect themselves from AIDS-carrying protesters. Where exactly were those cops planning to stick their fingers? Everyone nodded like gloves was a perfectly normal thing to do, even Dr. Trotter, who supposedly knew a thing or two about transmission and infection control. Clearly, they weren't worried enough not to push people down the stairs to get them out of the legislature building. Some politician had even claimed the homos used cattle prods for sexual entertainment. Club members loved the gory details, but *barely defeated* was barely defeated. The country was at risk.

It was late fall but hot inside the club house. The smell reminded Sarah of church. The windows were steamed up from all the heavy breathing. Some folks got suspiciously over-excited about the topic. Any minute, mini doughnuts would start flying.

"We need action, or this abomination will quash any vestige of decency across the country."

The speaker whom Sarah hadn't met, another average guy

dressed like her uncle in khakis and a golf shirt, seemed proud of himself for using words like quash and vestige.

"Too many folks are apathetic and lazy. 'My son's gay and it's okay.' It's not bloody okay. All you need is a bunch of confused kids with raging hormones who'd be happy for anyone to yank their chain, and there's no stopping it."

Gasps and laughter, then clapping.

He might have looked bland, but his reference to hand jobs was genius. People liked being shocked and titillated. He understood that and worked it.

An older man started grumbling about Quebec eroding the traditional family. Then got onto the Catholics and men who wore dresses, like the Pope. Mr. Khaki Pants coughed loudly, thanked him for his thoughts, and moved along. "Disrespect for traditional values is trouncing the economy and decent White folk are leaving Montreal."

Then they started reviewing a draft letter to the Premier of Quebec. Someone fumbled with the knob on an overhead projector until it came into focus. It would have made as much sense out of focus.

Sarah was going through papers in the library, feeling like it was all a total waste of time, when Carl arrived with a kid named Madeline McBride he told her would be a big help. With what, exactly?

The girl had shown up at a meeting one night a few weeks earlier with a boy named Bradley who'd mumbled and squirmed in his chair, clearly hoping something more exciting might happen.

Whenever Carl found someone a little too eager to kick some ass, he put them to work addressing envelopes and licking stamps to test their patience. Carl liked enthusiasm, but he understood one head-banger with no self-control could bring down an entire organization.

The boy didn't last long. After fifteen minutes, he started yelling about *pussies willing to be cowed by the Government.* When a rude gesture insulting the Premier of Quebec knocked tea all over a pile of sealed letters, Carl thanked Bradley for the night's work and escorted him out.

Sarah handed Madeline some envelopes. The girl licked each one carefully with a pierced tongue.

"They should make these taste better."

"My brothers had a friend who loved the taste. Use the sponge," Sarah suggested. "That's what it's for."

"Doesn't stick as well."

The kid was short and clearly gave her appearance only enough attention to guarantee it unremarkable. She hid in dark baggy jeans and a hooded dark grey sweatshirt with the words *Bring It* in red. The reddish-brown hair that hung in her face masked the only splash of colour—bright green eyes she could do nothing to mute.

"What brought you here Madeline, besides a taste for envelopes?"

"Call me Maddie. Please. Fucking Madeline, what kind of a priss name is that? I'm friends with Bradley. He's kind of a freak, but mostly he's alright. We're in social studies together. We were doing multi-culturalism. Immigrants who built the railroad and all that shit. Bradley yelled something about how they're taking jobs from real Canadians. Not that he wants to be building railroads. He wants to start his own White skinhead band."

Unlikely that a lot of Black and Asian immigrants would be competing with Bradley for that particular job, Sarah wanted to point out.

"The teacher asked Bradley where his parents were from," Maddie said. "She knew they were British. Asked him if that's what he meant by immigrant. He told her she knew exactly what he meant but he'd be happy to spell it out. The teacher said it wasn't necessary. But he started in anyway, and then there was this argument with some lezzy and two Chinese guys.

"Bradley says we're only entitled to an opinion if it's popular, and ours aren't. It's discrimination against White people. Anyway, he got sent to guidance because the teacher said he was prejudiced. But I agree. My dad keeps applying for management jobs that go to pakis and Arabs. They can't even fucking speak English. They're working there for like fifteen minutes and then look who's boss."

"Your dad's pissed off?" Sarah was trying to get the story straight. It was coming out really fast.

"Well ya, duh, what do you expect? But he won't do anything about it. He's a doormat. Every night at dinner, he goes on about work. All the *multi-syllables* and *gutturals* as he calls them. 'Ahmed. You've got to bloody hork in the middle of that name. Can't they just have names I don't expectorate over?' So I said 'I don't know Dad, Yu and Wa. Those seem pretty easy.' One less syllable than McBride. He didn't think it was funny."

"I think it's funny," Sarah said.

"Right? Anyway, I thought he was going to blow a gasket when he came home the other day from some anti-racism training. 'Anti-White training more like, and they served Jamaican for lunch. Jerk.' He won't do anything about it, but I will. Bradley shoots his mouth off. I don't. Not interested. Now he's stuck in the *Building a Rainbow* workshop at school—how faggy is that? He can't afford any more suspensions so he's going. Anyway, one day he tells me he knows this kid whose uncle is in a group, like a White pride group. So we came. Didn't work out so well for Bradley."

"Clearly," Sarah said, a bit overwhelmed by how much the kid talked. "Maybe he should take up boxing or something."

"He's not dumb, you know. I tell him he's going to end up in jail. One dead fag or kyke is gonna change his world in all the wrong ways. Not worth it. I want to change things. Get my dad that job. If we don't do anything, one day there'll be some ni———er as president of the United States."

Maddie glanced at Sarah, like she was unsure of the word, like she was testing it out, but it wasn't quite the right fit. Sarah didn't offer anything in the way of reassurance. The kid would have to sort that one out for herself.

She understood the anger and how Maddie got there. Rolling with the punches from all the job thieves was a recipe for a sense of indignant entitlement. The fact that the kid had to fight her dad's battles and that he wasn't remotely interested in anything beyond whining might eventually force her to see things differently. Or not. If she hadn't had the library, Sarah might have stayed the course too.

"How about you? How did you get here?"

"Carl's my uncle."

"In your blood, huh?"

"A place for every man and every man in his place, my grandfather says."

"And that place is somewhere else." Maddie banged her hand on the table. They both laughed.

Go home. Your dad's not worth the trouble. Sounds like a jerk who doesn't deserve a promotion, Sarah wanted to tell her. Exactly the kind of person her grandfather couldn't stand.

"I'm not complaining about stuffing envelopes. I know it's all important. But I want to do other things too—real stuff, fun stuff."

Fun stuff. Right. Sarah understood the pull towards something bigger.

22

MARCH 1995

Sunnyside Mental Health Centre

"I DIDN'T EXPECT MY FIRST ENCOUNTER WITH KATIE, or at least her art, to happen in front of Luce, who I still barely knew. And then being accosted by Micheline, a total stranger with all this insider information about Katie, her life, and her girlfriend. I hate people knowing my business. Even you, knowing people's names before I told you, felt like a violation."

Sarah was thinking a lot about her aunt's paintings. She spent arts and crafts that morning cutting people and animals out of magazines and exchanging their heads and bodies. Humans desperately needed help and thinking like animals might be the answer. She wondered if this was how Katie came up with her ideas and how much her finished project might sell for.

"In a nature documentary I once saw, someone was gutting a deer and the insides spilled out on her boots. The woman with the knife was smiling because that was her goal, to clean out the deer. I felt a bit like that deer. Insides dumped on the ground."

"Are you trying to shock me Sarah? That's an awfully violent metaphor."

"It wasn't about the violence. It was about the emptying. You want violence. There was a shoebox filled with images of lynching in my grandfather's attic. Most were postcards people sent to his father and grandfather. A couple were made out to him. But some of them were photographs, probably taken by family members. My family. Violence is nothing new for me. The deer was just an image I chose. Sorry it upset you."

"Sarah, you felt literally gutted by someone knowing things about an aunt you've never met."

"To you, this seems like a little thing, but to me it isn't. I have an aunt I don't know. Someone who is out in the world making and selling art that reveals horrible things about who my family is. Someone who probably knew I lived in Montreal and didn't bother to contact me. Do I care that Luce or Micheline know my aunt is a lesbian, when I don't even know how tall she is? I don't. But I hate being ambushed to the point of tears then asked if I'm okay. I felt obligated to explain the swastika art to Luce, to expose my family and myself to her. I may have told her eventually. Instead, I'm sitting there drunk in a bar babbling on about my mother and Mrs. Broder and my uncle. And of course, she's going to think it's fucked up and feel sorry for me."

"You trust Luce. You may not have known that at the time, but you do now. Maybe part of that instinct came because of what happened at the gallery and at the bar after. You took a leap of faith, and you know she'll protect your secrets."

"Maybe my problem isn't about finding other people to trust. It's that I don't trust myself to keep it together. I don't trust myself not to sell out my friends or put them in danger."

"Oh Sarah. You take any opportunity to make yourself out to be bad. You twist what is a positive, like building a friendship, into a negative, about how you ruin things. Or, how you will ruin them in some imagined future. That's not what you've done."

Sarah looks at her like she's full of crap and gets ready to say so, but Mona continues.

"Don't tell me it was your fault. Spare me that hamster wheel this one time. You can unearth the shit in almost anything, Sarah. Caring has thrown you for a loop. You suddenly found yourself in a world that involved more caring than you'd planned for. And that's not a bad thing. It's just a human thing."

23

LATE OCTOBER 1993

Montreal

DR. PICHON'S DOOR WAS SLIGHTLY AJAR. Sarah knocked lightly. The prof glanced up, then back down at a paper, signalling her to wait. It was a minute before she looked back at Sarah.

"Sorry about that, had to finish writing the thought before it disappeared. They do that these days."

"I'm Sarah Cartell."

"Yes, you are, and I believe you owe me a research project outline."

There were at least sixty students in the course and she remembered that? "Your memory seems fine to me."

Pichon laughed. "I'm good with names and assignments, particularly if they're outstanding, in either the exceptional or the *still due* sense of the word. I hope you're here to hand it over?"

Sarah couldn't help laughing. "Not exactly." She pulled a pile of papers out of her bag.

"That's more than three pages. Is this your hand things in to everyone day, or are we still at the discussion stage?"

"Unfortunately, the latter."

"Unfortunately, it's going to cost you marks." She pointed to the empty chair.

"I've been doing my own research. Can I tell you a bit about it?"

Best to just plow ahead. Sarah mentioned a few names and events, some of which the woman seemed to recognize. Not enough stuff based in Quebec yet, but she was only starting to gather that. The professor seemed interested enough, although a little impatient. Her time was valuable. Then Sarah mentioned Arthur Butz and *The Hoax of the Twentieth Century*.

It was a bit of a test. If the banned book got the prof's attention, then Sarah had made the right assumption about what she already knew. If not, Sarah would drop it. It would be disappointing, but that was fine.

Pichon leaned forward surprised. "Where'd you get hold of that? It's banned here."

"It was in my grandfather's attic."

She chose to mention the attic because it sounded almost accidental, like she'd stumbled upon it, like maybe even her grandfather hadn't known what was up there. It wasn't in a prominent place on a bookshelf in his den. It could be one of those skeletons in the closet type things. Sarah would wait before blowing her family wide open in front of this woman.

"You're not taking this class because you're keen on Quebec. You're here because of my other work."

"I like Montreal. But hate is my real interest. I–"

Professor Pichon cut her off. "You'll need to complete assignments for me, Sarah, on Quebec. I can't grade you on anything else. But if you want to meet and talk about other things, I'm interested." She asked nothing more about Sarah's family or how her grandfather had come into possession of the book.

"I'll have the research outline for you on Friday. I almost did it on Leonard Cohen."

Pichon laughed. "If I had a dollar for every student that suggests Leonard Cohen.

"I'm doing the Jews in Montreal 1900-1930."

The professor picked up her pen. "Friday," she said and looked back down at her papers.

Marc Scott, the one who prompted Carl's little fit at Aryan Fest, stuck his head into the *library*.

"Seen my dad?"

Under a leather jacket, his white t-shirt read *fuck the mosaic*. It shouldn't have made her laugh, but it did. Grade 10 history: *The American melting pot and the Canadian mosaic. Pick one. Argue the merits.* Neither worked. The bits never fully melted, and the tiles were only allowed to be colourful once a year. *Please bring your costume and spicy dish to the multicultural party and cross your fingers no one chokes on it.*

"He's due to drop off sermons to send out. We do his licking for him. If I see him, should I tell him you're looking?"

"Don't bother. I'll find him."

"I'm Sarah by the way. We met at Aryan Fest."

"I remember you. Master of White Power trivia." Marc turned an aluminum chair around and sat on it backward.

Sarah laughed. "Why do guys do that?"

"Do what?" Only the right side of his face smiled. He seemed unsure if he was being mocked.

"Never mind."

"So, you're responsible for this so-called library? Do I need a little card to take something out? Can I borrow some of your powerful *banish the scum* letters to the government? I'd like to use one as a prototype."

"Sorry, too precious to lend out. You'll have to review them in here." She patted the table.

Marc leaned back balancing the chair on two legs. It was probably meant to be cool, but the effect was more *ride 'em pony*.

"I'd better get back at it." There was work to do. Someone dropped off two boxes of what Carl had already determined was likely junk, but better check anyway.

"Your uncle's a real slave driver, huh?" Marc winked and came down off his perch. "We should grab a beer some time."

Maybe like the boxes, what she'd find was mostly junk, but it was only a beer. And Marc *had* been allowed in the inner circle meetings at Aryan Fest.

Then he began rhyming off a few fluent sounding sentences in what Sarah assumed was German.

"That . . ." He smiled all cocky. "Was a formal request. In case you don't speak the mother tongue."

"I do not. But I'm up for a beer."

"*Fett.*" He smiled. "That's slang for cool."

Harrison dropped by on Monday with a container of something Ara claimed he'd made too much of. Sarah had dinner with them three times in the past two weeks, and Ara was gleeful that he had Sarah on a path to conversion. From bland to not as bland. He had high hopes for red and green chilli in the near future. Harrison and Ara both laughed at how tentatively she lifted the fork or spoonful of something unfamiliar, sticking out her tongue to meet it before letting it past her lips. It was the reason she'd hesitated to accept the invitation in the first place. They'd make fun of her for sure. And what if she hated it? There was always naan bread, Ara insisted.

"He never accidentally makes too much," Harrison said. "He's started including you in his calculations of what we'll need for the week. I know how much you hate being pitied, but he might feel sorry for you."

"If the pity comes with containers of food, invitations, and tolerance for my predilections, I'll suck it up. It's a bland world over here."

Harrison looked her up and down. "At least your food matches your wardrobe. How do you actually dress like a bagel and baloney?"

Sarah laughed. "That was so mean. True but mean."

While she was putting the food away, she told him about her plan to have a beer with Marc Scott.

"That dick you met at Aryan Fest?"

Had she mentioned that? She couldn't remember.

"What the hell, Sarah. Isn't True Canadian Heritage enough infiltration for you? Why go out with this guy? He's a skinhead jerk, not some mastermind lynchpin for an international Nazi cabal. And it's not like you have piles of time to waste. Have you even done the assignment for Pichon yet, or started that paper on the Spanish Civil War?" Harrison was angry.

"The assignment is finished. I just need to hand it in. And the paper is on its way." An exaggeration, but she had started. "It's only a beer. And he approached me. I want to know what he knows. Why are you being so judgy?"

"Judgy? It's just an opinion, Sarah. Can't I tell you what I think without you getting all defensive? I'm trying to help."

With what? she wondered. "Marc's not dumb." Why did she say that? Because he spoke another language? Uncle Carl would completely agree with Harrison that this was a bad idea, which was funny. "My work is important. It's not some stupid hobby. If it's upsetting, I'll stop talking about it."

Harrison's so-called help felt like condescension. Sure, she was a little behind with classwork, but she was handling it.

She put her arm around his shoulder. Harrison glanced at her hand. It was a stupid move. He knew her well enough to know that if she was touching him, it was meant as distraction, not affection.

"A little fact-finding mission. I'll be fine. And I'll get the paper done. We can go to the library this weekend. I'll skip my uncle's on Sunday and have dinner with you two. Ara invited me again. It'll be like a White supremacy cleanse." Sarah smiled.

"Fine. But when you come over, the food's never spicy enough."

It was meant to make her feel a little bad. She deserved that.

She was doing him no favour by offering a trip to the library that she needed but he didn't. Something felt forced. No one knew her like Harrison did. She didn't want to alienate him, but she couldn't stay that close either. There was no right choice.

They went to a dim, wood-panelled pub in the north end of the city called The Pen, where Marc said *our people* like to hang out. Mostly country and western with the odd heavy metal tune. The smells were layered; cigarette smoke, beer, and a faint odour of the disinfectant bars that go in urinals. She glanced around. *Our people* looked a bit rough.

Marc leaned across the table to light her third cigarette. "You're making me nervous. Slow down man."

Sarah laughed, dribbling beer. She was drinking too fast. She kept pulling the crepe soles of her desert boots off the floor one at a time, mesmerized and grossed out by how they stuck.

"It's our time you know. I can feel it," Marc said.

Then he started in on his entire shit-disturbing history. Was he interviewing for something? He went on about the seventy-eight-day stand-off between the Mohawk Indians and the town of Oka, Quebec that turned violent in the summer of 1990.

"Who did they think they were road blocking? People need golf courses." He laughed. "You only get a say if you pay taxes, and we all know they don't. Everything they got, we gave them. Hands in *our* honey pot."

Sarah felt quite certain Marc paid no taxes. "They'd say everything we've got they gave us, or we took," she said.

Marc looked suspicious then confused. It was probably stupid, but she got a little kick out of making him question her, then pulling it back. "That is their argument, right?" She raised her glass. "To the victors."

He took an enthusiastic gulp. "Sacred burial grounds and all that shit, whining about those residence schools or whatever. Who didn't get a fucking wrap on the knuckles when we were growing up? You should hear my mom go on about the nuns. At least we got those little Mohawks in their motorcade. I know some kid got hurt. I'd never hurt a kid. But they grow into big red, don't they? You know what's wrong with us? No pride."

She took a sip and nodded. *So much to be proud of,* she wanted to say but changed the subject instead. "What's your problem with my uncle?"

"He's a pussy. No offence. But where was he at Oka, man? Old Carl protects his ass in his split-level, with his know-nothing wife, and his fancy reno business, taking cash from rich Jews and having a bunch of pakis on his crew put up drywall. He shows up at Aryan Fest like he's all tight with Nerland and them. I'm sure you think he's great. But you gotta take risks, put yourself out there. The guy's an envelope licker. Envelopes of money." Marc was one to talk with his constant begging for handouts. At least according to her uncle.

The more he drank, the looser Marc got. He tapped his feet and nodded along with the music. She'd insisted on pitchers over pints, and he didn't seem to notice she'd slowed way down.

"Hey, let's dance. It's *Boot Scootin' Boogie.* I love this song."

She glanced over at the dancers doing complicated steps in unison. "I don't dance."

"I could teach you."

"Really, I *don't* dance."

"You will." He reached under the table and squeezed her knee long enough for her body to overreact. What the fuck?

Marc told her about the time they were going to swastika Jewish graves. How his cellmate Declan, not like prison cell, like revolutionary cell, had smoked a doobie that might have been laced with something, then tripped outside the *Share Hash* Jew cemetery. The can of red paint hit the pavement and burst open. They didn't swastika as many tombstones as planned. Enough to make the news, but not enough. In Marc's circle, it seemed swastika was also a verb.

He told her he was bummed that he'd had too many run-ins with the cops and now he couldn't get into the US where the real action was happening. Best time he ever had was with a guy named Tim he'd met at an Aryan Republican Army meeting. A bunch of them snorted crystal meth and stayed up all night fantasizing global domination scenarios, casting themselves as White-Power vigilantes. He raised an imaginary gun and pointed it.

Sarah wasn't sure when she decided sex would be her next move. It hadn't been the plan, but it wasn't not the plan either. Maybe she shouldn't be feeling anything, but she was. When he'd put his hand on her leg under the table, not in a creepy way, but for sure in an intimate way, the unexpected current startled her. She was hoping he'd do it again. As she listened to his stories and made mental notes, she considered her virginity—not sacred, simply hanging around because no compelling occasion to dispose of it had presented itself. Exchanging it for access to Marc and his gang seemed a fair trade. He slid his hand up her leg again. If fucking him dealt with horniness at the same time, that was convenient.

When Harrison's words of warning crashed their date, she parked them with her overdue assignments. For the moment, Marc was her job.

Once they started, with unexpected force, it was hard to stop. They barely made it in the door of her apartment. Who grabbed who first was debatable. She bit his lip as soon as he kissed her. He shoved up her sweater and put his mouth on her nipple. She pushed his head into her hard. He got a message she didn't realize she was sending, and bit down. She groaned.

The weight of his body, his prick against her pelvic bone, hurt. Getting her pants off was the only thing that mattered, and it seemed insurmountable.

"Condom, condom," she groaned.

He pulled one out of his pocket. Did he carry a ready supply or were there expectations of how the night might end?

After three panicked tries, both laughing because he was so much taller, she wrapped one of her legs around his hip.

"You're a fucking wet mess." He finally pushed up into her, filling all the space there was, hitting the back of her. What hurt and what felt intensely good fused.

He threw his head back and made some sound between a grunt and a whimper that reverberated in her cunt. He came in seconds. "Sorry, sorry. Fuck. That was crazy. You'll get your turn. Promise."

"When?"

"Did you just ask when?" He laughed. "Fuck, you're different."

They lay blowing smoke rings upwards, not looking at each other. The pain, a kind of pleasant throb, was overshadowed by a desire to do it again.

"What the hell was that? It was crazy, Sarah. You learn that somewhere?" He was still breathing hard.

"Learn it? Like in a book?"

Sarah would never admit it, but next to White supremacy, she'd read most extensively about misfits and outsiders. Sexual proclivities came up a lot. Anything you could imagine, someone was doing it. More than just someone, loads of someones. Sex with animals and vegetables. Pain. Bondage. People even fell in love with inanimate objects. Plain old homosexuality was downright run of the mill. It was a wonder it even got categorized as *deviant*. Sarah suspected there was no normal, only an idea of it that got used to control and force people into line.

She decided not to tell Marc it was a first for that type of sex, or any sex, or that she *might* have read something. Not that she'd gone looking for the information specifically. He'd handed her a power card. She could tell he regretted saying anything.

"I usually like bigger tits. In fact, any tits at all." Marc was trying to take back control.

Sarah patted her chest and smiled. What little she had

did almost disappear when she lay down. "I've had very few complaints."

"You're not my type, Cartell." He got up and strode around the apartment and tried the door to the middle room. "What's in there? Some kind of dungeon?"

"Junk. Go in if you want. Door sticks." She thought about what was in there and whether any of it was incriminating. Marc dropped back on the futon.

His dick was hard again. Sarah smiled. "Not your type?"

"What do you want? I'm a fucking guy." He seemed irritated.

Sarah pushed herself into a kneeling position and threw her leg over him. "Well then do your fucking guy thing."

He grabbed her ass, all sign of irritation gone. "Your turn."

Marc was full of surprises. Before tonight, she wouldn't have taken him for a talker, or a dancer, or a fluent German speaker.

"It's Marc with a 'c.' My mom's a frog, insisted on the French spelling. That's the last thing she got her way on. She's Catholic, nine brothers and sisters. One's a nun. One's a priest. So, neither of them is contributing to the family pool, at least not the nun. Still, I have about fifty cousins. Bertrand's the only one who's part of my gang. My aunt would kill him if she knew. Dad baptised my mom in a river in Ways Mills in the Eastern Townships. Tried to wash away the Vatican and the Hail Mary's. He wanted to be her only confessor. But she still crosses herself when he's not looking and sneaks off to mass. She took me with her a bunch of times to visit her sisters, and my Mémé. There were so many grandkids I'm not sure she even knew who I was, but she was always pinching my cheek.

She made a huge stew from vegetables in her garden. It was nice. I haven't been in years. My grandfather won't talk to my mom. I once told my dad we'd gone to mass. I was a kid. Just blabbing. He hit her. She never took me again. After that, I didn't tell him anything she said or did. Now it doesn't matter, she can cross herself all she wants, he's never around except to change the clothes she washes."

"So she's not onside?"

"Not exactly. She knows what he's about. Doesn't get in the way. Mostly he's just a big talker. I guess that's the job of a preacher, bring the flock along."

Sarah thought about what her uncle had told her about Marc's charismatic dad spreading legs and seed in the congregation. She felt pretty sure that her grandfather had not *lain* with a single member of his flock. Marc was still talking.

"When she was young, it was some kind of rebellion. She says my dad was a combination of Jerry Falwell and Jimmy Dean. She was a bad girl. He supposedly saved her from too much partying and screwing random men. She got a house and me to take care of. Now she's mostly alone."

"She knows about you?"

"I don't talk about it much. I feel bad for her." He looked genuinely sad. "Your dad's cool, right?"

"He's a bit of an asshole too actually." She wanted Marc to feel they had that in common.

"What about your mom?"

"She's dead. Died when I was two."

Marc looked sorry for her, then nodded like it explained a lot.

"My dad was tough on us when we were kids, but we're all onside. It's in my blood." *In my blood* was the perfect phrase. People could interpret it the way they wanted.

"Sorry, Sarah." It wasn't clear what he was sorry for. Her mom? Her dad? "I do so much for the cause. You'd think my father would pay some attention to his only kid."

Sarah thought about the Scott progeny scattered throughout the congregation. It was curious what made Marc feel vulnerable. Saying he liked the rough sex was a problem, but admitting how badly he wanted his father's approval wasn't.

"Time to go." She got up from the bed and handed Marc his jeans.

"Seriously?"

"We're not at the sleepover stage yet." Or any stage. If she had her way, they'd never get there. "I'm tired and I'm not your type anyway."

Surprised, maybe disappointed, he grabbed at her, but she pushed him away. He got dressed too slowly then left.

In her dream that night, she and Maddie watched a cross burning at The Pen. Her feet were stuck to the floor.

24

NOVEMBER 1993

Montreal

HAVING SENT NO REGRETS, SARAH HAD BY default decided to meet her aunt for lunch. She learned what she could about her. Mostly jargon-filled, high art noise. An article in *FUSE: Art, Culture, and Politics* Spring 1991 had her aunt's photo on the cover. Katie's gaze off to the left of the camera seemed calculated to meet no mark. The artist who wouldn't be known.

Katie had been in Berlin for six months at that time and was having a show at the Berlinische Galerie on Alte Jacobstrasse. Sarah said the words out loud—butchering them intentionally.

Who cared if it was some post-post alternative progressive hotbed. It was still Berlin. Germany. How could she live there?

The review focused on Cartell's feminist, *anti-colonial esthetic, layered works that probe the depths of women's marginality, experience, presence and absence, playing with and complicating notions of appropriation, rupture, resistance, complicity.* The art show opened with a panel including Helene Cixous, Paris VIII, mother of post-structuralist feminist theory. *The artist and the writer/theoretician examine the interplay between sexuality and the sexualized, gendered imaging of language.*

Despite all the supposed play, it sounded like a dead bore that made Sarah laugh and gave her a headache at the same time. There was a reason she liked library sciences. Who goes looking for rupture and absence?

The piece on the cover, blocked in good part by her aunt's angular face, was reproduced in the body of the article. Sarah looked at it closely. A faint photograph of a pointed white hood reproduced hundreds of times made up the background. Sarah was sure she remembered one just like it in the box of lynching photos in the attic. Had Katie known they were there, gone through them and selected what she wanted?

Piles of swastikas made to look like candlestick holders lay next to 1930s style kitchen tables, blonde Aryan housewives polishing them. Along the border, forming a reddish orange horizon line, were burning crosses. If Sarah had any doubt about her aunt's grasp of family history, this removed it. Beside each table was a tiny picture she vaguely remembered being taken while she was playing in the sand box, wearing a striped navy and white jersey. Keith took it, and her dad got angry at him for wasting film. She was four. Keith was six. How would Katie have gotten her hands on that? She was long gone by the time it was taken.

She shoved the magazine into her backpack.

A quick glance in the mirror at her very blonde hair, blue eyes, and pointy chin. Katie was beautiful, Sarah just plain

Aryan. She was nervous about lunch and changed twice before settling on the brown sweater and dark orange corduroys that hung loosely. Why did she care what her aunt thought? Shouldn't it be the other way around? Melrose came running at the sound of the tin being opened. Sarah patted him. While he was eating was the only time he let her do it. She pulled on her desert boots.

"I'll be back in a few hours, Mel." She had made a habit of telling the cat where she was going and how long she'd be. Someone needed to know.

She arrived at the restaurant in Old Montreal early and sweaty. One look at the oversized glass door and she knew she was dressed wrong, not that dressing right was possible. She made a mental note to ask Ara to take her shopping at Value Village. In French, it was called Village des Valeurs, Village of Values. That's where she wanted to shop. The ridiculously high ceiling in the restaurant suited its name—Air. She was led to their table and handed a huge menu that was long on unfamiliar details—all supposedly edible. Lots of foams and mousses. *Just add air* seemed to be the theme. Rereading it didn't help.

Words from intimate conversations bounced unabsorbed off the stark walls and concrete floor. Sarah felt ridiculous in the huge chair. She remembered a trip to a provincial park that had massive Muskoka chairs. Her dad had pushed the three of them up, then climbed up himself. Even *his* feet barely cleared the seat, and he started yelling, *My name is Edith Ann and I'm five years old.* Supposedly an imitation of someone named Lily Tomlin from a 1960s TV show.

"Sorry I'm late."

Sarah looked up. Wild colourful fabric hit her first, then movement. Katie seemed to glide. She was bigger than Sarah expected.

"Let me hug you."

Katie leaned in toward Sarah. Why would she even want to? Sarah wondered. They were strangers. Katie must have sensed her reticence and stopped. Her bent body jerking upwards reminded Sarah of the doll on a music box scene in *Chitty Chitty Bang Bang*.

"Fair enough," her aunt said. "I'll wait and earn it."

Got a few years? Sarah wanted to say. "I thought I was having lunch with your assistant."

Katie smiled apologetically. "Sorry it was so impersonal. That's the only way things get done with no screw-ups. I'm pretty disorganized."

"I thought feminists liked the personal touch."

"That's a generalization. How about you? You don't seem the personal touch type at all."

Sarah smiled. "Or even the feminist type."

"Hmm." Katie tossed a woven bag on an empty chair and sat down in what didn't seem the least bit big for her. She shook out her napkin and placed it on her lap. "So here we are."

Sarah glanced at her own still folded neatly and wondered if following suit would seem childish.

Her aunt picked up the menu. "Let's order before we talk. Did you have a chance to look?"

Sarah's leg was shaking. She wanted to leave. Any urge

to know Katie's version of family history had evaporated into air. "Sort of. What do they do to the chicken? What's a chiffonade?"

Katie laughed. "You want a plain sandwich? I'll get them to make you one."

No use picking something she didn't like and wouldn't eat just to prove a point. Sarah nodded, feeling like a bumpkin. The book *Country Mouse, City Mouse* had always been a crowd pleaser at story circle. She'd wrongly assumed she was the city mouse, not the country bumpkin. So far, Air was proving to be a trip down some memory lane of books, movies, and TV shows, none of which included her aunt.

"Are we ready to order?" The waiter put a basket of bread and a plate of olive oil with a heart-shaped vinegar design on the table. It evoked Sarah's failed attempts to decorate coffee. The things people wasted time on.

His solicitous smile and raised eyebrows confirmed she was out of place. Her aunt's efforts to translate his words only made it worse.

"A few more minutes. But we'll have a carafe of white. House. All right with you?"

Sarah nodded, whatever *whitehouse* was.

"Does your daughter have some ID?"

Neither of them responded. He gave it a few seconds then left.

"Sorry about that." Her aunt buried her head once more in the menu.

Sarah pulled the *FUSE* magazine out of her backpack. "Looks like we work from the same material."

Katie looked up. "That's one of my themes."

Theme seemed an odd word, like hate could be reduced from its hideousness to a simple choice of topic. Was hate the *theme* of Sarah's life?

"Did you get the Cartell Sunday school lectures or read Grandpa's books? That piece from your show, the one that didn't sell with the KKK guy in the white hood, was that from Grandpa's attic from the shoe box of lynching pictures? Your bio says your materials are sourced from family archives."

Katie picked up a piece of bread then put it down. "I did see those photos. I will never unsee them. And yes, I guess I stole that picture of the KKK guy, some cousin maybe. There was a name on the back. The others, I would never use any of them in my art. Life with your grandfather was one big fucking lecture. I wish I could say it was his worldview that sickened me most, but back then, it was more about being controlled. Maybe if he was nicer, I'd still be there believing those things."

The waiter arrived and put two huge glasses—everything was so big—on the table, then poured some *whitehouse* into each. He turned to Katie and leaned forward, a look of anticipation on his face. Once she sniffed, took a sip, and nodded (like, yes, this is wine), he straightened up.

Her aunt ordered *canard* salad, duck she explained to Sarah, then shut the menu.

"Dad hunts. So I've had duck. But never any canard." Sarah emphasized the d, then asked for a plain chicken sandwich.

The waiter flashed a patronizing smile, turned with a twist that made a squeak on the floor, and flounced off.

They both laughed. Katie cleared her throat. "No idea why waiters act like that. Maybe they hate waiting. I sure did." She dragged a piece of bread through the oil. "Sorry about this place. It's a bit pretentious. My assistant doesn't know Montreal."

"A bit."

A strand of Katie's hair fell into the plate. She laughed and wiped it with her napkin. Was she trying to make Sarah feel less out of place? "It gets easier once you've been gone a long time. It took me years to figure out I even wanted to do something about it, about what I knew."

"You mean make art?" How that was *doing something about it* was unclear to Sarah. "That's me, isn't it?" She pointed at the tiny figure in the sandbox.

"Must be. I got it from Jean. It doesn't show your face. It was meant to be an image of innocence, the blissful ignorance of a child stuck unknowingly in a bad place."

"Seriously? Innocence and blissful ignorance. Not my life."

"I know. I just needed an image like that and since it came from the family archive."

So that was how making art worked.

"Why didn't you ever try to contact me?"

Katie took another piece of bread, chewed slowly then finally swallowed. "I always asked Jean about how you kids were doing."

"That's not an answer. Were you in touch the whole time? Aunt Jean implied that you weren't. After that, I probably never asked. So I guess she lied."

"We're not very close, but we keep in touch. Phone calls every few months, the odd letter." Katie sighed. "She made a choice to stay. For what? I don't get it. He never appreciated what she does. Not that she complains."

"She's got a life, you know." Sarah couldn't describe anything particularly good about that life, but who was Katie to judge? Not everyone lived *between New York City and Berlin*. And the man *was* their father. Alone in the world.

"We're different. That's all I'm saying."

She looked grateful when the waiter put the food in front of them. "Let's eat."

Sarah bit into the sandwich. Something that tasted like garlicky mayonnaise dripped onto the napkin in her lap. Good thing she'd followed her aunt's example.

Katie picked at a piece of spiky looking lettuce then offered Sarah a bite of canard.

She shook her head no. "What about your mother? How could you even go there? Didn't you hate her?"

"She's nice actually. She might even be a great person. She just stopped being a mother. At least to us. When I lived with them those few months after I left Goderich, we fought the whole time. I liked Diallo and the kids Yannick and Evelyne, but Charlene made me nuts. No way I was following any rules, and she had a bunch of them. Nothing unreasonable. But all I could think was, what gave her the right to impose any on me? Of course, she had every right. It was her home. I couldn't see it that way at the time. I never hated her. I was angry, maybe I still am, but I always understood that she did what she had to do. Jean understands that too. Those two clash even more than me and Charlene. But quietly and almost never. You have to see someone to really clash with them."

The idea of contact between Katie, Jean, and Charlene all these years, no matter how rare or brief, made Sarah feel more alone in her family than she already was. At least there was some fucked up comfort in the fact that she was not the only liar.

"My plan for contacting you was to wait until you were in high school. But by then, I guess I wasn't sure you'd want me to."

"Maybe you just couldn't be bothered. Same way you couldn't be bothered writing me a note."

Katie stared out the window. "Look, everything's changed. You reached out. You made it clear where you were at. I wasn't sure where you stood."

The colours her aunt was wearing suddenly made Sarah dizzy and nauseated. Throwing up in the middle of the restaurant was only appealing if their waiter had to clean it up. She shut her eyes to stop the spinning, but it didn't help. "You thought I believed what they believe? But you talked to Jean."

"I did."

The picture got clearer and that made it worse. Sarah laughed then covered her mouth. It was all crazy. Impossible but totally possible.

"Guess you fooled everyone." It wasn't meant to be nasty. If anything, Katie sounded impressed.

"I guess I did." She pushed the sandwich to the far side of the stupidly large plate and picked up a fry.

"I'm sorry."

Sarah waved her hand. More apologies. What was it with people and apologies? Like it helped. "I had a plan that got me here. I knew I'd find out more by helping Carl. And I have. He even took me to an Aryan Nations get-together in Alberta." The last piece of information was meant to upset her aunt.

Katie cringed. "Get-together. Is that what they call them? Why would you even go?"

"To understand what's happening, what's being planned. Not many people get to witness this kind of shit up close."

"I'm sure that's true. And did you uncover any big plans?"

"No." Sarah wasn't sure what prompted her to answer honestly. "Not yet. I met someone who might lead me there."

"Sounds pretty iffy. And scary. How much more do you need to know?"

"A lot. You can't just stop. What if you decide not to continue right before that thing happens that you could have prevented? And anyway, what's not iffy? You're lucky your work can be from memory or research. That's fine for art, I guess. But it wouldn't stop anything. That's what I'm hoping to do."

In the end, gatherings like Aryan Fest seemed less about planning and more about grown men playing silly games and burning crosses. "I fit right in," Sarah said. Close enough to the truth. "Don't tell anyone. Or use it in some art piece."

"I'd need a picture for that. Take any?"

Sarah laughed. If her aunt was offended, she didn't show it.

"And Aunt Jean, I didn't mean to deceive her. We hardly talked. Sometimes it felt like one of us was going to open up, but it didn't happen."

"She's never been a big talker. Don't worry about her.

Worry about yourself." Katie finished what was left in her wine glass. "You drinking that?"

Sarah shook her head and Katie switched the glasses.

"What if she slips up and gives me away?"

Katie laughed. "How many years do you think she's been keeping her contact with me and Charlene a secret? She's at least as good an actress as you."

That was true. Anyone who dismissed Sarah's acting talent based on her performance as the pineapple in the kindergarten Christmas pageant just hadn't seen her in the right role.

"Aunt Jean always looked out for me, even if she thought I was with them. She never seemed disappointed, although she did want me to go to University of Victoria in BC. I guess she wanted me far away."

"For your own safety and to give you a chance at something different. Blood's thick. Fucked up right?" Katie smiled at Sarah like this conclusion was universal and comforting.

"What about your blood? You barely have a relationship with anyone. Doesn't family need to give a shit?"

"Look Sarah, nobody won here."

"Really? Look at you, then look at my dad and Jean. Don't you think you kind of won?"

Katie didn't answer.

Other people's words filled Air—*summer place in Hudson, great investment opportunity, it's one of a kind, handmade in Italy.* Then there was *pulmonary embolism* and *his own daughter, can you imagine doing that?* Sarah wasn't listening, but she couldn't help hearing. She took another fry.

"We make choices, Sarah. I chose art and life."

"Jesus, Katie. And the rest of us chose death?"

"No, but *you* picked a dangerous, more hidden version of the life you had growing up. Instead of breathing fresh air."

Where might one find that air, Sarah wondered. Everyone had an opinion about the somewhere else that she should be going or the something else she should be doing.

"What was my father like as a kid?"

"When we were little, he was loveable," Katie said. "We were a gang, along with Charlene. Secrets, and games to keep the secrets we hid from Thomas. She tried to make it fun, but eventually when Thomas got hold of Frank and Carl, it was no more sissy bullshit. Only sports and building cabins. We still goofed around when he was at work or out hunting with the one friend he had, some old guy named Robert Mintleig, who willed him an old church on a farm."

Katie took another sip of wine then leaned back in the chair, expansive. Sarah looked at her aunt and thought of the pictures Aunt Jean had shown her of all of them as kids. How even standing still, in black and white, their personalities had been so clear. Katie smiled as though she were going to say something like, *a penny for your thoughts*. Thankfully she just went on.

"I only remember the name Mintleig because Thomas went on and on about him. *Such a great man. Such an inspiration*. For a few months after he died, Thomas led services at that place, but then people refused to drive that far. It was around then that everything changed with Frank. He was ten, maybe eleven, and it was like all the joy got sucked out of him. It was like he became a bully and a coward at the same time, always grovelling to please Thomas. I figured he just couldn't take the teasing anymore. He was the favourite target, always mocked for being too weak or too passive. He was better than Carl at most things, but that didn't seem to matter. Charlene was always trying to cheer him up. Occasionally she could break through the sullen shit, but not often. I remember missing him, missing the kid he used to be. We barely spent time together. We grew up and went through puberty and did our own things. Then Charlene left and we were all miserable."

Sarah thought about her dad as a happy little kid, then of the suddenly sullen boy he became, about Charlene's battle to make their lives lovely despite her grandfather. It made Sarah realize how much effort her father put into making things fun for them. It didn't come naturally to him. Why would it? Katie may not have escaped that childhood, but she and Carl, maybe even Jean, had escaped something, and it wasn't clear what.

"The day Bunny came by the house," Katie said. "I was in the kitchen with Thomas and Frank. Jean answered the door. When Frank heard the woman asking about her son, he started pacing around, all frantic. Maybe it brought back the upset of Charlene leaving and his betrayal. The look on his face was terror. It was odd for me because I hadn't talked to him since he'd told Thomas about the escape plan."

"Aunt Jean told me that too. She said my dad didn't know the boy."

"I don't think it was about the missing kid, because later in the day, after he was back from wherever he went with Dad, he was better. Not like his old kid self or anything, but fine."

Katie took a sip of wine. "But Dad, it was like he was even angrier than when Mom left, if that was possible. He slammed around the house. We stayed out of his way. All of us except your father, who kept asking if he could do anything to help and spent the week fixing things in the cabins that Dad hadn't even asked him to do. That's when I decided I couldn't stay. It would take over a year to plan and find an opportunity, but it was right then that I made up my mind."

Sarah watched her aunt dab her napkin against her lips, rather than drag it across her face the way she and her dad did. "He bought me a computer. He thinks I'm smart. He stayed."

"You *are* smart. Everyone knows that. And I get that you're angry I left." Katie pulled at her hair with her thumb and forefinger. "We all made choices. I never stopped running. Your father never started."

"You left when you were so young. That takes balls."

"Staying took a different kind of balls." Katie looked tired.

The restaurant was almost cleared out. The waiter finally gave up hope they would order something off the dessert menu.

"Do you think your art changes anything, like people's minds?"

"Hmm." Katie kind of grunted. "That's a depressing question. I'm primarily preaching to the choir. People show up to my shows because they're feminists or lesbians or both. No convincing required. Others try to get it. Some like the colours. It matches a couch. Once I got a letter from someone who wanted to return a piece. She hadn't looked closely enough before buying it. A Jewish man she'd started dating, the son of a Holocaust survivor, was over and noticed the swastikas and was appalled. I gave her the money back. Maybe take a closer look next time you drop a few thousand on art. I like to think my work adds something to the dialogue about misogyny and hate. But does it change beliefs? I doubt it."

"You glue together torn pieces of paper and photos, then paint it, and it sells for $7,000. Pretty sweet gig."

"I once got $16,000. There's a lot of gluing involved you know." Katie smiled and ran her fingers through her hair again. "Some of us are driven to do things. We can't not do them. For me, that's making art. It's a compulsion. Even when Thomas destroyed what I made and called me an aberration, I kept going. Can't stop."

"Neither can I." Sarah talked softly, not wanting her own words to land on anyone else's table.

"Until it's done."

"And it's never done, right?" Sarah said. The idea of the endlessness of it was exhausting.

"I guess we're alike in that way. But you're young. Lots can happen. Lots will. It took me a long time to figure out how to be mostly happy. I might have some tips for getting there faster."

Tips. Sarah almost smiled. Did she want to be more like Katie? Unclear. Somehow it felt like her aunt and her grandmother had cheated and gotten away with something they didn't deserve. Maybe that was stupid. Did Carl deserve his life? Wasn't getting out from under Grandpa Thomas and finding happiness a good thing? Did there always have to be someone to blame? What if certain things just weren't anyone's fault?

"I have your paintings. The ones you nailed to the wall before you left. I kind of like them."

"I thought those were long gone," Katie said, surprised.

"They're on the wall in my apartment. Didn't Aunt Jean ever tell you she rescued them from the garbage? I found them in the attic. If I get desperate, I could sell them."

"Doubt you'd get much."

"That gallery woman Micheline, she's a bit of a pompous ass, said your private life is a big secret. But she did out you, and she asked if I was your daughter. Wanted me to spill the beans on some big secret you've kept from the world."

"I'm sorry," Katie said. "That sounds unpleasant. Micheline had a crush on my girlfriend for years, a long time ago. What I'd really like to know is what you thought of my work?"

"You don't want to know. Lucky I had someone to explain it to me. I was clueless. But from a distance, it was attractive."

"Well thank you." She rubbed a finger along her eyebrow. "So Micheline told you I'm a lesbian."

Sarah nodded.

"And that my girlfriend's from Berlin. That's partly why I spend so much time there. I leave again on Friday for a few months."

"Germany." Sarah made a face.

"It's a great place actually. People there *do* take responsibility for what happened. Maybe you'll visit. You'd love it. It's very progressive. They seem to have less need to label or categorize everything."

Just her kind of place. No labels, no categories. No clarity.

There didn't seem to be anything else to say. "I have to go.

Lots of work to do." Sarah stood up and pulled on her pea coat.

"Your coat." Katie pointed at it. "It was mine."

Sarah had been wearing it for years, long before it fit her properly. "I assumed it was Aunt Jean's."

"Suits you." Katie paused, like she wondered if this ending to their get-together might be too abrupt. "I'm staying at this great little hotel. Super plush bathrobes you never want to take off and a great soaker tub. Want to have breakfast tomorrow? You can take a bath if you want."

"Thanks for the weird offer but I've got a lot to do." She stood up.

Her aunt looked a bit relieved. Shadows stretched across the room. Katie left the waiter a big tip that Sarah was tempted to grab back, but she didn't.

25

MARCH 1995

Sunnyside Mental Health Centre

"MANY PIECES ARE FALLING INTO PLACE. All these things you wanted to know for so long, you got to ask Katie. And she didn't have to peel a thousand potatoes for you to find out."

Bit of a dig. Or maybe Mona, a natural chatterbox and way more like Katie than she was like Jean, just couldn't relate to silence.

"Maybe Jean wasn't stingy with information after all. Maybe she was trying to protect me from a story than wouldn't help. Or at least she didn't think it would."

"Your dad and his siblings carry a lot of pain. Seems like your grandfather's only job was to dole it out."

"But it's not equally divided. Katie has this big happy jet setter life. She isn't dragging all the baggage around with her. May not have unloaded it completely, but she left most of it locked up in an attic with her sister and her niece as the custodians, and only looked at it again when she needed material.

She claims she's still working out our 'family stuff' in her art. But she calls it 'themes.' She didn't leave because she hated what Grandpa Thomas believed, she just wanted out. Even if the picture of the KKK guy that she used in that piece from her show was from up there, and she claims she'll never forget, I can't tell if she's just trying to build common ground with me."

"Everyone handles trauma differently. She may have taken what she needed and buried the rest so she could go on. I'm sure her life isn't as easy as it seems. I'm guessing your lunch together was hard for her too."

"She actually told me she wasn't in touch because she thought I was a White nationalist. Do you think that's true or just an excuse?"

"I wouldn't know Sarah."

"She said I had Aunt Jean fooled too, but unlike Katie, she never stepped away. Even if she thought I was a full-on Nazi, Aunt Jean was still there. But it's weird, because when my dad got Curtis's father fired, I thought she really knew what I was going through."

Sarah remembered how embarrassing it was when her aunt brought home a bunch of pamphlets about sex and feminine hygiene. Better late than never. Sarah had already had her period for over a year.

"She for sure didn't look at them that closely. One was about the right way to wipe. That was a conversation we should have had a few years earlier. Then we had the opposite of a staring contest. An eye avoiding contest. She mumbled something about a penis. And I said I knew that already, then she said something about prophylactics. That's what she called them. It was over pretty quick. But why would she have picked that time if she didn't suspect I might be doing something?"

"Jean was always there for you, but try not to resent Katie. She didn't abandon you. She was long gone. She saved herself. That might have been a selfish choice, but she was sixteen. She never knew you."

Even Carl said he wasn't angry at Katie anymore, so why should she be? "All that talking at the restaurant, and I still have no idea why my dad and Aunt Jean stayed. My grandfather wasn't an invalid. He wasn't even old. He was just awful. It's no wonder no one else married him."

"Did you like Katie?"

"She's really big and bright and confident. She strutted across that restaurant and went in for a hug, which I refused. But she seems to think we're a lot alike. I don't see it."

"Maybe you're like her in less obvious ways. You're both seekers. You're both out in the world, looking for answers, creating things."

"I'm not creative."

"I thought Luce compared your mural to a Jackson Pollock."

Sarah laughed. "Oh right, I forgot. I take it back."

"There are different ways to be creative. It's not just about making art. It's about finding solutions and answers. It might be worth thinking about the ways you want to be more like her. Sounds like you liked her."

"I guess I kind of did."

"Well, that's our hour. I hope your visit with Charlene goes well. Remember, you're not obligated to do or say anything. You can stay as little or as long as you want."

"I don't know if I'm ready for this."

"Letting something happen, something that you've chosen, can make you ready for it, and then ready for other things. I'm proud of you, Sarah."

She was freezing as she waited for Charlene to arrive. The dress she'd borrowed from Becky, loose and impractical for anything other than quick peeing, left her exposed and goosebumpy. The jacket did little to help. It was meant as a disguise. Sarah never wore dresses, but for some reason, she wanted Charlene to think she did. Keeping parts hidden, even the ones that didn't matter, was a habit. She glanced at the door to the yard every time it opened.

A woman strode towards her, a beige overcoat flapping—strong, purposeful, dressed for the weather. Until then, Sarah's height had felt tall enough. Charlene closed the distance between them in seconds. Not long enough for Sarah to gain her composure but long enough for the woman to read shivering as fear. No time to flee.

"You look like Katie," Charlene said, grabbing Sarah into a hug for the full two seconds it took to get over her shock and push away.

"Are you fucking kidding me? You don't get to do that."

"I'm sorry. You're right. That was rude. You really do look like her. It's disconcerting. We can go in. Must be cold in that flimsy dress."

Definitely a ridiculous choice. "I'm fine. I need a cigarette."

If that bothered her, and it was meant to, she didn't show it. Sarah called over the guard who was the keeper of the matches.

Her grandmother's thick grey ponytail hung just past the base of her neck and was held in place by a fat purple rubber band that might have come off a broccoli. She wore a man's orange cotton shirt over light wool pants. The laces on her dark oxfords didn't match—one brown, one white. Was that a metaphor?

Charlene looked down and laughed. "The other one broke this morning. Walk or sit?"

They circled the yard twice without saying a word, Charlene's composure broken only by large hands that moved in and out of her pockets.

"Someone needs to start."

Sarah lit a second cigarette off the first. "Or not." She took a long drag. "I didn't ask for this meeting. I don't even know why you're here."

"I thought maybe I could help," Charlene said.

"So I keep hearing. Well, here's a newsflash, you're about nineteen years too late. I could have used help a long fucking time ago. My dad too. You don't get to just show up and make yourself feel less guilty."

"Can we sit?"

Sarah pointed at a bench. Charlene sat and folded her hands in her lap. Even from the opposite end, she could feel the heat rising off her grandmother like a furnace.

"Why are you really here? You think coming to visit or begging to see me equals being in my life? It fucking doesn't."

"I'd expected your vocabulary to be colourful, but perhaps a little more varied."

"Fuck you." Sarah absolutely did not mean to smile.

Charlene smiled back, wedging her oxford into the crack Sarah hadn't meant to open.

"It's a start. I have explanations for what I've done and haven't done since I left Goderich, Sarah."

The sound of her name coming out of this woman's mouth stung. "You know what you can do with those."

She ignored the comment. "They're not justifications, simply an accounting of sorts. I know you're not interested in my regrets, nor should you be, but I'll say this; no matter how desperately necessary it all seemed at the time, what I did was wrong."

"But you've been happy. You don't get to start feeling bad now."

"I have been happy. But I've also been dreadfully sad and consumed with regret and guilt. You can be all those things at the same time. I don't expect you to ask, not now, or next week, or ever. But my story is yours, if you want it."

This was not how the conversation was meant to go. In the versions Sarah had constructed since deciding to let her grandmother visit, there was messy contrition, crying, snot, fishing for handkerchiefs in some old leather purse, and begging forgiveness. She'd briefly contemplated Charlene on her knees, but discarded the image as awkward, not clear how she'd get into the position or out of it.

The woman anticipated how Sarah would react, put up no resistance, and said all the right things. Mona couldn't have choreographed it any better. It made Sarah want to scream. She pushed her fists into her thighs, making an imprint to study later. Like the rocks on the kneeling beach. The pain was grounding.

Sarah finally spoke when she felt Charlene stir, fearing the woman might leave having had the last word.

"I'd never do it to a kid of mine, what you did to them. I had an abortion to avoid being the shitty mother you were."

Sarah couldn't see the expression that accompanied the sharp intake of breath. If it was pain, it didn't make her feel as good as she thought it would. The hate she was trying to reignite was dead. It was like she was reciting lines in a performance. Her grandfather's tight controlled way of humiliating his children flashed by. Escape was the only way out and it did its own damage.

They sat in silence as it grew colder.

26

NOVEMBER 1993

Montreal

"ALL THOSE STUPID WHITE SUPREMACISTS you're tagging along with. They're fucked up Sarah. You've got better things to do."

Now Luce was on about it too. She hadn't reacted that way to Sarah's uncle, or Maddie, or TCH. And it had nothing to do with the fact that she was having sex regularly with Marc, since she hadn't told anyone about that.

"It's not like what *you* do is so safe."

A week earlier, Luce was hit in the face by a dead cardboard fetus mounted on a piece of plywood. Four stitches above her left eye. Some woman in a brown tweed coat claimed the crucifix she was clutching made her lose her grip. On reality? Decency?

"It's not the same thing."

"What happened to your t-shirt?" Sarah wasn't interested in Luce's opinion, or Harrison's, or even Ara's. It wasn't up for debate.

"Washed it with a red sock. You're changing the subject."

"You think what you do is important. I feel the same about what I do. I've been at it since I was a kid."

"I'm sorry for you about that."

Sarah cringed. "I can handle myself."

"So can I, but that doesn't mean you have to. Marc Scott and his friends. It won't lead someplace good."

"That's kind of the point."

"Why do you want to be anywhere near these people?"

"Because I can. Because they trust me. Jesus. I didn't expect duck and cover advice from you. I thought if anyone would get it." Sarah grabbed the damp rag from the sink and started wiping the espresso machine. "Do I really have to justify myself? You're the one who wears the little anti-Nazi pin."

"Marc and his friends are jerks, and bad shit can happen."

"Turns out Professor Pichon is interested in this information I'm supposedly risking my life to get. She might write a book."

"Why her? You could write it yourself. Don't give it away. Why are you even at McGill? According to Harrison, if you keep going this way, you'll flunk out."

At least what Sarah knew about professional haters was important to someone. As for writing it herself, she couldn't even finish an essay on the Spanish Civil War.

"Groups like the Heritage Front and Aryan Nation get money from respected people who are happy to write cheques but not get their hands dirty. I'm trying to figure it all out. I do the digging. Make myself useful. The closer I get, the more I know. If something's being planned. I'll be able to stop it. Writing an essay about it won't help."

"If stopping these guys is your reason of being, you'd better be careful. Passion is not so good in the driver seat."

Sarah had never been accused of too much passion. But she did wonder about Luce's choice of words and whether she suspected something. Sure, sex with Marc was happening a little too often, but it was more a craving. Luce was right though, passion or whatever it was, was not so good in the driver seat.

"Do I have to worry for you all the time, Sarah?"

"I'll let you know when to start." She felt herself tear up and turned away. It was easier to be judged or criticized than cared about.

"*Ferme la porte, merde!*" Luce yelled. The temperature went down five degrees every time the door was opened.

Sarah looked up to see Ara and smiled.

"*Ça va chérie?*" Luce kissed him on both cheeks. "You are chilly."

Aravinda kissed Sarah and pulled out the stool beside her. "Just dropping these off." He pulled a stack of flyers out of his bag. "You gals can give them out at McGill."

"You're like a drug dealer with those things."

He lowered his voice to a whisper. "Hey, I got some nice abortion clinic protection for you. Next Friday."

They talked about the demo. Aravinda fiddled with his necklace, two silver male symbols on a piece of leather.

"How's my kitten doing?"

"Oh I'm just fine. Thanks for asking," Sarah said.

Ara laughed. He'd been by the week before with some cat toys and treats for both Sarah and Melrose. The cat needs to be indulged, he'd said. Otherwise, your couch will be shreds. They played with Melrose for hours, trying to wear him out, and Sarah had told him about Curtis. She hadn't talked about her first boyfriend, only boyfriend really, with anyone. Maybe the whole Marc thing made her think about him. She had to kick Ara out because she had a date. She would have rather stayed put.

"Melrose is liking his toys. But honestly, he's a total terror. When did you say he'll grow out of it?"

"Give him a couple of years."

"That is a serious commitment. Hey, do you think we can schedule our computer filing tutorial? Like deep."

"Anytime. I am your deep filing superhero. Mild-mannered boyfriend, chef, and architectural student by day. Wild activist, computer genius by night."

"I will call you on your bat phone."

"Perfect. Got to fly girls. Harrison's waiting for me at the gym." He flexed his arms.

Luce leaned over the counter and kissed him again. So much kissing in Quebec. He didn't seem to expect anything from Sarah. Once was enough.

It had been a month since her last TCH meeting. Sarah had left Maddie to file a bunch of things she'd sorted through.

"If there's anything that gets done around here, it's buying envelopes and licking envelopes, buying coffee and drinking coffee." Maddie put a box of envelopes on the table.

"Management of stationary, petty cash, and office supplies goes on my resumé for sure."

The kid was going to bail any day and probably follow her friend Bradley, who supposedly landed some gig running errands for Aryans. Sarah wouldn't blame her. The never-ending group-reviewed letters—offensive, but not offensive enough—were mind-numbing.

The only reason Sarah was still hanging around TCH was because of Carl. She was reaching the bottom of the hockey bag papers and still hadn't found much of value.

"Ernst Zundel's coming in January. You're helping with that, right? It's a big deal," Sarah said.

Battles about hate speech and free speech were fought between the Canadian Civil Liberties Association and the Canadian Jewish Congress, while Zundel kept spewing Holocaust denial in his iconic hard hat.

She wanted to keep Maddie there. Once the kid left TCH, she'd be lost.

Maddie had heard about Shaar Hashomayim, Oka, and Aryan Fest from Marc, who liked to go on about past conquests while sitting backwards on chairs. But she was tiring of old stories and looking to the future and how she could get in the game.

Never mind Maddie, Sarah was waiting to get in the game herself. Until a few days ago, Marc had seemed hesitant to introduce her to the cellmates, even though she'd convinced him, without pushing too much, that she could be helpful. She suspected his reticence had less to do with trust, and more to do with the way she looked and her missing knack for making *regular* people feel comfortable. Marc's gang, despite being neo-Nazi skinheads, qualified as regular. He hadn't mentioned her not fitting in and kept promising soon. Additional smarts could only be a good thing, he claimed. There was a meeting in two days, and they were giving it a try. He didn't directly suggest a push-up bra, but he had bought her a sexy underwear set as a gift.

Marc and Sarah stopped by the apartment he shared with two other guys to pick up the dirty laundry he kindly *let* his mom do once a week. He asked Sarah to wait in the car but she insisted on coming in. They had never hung out at his place, and she wanted to see it before she met the others there.

"It's a bit gross," he warned, pushing the door open into a surprisingly sunlit space that suffered from complete neglect.

It was immediately apparent why they never came here. In the kitchen sink, three oily circles marked water levels from historic dishwashing attempts. A pot with what looked like mac and cheese soup was soaking on the counter. At least someone had bothered. A burnt frying pan fared less well. The place smelled of sweat and stale smoke. Better not to think about what was lurking in the carpet.

"Nice lighting," Sarah said, her nose wrinkling in a reflex she couldn't control.

A faint flush spread across the top of Marc's cheeks.

Sarah jumped when she heard a grunt from the direction of the couch, a greeting from under a Starship Enterprise comforter. An arm emerged from the pile, knocking a full ashtray to the floor.

"Shit! Sorry dude. Don't worry. I'll get that later." A man boy grabbed a pack of Gitane cigarettes off the coffee table.

"Jesus, Declan," Marc yelled, glancing at Sarah. "That's disgusting. Clean it up now."

More of Declan became visible. A look of surprise suggested the request was a breach of no protocol. He lit his cigarette and started gingerly putting the butts back in the ashtray.

"I'm not exactly dressed here, man." Declan turned toward Sarah. His face was pudgy and spotted with acne, but he was cute in the way a bear cub is. His shaved head was lumpy. "This her?"

Marc ignored the question.

So he'd mentioned her. She smiled. "Guess I'm her. Sarah. Hi."

Declan waved. Nothing about his cockeyed countenance and slow movement felt threatening. In fact, the opposite. And *he* seemed unfazed by her.

"Declan doesn't live here, just likes to crash with the grown-ups instead of at mommy's place. We need a few rules around here. This place is a pigsty."

"But . . ." He looked confused.

"Listen man," Marc interrupted quickly. "You don't pay any rent so maybe you could get off your fat ass and help out once in a while."

"I buy beer and chips." Declan grabbed at jeans with a heavy skull and cross bone belt buckle that were lying on the floor.

Sarah turned away to let him pull them on. When she

looked back, he was waddling down the hall to what she presumed was the bathroom. Thankfully she'd peed earlier.

Sarah would only be of so-called help to Marc and the mates if she upped her computer game. Ara was finally coming over for their first subterfuge meeting. He brought his mother's famous lentil dish. Until recently, Sarah hadn't known what a lentil was. She'd heard the word only once when darts were being aimed at Barbra Streisand. Supposedly, that was the name of a movie she'd directed and starred in.

"It's not lentil," Ara said laughing. "It's *Yentl.* I grew up in Sri Lanka, how do I know this and you don't?"

"You really need to ask?" Sarah rolled her eyes. "I'm the one who should be making you a meal, Ara."

"I'm wary of your cooking."

"As you should be. I should put up a warning sign."

He laughed and spooned the brown mush onto naan. "One bite. And stop making a face."

She didn't mean to make a face every time she tried something foreign. *To her*. Ara had suggested she add *to her*, so it was less offensive.

She took a bite, then two more. "This is good. Really good."

She let him pack up what was left and put it in the fridge.

Ara's comments on her messy computer were more embarrassing than how she approached new food.

"It's like the computer is your bedroom. Right now, you open the door and throw things in anywhere. Occasionally you use a drawer, which is good, but for nothing in particular, which is bad. Underwear, sock, t-shirt, extra shampoo bottle, cigarettes, all in together. When you need to find something, you run around like the chicken with no head. If you understand how your computer works, you can have as many drawers or cupboards with shelves as you like. Make sense?"

It made complete sense. She told him about the lost Spanish Civil War paper, only three pages, but still, and how she started it over then found the original saved with a letter she'd written but never sent to Mrs. Broder.

Sarah looked nervously from the screen to Ara.

"It's a wonder you can find anything on this computer. And please stop looking at me like I'm going to steal your secrets. If I don't open things, I can't show you how to make subdirectories so you can hide this *Tightey White* thing."

It wasn't that she didn't trust Ara. He pretty much oozed trustworthiness. It was just habit.

"Apply the logic you use with a paper system. Harrison told me you came up with a brilliant way to categorize all the materials when you were in Goderich."

They spent a couple of hours burying things. He taught her how to rename them and hide them so they couldn't be found.

"These people that you plan to do this for are not whizzes, right?"

"Very not."

"Then you will likely be many steps ahead. One thing about the computer, though, you have to use what you learn all the time, or it won't sticks."

Sarah laughed. "Don't worry. I'll practise."

Between Luce and Ara, she was learning how fun the English language could be.

"But *I* want you there," Marc said.

Now he was pushing, and Sarah was feeling hesitant. She knew nothing about these guys. Unsmitten as they were likely to be, they might get suspicious. Marc's arm hung around Sarah's shoulder. They were heading to his apartment for an actual meeting. "They'll get over it once they see what you're capable of."

Given how he constantly mocked what she did at TCH, it was interesting that it suddenly constituted skill.

"I don't want to piss anyone off. Maybe they should get to know me first."

"Is that really the best idea?" He sucked air in between clenched teeth.

She punched his arm. He pulled her against him. She stood on her toes and pushed her hips against his instantly hard cock.

"Dirty girl," he whispered.

Everything tingled. She shoved him away.

He looked pleased. "I vouch for you. That's all they need. It's my cell."

He couldn't vouch for her. But then, no one could.

From what she'd figured out, there were seven guys in total who discussed mayhem that rarely went anywhere. The loose plans involving broken windows and threatening phone calls that less alcohol might have made more convincing. They were knee jerk rather than strategic.

Their preference for beer over hard work led to half-baked schemes that never took off or simply fell flat, but now, Marc claimed, they were ready to get serious. Sarah pushed aside the thought that she might have anything to do with Marc's newfound desire to become his best self.

Before Sarah came on the scene, there was Isabelle, who Marc described as big and small in opposite proportions to Sarah. Tits and brains. Sarah understood, in a way Marc didn't, that the guys liked Isabelle precisely because of that.

She'd left behind lipstick marks, nail polish remover, and a tiny t-shirt that said "pure laine" which translated as pure wool but was basically the equivalent of her dad's *stop the dilution*, or Marc's *fuck the mosaic* t-shirts. How it fit over her rumoured huge boobs was a mystery to Sarah.

Everyone stopped talking when they walked in. Four guys she'd never met were sitting with Declan. Marc introduced them. One was his cousin Bertrand.

The room was smoky, the windows covered in condensation. Sarah waved, then banged her mittens together, trying to give an unthreatening kid-like impression, but quickly reconsidered—a child at a White supremacist meeting might be worse. Surely, they had their standards.

Black t-shirts, jeans, and plaid flannel. Pretty much Luce's wardrobe. She looked at Marc, then took off her shoes and stepped over the pile of black boots. The place didn't look too bad. New hygiene rules were in effect for sure. It was hard to feel threatened by bald, tattooed guys in socks.

Marc pulled up two chairs and motioned for Sarah to sit.

One guy started talking about taking his girlfriend to see *Scarface* at a rep theatre the night before. "Not for the ladies," he said. "Can't hack the violence."

Marc ignored the comment and started talking about an attack they were planning on a Jewish School in Outremont. The others cleared their throats and glanced around nervously.

"What the fuck's wrong with you guys? We're having a meeting here." He started again, and again someone changed the subject, this time to his car problems.

Was it possible that Marc wasn't getting it? Or was it a power struggle he didn't want to lose? She was his *squeeze*. This was *his* cell. He made the rules. Shoes off at the door was clearly easier to swallow than *I'm going to ram my sort of girlfriend (with the smallest tits ever) down your throats*.

After forty-five minutes of Marc starting conversations and others derailing them, Sarah stood up.

"I'm going to go." She knew Marc would be mad, but the stand-off wasn't ending. She had better things to do. "I've got schoolwork."

She didn't say papers or assignments and Marc had asked that she not mention McGill.

She grabbed her backpack. The rest of them looked relieved, grateful even.

"See ya Sarah. Good luck with the work."

They waved, suddenly all friendly.

The next day over a beer, when Sarah pointed out (again) that dropping her like a bomb into their cell was an unlikely recipe for kinship, Marc agreed and proposed a change of approach.

"You should start with the ladies meeting at Connie's. You'll like them. They're very easy to be around."

Connie was Marlin's wife. She ran the women's group. They had a three-year-old kid, Celine. The ladies, as Marc called them, were the keepers of information so it didn't get lost. Sarah thought of the feminism works t-shirt. It should just say *women do all the work.* Marc assured her that the group was not like TCH. No envelope licking.

"Have I *ever* talked to you about hanging out and gossiping with my girlfriends?"

Marc shook his head.

"That's because it doesn't happen. Ever. I'm no good at it. Women think I'm weird. Well not just women. And you said *you* could use me. Maybe we could just give it a little more time."

"We can, but the guys think you're a bit, I don't know . . ."

"Flat?" Sarah offered.

Marc laughed. "Look, you take a little getting used to. That's not a bad thing. Maybe if you hung out with the ladies a bit."

"It would prove I'm normal?"

"No."

They both knew he meant yes. "Maybe."

A week later, Sarah went to a meeting to appease the boys and lower her misfit score. A bunch of women were sitting around in Connie's living room.

"Where'd he take you, Mr. Fancy Car?" one of them asked. Pam maybe, but Sarah wasn't sure she had the name right.

"Chinese. I get all dressed up and he takes me to Chinatown. Plastic fucking tablecloth, and he's all like 'But baby, I love the bobo balls,' and then he stares at my tits."

Sarah could certainly see why they were attention grabbers, as much for how close they were to the woman's shoulders as how big they were.

"Isn't that why you got them done?" someone asked.

"They look good, eh?" Pam cupped her hands under her breasts and smiled around the room.

Connie looked irritated.

"What did you do with all your fancy lingerie?" another woman asked. "Wish it fit me."

"Tell me about it, a thousand bucks worth of underwire and lace from that place in Vermont when Roger crosses the border for one of his Burlington meetings. All useless. What am I going to do with a pile of unmatched panties?"

"Donate it to one of those homeless shelters."

Everyone laughed.

"I read something about underwire the other day. It's bad for you."

"Fantastic. I'll get myself a pack of sexy sports bras instead."

"Did you end up buying that floor cleaner? The lemon one?"

It was sounding a lot like the guys' meeting, except different topics to avoid getting to the point. Or maybe women just talked like this.

"I got it on the promo. Regular price, it's too expensive. Vinegar works good."

"Tried that, the apartment smelled like a fish and chips shop."

"Jesus lady. You have to rinse it."

"What's the problem with the underwire anyway?"

"Cancer or something."

"When's his next lingerie trip?"

"Next week. Montpelier."

A nervous glance at Sarah, or had she imagined it?

Chinese, no decent alternative to underwire, hemlines, linen sales, bad breath, bad attitudes, bad hair, yeast infections, spying mothers-in-law, cheating boyfriends, bowel movements, sippy cups, spots on linoleum. On it went. It was like Double Dutch, with Sarah rocking back and forth, trying (not hard enough) to figure out how to leap in between the ropes.

"I'll get more beer," Connie said.

New Tits stood up. "I'll help."

Sarah asked where the bathroom was. On the way back to the living room, she heard the two of them talking quietly in the kitchen.

"What the hell does he see in her? And I don't mean the obvious."

"Isabelle was dumb as a doorknob but at least she laughed and made nice. And that tarte au sucre. So good. I miss that. This one's a cold bitch. Barely smiles. She gives me the creeps."

"Creepy or not, she's doing something for him." Pam probably made some gesture because Connie laughed. "Until further notice, I guess she's in."

"Marc may play tough, but he's a softie. And taking care of his mom like that. I ran into them at the movies last week.

He's her whole life. Remember he brought her to Celine's birthday party? Here, take these. I'll bring the chips."

Sarah hurried back.

At home after the meeting, she thought about the conversation she overheard. These women wanted her there even less than she wanted to be there. Sarah glanced over at Beans on the pink couch. Even with his face mostly worn off, he seemed to be smirking. Unless she made an effort (what would that even look like?), she wouldn't get shit from anyone.

She took out her notebook and started sifting through her recollection of the evening's discussions. They'd said a few things. Montpelier, Vermont, Robbie Iverton—Pow Wow, RaHoWa. Sarah hadn't asked what RaHoWa was. She just waited for the blather to sort it out, which it had.

"I know I'm not supposed to say this, but I hate that head banger shit. I like Hall and Oates, and The Cure."

Not one of the skinheads who corresponded with Ellie Mae Tucker had invited her to a RaHoWa concert. RaHoWa, she figured out, stood for Racial Holy War.

Sarah had been so intent on blocking out drivel, she nearly missed something important. She managed to retrieve it this time, but it could just as easily have passed unnoticed. South Carolina or maybe North, friend of Marlin and Marc's. She was pretty sure he'd been at Aryan Fest. An American. "Planning to come up for a secret pow wow the weekend of the RaHoWa concert. There'd be work." That's what jogged her memory, pow wow, then they'd all laughed. Sarah had looked over at Connie who looked back at her, then quickly at the others, as if to say button it, and they all did.

Both the meetings reinforced what Sarah already knew. How hard it was to fit in, and why she wasn't a joiner. Things like the math pack had been different because no one was there for any other reason than math. These folks were close friends and Sarah was an intruder. They didn't know her, and they never would.

She'd better learn to chit chat or make something as good as Isabelle's *tarte au sucre*. She doubted showing up with Ara's lentil dish would cut it. If she didn't up her social game, which felt almost impossible, she'd get nowhere with these women. And for the moment, they were the place to get.

Sarah missed her dad and Blair and Mrs. Broder, people that required no effort and just let her be. Well Blair didn't quite let her be, but she didn't need to change anything for him. She felt tired of pretending and guilty about not being in touch more, especially with Mrs. Broder. She grabbed a pen and paper and started writing. The computer felt too impersonal.

Dear Mrs. B,

Sorry it's been so long since I've written and sorry for starting every letter with sorry it's been so long. Long enough for my kitten to almost be a cat. That happens fast, but not fast enough that I couldn't have written at least once during his early adolescence. He was attacking Mrs. Pinky, the pink couch I told you about, so Ara and I went to Value Village and bought something called a scratching post. That didn't work, so he found some matching fabric and Melrose seems convinced it is a younger more fun cousin of Mrs. Pinky.

Harrison continues to be embarrassed that I eat the world's most amazing bagels with baloney. He'll just have to deal.

I'm loving Montreal but have almost no time to take advantage of anything cultural, although my friend Luce is an artist (so that's kind of cultural). She got me a job at the café where she works. A weird thing happened the day I started working there. I found a postcard for an art show that opened the week before. Guess who the artist is? Katie Cartell. Let me say that again Katie Cartell. As in MY aunt. Luce and I went to see the show. Wow people pay a stupid amount of money for this stuff. The one with tiny swastikas on it (you have to look close) was the only one not sold. I'll mention that at the next TCH meeting. Maybe someone is interested.

I'm still going through the hockey bags and some boxes for my uncle. The library is taking shape, but I haven't found much, which is frustrating. I may start barking up a more radical tree.

Talk soon,

Love, Sarah

27

MARCH 1995

Sunnyside Mental Health Centre

"GOD, THIS HEAT," MONA SAID.

It was worse in the tight closed space of her office than anywhere else. The therapist had complained about the heat even before the heating system went full blast bananas, with patients quickly following suit since it was almost impossible to breathe and self-control was already in short supply. She'd been on about the *change* and the hormones for weeks, dabbing her forehead nonstop with what she and Mrs. Broder called a *schmata*. A rag. Couldn't she keep the thing on her lap, rather than on the desk with the crumbs and the sweat?

"How long can it possibly take to fix a furnace?" She continued furiously fanning herself with the paper fan. "I'm sorry. Go on."

"I thought if they had a computer, they wouldn't accidentally lose or destroy critical information. They kept all that shit on scraps of paper. I told my uncle the same thing. I should have considered the fact that a neo-Nazi with a computer could be a lot worse than a neo-Nazi with a pencil. Of course, they didn't get a chance to prove that, but all I could think about was making it easier for me to keep track. If I hadn't opened my mouth."

"Something else would have happened."

"Sure, sure. Maybe. But here's what's even worse, and I tried to ignore it, even though part of me knew. I knew it when I walked into Marc's apartment for the second time, and everything was so much cleaner. He cleaned it up because he cared what I thought. I made Marc a better neo-Nazi."

Mona's expression suggested this might be a stretch, but she let Sarah go on.

"He always talked about the things they'd fucked up because they were too wasted or lacked commitment and motivation. They believed in the idea of White supremacy but couldn't be bothered with what was needed to get there. It was kind of a joke to them. You can't change the world with insults and graffiti. Like going to the Jewish cemetery stoned and dropping the paint can. He laughed about it, but he seemed embarrassed too. When he came by TCH and hung around while I was doing my organizing thing, he'd laugh at me, but I could tell he respected the effort. That he knew I was serious. And I could feel things start to change. The hygiene was just the beginning. Being around me made him see how foolish they might look. And maybe he thought that's what I thought. So, not only did I float the idea of computers and organizing themselves better, but I made him want to be better. Usually that's a good thing, when someone wants to improve themselves, even if it's for someone else. This was not a good thing."

The room suddenly felt even hotter. Mona's paper fan was supplementing the electric one. What wasn't in motion, like leaves and pieces of paper, was sticking—Sarah's hair to her face, t-shirt to her ribs, damp jeans to the leather chair, bare arms to the arm rests. Sweat everywhere. It was like the office was a rain forest with its own ecosystem.

Mona pulled a bottle of water from her desk drawer and handed it to Sarah. "Drink." She seemed to be buying time so she could come up with the right response.

"I understand what you're saying. I get the logic. And it's possible that you inspired him to pull it together, maybe aim higher, but in the end, what did he achieve? They're a bunch of thugs, Sarah. That's what they'll always be."

"Thugs can do damage too. Don't underestimate them. And here's another fucked up thing. I was flattered. I felt smart and purposeful around them. I wasn't treading water or drowning. I was secretly running the show. At McGill, I always felt like I was failing. Probably because I was. And Harrison, I love him, and I know he cared and he believed in me, but that didn't help. Was Marc and his gang really where I belonged? Makes me sick."

Sometimes when Sarah was with Harrison or Luce, she felt dumb, ignorant, like she'd lived her life in a narrow shaft she hadn't ever bothered climbing out of. Ara was the exception, he never made her feel like that, but one exception wouldn't change what she saw when she looked at herself.

Sarah was using a full scholarship at one of the best

universities in the country as a front. It was like she wasn't there. All the years of research didn't undermine a hate movement at all, it just guaranteed her no escape.

Mona reached out her hand. She didn't touch Sarah but came close. "Let's be clear about one thing. You didn't do poorly in your courses because you weren't capable. You weren't present. You had other priorities, sure, but also, you didn't think you were worthy of being there. In your mind, you don't deserve to be part of the world you're trying so hard to create, only the one you're trying to destroy. Blaming yourself for something that's not your fault is part of keeping yourself down. Doing well at school would prove you're entitled to move on, but you weren't willing to let yourself do that."

"I didn't even fucking try. I'm not sure I ever planned to." Sarah pushed her palm against her forehead. It was worse than pointless and so much to take in. She'd think about it more later.

Becky and Sarah lay in the dark debating the advantages and disadvantages of anti-depressants. Her roommate was a pro.

"It's like a timeout from all the stress and shit. I can't make a goddamn decision. After strokes, some people forget how to swallow. Imagine if you had to choose to swallow. And it's not like the decisions that freak me out are weighty, life-changing, or life-sustaining. They're inconsequential. I stand in the produce section staring at the fruit. Only one kind of banana, thank God, but how many to get and should I get green and wait for them to ripen? Or yellow, then have them go black within two days? My freezer was full of black bananas. So

I collected recipes—cakes, puddings, power shakes, muffins, curry—then couldn't decide what to make.

"Apples kill me. Golden Delicious, Cortland, Mackintosh, Gala, Matsu—where did Matsu come from? Suddenly out of fucking nowhere, there's Matsu. Oh, and Asian pears. Is it an apple or a pear? Who can cope? Sharpness is overrated. I can be sharp later. I think of meds as a holiday from myself. You could use one of those."

Was it that obvious? What would a holiday feel like? Not fuzzy, that was for sure, and meds made her fuzzy. It occurred to Sarah that she'd never had a holiday.

28

DECEMBER 1993

Montreal

THE TURNER DIARIES WAS A TEST SARAH gave to Maddie to see if there were limits to what she found acceptable in the fight for the desired end. Sarah's assumptions about who the kid could be, about how she might be steered off the current path, were getting dangerous for them both. The idea that she could be subtly or maybe subliminally convinced to change her beliefs or be rescued was based not on evidence, but on Sarah's judgment that was clouded by Maddie's adoration. For them both to be safe, Sarah had to fight her desire for Maddie to be redeemable.

"It's a novel about a White revolution for world dominance. A bit apocalyptic, super violent. It's pretty well-written, not like most of the junk out there that's full of spelling mistakes and historical inaccuracies you can disprove in a second."

Maddie looked surprised by the criticism.

"We might have the ideas right, but we don't always say it

right. That's probably why we're so misunderstood and vilified. The so-called movement could use some communications skills. Maybe you'll help with that."

Sarah's worry that Maddie would head off to whiter pastures had not yet materialized. She was both relieved and disappointed. The longer the kid stuck around, the more Sarah liked her and the more responsible and torn she felt. If Maddie disappeared early, it would have been like anyone who dropped in for a few minutes, got bored, and took off. Where they went and what happened to them, sad or wonderful, was of no concern.

Maddie was sticking around. Girls were so outnumbered there, maybe one in every twenty-five young people who showed up. That fed Sarah's worry.

Maddie finished the book in two days.

"What'd you think?"

"It was heavy. Not that I don't support the . . . you know, changes or whatnot." She hesitated. "Do you think that's what most people want? What *we* want?"

Maddie's questions confirmed for Sarah that she could trust her instincts, at least for a while longer.

"Most people don't think about what it would actually take, and even the ones that do aren't willing to martyr themselves for what they believe. It's not a cohesive movement. We like to think it is, but people are motivated by what irks them day to day, like your dad or mine. Most of them would find that kind of blood and gore repulsive, but if you offered them the end state, they'd be all for it. Your friend Bradley would probably love the book."

"I don't think I'll give it to him."

Sarah didn't have to lie to Maddie, just float ideas that let her make of Sarah what she wanted. Even with Carl and Marc, lying was almost never necessary. People heard what they wanted to hear and mostly talked about themselves. Maddie was one of the rare listeners.

"What's Carl's deal? He seems to know everybody. Why isn't he more . . .?" She hesitated.

"Radical?" Sarah suggested.

"Ya, I guess."

"Maybe it's having kids. He was more deeply involved when he was younger. Went to the fifth world congress at the Aryan Nations compound in '84. You make choices. Carl's good at hooking people up and bringing in money."

If only she could track the donors. She'd never asked Carl directly. Not that he'd tell her. It was better that way. If this all blew up in her face, he wouldn't have to blame himself for having trusted her with confidential information that exposed others. Money was strangely personal, unless it was big money. But in the world of White pride, no one put their names on buildings. It would be helpful if they did. *The Horst Von Beuller Advanced Racism wing in the Thomas Cartell School of Neo-Nazism.* Sarah laughed.

"What's funny?"

"Just a little fantasy about a world where our beliefs were out in the open."

"You're dating Marc. He's pretty Aryan Nation. That makes you more radical than Carl."

Far more radical.

The dating information must have come from Declan, who'd been sniffing around. Neither Marc nor Sarah described what they were doing as dating. As for *pretty Aryan Nation*, what did Maddie think that meant? Shared beliefs? Wearing the t-shirt? Blowing things up? Aside from *more* and *real*, the kid had no idea what she wanted to do.

"Marc said you two met at Aryan Fest. That's so cool."

"Very cool," Sarah said, thinking, *not cool at all*. "I'll tell you about it sometime. And don't say anything about Marc in front of my uncle. They don't get along. We're not all one big happy family."

"Families are barely ever one happy family, why should this be?"

The kid was smart.

When Maddie was gone, Sarah turned to the dregs from the hockey bags. She'd gone through almost everything, had a few more names and knew who'd travelled to what supremacist gatherings in the US and Europe, but to what end? Had she expected blueprints for world domination and bombs?

What was left was a pile of faded receipts and a couple of envelopes she'd set aside weeks ago in a safe place, and completely forgotten about.

She looked at the first unfolded paper and felt a jolt of excitement. Records of donations. Big donations. The largest was for $20,000. Merry fucking Christmas. She didn't recognize any of the names but made a note to look them up.

Sarah spent the last three weeks before the break in the library, studying for exams and busting her ass to hand in at least something for each of her courses.

Despite his annoyance that they hadn't fucked in ages, Marc helped Sarah pack and drove her from department to department to hand in what could barely be called *completed* assignments on the last day possible. He dropped her at the train minutes before it left.

She slept most of the way home and for a good chunk of the break. Her dad told her she was way too thin and suggested she see the doctor. Even Blair and Keith commented, and not in a mean way. The circles under her eyes were like bruises, and her clothes hung off her more than usual. The rush to cram the semester's work into the early weeks of December left her wrecked. Mediocrity was an option. Failing was not.

Grandpa Thomas was a watered-down version of himself, so Christmas dinner and Sunday lunch was almost fun. Mrs. Broder pretended Sarah didn't look like shit, practically force-fed her bagels with enough cream cheese for a family of five. They mostly talked about Professor Pichon and all the research Sarah let her think she was doing. After a question about what her uncle had done before TCH went more or less unanswered, Mrs. Broder stopped digging. They categorized new arrivals and kept the conversation superficial. Sarah described the *bises*, and how despite all her efforts, she occasionally got accosted by a stranger, like someone she'd talked to briefly in a class. Being at the library a few hours each day felt good. Mrs. Broder started kissing her on both cheeks when she arrived and left, which made them both laugh.

Sarah waited for Aunt Jean to say something, but she never did. Neither of them made the effort. If she knew about Katie and their lunch, she didn't say anything.

By the time she got back to Montreal, she felt a lot better. Second semester would be different.

29

JANUARY 1994

Montreal

SARAH'S ROLE AT THE ZUNDEL EVENT WAS to troubleshoot, which meant looking around the room for anyone who might be disruptive, then let her uncle know. An impossible task since many had potential. Marc offered to do security, since, as he told Carl, he had a handle on the *rival* cells. But he quickly corrected himself since the word rival suggested gangs with fields of competition more like drugs than hate. But he could spot a rabble rouser.

Takes one to know one, Carl had whispered to Sarah, before rejecting the offer. He told Marc the perceived favouritism might be a provocation. Pissed off, Marc suggested he hire some of those Jew thugs from the JDL to guarantee neutrality. Carl decided to take it as a joke and told Marc he and his buddies were welcome to front row seats. But Marc had no interest in Zundel. Seeing that armchair supremacist once in British Columbia with his dad when he was a teenager was enough. Back then, he assumed the hard hats that Zundel and his followers wore suggested action. But he'd seen no evidence of that.

Despite Carl's slight, Marc and the boys had shown up and were leaning against the back wall waiting for something to get started.

All exchanges between Marc and her uncle were tense. It was hard to tell if they'd gotten worse over the past couple of months. If Carl suspected something was going on between Marc and Sarah, he kept it to himself.

Unlike him, Sarah wanted to hear what Zundel had to say about the Canadian Supreme Court decision that struck down prohibitions on the publication of false information or news. A total win that the far-right was cheering.

Hopefully Zundel would hint at what was coming next. Sarah had gotten it in her head that her next move might be a summer job at his Samisdat Publishing House in Toronto. She asked Carl to introduce them and put off Mrs. Broder's offer to work at the library.

Over a beer the week before, she'd mentioned the idea to Harrison and Luce.

"Like an internship? An intensive hate program? Sounds great Sarah. Maybe ask Professor Pichon if you can get credit for it. Cheers to that." He held up his glass.

Luce was equally snarky. "You want to move into his prison and do what? Edit? Organize? All he does is publish hate literature." She sounded like Marc.

"You have no clue what he does. It's naïve to think that's all. Anyway, he's a big fish. I'd get way more from him than from Carl or Marc."

"Jesus Sarah, don't you want to do anything other than climb the hate ladder? Grandpa, to Carl, to Marc, to Ernst."

That was exactly what she wanted. Moving up, gaining access, being at the centre of things. While she knew there was no cohesive whole or command centre, getting to Zundel would offer a lot more. She hadn't thought much beyond climbing.

Sarah was wearing something that passed for an interview outfit, just in case. She scanned the crowd. People were getting antsy. The TCH space wasn't big enough, so they'd rented a large basement that felt no different from a lot of places where White pride was celebrated. Carl believed drawing attention in a flashier venue was a bad plan. Marc thought it was a pussy move. He was sick of dank underground spaces. They weren't doing anything illegal. This should be happening at the Masonic Temple on Sherbrooke Street. He wasn't exactly wrong. It did send a certain message.

Zundel was already half an hour late.

"When will he be here?" Maddie asked, pushing back her hardhat. She looked less baggy than usual. Her clothes almost fit. "Is he even coming? I spent fifteen bucks on the hat."

"Never let a crowd influence your fashion choices," Sarah said, smiling.

"*You* sure don't." They laughed. "Everyone can use a hard-hat. It's one of those things you only buy once."

"You'll have it when you start your construction career."

"Engineering," Maddie corrected her, and Sarah felt something like pride.

"Where's your team spirit?"

"I was in the bathroom when they were handing it out," Sarah said.

"You know Marc's friend Declan?" Maddie was trying to be matter-of-fact, but excitement was plastered across her face. Her cheeks flushed. She looked pretty.

"Why? You're not interested, are you? He's a bit of a goof."

Obviously, that's why she was asking. The idea of Declan with Maddie was a bit nauseating.

"He's kind of cute. They're planning to firebomb some Jew place. He thinks it would be great if I got involved with you guys."

The ease with which one sentence followed the other, like flirtation and violent hate crimes were peanut butter and jam, made Sarah want to march her home and have her grounded. And who else had Declan been blabbing to?

"What other stuff did he say *we guys* were doing?"

"Planning actions, going to cool concerts, that kind of thing."

"Loose plans at this point. It's not for sure."

"But the concert, that's happening. Anyway, you know I want to do more."

"How about I take you to a meeting."

"Really? With Marc and Marlin and Bertrand and them?" Having all the names down meant she was ready to fly.

"It's with some women. Marlin's wife Connie and a few others."

"Sounds sucky. I bet they just lick more envelopes."

"I go. Would I go if it was sucky? And no envelopes, I promise."

"I guess not." Maddie swallowed that easily enough.

Carl got up on stage and cleared his throat before making excuses and introducing some no-name Zundel substitute. The crowd hissed.

"Like he was ever going to show," Marc said loudly, and his boys laughed.

Carl gave them a dirty look.

If she didn't meet Zundel, there was no chance of working for him. Someone who lived the way he did, in a fortress with cameras everywhere, would never hire a stranger. Of course, Carl had never met Zundel either, so it was a long shot anyway. Toronto and Samisdat would have to wait.

"Zundel was a no show. The whole thing was a total bust. He sent his supposed second-in-command. Some guy I've never heard of, Werner Schlagg, who had zero charisma but thankfully, a German name and accent. Otherwise, the crowd might have rioted." Sarah laughed and poured herself more beer, then looked at her friends.

Luce and Harrison were unamused. Ara was trying to give Sarah the benefit of the doubt.

"I'm just kidding. They wouldn't have rioted."

Someone did knock a box of donuts to the floor in a huff on his way out, but otherwise only grumbling.

"Jesus, Sarah. You're wasting your time."

"That's not fair, Harrison." Ara jumped in. "Some people

say our demos do nothing to change anything." He turned to Sarah. "If *you* don't know this Schlagg guy, he's not worth knowing. Some replacement hack with the right accent."

"Off the substitute Nazi speaker list?" Harrison quipped. "Maybe you need to get a hold of that."

"Thank you, Ara." Sarah glared at Harrison.

"Keep checking the classified section in the Toronto Star, just in case Zundel's second-in-command job comes open," Harrison said.

"Oh fuck off."

They all laughed, and Sarah was relieved to have things lighten a bit.

Harrison was almost as gleeful as Marc about the failed Zundel event, particularly the part where Sarah didn't meet the man. He acted like that would be the point of no return.

Sarah wasn't quite sure what compelled her to keep telling her friends at least the broad strokes of what she was up to. They never bought her rationale for *why*, and she dismissed their concerns as overcautious or missing the point. She gave Luce Marc and Connie's addresses. It wasn't that Sarah believed she was in any danger or that if she was, they could swoop in and save her. She just needed them to know, needed someone to know. Melrose was unlikely to call the cops.

"You're in a white rabbit hole," Harrison said. "I'm just worried if you get too deep, you won't see out anymore. Look what happened to Eli Cohen."

He'd been working on a research paper about embedded spies from organizations like the CIA, MI6, and the Israeli Mossad. He claimed Sarah inspired him. Spy seemed grandiose, but maybe the only difference between a spy and an infiltrator was a pension and cool gadgets. Harrison was currently obsessed with the Mossad agent who had risen to the top ranks of the Syrian government between 1961 and 1965, until he was eventually caught and hung publicly in Marjeh Square in Damascus. He was forty.

"Enough with the comparison," Sarah said. "It's ridiculous. He was an Israeli in the Syrian government passing along intelligence. I'm basically an ex-White supremacist trying to pass as a current White supremacist. Not a stretch."

"It's more about realizing, probably too late, that you're in a situation you can't get out of, or that the compromises you've made might destroy you."

"You're so dramatic. Maybe take a break from espionage stories. I'm fine. You can keep checking in, but I am. Can't we just get to the demo plans already. I have about an hour, then I have to work on my paper."

"Yeah, I'll take a break. I'm not seeing clearly," Harrison said.

"That's enough you two," Luce said.

Luce looked at the notebook in front of her. "Let's get Monique to lead the marshals, and someone should call David and that girl Viv, they're always happy to pull a crew together to poster."

"Activist night out." Harrison smiled at Ara. They'd met at a demo and had their second date at another one. They did go out for dinner afterwards. It wasn't just marching and chanting.

Luce and Ara had done more than their share of postering, lugging around buckets of wheat paste and paint brushes at two in the morning. They were happy to give that task to others. "I'll get armbands for the marshals, and the bullhorns," Harrison said.

"We'll tell them all to meet at Baked Beans, that coffee place around the corner from the conference centre. About an hour before."

Campaign Life was expecting over a thousand so-called delegates at their so-called conference. The international pro-life gathering would be crawling with neo-Nazis and sympathizers. Shake the family tree and father's rights, and Heritage Front boneheads dropped out every time.

The demonstration would be big. Luce pushed the chant cards across the table to Harrison. "Not that you'll forget, just so you can switch it up a little. You'll lead the yelling, right?"

"Of course."

Campaign Life, your name's a lie . . . you don't care if women die,
They say no choice, we say pro-choice,
This is what democracy looks like, that is what hypocrisy looks like,
Not the church, not the state, Women must decide their fate!

For her part, Sarah pulled together a package of background information on Campaign Life and its leadership.

"Are you coming?" Luce asked Sarah. "It'll be so fun."

Sarah and her friends had very different ideas about fun. "I can't. Can't risk running into Marc and his boys or Maddie." They were all planning to show up in solidarity with right wingers of all stripes. Sarah doubted Maddie had strong anti-abortion leanings, but it was an opportunity to hang with the gang.

Sarah was relieved. She didn't like outward displays of affiliation and wouldn't be caught dead chanting in the streets. *Hey hey, ho ho, (something creepy) has got to go.* Not her thing. "Melrose and I will chant at home."

"Maybe another time," Luce said.

The plan to bring Maddie to the next women's meeting kept getting delayed, so it was mid-March before they finally went. Not the excitement the girl was after, but it was something.

Connie nodded coldly to Sarah but broke into a smile when Maddie stuck out a bag of Oreo cookies. Celine, at her knee, was dragging a stuffed animal with a striped red, white, and blue hat.

"Is that Muffy the Super Squirrel?" Sarah asked.

Carl's daughter had the same one. But this kid, short messy hair and mismatched boy's clothes that Connie said the kid picked herself, was nothing like Sarah's prim little cousins.

"Muffy, soupy skirl!" she shouted in a gravelly voice, then grabbed Sarah's hand and pulled her into the kitchen. One by one, her menagerie of stuffed toys was brought forward for Sarah to name. Aside from Curious George and Paddington Bear, Muffy the Super Squirrel pretty much exhausted her knowledge, so she came up with Boris the Bunny and Penny the Panda, which had Celine rolling on the floor.

"You're great with her." Connie's observation was more surprise than compliment.

"I was sure she'd go for Maddie," Sarah said.

"Kids not your thing? Didn't you babysit?"

"No, worked in a library."

"That figures," Connie said.

After a moment's awkward silence, Sarah started laughing and the rest of the women did too. "I'm not exactly a kid magnet. Carl's girls probably feel obligated to like me."

It wasn't true but made them all laugh again. It was that easy to be drawn into the circle. A little effort went a long way.

"That's a nice sweater, Pam." It was tight, turquoise, and fuzzy. Nothing Sarah would have noticed, let alone buy. But when Pam smiled, the sweater looked good, and the compliment felt true enough.

"It's mohair. I got it at an end of winter sale, not that it feels like winter's over. I hate March. Twenty-nine dollars, can you believe that? They're nuts. How the hell do they make money?"

Maybe she could get the hang of this, get them to like her. Liking them back would be the unexpected part.

Working to fit in didn't get easier, but the moments when Sarah let herself forget to be on the outside were nice. And *nice* wasn't as benign as it sounded. She'd always figured it was something to say if there was nothing better. But that wasn't true. People who had a lot of nice on a regular basis didn't get that it was a break from standing guard. Very little in Sarah's life was like that. Luce and Ara were nice. Really nice. Even Connie was nice.

That Thursday, they were back at The Pen having an impromptu meeting about the concert weekend.

Marc refilled her glass and passed the pitcher to Bertrand. Thursday *jump on the weekend* night at The Pen was packed with people doing shots of tequila with beer chasers.

"You wearing it?" Marc leaned over and whispered.

A blue padded push-up bra and panty set had been added to her other underwear set. At least it wasn't pink. She hated the word panty. Saying it made her feel exactly the way it was supposed to, small and frilly. Men should be forced to wear them one day a year, or even a month. Marc didn't care if she wore the stuff when they had sex, only when they were out. She preferred undershirts.

"If you can't tell . . ." she whispered back, looking down at her tits that had doubled in size. "Then what's the point of my wearing it?"

He claimed he didn't care what people thought, but he did.

Sarah's presence no longer raised eyebrows. Hanging out with the ladies had done what Marc hoped it would. No one shut up when the still amorphous plans for the Jewish school attack were discussed.

It seemed to hang on Robbie Iverton's blueprint for constructing a no-fail bomb. He'd be in town next week for the concert and would explain in detail. *Not too technical. A seventh grader could build it.* The comment was meant as a challenge. Let's see what you Canadians can handle.

"Then there's a guy from Cincinnati who said he'd get us the stuff to build it. I met him at a party a while ago." Marc slapped a scrap of paper on the table with a name and phone number scrawled on it.

Sarah was certain they were being taken. Three hundred and fifty US dollars for the incendiary trigger.

"This is big. It's time for a hit of our own, not just piggybacking or showing up for the after party."

A hit of one's own was one of Marc's themes. Did he know Virginia Woolf? He was sick of being *Reverend Scott's son*, especially since it made almost no difference to the reverend. He wanted to be known for something *he'd* done.

"Bring the kid to RaHoWa," Marc yelled over the music. "Maddie likes Declan, and she's got real potential. It'll be fun for her."

Real potential for what? "I'm not even sure we can trust her."

"Trust her? She's dying to move on from Carl's kindergarten. I thought you liked her. Anyway, Declan likes her. It would be perfect. He'd grow up."

As though having girlfriends or wives had matured the rest of them. Declan reached across Sarah for the pitcher and knocked her glass over. The beer washed over the paper, blurring the name and number.

Marc jumped up. "Fuck. Declan, you dick. Now how am I supposed to reach this guy."

"Seriously, you don't have a copy?"

"*Seriously, you don't have a copy?*" Marc whined in a high-pitched voice. "Shut the fuck up."

Sarah was annoyed. Who doesn't keep this stuff somewhere safe? If he'd only given it to her or Connie. Maybe nothing would have come of the name, maybe the guy was just some small-time fake incendiary device trafficker. But at least she could have tracked him down.

"I think it's time to get a computer. Store everything on it. Then nothing gets lost or drowned. I know a cheap place. We can probably get a discount."

"Computers are for geeks," Bertrand said.

Declan nodded in agreement. Sarah was pretty positive neither of them had a clue what a computer did.

Rod and Marc rolled their eyes.

"You're fucking Neanderthals. Seriously, what's wrong with you?" Marc didn't know much either, but he'd heard enough from Sarah.

The guys threw her dirty looks. But the humiliation was fleeting and easy enough to dislodge. She felt quite sure that the next time she brought up the topic of computers, they'd be eager.

It was pissing down rain the weekend of the RaHoWa concert. Sarah thought of the day they'd arrived at Aryan Fest. Some higher power was giving her a sign that these fuckers deserved to stand in mud up to their ankles. Harrison's kind of God in action. Of course, she'd be standing there too, but it was worth it. And she was wearing rubber boots.

Walking from the car, they passed a bunch of anti-racist activists gathered at the far end of Java Bingo's property in Laval, Quebec, where directions to the concert's secret location would be handed out. Sarah gave Luce the Robbie Iverton blueprint information.

Marc was angry. Iverton had been refused entry into the country. He'd left a message.

No idea why I was singled out. Probably my ex. The bitch hates me. So I'm back in Cleveland, pal. You'll have to hold off on the northern lights until I can get there.

Border patrol had gone through his stuff and found the blueprints he claimed were part of a game he and some buddies were designing. The Star of David tipped them off. No one's name was on anything. Nothing traceable. But offensive enough to draw attention.

"He thinks we're a bunch of pussies who can't do anything without help from big brother. Fuck that. We'll do it ourselves." Marc swiped at the rain on his new leather jacket.

Declan and Maddie were right ahead of them.

"Hey P Squared, check out that bunch of faggots." Declan had taken to calling Maddie P Squared because she kind of looked like Peppermint Patty from Peanuts, and she loved it. Sarah could relate to the thrill of a nickname.

"How did the cops find out? There's like twelve cars," Maddie said.

Luce and Harrison stood with a small group of people. Sarah recognized some of them, but they wouldn't know her—a perk of being unremarkable. People often asked if they'd met her before and couldn't remember if they had. Sarah didn't find that insulting, only helpful. Two of the guys wore faded leather jackets and had shaved heads. One of them had a t-shirt that said *not a skinhead, just a fag*. The protesters, in their black or yellow rain jackets, looked like a swarm of bees huddled together.

Sarah passed on the information about the concert but Luce hadn't shared the part of the plan where they show up. After they'd told her how stupid it was to get involved with these people, she'd stopped saying much of anything. What was the point of coming here other than to make trouble? Her stomach cramped. Sarah put two pieces of gum in her mouth. Connie told her it helped with an upset stomach. She was going through a lot of gum.

Luce looked at Marc, catching Sarah's eye for only a second, afraid she'd blow her cover or maybe just piss her off. Then out of nowhere, she lurched forward. "Fuck you, ya you in the squeaky jacket, you Nazi bonehead."

With no hair to absorb it and no umbrella to block it, the rain poured down Marc's face. He claimed umbrellas were for fags. He looked around, then pointed at himself, smirking.

"That's right." Luce kept going. "Feeling all big and important. Is there a single original thought in that brain, or are they all borrowed? Go on. Go to your Nazi concert, do your little Heil Hitler goose step dance." Luce pointed at the guys in the leather jackets who were now making out. "Who wore it better?" she yelled, and her crowd started laughing. Clearly, their goal was humiliation.

Marc was rattled. Maybe only Sarah noticed. "How the hell did they find out about this?" he asked her. "You recognize those queers?"

Sarah shrugged no.

"Fucking dyke," he yelled.

"You got one thing right," Luce shot back.

The cops stepped in front of her. Doing the job they always did so well, protecting the Nazis from violent anti-racists.

Sarah glanced back at Luce for a split second and shook her head, like what the fuck.

They moved inside the building, where a teenage skinhead wearing a Ku Klux Klan baseball cap and a RaHoWa t-shirt pulled a map out of his bomber jacket. Sarah wouldn't have recognized him if Maddie hadn't shouted, "Hey Bradley."

The boy had a puffed up *I'm on the inside now* look about him. He pointed to a spot marked with a swastika. "About an hour north of here in La Plaine. It's a huge heated barn. Very cool." He handed it to Sarah and lowered his voice. "Once you get there, destroy it."

The wipers were on high and the heat was blasting. Declan gave a heavy metal music tutorial to pass the time.

RaHoWa front man George Burdie followed an anti-Christian religion called "Creativity" that replaced God with the White man and encouraged insurrection. Well beyond where Sarah's grandfather or maybe even Marc were willing to go. She'd researched Creativity. The founder had written *Nature's Eternal Religion* and *The White Man's Bible*, as well as inventing a wall-mounted electric can opener. No waiting around for God to start the revolution or open the baked beans.

Goth metal was neo-classical with epic metal influences, Declan explained while doing his best to rock out in the crowded car, the way he thought Birdie liked to do it. What was it with guys and air guitars?

This event was private, he said, and there was supposedly a bigger one planned for Ottawa in May. Ninety skinheads paid twenty-five bucks to stand in a barn. When RaHoWa played *Third Reich, Resistance—White People Awake* and *Triumph of the Will*, the crowd went wild, pumped and angry, jumping up and down.

There was plenty of space, but they opted for a tight Nazi mosh pit, arms raised in stiff salute, like they were worshipping. Same energy as Aryan Fest. Sarah glanced over at Maddie. Wide-eyed, face frozen, somewhere between terror and excitement. She kept looking back, as though seeking assurance that the emotions made sense.

Sarah mouthed, "You okay?"

"I think." Maddie's body was pulled along by the pack of bouncing skinheads.

Sarah forced a smile and gave the kid a Carl Cartell-style thumbs up.

30

MARCH 1995

Sunnyside Mental Health Centre

"WHEN I SAW MY FRIENDS AND THOSE other activists at Java Bingo, it felt aimed at me as much as at Marc or the other skinheads. Marc was thrown off for a few minutes, and that comment about *Who wore it better?* It's lucky I was too freaked out to laugh. It was really funny. But what point were Luce and Harrison making? There was nothing to be gained by showing up there. We'd stopped Iverton. The plan was never to stop the concert, and anyway, they had no idea where it was, and it would have been dangerous to try and follow us. I was relieved that Ara wasn't there."

"Why didn't he come?" Mona asked.

"Certain situations are way more unsafe than others if you're not White. The police tend to target you. But I never asked him. I know it wasn't Luce or Harrison's intention, but they were exposing me as some kind of double agent or worse. There I am, walking along, Marc's arm around me like I'm his girlfriend. Not sure what happened to *we're not dating*. Aside from those three, no one else knows what I'm up to. If any of the other activists recognized me, I'd have been outed. Maybe I was."

"That must have been awful."

"I don't know what part felt worse. Being caught like that with Marc, not exactly in public but kind of, or being trapped like that by my own friends. I've worked hard to keep everything separate, and they know that. It's why things like the Campaign Life demo are a big risk for me. Not that I'm sad to miss it."

"Sounds like it was getting harder and harder to keep yourself safe; from getting attached, from being exposed, from embarrassment. And maybe Marc was feeling things for you. Despite what he was saying, he considered you his girlfriend."

"I wasn't having attachment issues. At least I don't think I was. Maybe I felt guilty because *he* was getting too attached. It confused him because I really wasn't his type. Initially, it was easy. He probably figured it was a wild sexual experience he'd never had. Out of control. Exciting. He was relieved he couldn't hurt my feelings by missing a date or wanting to leave right after sex. His ex-girlfriend cried and complained a lot. I never did. Of course, I was always the one who wanted him to leave right after. I thought his push back was ego, not dependence, that he wanted to be begged to stay."

Sarah knew as she said it, that it wasn't quite true. Marc's words and feelings were at odds very soon after they met. It wasn't a reason to end things. So long as he insisted, she could ignore the rest. And she found any concerns about the unfairness to him, annoying. He was exactly what her friends claimed he was, so why should she care? But it wasn't that simple.

"In the beginning, I was everything some guys fantasize about. No strings. I wanted what he wanted, until he wanted more. And then he was stuck. He couldn't ask for it because he'd claimed there was no relationship. The danger you think I was in, that wasn't of becoming attached. It was feeling confused that I cared about hurting him. The day of the RaHoWa concert, I could feel this possessiveness. His arm around my shoulder was so heavy. And I'm sure Luce and Harrison could tell, even from that far away. I felt ashamed. My friends put me in that position."

"You were fine being perceived as his girlfriend, as long as it was only in that closed world."

"It was easier to deny what was happening. It was a game I was playing that no one outside could judge."

"Maybe you stayed that long with Marc because somewhere you believed he was all you deserved. You can tell yourself you were getting what you wanted, good sex and information, but what about something deeper, like love? Don't you want that? We've talked about this. About you trapping yourself in a world you wanted destroyed. The logical conclusion is that you don't survive its destruction."

How the hell had they gotten from the Java Bingo encounter to here? Mona started by asking how awful that day felt, stuck between her two worlds, which it did. Then whether she was attached to Marc or not, and now she was almost suggesting that falling in love with him would have been way less fucked up than what she was doing. Sarah put her hands over her face.

"I don't understand. It sound like you're calling what I was doing a suicide mission. Something I knew I couldn't come out of alive."

"What I'm saying is that I don't believe you've figured out how to find a place for yourself. With the good guys. A place where there can be love, maybe a relationship. You love Ara and Luce and Harrison, but you created barriers to how far those friendships could go. I'm not even talking about romantic love. It keeps coming down to what you believe you deserve. It's not that you won't come out alive or that you can't envision a way out. It's that you don't bother. You have convinced yourself that you're too busy rooting out an evil that can't be rooted out."

Maybe Mona was right that she hadn't considered anything like love or even a career. A path out, rather than the same path around the inside. But she'd assumed it was about being busy with a mission, not that she considered herself undeserving. Why think that far ahead? Now was not the time. And if, at least for now, she wasn't ever who she claimed to be, how would a romantic relationship even be possible?

"Maybe I'm hardwired to misrepresent myself or point people in a different direction. Maybe that will never change. That first time I met Charlene, when I wore Becky's dress. She saw right through me. That doesn't happen very often. I'm good at it after so much practice. When we were little, we pretended not to believe what we believed. Then later, it was convincing my family that I still believed, and not being completely honest with Mrs. Broder about the infiltration plans. I was only ever honest to a point, because the whole truth was too much."

"For them or for you?"

"I thought it was for them. I'm a professional liar. Fundamentally dishonest."

"You had your reasons."

"An honest person couldn't do what I do."

"I don't think the liar/truth teller distinction is useful."

"Shouldn't it be hard to lie? Shouldn't you feel shame or something? It's so easy for me. The game became 'how few lies does it take to create a story that's the opposite of the truth?' Even with people I care about."

How much did she lie to Mona? In the end, she'd leave Sunnyside, and the therapist would see a new fucked up person. How Sarah made sense of things or didn't, or told the truth or didn't, would be irrelevant. Every person who stepped up to be her friend triggered the calculation of what bits of her story they were entitled to or could manage. Where would love even fit in?

"What you chose to do required constant deception, so you had to find ways to be okay with it. I guess keeping your distance helps." Mona sounded unconvinced that anyone could come through that much fakery unscathed. "Emotional distance feels like safety, but it might even be the opposite."

"Or this is the perfect job for someone who prefers distance. Maybe I'm just lacking that gene." Had Sarah ever found a way to be okay? Had she even paid attention to the being okay part?

"Here's a fact," Mona said. "Some things *are* evil. What you've been fighting is a form of evil. That's why you do it, not because you love a good lie."

Sarah laughed. "Thanks." It felt comforting to have Mona believe the best of her, even if it only lasted a few minutes. "I guess people are capable of good and evil simultaneously."

"The contradictions hurt. Most people don't live with as many as you do. And maybe drop the word evil. Some people are capable of good and bad. Evil feels like it belongs in a category of its own." Maybe Mona understood more than Sarah gave her credit for.

"Why do you think you need to see yourself as bad?"

"Do I?" Did she? Maybe bad was the wrong word, but deceptive. Weren't all these concepts somehow related?

"I'm more worried that I get off too easy. There are no consequences for what I brought about."

"No consequences?" Mona choked out the words like she couldn't believe what she was hearing. "You call this easy? For a smart person, you're incredibly dim."

"I never take the risks. I'm always behind the scenes or protected by someone else. That's why I wasn't there that night. Other people took the risks."

"Aryan Fest, passing as a White supremacist, and ratting out your Nazi friends, feeding information to the cops? That's the easy route? If the roles were reversed, and Luce was doing what you do, you'd call it easy?"

Sarah pulled at her t-shirt.

"You have no perspective when it comes to yourself. Most people have at least a little. That's the common denominator for everyone in here. That's how I know you belong. You need perspective to have perspective."

Mona sipped her coffee then pushed some crumbs to the floor with the side of her pinky. "You are so frustrating. You're either the queen of bad or you're la dee da kicking back in easy-chair land. Why do you think you spent so much time on that mountain in Montreal, staring at the stars? You were trying to cope, hide from a life that was almost impossible."

"I love that mountain. Look, all I'm saying is there are riskier things."

"There are always riskier things. And hiding only works until it doesn't. You're smart enough to know there's a price for secrets and lies. Do you really think there's anyone who doesn't lie or misrepresent themselves now and again?"

Mona was right about that. Good thing not lying wasn't one of the ten commandments. It was unsustainable, not that the others were working well, but they weren't violated constantly. Adultery, murder, idol worship, taking the Lord's name in vain, keeping the Sabbath, honouring your mother and father. If your father violated three, nine, and ten, did he still deserve to be honoured?

"People always tell me I have an honest face." Sarah laughed. "Lucky me."

Mona looked sad. "Yeah, lucky you."

31

APRIL 1994

Montreal

THE FIREBOMBING OF THE JEWISH SCHOOL WAS an elaborate plan by their standards. Despite Robbie Iverton and the foiled border incident, and despite the glass of beer that washed away the three hundred and fifty dollar incendiary device trigger, things were coming together. Declan (to everyone's surprise) had researched, bought all the materials, then built an actual bomb. A little bomb, but a bomb nonetheless.

The device would be launched through the library window. They had scouted it many times. Connie and Maddie, with Celine in a stroller, had even been sent in to find the right room and window. When some *freak with ringlets and a black gangster hat* heard Celine screaming that she was too old for a stroller, they were asked politely to leave.

"I told him we were looking for a bathroom for Celine," Connie said.

Maddie laughed. "Then she starts yelling 'I don't need to pee.' Almost blew our cover."

"Freak probably wanted to jump your sexy white ass," Bertrand said, and Connie gave him the finger.

"He was actually nice. He gave Celine a candy," Maddie said.

"To choke on," Bertrand said.

"Shut up Bert," Declan said. "You're an asshole."

Connie and Maddie drew a floor plan of the library, carefully marking the windows. Sarah listened to hours of strategizing, peppered with *kyke* jokes no one tired of. It was past eleven before they landed on a date.

Sarah would have been happy to head home alone, but Marc was all revved up and wanted to fuck, so they went to her place. Bertrand and Mireille may not mind doing it with the roommates around, but Sarah was not interested.

She didn't really care whether it was her or the bomb that made Marc that hard; once she felt it, she was all there. He thrust in and out of her from behind, wanting it so badly it was out of his control, and it hurt. It was the moment she knew he'd lost his ability to care that made her the craziest.

She whimpered and he stopped to ask if she was okay.

"No, no, no . . ."

His concern turned her stomach. What the hell?

"Fuck. Fuck you." She rolled off the bed, leaving him dejected and soft. In the bathroom, she sat on the floor and leaned her head against the cool toilet bowl.

He was sitting up when she came out, his socked foot crooked against his dick.

Her eyes drifted across the computer, the bookshelf, the Happy Face mug: objects that would retain their form, not collapse in front of her, like he had.

She pulled the fridge open and leaned against the door. He came up behind her, took a handful of her hair in a slow fist and tightened it, pulling her head back and bringing his damp mouth to her ear.

"Don't fuck with me," he whispered.

She leaned away from the tug of his arm, wanting him to tighten it. He pushed his hand between her legs, then laughed as she started to rock.

"I don't think so," he said, wiping his fingers in her hair. She pulled them into her mouth. He forced the fridge closed with her body and made frantic attempts to get inside her, ramming against the outside of her cunt until she made sounds that cut into his oblivion. He slid into her then pulled out.

"Way too easy. You don't deserve it." He stared down at her. "Go on. Show me how badly you want this. Do yourself." She held his gaze and spread her legs wider.

His smile claimed victory. "Nice."

"You fucker." Sarah moved slowly then faster against her fingers. She glanced over his head out the window, hoping for a moment that someone else was watching too.

After she came, he handed her a kitchen towel then pulled her down on her knees in front of him.

"My turn," he said.

He could push her head down and laugh cruelly, but no amount of feigned disregard could cover Marc's need for Sarah. She could feel it coming through in everything he did. And it was starting to worry her.

Sarah waited a few days for the plan to solidify, then called Luce. "Who calls the police?" She'd never asked who ratted out Iverton.

"Not me. I don't call cops. But I know who to tell. It works out," Luce said.

"Will they believe it? What if they think it's a crank?"

"They can't afford not to take it seriously." Luce didn't say anything for a few seconds. "I'm worried about you. You're not at class, you're barely at work. You're up to your ears in this shit. You need a rest. Maybe we can go to Lac St. Jean for a weekend. It's quiet. You can bring your books."

"That sounds nice." It really did. "I'll think about it for sure."

In the end, all she thought about was how she repaid Luce's kindness with less than nothing.

She had early class the next morning, but Sarah went to meet Luce, Harrison, and Ara for a couple of beers anyway. They had cleared the air somewhat since the whole RaHoWa fiasco, but only somewhat. Luce admitted that showing up there, as though it were a regular counter demo, was stupid and risky.

It was the wrong approach. She had wanted Sarah to see how horrible Marc was, in the light of day.

"You were frustrated that I wasn't listening to you guys, so you thought you'd take it public?"

"Something like this," Luce said. "I'm really sorry. But you have to admit, I did stick it to Marc."

They all agreed she had. While Sarah needed the apology,

it also felt messed up. Luce owed her nothing. She hadn't meant to shame Sarah, that was clear, but shame was the result and Sarah didn't deserve that.

She understood the *concerns* they threw at her, but still resented having to justify her choices. If she failed, she failed. That was on her.

But after two beers, she was back to justifying with a quick impromptu history lesson on what she liked to call *the rise of the extreme White.*

"Adrian Arcand, National Socialist Christian Party, interviewed by *Life* Magazine in 1938. Called for the forced resettlement of Jews to a concentration camp near Thunder Bay, Ontario. Thunder Bay. And what's totally fucked up is the respect he gets. Close associate of R.B. Bennett, the fucking Prime Minister of Canada. The guy was his paid publicist. I know, I know, there were tons of fascist Hitler supporters back then. But look at Jud Cyllorn. Fucking 1980s. Wrote and printed thousands of copies of a White supremacist manual, then sent it to federal and provincial politicians. Close aid to Bill Van Der Zalm, once premier of British Columbia. Can't fucking trust anyone, not even lefties. Some guy named Carlysle called Jews 'slave masters throttling the throats of White people to enrich themselves.' A couple of years later, and he's helping Tommy Douglas, the father of Canadian Medicare, win his campaign." Sarah stopped to take a breath.

Her friends broke out clapping.

"If you applied yourself to your university courses the way you do to your extracurriculars," Harrison said.

"Don't fucking start."

"You're a machine, girl. It's crazy what you know. I bet you can go back to the time of Christ. John the Baptist—White supremacist or anti-fascist?"

"How about those bored kids who started the KKK," Ara said. "Gave themselves titles like Grand Cyclops, Grand Magi, Grand Scribe. Like the stoned college guys that came up with *Teenage Mutant Ninja Turtles.*"

"Ya, but this one really mutated. The Klan didn't start off as White supremacists."

Even Sarah was surprised by her instant recall. Why couldn't she make room in her brain for stuff that would get her marks so she'd pass the year?

"You need to get out, Sarah. Seriously. See a movie. You're in too deep." Luce looked at Harrison and Ara for support.

"I'm not stuck. And I go out with people."

"Barely," Ara said.

Damn, she could usually count on him not to gang up on her when the others did.

"And how would you know how much I go out?" Sarah said.

Luce and Ara started laughing.

"Fine, we'll disable the cameras in your apartment. But come on. I'm kind of right, aren't I? You don't know how to relax," Luce said.

"Lay off. I'm fine. People relax in different ways."

"A night at The Pen. Sarah and the Supremes. Sounds totally chill." Harrison wasn't joking. "I got a letter from Mrs. B. She doesn't think you're fine. None of us really do. At least write her."

"Fine. We'll go to a movie." But it was too late to dial it back. Sarah turned away. Now would be a really bad time to cry.

She reread the arty postcards and letters Katie sent from Berlin. They were arriving at least once a week. Analysis of their conversation at lunch. How similar they were. How Sarah could do amazing work while still protecting herself. A million questions about what she was up to. Threats to send a plane ticket. *Give me some dates. How about this summer? Please stay safe. Thinking of you a lot.* And plenty of *xox*. The weight of Katie's concern added to the pile.

Her aunt was doing what she was good at. And so was Sarah. Maybe the feminist, anti-fascist art was a form of engaged confrontation, but was Katie any better off? She was also on the run, avoiding Cartell shit. A coward's choice or a hero's choice. And which one was Sarah? It was too complicated to answer Katie. Too many tangents. At least she could try reassuring Mrs. Broder.

Dear Mrs. B.,

I know you've been worried. I haven't been exactly straight with you. I've been pretty tired lately because I'm burning the candle at more than both ends. I'd love to tell you that it's too many parties or nights out at the pub, but you know me. Harrison and my other friends say I need to relax more. I will try to find a book on relaxing or maybe meditation. But who has time for that?

I feel like I have two full-time unpaid jobs at the moment. Both are being subsidized by McGill, or the Quebec government, and, I guess by Charlene Duoma, but screw her, let her pay (sorry). The student job needs more of my attention than it's getting. But I have already started to turn that around. The other job is our research project, part two. There's so much to figure out. I'm still organizing stuff for TCH, but I've met some other people, who uncle Carl knows, and have gone in a bit of a different direction. More hands on, I guess you could say. And of course, I still have my paid job making coffee. So it's all a lot.

You would be blown away by how incredible my computer skills are getting. Can't wait to apply them to Goderich Public Library this summer.

Please try not to worry. I feel perfectly safe.

Love, Sarah

The firebomb never happened. Marc and Rod went by the school for a final check and noticed cameras they'd never seen before. They came back to the apartment slamming doors and yelling.

"What, what?" Sarah jumped up just as Declan leapt off the couch.

"Those are new. For sure they weren't there. We'd have noticed."

"Noticed what, man? What are you talking about?" Declan asked.

"Fucking cameras," Marc yelled.

"What cameras, where?" Declan asked.

"Seriously dipshit, where do you fucking think?"

Declan's mouth hung open.

Bertrand walked out of the bedroom with Mireille, who rubbed at her eyes. He smacked Declan's face lightly. "What's up stunned-o?"

"What the fuck is she doing here?" Marc barked.

"What's your problem man? It's not a meeting night. Everything all set?"

Mireille rolled her eyes and sucked on a strand of hair. She pushed past Declan to grab a beer out of the fridge.

"Hostie Marc! *Franchement*." Mireille's hip bumped against his.

"'Scuze Mireille," he said, then turned to Bert and mouthed, "Get her out of here." Bert shrugged, like how was he supposed to do that?

"I don't care," Marc whispered back.

He placed a hand on his girlfriend's shoulder. "I'll take you home baby."

"I just open my beer. I thought we'll stay at your place. My parents are home," she whined.

"Sorry, Marc needs to work. He needs quiet."

"He comes in here screaming and wants quiet? Marc, Marc, always Marc to say what goes and what stays. You pay rent too, no? Maybe you'd like to fuck *him* instead?" Bert's cheeks went bright red, and he raised his hand. Marc grabbed his wrist. Bert wrenched it back.

"Look, I'm the asshole, Mireille," Marc said. "Just tonight, okay? We have business." She flipped her thick hair and stomped towards the bedroom to get her bag.

"Take the truck," he said, throwing Bert the keys. "But come right back."

The whole Mireille scene had taken the piss out of Marc's anger.

"I don't get it. How could we have missed that? I know they weren't there. Maybe Connie. . .?" Marc paced.

"Do you know what she risked to wander in there with our kid? Jesus, Marc," Marlin said.

"Sorry. You're right. I'm just upset. I don't get where it fucked up."

No one said anything. There was nothing to say. When Bert came back, he bitched about having taken Mireille home since there was nothing to be done. Sarah was quiet.

Declan finally broke the silence. "What's up for tomorrow?"

Marc grabbed his beer off the table then put it down again. "Nothing's fucking up for tomorrow. I'm not ending up on the six o'clock news, balaclava or no, and neither are you guys."

"We can throw it somewhere else, like another Jew place or something. Plenty in the Yellow Pages, I bet. Find a window and pop." Declan raised his arms like he was tossing a basketball, trying to reignite some of the enthusiasm of the past few weeks. He was so proud of the bomb, he'd signed up for an electronics course at Dawson College. He told the guys that maybe he wanted to be a sound engineer or an electrical engineer even.

Sarah had watched him change, hold his head up higher, suck in his gut with purpose, as though he had a paying job.

"Don't be an idiot, this shit takes planning. You have seen us plan, right?" Marc said.

Declan shrunk back. "I was just sayin', you know, we could find something else." His voice fell away and he lit another cigarette.

"I'm going to sleep," Marc said, after they'd circled the failure too many times.

He slammed his chair against the table and didn't look at Sarah as he walked by. The Jew School plan was dead. At least for now. She waited until Marc was asleep before getting into bed.

32

APRIL 1994

Montreal

SARAH DID GET OUT OF MONTREAL FOR a weekend, but not with Luce.

Marc took her to his uncle's cabin in the Eastern Townships. He insisted they both needed the break, which maybe they did. The collapse of the Jewish school plan left him sullen and at loose ends. Because breaks—what other people referred to with anticipation as vacations or getaways—were mostly unfamiliar to Sarah, it was hard to imagine what good it would do.

The lesson learned was keep away from anything that passed for romantic—the tub in the middle of the room where he washed her hair, lying on the couch together reading old *National Geographic* magazines, Emmy Lou Harris and Johnny Cash on the record player, standing outside in the cold night pointing out the constellations, too much scotch and sex. When Marc pulled a twelve pack of candles out of his bag, placed them thoughtfully around and lit them before they got in the bath, Sarah realized she barely knew him. It wasn't love, but it was a facsimile.

The spell was shattered when they were packing up to leave and Marc told her matter-of-factly, that the fat chick with the orange hair and the huge tits at Aryan Fest, Klaudia, was dead. An *accident*. He made quotation marks with his fingers.

"You remember her, right? Seemed like the perfect Nazi Frau." He laughed. "Nope. A fucking spy. For the JDL or the Friends of Simon Weisenthal or something."

Simon Weisenthal? Marc always knew more than he let on. Dumbing it down was apparently a strategy. Seemed Klaudia had been infiltrating too. Another girl who passed, in this case, until she didn't. *Sneaky bitch* had gotten three guys busted in Drayton Valley, Alberta with evidence she'd managed to scam of a plan to blow up Beth Israel Synagogue in Vancouver. The shit was meant to have gone down during some Passover party a couple of weeks earlier. Unlike Robbie Iverton and his blueprints, there was no explaining away the sophisticated bomb in their apartment.

The buzz of too much coffee added to that news was wreaking havoc with her stomach, and Sarah was afraid some kind of terror might be visible on her face. She averted Marc's eyes and busied herself sweeping. Any trace of mice when the uncle next came up might result in them not being invited to use the cabin again. And she wouldn't want that, right? Sarah felt certain she'd never agree to come there again. Marc hummed as he put away the breakfast dishes, light and easy, as though the Klaudia story was some fun gossip he thought she'd like to hear. Or was it a threat. Did he suspect her?

When everything was done, Marc came up and grabbed Sarah from behind, kissing her neck. "Maybe there's time to fuck once more." His voice was playful.

Sarah felt desperate to read *all's well* in his tone. She should agree to sex but she couldn't. "Sorry baby. I really need to get back. I have an essay due, and I can't afford the late penalty." She'd never called him baby. It was such a stupid word for anything other than an actual baby.

"You should quit that university shit. Look, get a *higher* education if you want, but you're always behind. You don't seem to really care. Do you even want to be there? Seems like a fucking waste of money to me."

"Full scholarship," Sarah said weakly. One minute he's a threatening monster, maybe, the next he sounds exactly like Harrison. It was dizzying.

In the car on the way back, Marc's hand on her thigh felt heavy and possessive. Sarah chain smoked and chewed her gum. She knew she wasn't safe, but it wasn't clear where the danger lay.

Luce passed Sarah three bags of espresso beans. They'd been unpacking the delivery for half an hour. *Put that on the shelf over the sink* or *don't try to carry all those at once* was not conversation. It was their first shift together in weeks and only two days since she'd gotten back from her *vacation*. Sarah was completely preoccupied with thoughts of Klaudia. She reached for a box of sugar cubes, trying to catch Luce's eye.

In the rare moments when the café was quiet, Luce usually told stories about the regulars, wanna-be writers, academics, corporate types who dressed like artists, renegade high school students, lefty activists, and joggers who fished damp bills and loose change out of bras. But that day, she was saying nothing.

"What's up?" Sarah finally asked. "I know I haven't called or been around. I've been so busy." It was hollow and stupid-sounding.

"Call, don't call. I don't care. But I am thinking you're dating that Nazi for real." Luce finally looked at her.

"What? No. Are you kidding?"

"Yeah, that's my idea of a joke." She hesitated for a second before going on. "I saw you outside your apartment on Sunday. You were all over each other. Either you're amazing at faking it or you're into him."

Neither. At least not exactly. Sarah knew that what Luce had witnessed was the lone violation of her no kissing in public rule. Kissing was understating it a bit. She remembered them up against the wall. He'd begged to come up and she was trying to make up for insisting he go home. Did Luce just happen to walk by or was she stalking her?

A woman wearing a fur coat and carrying a violin case waved a bangled arm at them and ordered a café au lait.

Sarah started making it. In a lowered voice, she said to Luce, "He's not my boyfriend."

The woman smiled stiffly like she was witnessing some high school confidential she had no time for and pushed a ten dollar bill across the counter. "Change, please. I'm in a rush."

Like Sarah would keep the six bucks. Fucking coffee drinkers.

"No boyfriends, no girlfriends. Maybe it wasn't even you." Luce picked back up after the woman left.

"I didn't say it wasn't me."

"Tell me you weren't into it." Luce hissed. "I'm not hard of seeing, you know."

Sarah tried not to smile. Ironically, that kiss was one of the few times she'd been pretending, or at least exaggerating. But the sex, she wasn't faking. "It's the only way."

Luce rolled her eyes. "Look, I don't really care who you fuck, but I need to know you're not playing both sides."

Get in line, Sarah wanted to say. The number of people she had wrongly assumed had no doubt where her allegiance lay was growing. She leaned against the counter, feeling vomit rise in her throat.

Maybe the tears gave Luce some answer she wanted because she moved towards Sarah looking regretful. "Look, I . . ."

Sarah pulled back. "Here's the deal. It is harder than I thought. And I happen to like the sex. It's a release and it gives me a break from pretending to be like them. But mostly, it's a strategy."

The more Sarah thought about Klaudia, the more she knew she was doing the right thing. She could never know when some horrible plan would emerge, even out of the fumbling train wreck of Marc's little cell. Someone had to look out for it.

"But that day you saw me; we'd been at some cabin for two days and I needed him to leave. That was the way to do it. Jesus, Luce, do I really have to give some sworn affidavit that we're on the same side?"

"Maybe you think we're so close friends that it's not possible I could make this mistake," Luce said softly.

She was right. For normal people, friendship wasn't a set of data that had to be analyzed, calculated, and labelled. Sarah misread the cues.

"I'm sorry," Luce said. "That was a shitty thing to say. We *are* friends. It's just you keep all these secrets. Friends usually trust each other more."

"Sometimes it's easier not to tell you things. You, Ara, Harrison—you get upset. And since this is the plan, at least for now, I don't want to constantly defend myself. I didn't expect it to go this way. But now Marc trusts me, or I think he does."

Luce raised her eyebrows. "You think?"

"It's a long story I can't go into now."

"We worry, that's all. And about this sex you say is just sex. Be careful. Some part of you has to really want it, even if you say it's for the exercise."

Sarah laughed. "Like I ever exercise."

Luce handed her a damp rag. "Can you do the tables?" She seemed to want this conversation to end as well.

"Look," Sarah said. "I only want one thing. To get in the way, to ruin the plans I find out about, even one little thing at a time. Everything else is the means of getting there."

Sarah could only hope that Luce didn't see *their* friendship as a means to Sarah's ends. She thought about how she'd spotted her little anti-fascist pin, then followed her. "We can talk about it more if you want, maybe hang out. Are you busy tomorrow night? You all think I should have more fun." Sarah wasn't sure if she wanted Luce to agree or tell her to fuck off. But the girl didn't hesitate.

"I'm done work at seven. I'm going to a documentary. You'll come. *Grey Gardens*, it's about some strange Kennedy relatives in a decaying mansion."

"Sure. Sounds good." It sounded awful.

"You wanted to hear about my childhood. Now you know." Sarah poured more wine into their coloured glasses, a gift from Ara that he found in a Moroccan shop. Each one had a silver minaret and dome, like the top of a mosque.

Sarah and Luce leaned against the pink couch, legs outstretched, staring out the window. It was easier not facing each other. Luce had on her accidentally pink *Espress yourself* t-shirt and jeans. Sarah was wearing her own uniform; beige cords, brown long-sleeved t-shirt.

She followed the downplayed horror stories (why was she telling her about kneeling on rocks?) with good ones (smaller, harder to find), as though it mattered what Luce thought about her family. Only Grandpa Thomas deserved no mitigating anecdotes.

If Luce was freaked out, she didn't show it, she just nodded and refilled their glasses. Her own stories, poor, Catholic, overcrowded, and homophobic, but not to the point of expulsion, were much lighter.

She wanted to tell her friend about Klaudia. Sarah had gone to the Humanities and Social Sciences library, where she was certain not to run into Harrison, and looked up the story about the Drayton Valley bust in the *Edmonton Journal*. The details were vague—a bomb meant for a synagogue, but no Klaudia or how the police found out. Maybe it was still being investigated. Regardless, there was no way to tell the story that wouldn't make Luce worry even more. Sarah didn't believe Marc was capable of anything like what supposedly happened but she decided not to trust that instinct.

Too many words later, Sarah finally got them off the hard stories by offering up an uninformed but detailed critique of *Grey Gardens*. They were both laughing, and Luce was leaning her head on Sarah's shoulder. Sarah was suddenly aware of how little space there was between them, and that she wanted Luce to kiss her.

Any cogent opposition to that idea couldn't get past the wine-soaked brain/cunt divide to form a successful argument. Luce wasn't making a move, so Sarah did, and she was kissed back. It felt totally different and exactly the same. Of course, she only had two people to compare it with. Curtis, with whom she had kissed for hours, both of them mesmerized by it all, had been as inexperienced as she was. With Marc, everything had this frantic quality, and she did her best to limit the kissing.

"I wanted to do that since you first tripped over me," Luce said quietly.

"We could keep going."

Luce put her hand over Sarah's mouth and Sarah grabbed it gently with her teeth then ran her hand up Luce's leg. Luce stopped her.

"I thought this is what you wanted," Sarah said.

"You're doing this for me?"

"No, I . . ." Sarah wasn't doing it for Luce. But it did feel like somewhere to hide.

"This is what I call unsafe sex," Luce said, straightening up. "Let's just talk."

"Haven't we talked enough?" Sarah's leg started shaking. She pushed her hair behind her ear. "More chips?"

Luce put a hand on her leg. Not to turn her on, just to calm her down. "It's not easy for you, being still?"

Sarah sighed. "It's harder than anything."

The plan to give Professor Pichon some of the material she and Mrs. Broder had gathered, as well as the donation records, felt suddenly risky.

But there she was, having forced herself to leave the apartment, get on the bus and knock on the prof's door, without thinking too far ahead to some unfortunate consequence. She handed over the neatly organized orange file.

Her professor looked confused. "Is this for the final paper? You're never early."

She was grateful for people's optimism, but it often led to disappointment she had to manage. Early April in Montreal wasn't that hot, but Sarah was sweating. "I'm getting close, but I wanted to show you something else, related to what I mentioned last term.

"*The Hoax of the Twentieth Century*?"

"Yes. I might have underplayed things a bit. I've been researching White supremacy for years. I have more material in Goderich, at the public library, but I want you to look at this."

Pichon opened the file and glanced at the papers, her eyes widened. "This is exciting, Sarah. You might have something here. I'll take a closer look, then we can talk about it. Maybe we could collaborate."

Collaboration sounded important, mature, exactly what Mrs. Broder would want. It also described the Vichy Government's relationship with Hitler. The professor seemed too keen. Sarah was barely getting through first year, so what exactly was she dangling? "I have a lot of work to finish, like your essay."

"How about when you're ready, you let me know. Can I keep this?" She held up the folder.

Sarah nodded. It was kind of a relief to give some of it away.

When Sarah got home, she wrote Mrs. Broder a letter. Finally, there was something she *wanted* to tell her. What passed in her world as fantastic.

Dear Mrs. B,

I have exciting news. Or possibly exciting. I brought a bunch of our research in to show Professor Pichon. I didn't give too much detail about my family, but I think she got the point. I also finally found something significant in the piles and piles of donut receipts and other junk I've been sorting through for TCH. Donation records! I gave those to Pichon too.

She only had a chance to glance at everything. Honestly, I think she's a little frustrated that I never come in to see her with completed assignments, only with my own unrelated research, but she seemed really interested. I told her I'll gather more over the summer. I've saved the best for last. She thought maybe we could collaborate on something. I thought you'd love that!!

Looking forward to getting back to what I do so well. Organizing the library!

See you soon.

Xo Sarah

The last few weeks of term were spent in the library or holed up in her apartment with bagels, baloney, and often Ara and his juju magic cheering her on. Harrison helped her structure two papers despite all the reasons not to, mainly that she was a shitty friend.

Astronomy was no problem, a visual essay and an exam. That class never felt like work. Pichon's paper on the Jews of Montreal Post WWII was a slog. She'd actually gotten a decent mark on the one last term that focused on the first wave of European Jews. Political science, sociology, and psych were all exams. Most people hated statistics, but Sarah found the order of bar charts, histograms, dot plots, scatter plots, and box plots comforting.

33

SUMMER 1994

Goderich

SARAH NEEDED THE SUMMER TO BE UNEVENTFUL. It turned out she worried unnecessarily that what hung in the air unsaid would make the days at the library long and uncomfortable. But they were busy and there were other things to talk about. Whatever Mrs. Broder suspected, she kept to herself. Sarah finally decided to trust that Harrison had shared no details. After the third time asking him, he had told her to fuck off, that she was the one who lied for a living. Which was true. When marks came out, she was happy to have passed all her courses with C's and C minuses. Unimpressive, but a pass was a pass.

There was a lot of sleeping in, hanging out at the Pinery, and getting stoned. Blair had a new girlfriend named Cindy whose family went to the United Church. She liked clutching Sarah's arm, calling her *Sis*, then laughing like it was meant to be a joke.

Sarah painted her room bright yellow and went to parties with people she'd barely known in high school. Marc called every week with new ideas, tensions between the guys, stories about the delivery company he was now driving for that had him constantly dropping packages in the wrong places, frustrations, and disappointments with his parents. The fact that he turned to Sarah for emotional support was both misguided and funny. He didn't say it, but she could tell he missed her.

Her grandfather's lapses in memory and other quirks had made Sunday sermons more entertaining and less painful for those listening, but congregants and family finally agreed that it was time he retired. Thankfully his anger over it being his church didn't last long. The new fellow, with his cheerful manner, colourful collection of seersucker summer weight suits and straw hat, was what Ara would call a dandy, and what Grandpa called a faggot, even though he had a wife. The Cartells stopped going to church and that suited them all fine.

Easy and uneventful, the weeks stretched in front of Sarah, until they didn't. And then it was the last Sunday before heading back to Montreal.

"Where's the cabbage? I asked for cabbage?" Grandpa Thomas's comment came out of nowhere. They were almost finished lunch.

"You asked for lamb chops and potatoes, Dad. That's what I made. Don't you like it?" Aunt Jean's voice was gentle.

"I asked for cabbage, Charlene," he yelled.

"Who's Charlene?" Cindy asked. She had started coming to lunch most Sundays.

Keith glared at her.

"I must have misheard you, *Dad*," Jean said loudly. "I'll make it tomorrow."

"I don't want it tomorrow. I need a wife who listens to me, not someone who humiliates me and brings shame on my family. You race traitor cunt. Why did you leave?"

"Dad, I'm Jean, your daughter," she snapped.

"Dad. That's Jeannie." Frank's voice was shaking a little. "We're having a nice lunch. Blair's girlfriend Cindy is here. Sarah's home for the summer. Isn't that nice?" He turned to his sister. "Isn't there cake for dessert?"

Jean looked stunned. "I'll get it." She didn't leave the table.

"We got a new puppy," Cindy chirped.

Grandpa Thomas stood up. "Why do you even talk, Frank?" he yelled. "Charlene can fuck herself. I don't care. But you, you're my greatest disappointment. I showed you the way. Jesus, I practically paved it for you, stuck the tools in your hand, and what do you do, nothing. You're a weak pussy, Frank. It's a wonder you can even throw a dart and hit anything. Can he?" He turned to Blair and Keith. "Hit anything?" His laugh was brutal. "You stand for nothing. Never did. Never will. At least Carl, that prick of an ingrate who never shows his face around here, stands for something. Right, Sarah?"

Suddenly, he could identify everyone.

She said nothing. No one moved. Aside from the time in the old church basement, she'd never heard him swear. She didn't look at her brothers, worried she'd start to laugh out of shock.

Then it was over. Grandpa Thomas sat back down in his

chair. "Alright then. How about cake. Jean, can you bring the cake?"

They ate in silence.

"What kind of a puppy did you get, Cindy?" he asked.

"A shih tzu."

Sarah, Blair, and Keith started laughing and to their surprise, Grandpa joined in.

"Will we all fit?" her aunt asked.

Her grandfather stayed home, but the rest of the family came to drop her at the bus. No one complained about the tight squeeze. They hadn't discussed what happened at Sunday lunch, but Sarah felt they were closer because of it.

"You've still got this year to fuck up," Blair whispered in her ear. His hug was warm.

Sarah punched his arm and laughed. He was kidding, but he was right.

34

OCTOBER 1994

Montreal

SARAH AND MARC HAD BEEN AT IT, whatever *it* was, since she got back from Goderich eight weeks earlier. Life without him had been less complicated for sure.

She tried not to slide back into the habit of too many drunk nights at The Pen with the boys (and now Maddie), but gave in occasionally.

Barely inside her apartment, Marc caught her arm.

"Shut the fucking door," she croaked. He kicked it with his foot while he grabbed her nipple and twisted it. Sarah winced.

"You okay?" he asked.

"Don't stop. It's good, it's good."

He bent down to take the other nipple between his teeth, and she cried out in pain.

"Jesus, Sarah. That didn't sound like the usual *good*."

"Work around the tits. Must be my period coming." He

pushed her onto the bed, shoved his hand down her jeans, and laughed like he always did when he found her wet. Like he'd done a magic trick. He yanked off her pants, flipped her onto her stomach, and pulled her up on her knees. She slammed her ass against him, meeting his hips. When his cock slid out, they both groaned then laughed, frantic and frustrated.

"Maybe there's such a thing as too wet," he whispered grabbing her hips tighter.

"Really?" she asked.

"Actually never." She was drunk but not too drunk to notice that the way he kissed the back of her neck was out of sync with the rough fucking.

Sarah fell asleep before giving the usual order to leave.

It was ten in the morning when she ran to the bathroom and threw up. Marc was standing naked at the fridge gulping orange juice from the carton. He laughed as she dragged herself into the kitchen.

"You didn't leave," she said.

"You didn't ask."

"Did we really drink that much?"

"Oh we did, and you ate about thirty chicken wings." Marc burped. "Gross, I can still taste them."

"Shut up or I'll puke again."

"Coffee?" He was already making some. She'd graduated from instant to drip.

"Do you have to ask?" Sarah pulled off last night's t-shirt and grabbed a clean one from the laundry basket.

Forcing him to leave required too much energy. They lay on either end of the couch, Sarah reading a book for Modern European History, Marc thumbing through *Hoax* and throwing out random comments.

"My dad's got pneumonia and guess who's waiting on him like Florence fucking Nightingale? I don't know what's more pathetic; how depressed she is watching him run in, grab clothes, and leave, or how ecstatic she is when he's sick and lets her fawn all over him. She takes any scraps he throws at her."

Sarah knew that what upset him most was how quickly his mother's allegiance shifted back to her husband, when it was Marc who always showed up, Marc who took her out for Chinese or Lebanese, Marc who fixed the dryer.

At about seven o'clock, he made them mac and cheese and laughed when Sarah drowned it in ketchup.

"Want a few noodles with that? At least you're feeling better."

"It's the only way it's good!" She licked the ketchup off the shallow bowl. She'd never shared the cheese puff recipe with him. They stuck the dishes in the sink and went back to bed.

He leaned over to kiss her breast. "How are the ladies today?"

"Like me, they're not ladies, and they're still sore."

"They look bigger." Marc sounded pleased with the observation.

"Wishful thinking."

"No. They're bigger. I mean really bigger. Not just PMS bigger. I'm a guy. We notice that shit." He stopped smiling. "Jesus Sarah, there's no chance . . .?"

"No chance what?" She glared at him. "Are you kidding? Like I wouldn't know?"

"Isabelle told me that once in high school . . ."

The look she threw shut him up. It was getting dark in the room. Marc went to turn on the lamp.

"Don't. Just leave it," she croaked.

"What about the barfing? Didn't you say you've been barfing a lot?"

Was he still fucking talking? Her mind was racing. How many times had she thrown up lately, once or was it twice in the bathroom at the café? "I barf easy. I always have."

Sarah pulled her legs up to her chest. She couldn't breathe. The idea was so grotesque it hadn't entered her mind.

"You're probably right. You'd know if there was a bun in your oven." He was trying to make her laugh.

Sarah was no longer remotely convinced by her own bullshit. She wouldn't know a thing about her own body. She realized that she'd puked most days in the last week. She put her hands on her breasts. They were swollen and sore. "You need to go."

Marc put his arm around her. "It's okay, baby. We can do this."

Do what? she wondered. "You need to leave." She pushed his arm away, jumped off the bed, and pulled on jeans and a sweatshirt that smelled like smoke. "Please go."

She picked up his backpack and used it to push him toward the door. "I'll call you later." He leaned in to kiss her. She turned and his lips hit her eyebrow.

He shut the door quietly behind him and she locked it.

Once the question was out there, Sarah knew. She was as certain that she was pregnant as she'd been doubtful minutes earlier.

She dug through the pockets of her pea coat for a cigarette and lit it, glancing at the warning on the package as she blew smoke out the kitchen window.

It was cool and drizzly when she ventured out for a pregnancy test, not to confirm what she already knew, but so she'd have the stick to wave, in case the clinic asked. The apartment was unlocked when she got back, which freaked her out. It took half an hour of frantic searching through the boxes in the unused bedroom and closets to convince herself it was *her* mistake, and no one had broken in.

After listening to a message from Marc reassuring her that she wasn't alone, Sarah turned off the volume on the machine. When she checked two days later, he'd left a bunch more messages, and so had Maddie, Luce, Harrison, Carl, and Katie from Berlin.

Why was everyone suddenly calling? Sarah accumulated more people that gave a shit about her than she'd realized. All the baited hooks and lines she'd cast to catch what she thought she needed for some undetermined battle were getting tangled. Demands for attention, for love, for answers. Are we friends? What are you doing? Why aren't you doing this instead? Are you crazy? Agnes Pichon had also called. Sarah was taking her advanced research methodology seminar, a third-year class but the prof let her in. Either she was impressed with the evidence of solid research skills, or she wanted what Sarah had brought back from Goderich. The message said urgent.

A bath. Campbell's tomato soup. Bed.

Monday morning, she called a clinic.

"You'll have to come in for a counselling session, dear. These are emotionally charged decisions." The woman's voice was nasal and high pitched.

Someone else trying to get all intimate with her. "It's Sarah."

"Pardon?"

"My name. It's Sarah, not dear." She walked in a circle trying to unwind the telephone cord. In the middle of conversations she didn't want to be having, she'd hang the phone down and let it twirl. This was one of those calls but unfortunately, she had to listen.

"That's the protocol, Sarah. We can't schedule the procedure until you talk to a counsellor. Nobody's trying to influence you, we just need you to understand your choices and their implications."

There *was* no fucking choice. This being, whose life she could end painlessly now or utterly mangle later, needed to be gone. Keeping it or giving it to someone else was out of the question. DNA was DNA. How had she been so careless?

"Fine. Can I schedule that appointment then?"

"Do you know how far along you are? Have you taken a pregnancy test?"

"I did. Maybe five, maybe eight weeks."

Had they used a condom that first time after she got back? They always did. It was an obsession of hers, no matter how much beer she'd had, she never forgot.

"We'll have to do blood work to be sure."

"Glad I wasted twenty dollars." Sarah laughed. Wrong response. Silence on the other end of the line. "Hello?"

"Can you come next Monday at ten o'clock?"

"Can I come tomorrow? I need this to be done."

A sharp annoyed intake of breath. "You and all the others, Sarah. At the moment, there's nothing open."

"Will you let me know if there's a cancellation?"

"No. But you can call and check. Any time after nine. By then, I should know what the day looks like. Will someone be coming with you? It's good to bring a friend or a partner. For the actual procedure, you'll need someone to get you home."

"Are you kidding? What if I don't have anyone? Then what?"

"No, I'm *not* kidding." The woman continued slowly, like she was explaining to a five-year-old. "If you don't have someone, we'll get a volunteer to accompany you."

"I'll find someone. Thanks. Thanks so much."

"You're welcome, *dear*."

Sarah put down the phone and laughed at the well-deserved dig. She hadn't meant to be such a bitch. The receptionist probably dealt with freakouts every few minutes. She'd be nicer when they met.

There was nothing clean left to wear so she rinsed out underpants each night and put them on the radiator. If they weren't dry, they went on damp. After a few minutes, she stopped noticing.

Sarah told Marc she wasn't pregnant after all but had a wicked yeast infection and felt like crap. She didn't care if he believed her, although the bubbling bread factory description she conjured kept him at bay. She had three papers due but worked on her White supremacy mural instead. Finally. She'd get to the other stuff later.

The floor was covered with notebooks, highlighters, and markers to colour-code people, places, meetings. She taped up the paper she'd bought when she first moved in and started plotting everything with sticky notes and pencil.

She ached vaguely for company.

In the evenings, she sat in the tub for hours adding hot water and drinking rum and coke. She put little stock in the baths and booze spontaneous miscarriage tales, but there was no harm in trying.

She checked an electronic mailing list that Ellie Mae Tucker was on and learned that George Burdi, lead creep from RaHoWa, had been charged with assault for kicking an anti-racist protestor in the face after a concert. Sarah had heard about the march on Parliament Hill, George and his Heritage Front buddy Wolfgang Droege, the confrontation with ARA members, and the fact that the woman he'd kicked was already on the ground.

The night they heard Droege was expelled from Canada's new right wing *Reform Party* for involvement in racist organizations, Luce, Harrison, Ara, and Sarah celebrated. Not that the new party wasn't still crawling with fundamentalists and extremists, but most of them weren't known neo-Nazi drug dealers who'd tried to overthrow a Caribbean island from which to run their trafficking organization. They'd laughed and toasted his downfall with too many shots of tequila.

Sarah sketched out all the possible links, even the most tenuous of connections, identifying networks that might or might not be there. She filled pads with intricate diagrams and detailed notes.

Weaving it together was exciting. The first time she and Luce found a link they'd suspected—a Montreal businessman that showed up in a fathers' rights group, then again in an Aryan Nation letter—they swung each other around in a giddy two-person hora dance. Blowing holes, albeit silent and as yet unproven, in upstanding citizen facades felt important.

If she had to have an abortion buddy, she wanted it to be Luce. Of course, she'd have to tell her she was pregnant, which would lead to questions she'd feel pressured to answer, so she procrastinated.

Sarah called the clinic every day, but there were no cancellations. Abortion was popular. Finally, she left Luce a message.

"Listen, I'm okay. I'm really sorry I haven't gotten back to you. I need a favour. Can you call? Tomorrow's good. Thanks. It's been a rough few days. Please call. Did I already say that? By the way, it's Sarah."

Luce called back drunk at two in the morning. "I guess it's kind of late. Nice message Sarah. What the hell? You were stoned?"

Sarah was too sleepy for a prologue. "I'm pregnant."

Luce exhaled loudly. "Oh Sarah. Really? Fuck."

"And it's Marc's. Will you come to the clinic? They said I need someone. I'd go myself but that's the protocol. I have to do some counselling thing on Monday, then they pick a time for the procedure. The counselling I can do alone no problem, but the actual . . ."

"I can do both." There was silence. "I can come over now, if you want."

The offer almost made her cry. "No. I'm all right. Other than feeling like shit. Can I call you tomorrow?"

"Sure. I'm sorry."

Sarah wouldn't have minded an earful of what she deserved. But kind people rarely gave in to those inclinations, or maybe they didn't have them. Hearing Luce apologize felt fucked up.

"Sarah?"

"I've got to go. I think I'm going to be sick."

"Call tomorrow for sure."

She hung up and stared out the window.

The knock on the door broke her focus. She'd lost track of time and was still in her pajamas. She'd meant to tidy up. Luce was early as usual. No choice but to let her in. The apartment looked like an office supply store had been bombed. But there was an order to the chaos that would be impossible to recreate if she put shit away.

"Holy crap. What happened here?" Luce looked stunned, or maybe revolted. The dirty dishes and overflowing ashtrays didn't help.

"Finally working on the at-a-glance thing. It may not look like it, but I'm making progress. I'll get dressed."

"When did you last wash your hair?"

"I've been taking baths."

"Sarah, the place stinks."

"I'm pregnant. I'm not up for much."

"Looks like you've been doing plenty. Take a shower and wash your hair. *Si non*, I'm not going out with you."

Sarah laughed.

"It's not funny. It's disgusting. Look in the mirror if you want some clues."

From the bathroom, Sarah could hear Luce putting garbage in a bag and piling plates. "Stop cleaning! Leave the dishes! I'm not kidding, it'll piss me off."

If Luce heard, she ignored her.

When she got out of the shower, Luce handed Sarah the least offensive clothes she'd found and shoved the rest in a duffel bag. "We'll do laundry later." She ignored Sarah's protests. "Now breakfast."

"I never eat breakfast."

"Looks like you stopped eating altogether."

They went to a diner around the corner.

"They have good eggs."

"I don't love eggs."

"Scrambled, fried, or poached? Pick."

"Over easy. Broken. With home fries."

Sarah eyed the plates of food heading to tables around them. When her eggs arrived, she went at them with a hunger that caught her by surprise.

The woman with the unmistakable voice who'd called her *dear* was at the front desk. Sarah was glad Luce forced her to wash and dress decently. When the time came, she'd be drugged and vulnerable. Although she knew she didn't want a kid ever, she didn't want someone to take out her ovaries or tie her tubes while they were in the neighbourhood just because the receptionist thought she was terminally unstable.

She was handed a bunch of pamphlets, including one on adoption, then everything was explained. Emphasis on the potential emotional impact. Sarah waved this off. The counsellor ignored her.

"You have no idea how you'll feel."

She didn't ask if Sarah knew or had discussed this with the father. If they had, she'd have answered, *Why yes, he's a charming Nazi.* The abortion was scheduled for Thursday.

At the laundromat, Sarah stared into the dryer. Luce had offered to do the laundry alone, but she was already doing too much.

"Maybe we should drop this off, then buy food."

"I have soup."

Eating was a problem. More stuff rotting in the fridge would only remind her of another thing she couldn't get right. But maybe more saltines. World's least offensive food. She'd been through three boxes in a week.

"You need more than soup. How about lettuce or cucumber?"

"Can't do vegetables right now."

"You liked those eggs."

At the moment, her stomach wasn't entertaining words like *like*. Only tolerance. She and Luce had discussed many times how *tolerance* was never the goal. They both agreed that for now, it was perfect.

"Don't you have to be at work?" Sarah asked.

"Not until five."

"I talked to Marc." She owed Luce at least that much information.

"He knows?"

"Not exactly. But he did identify the telltale signs, like the tits. He said we'd do this together, like he could be a dad or something. I told him it turned out I only had a yeast infection that made me puke and caused my boobs to get big and sore. I doubt he'll look it up." They both laughed.

Luce started folding the clean laundry, but Sarah grabbed it and stuffed it in the bag. "Please don't."

"If we're not getting groceries, I'll head home." Luce looked tired or maybe fed up. "Can you manage the bag?"

Sarah regretted not letting her fold. "I'll call you later." She wanted Luce to hug her but crossed her arms instead. It was too hard.

"I'll see you Thursday. And take a shower before I get there."

Marc had left more messages. He sounded worried. If he suspected, he didn't say anything. She called to tell him she was still feeling awful and promised they'd talk in a few days.

35

OCTOBER 1994

Montreal

IF SARAH HAD BEEN ON TOP OF things like she usually was, she'd have known it was a National Day of Action for the Pro-Life movement.

At the clinic, there was a line of fundamentalist Christians and staunch Catholics to breach. Some were bearing wooden crosses mounted with cardboard cut-outs like the one that landed on Luce—big-eyed baby Jesus figures, bloody fetuses that looked like the mutant offspring of baby seals and diseased gums. Clinic escorts stood at the door waiting. Women often turned up alone when they'd promised to be accompanied.

"Look what we have here," Sarah said too loudly, grinning. What decent human being could smile before committing murder?

"Fuck. Just what you need," Luce whispered.

"Are you kidding? This *is* what I need. If I was feeling even remotely bad, this will take care of it. Let them try to stop me." Sarah had a flash of playing Red Rover as a kid. *Go on*, she thought, *call me over*.

Luce bent her head, raised her middle finger, and moved toward the clinic door, keeping her distance from the sign-wielding life savers. Two women in wool coats and thin cling film rain caps closed in on Sarah. Some fetal divining rod must have pointed them in her direction. Inspiring them through song, the rest of the group belted out a hymn that rhymed forlorn with unborn.

"It's not too late, dear," one crooned. "Jesus will provide."

Her sidekick echoed the refrain in a higher voice. "It's not too late. We can help with your little one."

Someone had propped open the door of the clinic and was gesturing at Sarah to hurry.

"We can find your baby a good home," Christian lady number one said, placing a hand on Sarah's arm.

Sarah pivoted, gripping the woman's wrist tightly in hers. "You picked the wrong girl to fuck with today," she hissed loudly. "Fragile, vulnerable, confused? Bet you were counting on that."

The women in the cellophane hats leapt back and were engulfed by their congregation.

"What's the big plan to help?" Sarah asked. "What will Jesus provide? Because I could use a car, a nice crib, and one more bedroom. If that's not too much to ask. Or should I expect my little darling to have a home with one of you perfect Christians and grow up to hate the right people? God knows how important that is. Just sign us up, because I can tell you are fine folks who invest time and whole hearts guilt tripping us. I'm sure not one of you covets your neighbour's wife, or sucks dick. Well maybe you sir, but that's okay. I won't tell. None of you ladies spends a little too much time with your best girlfriend, do you? Maybe think about that sir, the next time she comes home late looking a little flushed."

The raw rage felt unfamiliar. She was as angry at herself as she was at these athletic Christians out practising the indecent sport of kick-her-when-she's-down. She winked at a man in the group who looked aghast and started coughing. His wife banged him on the back, and he gave her a dirty look. Women whose arms were linked in solidarity inched apart.

"I grew up among you, a God-fearing Christian. *For behold as soon as the voice of thy salutation sounded in my ears, the infant in my womb leaped for joy.* Is that what you might offer up as evidence of my impending transgression?"

The crowd shuffled awkwardly. One man squeaked, "*Behold the inheritance of the Lord are children: the reward, the fruit of the womb.*"

"Psalms 127, nice choice," Sarah threw back at him, grinning like a maniac. "Better go. I'm late for my date with the vacuum." She pumped her fist over her head. "Let's do this!"

Some of the escorts were smiling but the clinic director was unimpressed with the performance.

"This is a medical clinic, not a venue for your guerrilla girl act," she hissed at her.

"World's a stage," Sarah answered.

The woman rolled her eyes, clearly tired of arrogant little shits who thought they invented radical activism. Sarah kind of agreed with her. She already regretted the outburst.

The waiting room was almost empty. A heavy-set teenager, mousy brown hair in a tight ponytail, head in her hands, was perched on the edge of a chair. Someone the girl seemed to barely know passed her a tissue and patted her shoulder—an act of intimacy from which the kid recoiled. Sarah vaguely remembered them scurrying by when she was outside. The girl looked over at Sarah through red, puffy eyes. Sarah smiled with what she hoped looked like support. The girl mouthed "asshole" and turned away.

Sarah dropped into a chair beside Luce, suddenly exhausted. "I'm glad you're here."

"I wish *you* weren't. But I'm glad I caught your act. Wow."

"No idea where that came from. I do behind-the-scenes. Have you ever heard me yell or say anything at a demo?"

"Those people were ready to turn on each other," Luce said. "Forcing them to break ranks is a brilliant strategy."

They both laughed weakly.

"This sucks."

Sarah said nothing for a minute. "It really is fucking horrible."

She barely remembered Luce bringing her home, getting her changed and into bed. What time was it? It was dark. The clock said 2:03 a.m., which didn't seem right. The light over the stove was on in the kitchen.

"Luce!"

Was she supposed to call later or come back? The cramps came in waves. Sarah clutched her abdomen. Luce had brought her a hot water bottle, but it was too much work. The large cotton pad someone must have stuffed in her underpants had shifted. She adjusted it and stumbled to the bathroom. It stung to pee.

Follow-up care specified nothing with synthetic fibres, no wings, no peel-off, stick-on. Luce, always thinking, had left a box of pads, all cotton, on the bathtub ledge. Sarah grabbed at one, knocking the rest into the tub. She held it in place while she searched through the laundry. Hadn't they washed everything? She found a pair of underwear and put them to her nose, then pulled them on anyway. Pins, she'd find pins later. She grabbed a towel to cover the bloody sheet and got back in bed.

6:30 a.m.

In the glow of the clock radio, she could make out the pink instruction pamphlet propped on the table between a glass of orange juice and ibuprofen—one every four hours as necessary. Sarah took two. No tampons, no intercourse—no problem. No douching, who the fuck does that anyway? No baths for one to two weeks, she'd miss that. No strenuous exercise like aerobics or running. As if. No alcohol or marijuana. That's what they always said.

The next time she looked at the clock, it was noon. The towel was bunched up. There was fresh blood. She took a sip of the orange juice and noticed a neatly folded stack of clean sheets on the chair under a note with a groaning stick figure and the words *If you need me, call!!!*

Aside from two more trips to the toilet, Sarah stayed in the mess of her bed for a few more hours. She felt a vague pressure to do something but couldn't think what. At four in the afternoon she finally got up.

It was over. Sarah suspected that empty was the way she was supposed to feel. She took the fresh pads out of the bathtub and gathered the used ones in a plastic bag. She changed the sheets, finished the lukewarm juice, then took a shower and got dressed. Loose pants. Someone had said loose pants. They were all loose these days.

A can of tuna and a bag of bagels were on the counter. Sarah made herself a baloney sandwich forcing her mind past the recent link between food and puking. Each bite required effort. She opened the tuna and put it on the floor for Melrose, who sprinted over like he'd won the kitty lottery.

She stared out the window, letting images of the past days knock randomly: the laundry, the outburst at the clinic, the chicken wings. Sarah pushed them away and a new set took their place: the girl with the ponytail, the bloody pads, cold tomato soup. She reminded herself to chew.

The cat rubbed against her ankle, offering rare thanks. Sarah bent to stroke him and started crying. Maybe empty was the wrong word.

She woke late the next morning to loud banging on the door. She stepped on the bag of used pads, then kicked it aside to let Marc in.

He pushed past her, smelling like beer. "You had an abortion, didn't you?" He expected her to deny it.

She hadn't meant to keep it a secret. "I did."

"Fuck. Fuck you. That was my kid."

"It wasn't a kid. It was a bunch of cells. And what did you expect anyway, that we'd raise a baby together? You live in a pigsty with a bunch of boys, and I'm basically a mess." She gestured around the apartment.

To her surprise, Marc started sobbing. "It wasn't your decision."

She felt confused by his reaction. Should she say something to make him feel better? Explain herself? There was no explanation. "It *was*, actually, and I made the only one I could."

"Without asking. You lied."

"I'm sorry, Marc. I couldn't have this fight with you. And I couldn't have a baby—not to keep, not to give away."

"What about what *I* wanted?"

"To raise a kid by yourself?"

He sighed, resigned, then bent forward and leaned his head against her shoulder. She took his hand.

"I guess sex is out of the question?"

36

NOVEMBER 1994

Montreal

THE ONLY PERSON WHOSE VISIT SARAH HADN'T discouraged was Ara. Luce told him and Harrison about the abortion, but only after the fact. Not that they would have tried to talk her out of it, just that their concern over her wellbeing and shock at the state of the apartment might have cracked her open. With Harrison, even if he didn't ask the questions, they would be there on his face, and it would feel like shit. Not exactly *I told you so*, but close enough.

In that first week, when Sarah was supposedly still an invalid even though she was back at classes, Luce came over whenever she felt like it. No encouragement needed. Sarah stopped resisting the offer to help clean. It was the only thing that would shut her friend up. Ara actually bothered to call first. They joked around on the phone, dark comments about Sarah's solo counter-demo outside the clinic, and how even Christian ladies in cling film caps had their own gangs. Then he passed the phone to Harrison who did the same, all of them knowing it was filler. Only Ara was invited to come by. Well not exactly invited, but she had said *sure, if you want* when he offered.

The place, still messy, was no longer repulsive. Sarah hadn't let Luce touch any of the mural bits. Ara didn't comment or signal any disgust, just went to the kitchen and put the containers of food on the counter.

"Want to eat?" She did. She was starving and tired of sandwiches and cereal on repeat.

Ara's stories about his childhood in Colombo didn't feel like an intentional distraction or a ploy to get Sarah to share hers. But it was and she did. Ara *also* had a funny brother whose attention he craved. As he'd gotten older and more himself, the teasing (that his parents did nothing to stop) became too unbearable. Rather than traipse around after his brother as he'd done for years, Ara took to hiding or *butching* it up to deflect the faggot comments, which didn't work. That brother was now in medical school and engaged to be married. He wrote Ara funny letters about cadavers and organs dropped on the floor of the dissection suite, as though the years of torture hadn't happened. Still, Ara accepted them as a peace offering. Maybe the apology part would come later.

It felt good to listen. People rarely told Sarah their shit because hers was so much worse. Or maybe she didn't seem receptive. But Ara opened himself to her. Not to prove to her that she was worthy, but because he trusted her. In that moment, Sarah understood that not everything that felt like pity, was pity.

"You might think you're fine. But it doesn't mean you are. That abortion doesn't end when the bleeding stops. Has it stopped?" Luce's voice was soft, and Sarah let her squeeze her shoulder. They were at work. Sarah's first shift back.

She was grateful for everything Luce had done to get her through the shit of it, and glad she was no longer coming around all the time. It had been four weeks. She wanted to be done, but the ongoing interrogation about blood and feelings kept it front and centre.

Luce insisted talking about it would help. "It'll come back whether you want it to or not. I know some things about this."

If she expected Sarah to ask about the "some things," it wasn't going to happen. "Look, I'm fine. There's very little bleeding."

"Blood is normal. Even up to five weeks. But after that, maybe get it checked."

Luce sprayed a rag with vinegar water and started wiping the counter.

"I just did that," Sarah said.

"I don't mean to bitch you, but you can't even wipe a table," Luce said. "It's sticky here and there are still crumbs. You do it, then I do it over."

"I guess I deserve to be bitched."

Luce took that as an invitation to go on. "You keep cancelling on Professor Pichon, your essays . . . Harrison says he bugs you to go to the library. And that apartment, I'm afraid to ask."

"So, don't." Sarah held up her hand to stop the rest of what was coming. "You're right about the counter." She dragged her fingers across it. "Not okay. Sorry."

"I'm sorry too. I only want to help. But have it your ways." Something seemed to drop out of Luce's voice. The part that gave a shit.

She wanted Luce around. Sort of. Sometimes. She suspected her friend would soon give up on her.

The café door opened, and Luce hurried over to kiss a woman with asymmetrical jet-black hair, not on the cheeks but on the lips, then threw an arm around her waist and pulled her towards Sarah. "Sarah! This is Françoise. Frankie."

Frankie. Figures. Sarah's smile felt too keen, her mouth stretched too wide. She turned to avoid the bises that she'd figured out the hard way also applied to friends of friends. Only the urge to flee seemed particularly useful.

"My shift's done. Library's calling."

Luce didn't seem to care much what was calling. She was looking at Frankie with a dumb grin.

"Nice to meet you, Sarah. This one has told me so many things about you."

So many things. Great.

Obviously, Sarah wasn't the only one being circumspect. Luce's new unmentioned girlfriend, or whatever she was, felt like a rebalancing of things.

Sarah left the café and caught a bus to McGill hoping not to find Pichon and just leave a note. Unfortunately, the prof was at her desk. Sarah stood outside for a minute, tempted to turn around and head for The Pen to find Marc. Instead, she knocked.

Pichon looked up, surprised. "Sarah. I've been trying to reach you for weeks." She didn't sound angry, just excited.

"Sorry. I've been sick."

Pichon looked like she should be polite and ask about it but didn't bother. "The file you gave me. What you've found may be huge."

Sarah felt relieved they weren't going to discuss anything personal.

"The donations. The one for twenty thousand. I traced the signature to a staffer that works for Bruce Gotteral. Do you know who he is?"

Sarah shook her head no. She'd meant to follow up on that.

"He's a member of the National Assembly of Quebec, a politician. He represents Gatineau." She passed Sarah a flyer. "That's him."

She knew the man immediately, despite the suit. Bruce, no last name, the middle-aged department store catalogue model in the stiff survivalist outfit who looked so out of place at Aryan Fest.

"I know this guy."

Sarah sighed. This meant having to tell Agnes Pichon a lot more than she had planned. But it didn't feel like a choice. She sat down and started talking.

Sarah was excited to tell Ara about Pichon's revelation. He'd come by that evening after she got home from meeting the prof for what was to be their final electronic hide and seek class. But there was nothing more to teach or learn. The student bypassed the master.

Scraps of paper, letters, editorial clippings, articles, and pamphlets, all susceptible to the lightest of breezes and spilled beer, disappeared into the computer. The two of them raised a few glasses to Sarah's brilliantly cryptic hard drive. An indecipherable non-code she hoped no one could break.

Ara joked that if she was ever desperate, she could make quick cash doing corporate espionage gigs or foiling them.

She threw her arms around him, and he laughed surprised.

"I have no idea how I can ever repay you."

"You just did."

Once Marc's gang approved project *technotack*, a combination of the words technology and attack that Declan had come up with, flyers for software and hardware invaded Marc's apartment, outnumbering take-out menus. As predicted, Declan and Bert went from ignorant naysayers to ignorant zealots in no time.

Sarah's mini lectures about computers taking their operation international and transforming them into heroes (not exactly what she'd said) stuck like glue.

Marc had already entrusted whatever information he had to Sarah. At the apartment one night, she pulled another chair over to the desk, ostensibly to show him all the electronic files. He had zero interest in the details. She'd counted on that. Knowing they'd be deeply buried was enough for him.

But the need for his cell to have its own equipment was now uncontestable. Sarah agreed to go through the flyers with Declan and Bert and pick the brand.

Until the day before the break-in, Sarah didn't realize they had no plans to pay for anything. Discounted or not. Why should they have to? Gathering flyers was simply an exercise in exhibiting their commitment to the project. She tried to find out what time and what store. Marc said it was better she not know. They'd made a list that met their only criterion—owned by *pakis*. Anyone brown fit the bill. Sarah felt sick that she'd mentioned Ara's cousin's place.

Wait at the apartment. That was her assignment. They'd be back later to celebrate.

Sarah left most of the mac and cheese she'd made uneaten and laid down on Marc's bed, trying to distract herself with Pichon's essay. The heavy backpack full of library books she carried everywhere was more habit than a guarantee of progress.

She and Marc had barely had sex since everything happened. When they did, the overriding sensation was numbness, onto which Sarah added a thin layer of fabricated enthusiasm. The pain, more from surgical leftovers than anything desired, was dull and uncomfortable. Caution would never again be thrown anywhere near the wind. Marc always managed to get it up, but he seemed distant, maybe even indifferent.

Maddie was with them. That hadn't been the plan. It was a last-minute decision, and Sarah tried to talk Marc out of it. His fucked up logic justified keeping Sarah on the outside while inviting Maddie in.

"She's seventeen. She's not ready for anything like this. I can do it." Sarah was quietly frantic but had no convincing argument to alter what was in motion.

"Exactly. Seventeen. She's a juvenile. She'll handle look-out.

No one will pay attention. Why would I risk something happening to you?"

Rather than thoughtful, the words felt punitive. There was no way to get Maddie out of it. She was a kid, but not a child. She made her own choices. Maybe the abortion was messing with Sarah's head. She felt constantly paranoid, guilty, and worried. Was this what being maternal felt like?

She twirled her pen over her knuckles but it kept falling on the bed leaving dots and lines on the sheets.

The library was her haven now, almost every day for the last two weeks since Luce had said her piece and Françoise had shown up. She arrived when it opened then spread the contents of her backpack across a large table, guaranteeing no company.

Harrison would be proud that she was hunkering down. The spot she'd picked, deep in biophysics, was not one of his haunts. The research was getting unwieldy, the pile of books too large, the scribbled notes and references on the yellow legal pad deep but formless. She started bringing scissors and scotch tape, cutting the pages into strips, and moving them around, trying to create a structure. If it made no sense, she'd peel them apart and stick them somewhere else. The tape tore words away with it.

It was better than being at Rue Rachel where she'd get lost in the chaos of the mural that consumed her from 11:00 when she got home, to 3:00 a.m. Even Marc, who thought the thing was great, commented on the mess.

It wasn't until a tenth student in the crowded, pre-finals library shot her a look for monopolizing an entire table, that

Sarah noticed their expressions of irritation were tinged with repugnance. Maybe fear. The floor around her was covered with yellow slivers of paper and rolled bits of tape. She finally gathered everything up, threw out the shreds, and fled the library.

The sound of a door banging open, loud whispers, and laughter woke Sarah.

"Fucking fuck, man. Holy shit. What do we do now?" It sounded like Marlin. She listened for Maddie.

"Just leave the stuff in the living room and get the fuck out of here," Marc said. "I want the place to myself tonight. I'm pumped. I think I've earned it."

"Shouldn't we hide the stuff? What if someone followed us."

"No one fucking followed us, Declan. Did you see anyone?"

"No, but . . ."

"No but . . ." Marc fake whined. "Go home."

"Is Sarah in there waiting for it?"

Giggles.

"Out."

Marc swept the books off the bed and grabbed Sarah. "Get ready to be fucked by a serious motherfucker."

She was groggy and still half asleep. "Wait. I really don't . . ."

"Sure you do." He put his hand across her mouth and pulled down her pajama bottoms.

Marc was quietly snoring. Sarah pushed his arm off her chest and got out of bed. The living room was filled with computer boxes. Unclear what they were all for. She plugged in the kettle and turned on the radio.

Electronic shop on Ste. Catherine Street robbed. Young man severely beaten. Aravinda da Silva, a Sri Lankan foreign architecture student and gay activist. Life threatening. According to his uncle who owns the shop, the victim was doing pre-Christmas inventory and was surprised by the intruders.

The news, the vomit, bright orange mac and cheese. It all happened at a piercing volume. How was Marc still sleeping? The radio announcer was yelling.

She must have called Luce then gone outside to wait because her friend was suddenly there, pulling Sarah up off the curb.

On the bus, people were staring. Luce's hands were also covered in barf. The seats around them were empty.

Then she was in the shower in her clothes. Sarah looked down at her socks. Luce must have pulled off her boots. Words resumed their attack. Prompts to brush her teeth, attempts to pull off her pants. She sank to the floor of the stall. A guttural sound cut into the high-pierced accusations. Sarah looked around for the animal. Luce turned off the water and covered her in a blanket.

It was unclear how many hours it had been when she woke up in bed screaming for Ara.

37

APRIL 1995

Sunnyside Mental Health Centre

WHATEVER THERAPEUTIC CORNER THEY TURNED, Ara was there, in all his generous graceful beauty, or broken and bruised on a hospital bed. Sarah saw him back in Sri Lanka, separated from love and a life he'd chosen, stuck with his judgmental parents maybe forever, while she sat around discussing her problems and choosing (or not) to eat shitty French toast.

She tried, like Mona suggested, to avoid explanations for what happened that all led to blaming herself, but it felt impossible. It was a waste of time, Mona said, going back over how she insisted on computers or didn't push hard enough to go along the night of the break-in, which might have led to an even greater tragedy. Following that logic, she would have to keep going back; why did she get involved with TCH? Why Aryan Fest? Why hook up with Marc? Why McGill? Where did it all end? Things just happen on the road to doing something worthwhile. That was what Mona kept pushing

Sarah to acknowledge she was doing. Unreasonable at times maybe, but still worthwhile. She tried to hold on to that idea for more than a few minutes at a time.

"You took risks," Mona said. "Some paid off. Some didn't. You chose the same sorts of people you grew up attached to. You broke away from beliefs that you had to pretend you still had."

"My project was based on replicating what I knew best. Otherwise, it wouldn't work."

"Maybe it didn't work because it broke you."

"I wish I was the only one it broke."

The months leading up to the attack, it was like Sarah had been riding a cart that was hurtling forward, piled high with papers and assignments, Klaudia's murder, then the pregnancy.

"After the abortion, or maybe when I found out I was pregnant, it all came apart. I was disorganized. I couldn't finish anything. It's like there was no more order. I need order. Even after it was done, that maternal hormone business was still raging. The way I felt about Maddie, suddenly all mushy and worried."

Mona looked irritated.

"I know things were awful," she said. "But the maternal instinct you're blaming for the chaos might be misplaced. Who are the world's greatest multi-taskers? Who manages jobs, homes, kids, schedules, injuries, food, and a million other things?" She sighed. "I needed to say that. Probably a bit of defensiveness. Sorry. Tell me more about the chaos feeling."

It occurred to Sarah that she knew nothing at all about Mona's personal life. Not that therapists were supposed to share, but she hadn't even bothered to ask. Did Mona have kids? Did she go home and deal with a huge pile of her own crap every day? Sarah suddenly wanted to know things about her. But this many months in, it felt odd to ask.

"What you felt about Maddie; that was guilt, not maternal instinct. She wasn't your child. She was only a couple of years younger. She arrived with her beliefs more or less formed. Mostly, I think you felt guilty about deceiving people who cared about you so much. Like Maddie and even Marc. There was no way to save *him*. But I think you saw yourself in Maddie and thought you could alter her trajectory.

The exciting thing is that you have a chance to change things in the new relationships you're developing. Like with Charlene. Flimsy dress aside, you can let her know exactly who you are. There's no reason not to. I'm not telling you to dump everything on her all at once. But you don't need to pretend."

Sarah told her grandmother bits of what she'd been trying to do in Montreal, details of how it all started with Mrs. Broder. She talked about Curtis. It was unclear if she was making a point about how she and her grandmother were similar, or maybe how they were different. Sometimes she wanted the information to sting. But making Charlene take responsibility felt more and more pointless. When her grandmother seemed despairing, she found herself repeating things Mona said to her about blame and fault that she hadn't realized at the time felt comforting.

"What's your husband like?"

Sarah wasn't sure she needed to know but things were feeling one-sided, and Mona had suggested she show some interest. Had that been a dig at Sarah for never asking Mona anything about herself?

"He's a good man with a big heart. One day you'll meet him. He thought my coming here was a wonderful idea. Maybe he just wanted to get rid of me for a few hours."

"This was his suggestion?"

"Actually, it was Katie's."

"So I guess she knows and he knows and your other kids know." Sarah cringed at the growing numbers. Her worst nightmare.

"She really cares about you."

"I know. Lots of letters and cards from Berlin. Everyone worried about Sarah. And who knew the Cartells were such a chatty bunch?"

"Better late than never maybe. And for what it's worth, Katie was worried before you got here."

Retroactive concern. Was that supposed to make Sarah feel better?

"I tried to protect my children. Thomas was so controlling. The rest of the hate wasn't as overt back then."

"Didn't he tell you about his own father? You must have met him, at least at your wedding."

"No one from the Cartell side came. He told me there was bad blood."

Bad blood. Well, that was accurate. "He always talked to us about his father like he was a star, hanging out with all these White superheroes."

"All I heard was that the man was a bully. It might have been true, but Thomas was likely fishing for sympathy. In the early days, he was on his best behaviour with me and my parents." Charlene shook her head. "I saw it coming. But by then, I was pregnant with Frank. I've gone over every detail of our lives together countless times."

"What about his books? You knew what was in your attic."

"I'm not sure all of it was there yet. I rarely went up, only to shove a box in now and again, and usually I sent one of the kids."

"Well, if there's anything you want to know. I can tell you what happened in every province and most states. I met Carney Nerland once. What a fucking piece of Nazi shit. He murdered Leo Lachance four years ago. The Cree man, in Saskatchewan? Charged with manslaughter, got four years for murder. Probably worth it to him."

Charlene nodded.

"Grandpa used to talk about all those guys. Nerland, Richard Butler, Ernst Zundel, Keegstra, Doug Christie, that slime who defended them all. Every Sunday, we heard the stories. 'Wish I was younger, I'd head out to Alberta right now,' he'd always say, and I always said the same thing back. 'You're not that old Grandpa, you should go.' I meant it with all my heart. Wished he'd disappear into some hole in the wall in rural Alberta, or Ohio, leave us alone, let Jean and my dad have some peace. The only time he came close to happy was when he fantasized about White global domination—always right around the corner. You ended up with two kids who are aspiring neo-Nazis. Although my father hasn't quite earned that distinction, more of a failed hatemonger."

When Sarah had nothing left to say, Charlene started talking like she'd been passed the relay baton.

"The last time I was up in that attic, it was to hide something from Thomas. I haven't thought about that in years. He came home one afternoon, all flushed and excited. He never got that way. Pulled off his shirt and started unbuttoning his pants. In the living room. Can you imagine?"

There was nothing Sarah wanted to imagine less.

"We were alone. Carl and the girls were with friends. Thomas had been out hunting with Frank. 'Come here,' he said and grabbed me, giggling. In all the years we were together, I can't say I'd ever heard that sound come out of him. 'We never have any time, Missy,' he said to me."

Sarah cringed.

"He'd never called me anything but Charlene. Not Char, not dear, and certainly not Missy. I asked where Frank was, and he told me he was working on a cabin and would come in when he was called. I suggested we go to the bedroom. I thought he'd take me right there. Instead, he looked at me, like I was the disappointment he could always count on, and he shoved his pile of dirty clothes at me and told me to wash it well. Seems there was blood on his favourite undershirt. Then he strutted around in his underpants ranting about what kind of man Frank would make if he couldn't shoot straight.

"I asked him what they shot. He said it was a deer, but he forgot to bring a tarp and wasn't about to strap it to the car.

"I don't remember ever seeing him that excited again. I didn't wash anything. Maybe it was payback for humiliating me like that. He was fussy about his clothes. Although they were all the same. The man had six or seven of everything. Pairs of trousers, shirts, undershirts, socks, and briefs. He never suspected. I stuck the stuff in a bag and hid it in the attic. That was the last time I was up there."

Sarah nodded, squeezed her grandmother's hand for a second, then let go.

38

APRIL 19, 1995

Sunnyside Mental Health Centre

THE TABLE WAS COVERED WITH HARLEQUIN ROMANCES, word puzzles, and easy to solve mysteries. Perfect for donating to sad sacs and the mentally questionable. Sarah had volunteered to turn a small meeting room into a "library." Mrs. Broder would be proud of this impressive side hustle. She spent hours categorizing the handful of classics and piles of airport and supermarket checkout books. It was taking shape. If she could only monetize it.

The TV mounted on the wall high in a corner was tuned permanently to CBC. Someone turned it on in the morning and off at the end of the day. The volume always set on low. Sarah was banging a dusty cover against her thigh, inhaling paperback dust, when news of the explosion came on. The entire north face of the nine-story Murrah building in Oklahoma City blown to dust and rubble. April nineteenth, the day before Hitler's birthday—an early present, as it turned out.

She climbed on a chair and turned up the sound. People were already at work. Children were at the daycare when it blew up at 9:02 a.m. It would take weeks to sort the debris and piece together the remains of 168 people, nineteen of them children. And that was only the ones who died; many were brutally injured. Thousands of lives shattered by five thousand pounds of ammonium nitrate fertilizer. Sarah stared at the TV watching the horrific details accumulate.

Before he was caught, the bomber had three hours believing he'd walked away from all those pieces. His triumphant first step in overthrowing the government, like in *The Turner Diaries*.

Those three hours ate away at Sarah.

When she heard his name, *Timothy McVeigh*, the force of it made her vomit. It wasn't until someone came looking for a mystery novel and she heard, "Jesus Christ, stinks like puke," and then, "You okay?" that she even remembered she'd done it.

Timothy McVeigh wasn't exactly a friend of Marc's, but he'd hung out with him at an Aryan Republican Army meeting. Sarah wrote down every name mentioned, never knowing what might matter.

Virgin freak with the right idea was Marc's description. *No cunt to distract him*, he'd said, then, "Sorry, babe," like suddenly the word was too much for her.

Kick ass, fucking new world order, nuclear war heads and *bits of kyke everywhere*. She remembered fragments of Marc's description that back then had a comic book feel. Sarah tried not to think about his reacting to this bombing news—glee, envy.

Those days had been wild ones, Marc told her one night, shaking his head, as though he was looking back at his irresponsible youth from the vantage point of middle age. Sarah heard about The Aryan Republican Army through his regrets that run-ins with the law had made border crossing impossible.

"Shot myself in the fucking foot with reckless B&E's for a few bucks and some booze. I could have been a big deal."

Sarah stumbled back to her room. What had she ever prevented from happening? Marc mostly tripped over his own ego, that's what got in *his* way. Maybe she stopped some asshole with a supposed bomb blueprint from crossing the border, a supremacist academic from making a presentation, some windows from being broken or books burnt at a Jewish school. A politician who liked playing White supremacist in his spare time would no longer get his rocks off. What difference had she made? Ara's life was destroyed. When would the next 168 people be killed? What purpose could she actually serve?

It was mid-afternoon, she was supposed to be in art therapy doodling her way back to health. In no time at all, she'd be missed. Someone was always looking.

39

APRIL 21, 1995

Toronto Western Hospital

PSYCH WARD. SARAH FIGURED OUT WHERE SHE was in the moments after she came to, or woke up. It wasn't clear which. Two nurses were talking quietly.

"Why Western? Why not Sinai?"

"I don't know. Damn paramedics, rush, rush, rush."

"My boyfriend's a paramedic. You think they pick the hospital? They don't."

"Right, sorry."

"She looks sixteen."

"Says twenty on the chart. Kid's a stick, I could use a few weeks on her diet."

"Maybe try Jenny Craig. Why's she here?'

"Suicide attempt. Supposedly at risk for another try," she said, an edge of sarcasm in her voice. "Sometimes it's better if they just move along to the happy place."

"Why do you work in psych? You can't stand these people."

The comments made Sarah laugh inside. At least it must have been inside since thankfully no one looked over.

"What are you talking about? I think she's perfectly lovely. You know me, I tell it like it is."

"No one wants to hear it. Anyway, she's a nice break. Quiet and respectful."

"Wait until she wakes up before you say that."

"If she wakes up."

Jump out of bed and join the party, was what Sarah wanted to do. She loved this nurse and was tempted to call out, "I'm awake! Say something else!"

But she stayed silent, and coma-like.

She hadn't stopped taking Zoloft once a day with the intention of swallowing them all in one go. She'd been looking for the sharpness that eluded her for the last two months and she set aside the pills in case she needed them again.

It was Becky who put the idea of recapturing acuity in her head, mostly by describing how great it felt to let it go, to give up the headaches that over-thinking decisions brought on. But a drug-induced vacation didn't work for everyone. It left Sarah discombobulated and eager to return to something sharper.

She'd expected Mona to notice the difference between her drugged and undrugged self. But she had only known Sarah a short time and might have read the return of her clear head as an adjustment to medication and life at Sunnyside.

After a few days, no one watched closely enough to make sure she swallowed. In retrospect, keeping the pills might have been a sign, but if she was building an escape route, it was subliminal.

Taking them all at once wasn't an idea or a plan. It was more like a blackout with no warning it was on the way. Not that Sarah had been working with an active desire to stick around. Did anyone regularly confirm the choice to stay alive?

Every day, she opened the drawer and tucked the pill in a sock. Maybe she'd sell them on the street or offer them to needy fuck-ups who lived off the grid with no access to prescription meds. She bypassed the growing stash daily on her way to underpants.

To the toilet to puke again was the direction her conscious brain sent her. But all those broken bodies among the toys and blown bits of concrete and rebar exerted their own pull.

Had she thought it through, she might have taken her handful of drugs to a supply cupboard, not washed them down in her room where someone was sure to come looking. But there had been no thinking at all, just reaching for the oblivion one pill at a time couldn't offer. If she'd known her actions might be construed as a cry for help, the mortification of that alone would have stopped her. But in that reactive, robotic moment when she reached into the sock, none of this crossed Sarah's mind.

The note was an afterthought. *Give my boxes to Professor Agnes Pichon. She'll know what to do. Give the last version of the mural to Katie to make something out of. Destroy the rest.* Not an explanation, but a will of sorts to address the fear that some cop who moonlighted with the Heritage Front would be given the task of sorting through it.

Scraps of overheard conversation amongst the nurses and an intern suggested she'd been out for a while. Whether it was hours or days was unclear.

She would have asked but she wasn't up for the chaos that might ensue, people rushing in poking and yelling at her like she was deaf. She'd watched it happen to the person in the next bed. The question could wait. Sarah fell back asleep.

Cartons of juice, containers of pudding, and an oatmeal cookie lined the table across the bed. Someone was holding her hand.

She squeezed. Mona jumped.

"Sarah?" She squeezed back too hard. "You're conscious."

"Conscious is a big word." They both laughed.

"I thought you might die." Mona's hair was wild, her eyes baggy. She rubbed Sarah's hand. "I'm sorry. I'm so sorry."

"For what?" Sarah reached for the oatmeal cookie. She was starving.

"I didn't see the signs."

"I don't think there were any."

Sarah looked around the room. Two empty beds and flowers in ugly vases on the windowsill.

"What day is it?"

"Thursday. You've been here since Tuesday."

"You couldn't have anticipated Timothy McVeigh," Sarah said.

"I figured if you'd survived what happened to Ara."

"Maybe survive is too strong a word," Sarah said.

"Who's the therapist here?"

"Definitely you. You won't catch me trying to sort people's shit." She took a sip of juice. "Who knows I'm here?"

"Your dad and Charlene. The whole family I think."

"Fuck. It would have been easier if it had worked."

"Easier for you, maybe. A disaster for me and a lot of others."

"A lot? That's kind."

"I like the idea of having you around," Mona reached for Sarah's hand again.

Sarah let her hold it. "So, I get my own apartment at Sunnyside?"

"In the world, I meant."

"Hasn't this happened on your watch before? You must have some experience."

"It has, but this time I was blindsided."

"Sorry about that."

"Was it planned?" Mona asked, clearly worried about the answer.

"Not that I knew of. It just seemed a waste to throw them out, so I kept them. I guess I accumulated quite a stash."

"If Becky had found them, she would have ratted you out."

"Fuck. Becky. I didn't even think about her. Like she doesn't have enough stress without finding me dead in our room."

"She didn't find you. But she knows what happened."

Sarah sighed. "What now? Back to the orange drawing board?" She sort of hoped so.

"I have no plans to kick you out. But I might change the colour."

"No. I love the orange."

"You'll also find security a lot tighter. You tried to kill yourself. Trust needs to be built back up before you can head out into the world with your mural and boxes."

"If I knew I built that much trust, I would have thought twice before squandering it. Did anyone else come to see me?"

"Your dad. Jean. And Blair was here too for a little while. The nurse told me he didn't know what to do. She told him he could hold your hand."

Sarah laughed at the idea of her brother awkwardly trying to do something to make her feel better. Visitors while she was sleeping or comatose seemed easier. "Figures he comes when I'm totally out of it."

"Maybe he'll come back when he knows you're awake. Or visit you at Sunnyside?"

"Were you here when my dad came? Did you talk to him?"

"Only on the phone. He's angry, asked what the hell's wrong with you and why we haven't fixed it yet. I couldn't explain in two minutes. *It takes time* seemed to piss him off even more. He thought you were getting better and I told him you were. He laughed at me. 'This what you call better?'"

Since she'd brought up the topic, this seemed as good a time as any to ask Mona about *better*. But she felt too tired.

Sarah put on the clothes Mona brought her and went out to the front of the hospital to bum a cigarette. The woman in the next bed who smelled of smoke didn't actually have any—not allowed, she said—and told her that's how it was done. Sneak past the nursing desk and then ask nicely once outside. A man in a wheelchair hooked up to an IV was happy to oblige in exchange for a quick chat, thankfully about their cats. Standing in the cool night, inhaling nicotine and the not quite fresh air of Dundas Street, Sarah realized this was the first time in months she'd been free. Just a walk, she thought. The next day, she'd be back at Sunnyside. It would do her good to wander a little. She headed east then just kept going, happy not to be walking in a circle.

She knew of only one bar in Toronto. The Tulip, a lesbian bar on Parliament Street Luce had mentioned. Dundas went all the way to Parliament. Once there, she asked someone who looked like she might know. At the entrance, she hesitated a minute. On the plus side, her pants had no drawstring, so she looked moderately un-institutional. On the minus side, she had no money for beer. A glass of water before heading back would be good.

Her feet were sore, so she sat on a stool against a wall. A tall girl with brown hair in a loose ponytail asked if she could buy her a drink.

"You are over nineteen, right?" the woman asked as she handed Sarah a pint of draft.

"I can show you some ID." She actually couldn't.

The bar was too loud for anything but choppy conversation. The girl had an easy grin and seemed comfortable saying little. They yelled basic information in each other's ears. Ellen was an environmental studies major from Saskatoon who had a car and lived pretty close to Bathurst and Dundas, where Sarah said she lived. She told her she had just moved back from Montreal and was looking for work. Library sciences.

One and a half pints did the job of three. By that point, the only thing that made sense was going home with the girl.

In bed, Sarah was focusing on an orgasm but too many things got in the way. Emotions fragmented, reconstituted, then fragmented again like mercury. The girl redoubled her efforts, tongue testing speed and pressure.

Lying with her head tipped off the edge of the bed, Sarah caught the world outside the bedroom window in some upside-down version of itself. She remembered the times in her dad's station wagon, seduced by his big laugh, and readjusted her position. She thought about kissing Luce then shoved Marc away and tried getting back to where Ellen—was that the girl's name?—was still working diligently.

"Stop, stop," Sarah finally said, touching her head. "I think I need a break, I'm getting a little numb down there."

"Sorry, sure, sure. Just tell me what you like." The girl looked embarrassed, but eager. Not one to quit with the job half-done. Sarah had no idea what she might like. Why she had assumed casual sex would be a useful distraction suddenly struck her as funny. Ellen looked up, unsure whether to take the laugh as encouragement.

Since there was no losing herself in this, she needed to wrap it up. It was the opposite of a distraction. Her failure to come would invite a far more intimate interaction. Sarah actually felt the opposite of numb. Too many nerve endings standing at attention, too many diffuse reactions collapsing in on each other.

"Do you want something? A drink? Some tea? Are you cold?"

The second it occurred to her that she couldn't fend off the comfort being offered, Sarah made an excuse and got dressed.

Ellen offered to drive her. *Do you know where Toronto Western Psych Ward is?* Sarah said she'd prefer to walk.

It was three in the morning. The police officer at the nursing station followed her into her room.

"You were waiting for me?" Was she really worth this expenditure of public funds?

"Where were you?"

"Is it illegal to go out? You going to arrest me or something? I was getting laid. Unsuccessfully. Not that it's any of your business." Sarah smiled widely. That shut him up. She put an end to their meeting by dropping her pants and grabbing for pajama bottoms before he could turn away.

Once he was gone, she lay awake thinking about her performance outside the abortion clinic, and how she'd just talked to the cop. Seemed all she needed was an opportunity to shine.

40

APRIL 24, 1995

Sunnyside Mental Health Centre

"NOT A GREAT START." MONA DIDN'T LOOK AMUSED.

Sarah wondered exactly what it was she was starting. Her life over, maybe?

"That was stupid and dangerous. What were you even looking for? Or were you just showing off?"

A dyke bar seemed safe compared to so many other choices she could have made. But she did feel stupid. Mona was probably right, the little break out was simply to show she could do it, not to actually have fun. It wasn't fun. The best part had been the walking.

"I just needed to get out. I haven't done anything for months."

"And how did that go? I'm not a prude who thinks casual sex is immoral. If it was great, great. But I'm guessing it wasn't so good."

"I tried for good, although not nearly as hard as the other

girl did." Sarah groaned and dropped her head into her hands. "I'm an asshole."

"You certainly are the opposite of a party girl. When did you last have a good time, or just lose yourself Sarah?"

Never, was the first word that came to mind. That was an exaggeration. Fucking Marc, maybe. There were times with Harrison, Luce, Mrs. Broder, Curtis, her dad, even Mona. Nothing sustained, more intermittent. Just flashes that poked through the overall not fun-ness of things. She didn't want to ask for a definition. Clearly the therapist already knew how little there'd been. That's why she asked. Sarah always assumed that some people just didn't have a lot of fun, and that was fine.

In the office on the leatherette chair, five times a week now instead of three, it barely felt like Sarah had been away, or that anything had changed. Pills left no scars.

That she'd jumped off the ledge so flippantly seemed in retrospect an embarrassing cheater's escape. Mona stacked up the justifications to explain why the Oklahoma City bombing had broken her—the pain and conflict seeded in early childhood, the culpability of betraying her family, the guilt of believing even childishly in the doctrine of White supremacy, friendships with bad guys, Ara's attack. It all added up.

The revised belief that she'd been teetering on the edge, waiting, hoping, for some event to send her over, was even worse than being stupid or complicit.

The failed attempt scared the shit out of Sarah, not because it didn't work, but because she didn't see it coming, which meant the self-control she relied on to guide her choices might be an illusion. The pregnancy, what happened to Ara, they'd derailed her, but she'd recovered her footing. This attempt at an ending was different.

Mona needed it to be the last straw or the nail. She needed to believe that Sarah's life was predictably a camel or a coffin. She was wrong. But there was no proving it. All roads led to that pile of pills. Maybe not inevitably, but with only retrospect as a forensic tool and Mona doing the science, the conclusion was forgone. And then there were the looks she got. Goderich-style pity was nothing compared to this. Even Simon had stopped threatening murder and adopted the sympathetic head tilt. The wackiest of her co-crazies gave her a wide berth in the yard and cafeteria, like suicide was contagious. In her first couple of months there, she tried so hard to be left alone. Now alone felt bad.

Becky was the only one who wasn't different. She grinned with relief when Sarah walked into their room.

"You motherfucker. Were you trying to recreate the produce section for me? Which option to save your life would you have had me choose? I was not about to stick my fingers down your throat."

She would have kissed Becky, except she wouldn't. Lesson learned. And anything too out of character might freak her out. Thank God they'd put her back in her old room.

41

MAY 1995

Sunnyside Mental Health Centre

IT WAS RAINING SO THEY SAT IN THE LIBRARY. No smoking permitted. Sarah's feet added percussion to their conversation. She fiddled with a pencil. Charlene didn't seem bothered.

"Thank you for letting me come again."

Sarah smiled at the game of make believe. Which stress toy to fiddle with in Mona's office? Cereal or oatmeal? A second cigarette? Those were more accurate examples of free will these days. Allowing her grandmother to visit was a requisite demonstration of improved health.

"You really scared us."

Sarah opened her mouth to comment about *us* and *our* newfound concerns and fears but changed her mind.

It had only been a week. She was still tired and inclined to pick her battles. The family wagons seemed to be circling, and snarky comments felt like an effort not worth making. Instead, she apologized for causing so much distress.

"No need for that," Charlene said. She must have had some idea how uncomfortable her tears would make Sarah, because she looked away.

"I suppose it's all a bit much for you. It certainly is for me. Since I've been coming to visit, memories keep ambushing me."

"Try being here for months. Pretty much all we do is memories."

For a moment, Charlene seemed to be considering whether to go on. "I was too spirited for Thomas, too gregarious. My mother had an inkling about him. Perhaps more than an inkling, a spidey sense. She thought his way of laughing in sudden spurts rang false, that his touch was more possession than affection. She said he had no people, no one to vouch for him, and that was suspicious. I told her she was being un-Christian.

"Once after services, I was telling a joke, my hands were flying. He walked up behind me and squeezed my shoulder in what my friends would have seen as a husbandly gesture of affection. I didn't turn around but felt his grip tighten. My hands dropped. 'Go on. Do finish the story, Charlene.' I might have mumbled the punchline. At home, he told me that waving my hands was unladylike, and even worse, ethnic.

"Sometimes a tree grows around metal or concrete, contorts itself into something misshapen but still alive. I didn't lose myself entirely, but I bent to fit around him and avoid him at the same time. Why had he wanted me when there were plenty of pliant girls to choose from? Turns out a penchant for crushing the human spirit or breaking will were the things that brought him . . . I wouldn't call it pleasure, but certainly satisfaction."

Sarah nodded. The layers of her grandfather's abhorrent behaviour kept getting thicker.

"I found my rhythm. When I was home with the kids or with friends, I almost felt happy. Thomas paid his children little attention until they were upright and talking. Ready to be schooled. The house was mostly a woman's domain and that suited me. The kids and I listened to music, danced to Jeanie's choreography, banged on pots, made up silly rhymes.

"Self-expression through art or affection, Thomas believed, would lead to lax values and soft sons. He commented harshly on signs of individuality in the girls, or effeminate behaviour in the boys. When they jumped into my lap for a hug, Thomas ridiculed their *sissy kissy* behaviour. God knows by six they should have been ready for military school.

"When Katie was nine, he tore up a painting she'd made him. No appetite for abstraction. With Jean, it was dancing with a silk scarf in the backyard that set him off. What purpose could that possibly serve? What did she have left to show for herself when the music ended? They were on the road to damnation. With Carl, Frank, and Jeanie, creativity and independence were suffocated. Fear requires little air to flourish.

"For his next birthday, Katie spent weeks painting a still life with flowers and fruit. He unwrapped the brown paper so carefully. He studied the gift, and all he said was *much better*. I have no idea what happened to that painting. I hated it. But the brown paper was cut into six even squares and used to wrap his sandwiches."

Sarah rolled the pencil on the table. It sickened her that she'd ever tried to please the man who lacked even a speck of humanity. His own children had grown up starved for the affection he was incapable of giving. Sarah realized how much her grandmother still suffered. Every accusation she'd wanted to hurl at Charlene, the woman had already hurled at herself.

"I've seen Katie's art," Sarah said. "At a gallery near the café where I worked. I don't understand it, but my artist friend Luce says it's really good."

Charlene nodded. Sarah didn't ask if she'd been at the opening. She didn't want to know.

"How did you leave Goderich?" She knew how it ended. But Charlene had her own story and needed to tell it. Sarah was ready to listen.

"The kids were all in school by then. Thomas didn't want me working, so I got more involved at church. We sponsored a family from the Congo and their integration became my business. Christian charity. Thomas hated Negroes but couldn't say that out loud."

"After you left, he said it all the time."

Charlene grunted.

"They arrived. Bunmi, Taj, their two children, and Bunmi's older brother Diallo, a teacher whose wife and child had been killed by government soldiers. When I think of what they tolerated in Goderich with no outward sign of discouragement. They made a lovely home out of a pile of furniture no one wanted. All of us Christians puffed up with the righteousness of our deeds. We gave them new names—Bunny, Tobias, and Darryl.

"The generosity was always theirs. Grace in the face of bumbling paternalism. Bunmi later told me how they laughed and yelled those made-up names from room to room. *Bunny honey, have we run out of cereal?* Their home was well stocked with all kinds of cereal. Someone at church had a cousin who worked for a big brand.

"People treated them with polite indifference—the work of God now complete—but a small group of us became friends. I was there at least twice a week drinking strong coffee in their kitchen. I loved our conversations and the sound of their voices. It was like music."

Sarah remembered lying in the park with Curtis while he told her funny stories about everyday life with his family—glimpses into an alternate universe she tried not to envy and saw no point wishing for. Maybe his leaving had been a bit of a relief. Then she thought about walking through Montreal at night, glancing into windows to catch families being families. Her grandmother had also managed separate lives, struggling to keep the pieces from falling into each other. They both paid a price. But Charlene never blamed emotions for the trouble, and in the end, despite having suffered, she had not been broken. The story she was telling now felt so different to Sarah than the one she believed she knew.

"Thomas asked me constantly whether the Africans weren't yet able to stand on their own feet without my meddling. *Give them a fishing rod, for Christ's sake.* Or a plane ticket back. When I realized I was falling in love with Diallo, I was sick about it. It was like nothing I'd ever felt. I stopped going by their house without explanation, thinking the feelings would simply go away. A doctor diagnosed me with depression and prescribed pills I never took. The apology I owed for disappearing weighed heavily. I finally went to see Bunmi. Warm smile and open arms. That was the greeting. I'd expected a door closed in my face, not the reception one gives a dear friend."

"I know that feeling well," Sarah said. "Sometimes when I didn't get the right angry response to my bad behaviour, I got even more irritated. Like, you're not playing your part. Luce and Mrs. Broder always gave me the benefit of the doubt or cut me slack. And Ara, he was my polar opposite. He knew nothing about my kind of self-protection and so much about giving without expectation. I'm sure you're much more like them than like me."

"I wouldn't be so sure," her grandmother said. "I have my moments."

"So you told Bunmi?"

"Yup. Spilled the beans. Then asked her not to tell Diallo. She said she'd wait a week, but insisted I owed him the truth, even if it meant not seeing him again. Turns out he felt the same way I did. Four weeks later, we left Goderich. Was it the wrong thing to do? Absolutely. Was it the only thing I could do? It was. Bunmi and Taj were appalled. They didn't talk to either of us until months after Yannick was born. We were completely isolated. We had regrets, but there was no going back. The damage was done."

Sarah and Charlene sat silent.

"It's a story, not a rationale. I wouldn't blame you if you didn't care, but I would have died if I stayed. It's that simple."

"You left your kids," Sarah said.

"I did. I realize looking back that my plan to get them out was absurd and unworkable. I couldn't see it then. Diallo and I had no money. I borrowed from my parents, who didn't have much either, to buy tickets and mattresses. What happened, happened. I don't blame Frank. Even if he hadn't told Thomas and they all arrived, it wouldn't have gone the way I dreamt it would. But that day, I waited at Union Station for hours watching trains empty of people. I couldn't bring myself to go home.

"I had no other plan. Having them live with us was as far as I'd gotten. I was already pregnant. How could I not have thought about the upheaval, about leaving everything they'd known and moving to some dingy flat in Toronto. Diallo suggested we wait until we had more to offer. I screamed at him for being selfish, that he should understand, that he'd lost a child. It was horrible. I was horrible.

"I threw all my anger at him, as though the mere suggestion of delaying their arrival had caused the plan to implode. I cried until there was no sodium left in my body and fainted at the corner store. It's a wonder I didn't lose the baby."

Charlene looked at her granddaughter. "As I said, I have my moments."

It wasn't the story that made Sarah cry. Although it was hard to hear, it was relief. She hadn't realized how terrified she was of being like her grandfather, unable or perhaps just too well practised at feeling nothing. But she wasn't like him, and she was finally figuring that out.

She leaned over and put her arms around her grandmother. Charlene exhaled surprise then hugged her back.

42

MAY 1995

Sunnyside Mental Health Centre

"DO YOU LIKE ME, MONA?"

Sarah felt like she hadn't regained solid ground since *the pills*, which was how she referred to what happened. *Suicide attempt* seemed too considered. Or maybe solid ground had never been there at all, which was worse. She cycled through past relationships, caring suddenly how much or whether she mattered. Since when had she needed this kind of certainty?

"Of course I do." Mona smiled the wrong kind of smile.

"Why did you say *of course*?"

"Because I do. Isn't it obvious?"

"Are you obligated to like all your patients? Do you have patients you don't like?" Sarah didn't want to beg but she couldn't help herself.

"Sure. Some I like more, some less."

"Would you tell them if you didn't like them?"

"No."

"Would you tell me if you didn't like me?"

"No. But I do. Does it feel like I like you?" Mona asked.

"I guess." Having given being liked so little thought unless it was calculated, as it had been for so long, Sarah wasn't sure she'd recognize it. "I don't trust my gut anymore."

Mona laughed. "I wouldn't trust your gut either. It's a muscle you haven't flexed all that much, so it's probably not very reliable. But pay it a little attention and it will be. Do you ask everyone if they like you?"

That was a dumb question. "No."

"Then why are you asking me?"

"Because it's important. I want to know if we're friends."

"That's a different thing."

"You're saying you like me, but we're not friends?"

"I'm your therapist, Sarah. I don't think about our relationship any other way."

"Well, I do. A lot lately. I think about how relationships are fucked because they're always imbalanced. Someone always wants more. Someone always gets less." Sarah had usually seen herself on the wanting less end of that scale. But lately, she was starting to revise the calculation.

"Most relationships are imbalanced, to some degree."

"Can't you stop being a therapist for one minute?" Sometimes she wanted to shake Mona. But she'd probably get that twinkle in her eyes. *Made you care. See, you're getting better all the time.* If this was what better felt like, there was a lot more pain coming her way.

"I guess I can't."

"Do you have children?" Sarah finally asked the question.

Mona smiled. "I do. I have three. One still lives at home with me. He's in high school. One of them is working. My daughter is at university."

"At McGill?"

"Not at McGill, and that's all I'll say. Therapists can get into trouble offering up personal information, as tempting or relevant as it might be."

Sarah knew Mona had used the word relevant intentionally.

"You mean you would, but you can't."

"There are boundaries. What's this all about Sarah?"

"I don't want to leave."

"Who's asking you to?"

"*You.* I don't want to leave you. I guess eventually I'll leave here."

"I hope so," Mona picked up her pencil and held it like a cigarette. She hadn't done that in a while.

"And then what?" Sarah asked.

"What do you mean then what?"

"What happens to us? To our relationship?"

"When . . ." Mona picked her words carefully. "When you're ready to leave, we'll have done what we need to do together. That's the point of you being here." Her voice was soft and comforting, which made what she was saying so much worse.

Sarah put her feet up against the table and started crying. Mona sat forward and reached out her arm.

"Don't," Sarah said. "I've never been big on touching. You wouldn't do me any favours by changing that now."

Mona leaned back in her chair. "Sarah, I . . ."

"It's just a fucking job. When I walk out of here for good, you'll put my file away in the done-drawer and close it. I bet you'd be happy if I left right now."

That last bit was childish. What did she expect Mona to say? They were both stuck in their places.

"I'm sorry you're so upset."

"I wish you were more upset."

Sarah looked down at her hands, suddenly embarrassed.

"Sometimes when I sit across from someone, talking, I can see where their path will likely lead," Mona said. "It's clear. This person will always need care or medication, never live alone. This one won't leave here. This one will be just fine. I'm usually right. But there's no science to it, no obvious route to healthy or better. You're at a crossroad, Sarah. You have to pick a new direction, figure out what *you* want."

"Or I could just hang out at the crossroad." Sarah laughed.

"Not for too long. Staying where you've always been won't work."

"You made sure of that Mona."

"We did that together. Look, you're strong. You're resilient. You had to be, to pull off what you've pulled off. Maybe leaving the White supremacy behind and applying your research skills elsewhere, at least for a while, would do you good. I know there's work you need to finish. I'm not suggesting a complete 180, like becoming a physiotherapist or a plumber. But a redirect."

Sarah groaned. Everyone was a little too invested in her strength. Carl, Mona, Katie. Maybe it made it easier for them. Less to worry about.

"I'm also an avoider, as you've pointed out. And I did just try to kill myself."

"But you don't avoid everything. You've been digging up all the buried history for months."

"I wasn't given a choice."

"Really? I'd argue that's how you need to see it because choosing to reveal yourself makes you feel weak. But pushy as I am, I don't force you to talk." Mona fiddled with her glasses. "Let me ask you something, Sarah. Is choice what you want most? Because what I want for you above all else is hope. Not this purgatory you seem stuck in where you're doing penance for wrongdoings that are not yours to atone for. You keep fighting for change. Where do you belong once you're off the battlefield? The ability to envision yourself in a better place, that's where living begins."

43

MAY 1995

Sunnyside Mental Health Centre

SARAH'S WAKING HOURS WERE INCREASINGLY spent panicking that the more she divulged, the more Mona might define her as better. The whole story would be out, and she'd have nothing left except a bunch of boxes.

She could move into a storage unit and someone might find her and make a documentary. It could be the new *Grey Gardens*. *Beige Gardens.* They'd give her money for an opening night outfit and people would ask stupid questions and tell her she was brave. Mona would be interviewed, and she'd pretend she wanted to protect Sarah's anonymity but ultimately share her story to help others. And Sarah could turn down generous offers to organize a few personal archives for rich people, then fade back into oblivion.

How many times over the months had Sarah arrived in Mona's office determined to make small talk and divulge nothing? Now she was spewing on a regular basis. She had yet to feel any better despite the crap-load of stories she'd dumped at Mona's feet. Unlike barfing when you've had too much to drink, once you've gotten your story out, it's still in. Catharsis was a flawed concept.

Sarah thought about Gita Lieberman, the Holocaust survivor she'd gone to hear with Mrs. Broder. Not that Sarah's own story was comparable in even the tiniest way. Only that the idea of telling a story to be free of its burden seemed impossible. Maybe she'd missed the point.

"Can we talk about what happened the night of Ara's attack?" Mona said it softly, as if that might make it easier.

Sarah had been expecting it, which made it worse, like bracing herself for a loud noise or freezing cold water dumped on her head. She wanted to shock Mona.

"Crazy fucking sex. That's what happened. Slam me down, fuck me before you even know or care if I'm wet. Hard and cold. No 'Hi sweetie, I'm home from the computer heist.' No words, no warmth. And if you're thinking 'Oh my God, he's a rapist too, how awful,' he didn't get there on his own. That was our thing. That's the way we did it. I broke him of the inclination for tenderness, detached it from the sex. At least I tried to. He didn't know he'd like it, but guess what? I barely remember the next morning. Just the radio. Puking on the bus. No idea how I managed to call Luce and get out of that apartment."

"Did he try to find you when he woke up? What did you say?" Mona seemed to think these were useful questions. What answers would they provide? Who cared if he tried, if it was out of embarrassment, a need to control, or something

Mona liked to call love? Where Marc was concerned, those things were indistinguishable.

The line of inquiry she faced in her chair at Sunnyside—the never-ending *so what happened next*-ness of a process that was meant to make her better—was exhausting. In the end, there was always Mona. Waiting for an answer.

"I didn't talk to him. Luce answered my phone. That pissed Marc off. She said she was my neighbour. Didn't he think it was odd that I'd never mentioned one? He said he was worried, that he woke up to vomit everywhere, and me gone. Luce told him I had stomach flu and had been barfing for hours. He offered to come help which made me sick all over again.

"I knew he'd head over so we went to Luce's place. Marc left my backpack and all my library books outside my apartment, which I guess was thoughtful. There was a note. *I'm sorry.* For what? That all happened a few hours before he was charged. The next day, I went to the police. But you know that. You've read my *confession*. And here I am, in a mental institution in Toronto safe and almost fixed."

Mona sighed. "You wouldn't have been arrested and you know it. The only person whose job it is to punish you is you. You've been doing that for a long time. Get yourself a new job." Her voice was flat, like she didn't much care whether Sarah bought it or not.

"Ara smelled sweet, like Chai and patchouli. I always smell like puke."

"You don't actually. Or maybe only to yourself."

Usually when Sarah arrived for their appointment, Mona was at her desk reviewing notes or finishing up a call. On occasion, when she was late, Sarah would sit on the floor in the hall and wait for her to come rushing up and say something like, "Oh Sarah, the floor's so dirty," which was funny coming from someone surrounded by crumbs who used spit to clean stuff.

The messy collection of moving items that was Mona in flight, reading glasses on the Barrel of Monkeys chain knocking against her chest, heavy purse swinging, a sandwich or a bowl of soup balanced on a notebook, always made Sarah smile.

This time, the office door was open. The *Globe and Mail* was on the desk beside a half-eaten muffin. The newspaper was always somewhere in the office, but Sarah rarely had the patience or inclination for news. She noticed the word "Goderich" printed across the front page, and she picked it up and read.

Skeletal remains of a child found in abandoned church near Goderich, Ontario

The skeletal remains of a male child seven to ten-years-old were found approximately 35 kilometres northeast of Goderich, Ontario. The body was located beneath the cellar floor of a church house built in 1877, recently purchased and gutted for renovation. Preliminary testing indicates the remains are African/Black, dating from the mid 1950s. The body shows signs of trauma. Fingers from the right hand were found a few feet away.

Interviews with neighbours revealed nothing about the prior owners of the property. Municipal records indicate it had been donated in the will of Robert Mintleig to the Church of Purity, a fundamentalist church group, in 1954. . .

There was a photo. She recognized the church building surrounded in yellow crime scene tape.

Sarah read the article three times trying to sound out and understand the words. When they finally took form, she dropped the paper.

That breezy drive in the green Cortina, the church with the broken windows and the shiny brass doorknob. Her grandfather's bright White future balanced on her eight-year-old shoulders. She remembered how he'd screamed at her when she came down to the basement and found him scratching in the dirt. And then she remembered Charlene's story about the hunting day and the deer he wouldn't strap on the roof of his car. What hunter doesn't bring home his kill?

She didn't realize she was screaming until Mona ran into the office. The container of soup toppled when she reached out.

Sarah pointed at the newspaper on the floor, now covered in bean and barley. Then Mona was on her knees wiping soup off the paper, scanning the damp mess. Skeletal remains near Goderich. "This?"

Sarah nodded and gulped air, then threw up.

44

JUNE 1995

Goderich

SARAH SAT ACROSS FROM HER FATHER IN the visiting room at the Elgin Middlesex Detention Centre near London, Ontario. That's where they'd taken him to await trial, but he'd likely be out on bail soon. Charlene, Katie, and Aunt Jean were getting the money together. Her grandfather was in a mental facility. He'd be found guilty for sure, too much evidence against him. Whatever instinct had made Charlene shove those bloody clothes in the attic had been a good one. But her grandfather was unlikely to serve time with many of the people he so hated, in some general prison population. Too bad. That would truly be punishment. But he was frail and unstable.

Her dad seemed almost relaxed, not at all angry that she, actually Mona on her behalf, called the police the afternoon that she saw the article. He didn't want to go into the horrible details of that day when he was eleven. It was enough that he'd have to do it on the stand when he gave testimony against his father.

But he did tell her what happened when he was sixteen, two months after Charlene left them and left Goderich. He was in the living room when that woman Bunny or Bunmi came to the door looking for her nine-year-old son who had been missing since the night before. Frank was in the kitchen with his father, maybe Katie was there too. Their dad was calmly drinking tea. They could hear the woman at the door. Frank heard Jean telling her they had no idea where the boy was. But Frank knew. His father had grabbed the kid, lured him into the Cortina with a few candies and promises of more. The boy was tied up in the basement of the hardware store. The plan was to take him out to the old church where this time, Frank would take the lead.

By some act of God when they got to the store, the rope had been cut with a piece of broken glass the boy must have found. There was blood on the floor. He was gone. It took all Frank's effort not to cry out with relief while his father stomped around yelling as though it was his son's fault. Another time, her grandfather had said, shaking Frank by the shoulders, "There *will* be another time for us." Frank never doubted him and from then on, he waited.

Suddenly, the whole story about Curtis Otonga and his father made sense to Sarah. Her dad *had* been the one who accused him of stealing and got him fired. But not because he found out that Sarah and Curtis were spending time together, because he was terrified her grandfather would try to kill him and his brother.

"You were trying to save them," Sarah said.

"I wouldn't go that far, I'm not exactly one for helping Negroes. And I couldn't have known for a fact what would happen. I just had a bad feeling. So I killed two birds with one stone."

"I guess you did."

The way he looked, the way he talked and held himself, it was clear to Sarah that her father no longer felt insignificant.

There was a *For Sale* sign on the lawn. Aunt Jean stood on the porch of *his* house, hands jammed in the baggy pockets of her old grey wool sweater. She looked years younger.

Her aunt's arms around Sarah felt tight and protective. Had they ever hugged? Her memories were more of being patted. Sarah froze as she always did when affection was on offer. She knew her aunt understood the instinct.

"Come on in." She opened the door, waving Sarah forward.

On the cusp of it no longer belonging to a Cartell, the house was finally her own. There were boxes in every room. The air felt light with her grandfather's absence.

"How's it going at Charlene's?" Aunt Jean asked. "I will get there to visit. As soon as I've finished with all this. There's a lot to sort through. Lucky we don't get rid of anything." She sighed heavily, her face a mix of relief and sadness. They'd never talked. Sarah had never asked why she stayed.

She wished she knew her aunt better. Maybe now with nothing left to hide, they could begin.

"Things are good. Diallo's really nice. And I met some of my cousins. I spent years hoping Charlene had a miserable life. She doesn't, and guess what? I'm happy about that."

"It's hard not to stay angry," Aunt Jean said. "I've spent my whole life working on that. In the end, it doesn't serve us well."

"You did a good job hiding it," Sarah said. "You know what I found at Charlene's house? A jar filled with stones from the beach my dad took us to. The kneeling beach. Do you think she had them all this time? Or did she come back and get some?"

"Maybe she came back," Aunt Jean said.

"Thanks for coming to the hospital. Mona told me you were there."

"I should have come more often to Sunnyside too, but Dad couldn't run the store anymore, and . . ." She paused, embarrassed. "Oh Sarah, there was so much to say, it felt easier not to say anything. Fatal Cartell flaw."

Sarah nodded. "You've always been here. It's alright that you didn't visit more. I still love you."

She'd never said those words to her aunt. Who had she said them to?

They both teared up then laughed it off.

"I met someone. I've been dating," her aunt said.

Sarah tried not to look too surprised. "You're kidding. Aunt Jean has a boyfriend?"

"It's early days, but maybe."

Sarah wouldn't have expected that to feel like such great news or to be so happy to see her aunt blushing.

"I went to see Dad. He seems good. I mean really good."

Everything moved so quickly once the police had been called. That short article in the paper filled so many holes in a narrative Sarah always struggled to piece together. With each story she'd been told, by Jean when she was younger, then by Katie and her grandmother, she'd expected to understand her family, but never really had. Everyone was still reeling, there were still gaps, and Sarah had no illusions that they'd all come together to laugh and fill in the missing bits over a big meal. But anything was possible.

"It's a horrible feeling, to have had no idea," Jean said. "Your dad bore the brunt of everything, all the pressure of what he was forced to be part of and the belief it would happen again, and it was his to stop. I always thought it was me and Frank in this together. We both stayed. We put up with Dad. But it wasn't. He was alone. At least this ends some piece of that hell for him."

Sarah touched her aunt's hand. "You were there with him. Even if you didn't know what happened, you knew he needed you. You could have left. But you didn't. You stayed for all of us."

"Thank you, Sarah." Aunt Jean wiped her eyes then smiled. "One thing I did know about was your friendship with that boy Curtis. I once had a chat with his mother at the hardware store and she let it slip. She told me that both her son and her husband thought you were wonderful. They were nice people. He was a smart boy. I wonder what he went on to do?"

"I knew you knew." Sarah laughed.

As for Curtis, she figured he was headed for medical school, or law school. Maybe she'd even track him down.

Jean poured them each a glass of lemonade.

"I have more pictures you might want to see." She gestured to the boxes in the living room. "I know I shouldn't feel sorry for your grandfather, but I can't help thinking that most monsters are created, not born. I kind of wish that monster was still in evidence, but he's been so confused. Although he remembers what happened. The old memories stay intact the longest. It didn't occur to him not to be honest when the police questioned him. Supposedly he'd said very sweetly, if you can imagine him saying anything sweetly, that *undoubtedly, they understood that those people needed to be taught a lesson.*"

Sarah remembered feeling specks of pity for old Nazis with cancer and grandchildren who were wheeled to trial, their crimes now ancient history. But it made her angry that her grandfather would never pay. He lived a full miserable life with blood on his hands, always holding out hope for another opportunity.

She thought of Timothy McVeigh, now known as the Oklahoma City bomber. A legacy that would never be forgotten. There were more McVeighs in the making, more Bruce Gotterals funding fantasies of mayhem and supremacy, more Uncle Carls playing back-up.

According to Mona, despite her best intentions, so much of what Sarah had been trying to do, undid her. The prison she was born into where, as the saying went, *if the only tool you have is a hammer, you tend to see every problem as a nail,* was not her forever home. She could approach the world differently, no longer sentenced to bang away at those same nails.

Mona and Harrison believed things were ever improving. That they were better and brighter than Sarah could let herself see. But with vigilance hardwired and everything she had witnessed and knew to be out there, she wasn't sure she could be someone who leaned fully into hope. But she could surround herself with those who did. She already had.

Sarah reached into her pocket and touched the letter she'd received that morning.

Dear Sarah,

I have been thinking about you. Maybe enough time has passed that you're not so angry at me. We are ordering many less sugar lumps at Olé. I'm guessing you have no espresso these days. I don't expect to hear back but hope this letter will find you.

I know about what happened with your grandfather. I'm sorry, is not enough words. So much hardness on top of so much hardness.

You probably hear that Marc Scott and that Rejean were both sentenced to two years for assault. Assault??!! Fuckers. Can you believe it? The rest of them got off with community service. Lucky Montreal.

I saw your friend Maddie McBride at a demo a few weeks ago. On the other side of course, but I swear she kept looking over, like she'd have more fun with us. (Ha ha). Maybe it's just my imagination.

I met with Professor Pichon and gave her the rest of your stuff. I hope this was ok. I didn't tell her anything about what happened. Let her have her own conclusions. She thinks you left school for too much stress. She wants you back so you can work together. And she exposed that Bruce Gotteral. He resigned. So that's great news.

I'm not sorry I spoiled your very stupid plan to be in jail like Marc. It wouldn't have worked anyway and what good would you have been to anyone even if you got in? You probably think what fucking good am I doing here? Getting healthy so you can do more work. Right?

Ara is a lot better. He has one more surgery, then lots of physio. I don't know if he will come back to Montreal. Maybe you know this from Harrison.

I have many things to tell you, but this is enough for now. I hope we'll see each other one of these day, and mostly I hope you will find the way to your own happy.

Love, Luce

P.S. Melrose is doing great and maybe misses you. But who knows with cats.

Afterword

AT ITS CORE, THIS NEAR HISTORICAL FICTION NOVEL is about the trauma of not belonging in the right places and belonging in the wrong ones. It focuses on struggles of morality, loyalty, betrayal, and the powerful pull of family.

I spent years working on this book. The world changed dramatically in the interim. The characters too have evolved, particularly Sarah and her father Frank, whom I now believe I understand far better—their motivations, questionable choices, and what they perceive to be lack of choices. While I have no desire to understand White supremacy or any form of supremacy as a legitimate alternative world view—as it is sadly emerging to be—I do have compassion for people who get trapped in its grasp and false promises. Underlying hate is often the deep fear of losing what people have been taught is their birthright. It is to our detriment as a society, that we ignore the strong pull of racist and anti-Semitic ideologies.

While it is grounded in the legacy of White nationalism in Canada, this is not a book about White supremacy. It is rather about the long and damaging reach of personal and familial attachments, histories, and entrenched beliefs. Many of the events and people are drawn from Warren Kinsella's thorough research in *Web of Hate: Inside Canada's Far Right Network* (Harper Collins, 1995).

I spent a number of years in the 1990's doing anti-fascist activism at a time when Ernst Zundel, Wolfgang Droege, and organizations like the Heritage Front were very active in my city of Toronto, and across Canada and the United States. However, other than legal battles over freedom of speech with the Anti-Defamation League and the Canadian Jewish Congress, these neo-Nazis functioned for the most part on the fringes of society. Their beliefs were perceived to be marginal and not representative of where much of the country was headed, legally or ideologically. Over the writing of this book, I have witnessed this changing.

Were this novel to have been published eight or ten years ago, it would not have been as frightening or familiar. I am horrified by the insidiousness of White nationalism and White supremacy, fascism, anti-democratic movements, extremism, and fundamentalism in all their forms. Too many leaders affirm and support exclusive and hateful beliefs that not only allow but invite them to move from the fringes to the mainstream. We find ourselves in a moment of false moral equivalencies, where one viewpoint or set of values is argued to be as legitimate as the next. It is a time that calls for bravery and nuance.

Acknowledgements

THIS NOVEL HAS BEEN A BEEN A LONG TIME COMING and I'm grateful to everyone who has kept me going so *WHITE* could tumble into this messy and complicated world at (unfortunately) the right time.

Thank you to Rebecca Eckler, Chloe Faith Robinson, and the team at RE:BOOKS for bringing my novel to tangible life and for guiding this old newbie through the world of publishing fiction. I'm grateful to Rebecca for taking a chance on me and championing this challenging story.

To my extraordinary editor, Deanna McFadden, for pushing me in all the best ways to think deeply about motivation and chronology, about where it's great to leave the reader guessing and where that's a recipe for derailment. Also, who knew I could use the word *just* so often? I *just* won't be doing that anymore.

I am grateful to my early readers who are too numerous to name, but made me question, consider, dump, and change bits of the story in helpful ways. Thank you in particular to Laura Trachuk, my ideal reader, who gave me the confidence to know this book was ready. To Ron Davis, James Hyman, Sarah Schulman, Natalie Atlas, and Shira Spector for the observations, support, and motivation to keep going.

To my dear friends, Brenda Cossman, Kathy Marinkovic, Fogel, Jen Garber, Paula Klein, Rena Swartz, Geraldine Cahill, and Ingrid McKhool, for always picking me up off the real and imagined floors.

To my beautiful sons Noah and Ari, who may or may not read this book. Thank you for teaching me that my own way of seeing and understanding, is not always the best way. To my mom for her unwavering and loving support, and my dad who offered to go door to door and find me a literary agent, or better yet, call (the late) Jack Rabinowitz—it doesn't work that way, Dad. He never stopped asking when this novel would get published. Here it is.